# THE MAD HOUSE

*Pagalkhana*

GYAN CHATURVEDI

Translated from the Hindi
by Punarvasu Joshi

THORNBIRD

NIYOGI
BOOKS

Published by
**NIYOGI BOOKS**
Block D, Building No. 77,
Okhla Industrial Area, Phase-I,
New Delhi-110 020, INDIA
Tel: 91-11-26816301, 26818960
Email: niyogibooks@gmail.com
Website: www.niyogibooksindia.com



Editor: Vibha Chakravarty Kumar
Design: Shashi Bhushan Prasad

ISBN: 978-81-19626-27-4
Publication: 2024



Printed at Niyogi Offset Pvt. Ltd., New Delhi, India

# Contents

*This work is for Kiya*

*Kiya is my grand daughter, all of two years and a quarter*

*She doesn't know about the Bazaar yet,*

*But every evening, she pleads,*

*For a trip to the mall*

# Those Days When The Whole World Was Turning Into A Market...

Nobody knew, and then one day it ensnared the whole world.

Not a single human being came to know about this, and the free-market forces took over the whole world. Their ever-widening reach extended across the whole planet in waves and turned the local communities, societies—and in fact—the whole world into a Bazaar. This tyrannical Bazaar, in its rampant and unchecked expansion, was colonising an increasing number of the planet's living places, gnawing away at people's livelihoods, ruthlessly displacing people from their traditional and ancestral homes—and most importantly—slowly turning the sacred institutions of a democratic society impotent. The free-market forces were sacrificing our physical, social, environmental and mental health at the altar of corporate profits.

In its unchecked march, the Bazaar never failed in reminding and assuring us, again and again, that incessant consumerism is the real path to happiness, that the governmental systems of checks and balances on market excess are the real cause of people's distress, and that the tsunami of economic globalisation is inevitable and an ultimate boon to the human species.

All of this happened with such efficiency that not even *life* could feel that it was being lassoed. A time came when thought and thinking, attire, clothes, emotions, love, smile, culture, art, music, literature, folk—everything in life moved according to the free market's will. Eventually, one after another, everybody fell under the market's spell and nobody had an inkling about what was going on. Neither were there any enemy paratroopers nor were there any battle cries. Nobody sounded any bugle calls. There wasn't any ammunition involved, and there were no marching bands. But the siege happened, just like that.

Such was the spell cast by the Bazaar and such was the allure of the promised happiness borne out of continuous consumption that the advocates of the Bazaar were increasing in numbers with every passing day. These folks who considered the Bazaar as the new God insisted, with the rest, that the Bazaar should be received as a new type of light. Whenever a bolt of lightning struck from the thickness of dark clouds, it blindingly illuminated everything. Then they would say, 'What a brilliant light!' This radiance was unique. This would illuminate everything yet it would keep things in the dark. The world could see a lot in the illumination of this new light; but in reality, it was being kept in the dark. The world was ensnared by the Bazaar and its thinking. The world was learning how to live with and within the Bazaar.

But even then, there were some crazies who considered life to be something more than mere consumption, and greater than the market. These folks tried to run away from this glittering darkness. They believed that the market is for life but life isn't only for the market...that it has deeper meanings.

These people were called Crazies.
This is the story of those Crazies.
This is the story of those crazy times.
This is the story of your time.

# A Plush Clinic Of The Healthcare Market

The clinic's physician is the most successful psychiatrist in this region.

People, who are under the illusion that they are not insane, bring those here who they think are crazy. Though, often after seeing somebody, it is quite difficult to decide who should have been rightfully brought here in the first place, and who is actually brought here. The standards of judging insanity are ambiguous. Anyhow.

The clinic is like a grand showroom.

Wall-to-wall glasses. An illusory play of light on the walls is such that it hides more than what it reveals. Many certificates that the doctor has received from time to time, over a long period, hang on one of the walls of the clinic—certificates with beautifully rich, heavy paper and fine printing; an array of them framed in elegant wooden frames. Their beauty so astounding that the moment one sees them, one is filled with the feeling that they are phoney.

The patients wait for their turn in the clinic's waiting room patiently; it has plush, elegant couches on three sides. The cushions are so soft and fluffy that the moment one sits on them, one sinks into them; and then keeps on sinking, further and further. Head in the heavens and buttocks on earth. The room has many designer chairs, too.

And there is a splendid nook in the waiting room as well. A beautiful receptionist sits there.

Magnificent marble tiles for people to walk on. And such a regal false ceiling above one's head that even the insane would be proud that they got to sit underneath such a royal ceiling.

Well, everything in this clinic is so resplendent, grand and marvellous that, for once, one can't believe that this place is for treating lunatics. But they *are* treated here. Although, how much effect this grandeur has on them is not known.

Anyhow, this is the clinic of the city's most famous psychiatrist. Back in the old days, he would have been known as the 'doctor of psychos'. Nowadays, somebody would have to be crazy to call him that. But he has kept this clinic of his glitzy and glittering. The doctor knows that he is in the market. 'In today's glitzy world, even a doctor has to keep his clinic glitzy. Otherwise who would be so crazy to come here and pay loads of money to have their insanity treated?' He, this same psychiatrist, was laughing and telling this to somebody the other day.

There are so many patients in the clinic waiting to see the doctor that it is kind of scary. Oh, my God! So many insane! What is going on in this world? Is the number of insane on the rise? Really? Or is it that even the wise ones are being declared lunatics?

On one of the walls of the clinic, the Hippocratic Oath hangs, framed in an elegant wooden frame.

An oath to selflessly serve the patients.

The Bazaar treats these oaths, declarations, slogans and aphorisms admiringly—and with the utmost respect. Just see for yourself, even here, where this oath is hanging…

No, no. The oath is not being hanged, like on a noose. It's just that it is imprisoned in a classy, black ebony frame. You wouldn't be able to tell if it is in distress hanging there. In fact, that expensive frame attracts all the attention so quickly that one hardly notices the *words* of the oath. There is a huge market for aphorisms, platitudes, and quotes, too, in the marketplace these days. The Bazaar loves that. People love to hang them in ornate, carved and expensive frames in prominent places in their offices, homes and shops. When the frame used is expensive, glitzy and engraved, there is no risk of somebody really paying attention to the real thought framed within it.

A portrait of Hippocrates is also in there, along with his oath in the frame.

Just look at his face in the portrait! He looks as if he is in great pain. Those who know say that the pained look on his face isn't because of the healthcare business, that he has had that look from the beginning. Anyway, anybody who has spent all of his life thinking and worrying about the world would end up having a long face.

And if you look just underneath Hippocrates' nose, there is a wholesale market of patients. One of them, who is waiting for his turn to come, just glanced at the wall with Hippocrates' portrait on it. He felt as if frame-restrained Hippocrates is wriggling within the frame. 'Yaar, I hope he doesn't fall off if he is wriggling so much!' The patient felt that he should share his concern with his wife, but he kept mum. Who is going to listen to him here? Everybody thinks that he has gone off the deep end. It is better to keep quiet. To hell with Hippocrates. He ain't my business.

However, he did notice that the old man sitting next to him also saw the same thing. 'Did you see that?', he asked, signalling towards the portrait. The old man nodded at him and put his finger on his lips, signalling him back to keep quiet.

Both of them broke into laughter. They both looked at Hippocrates and looked at each other, and started smiling. The receptionist stared at them closely and waved at them. 'Sit quietly, Uncle…' She conveyed this wordlessly by staring at them unblinking.

The young man accompanying the old man, too, stared at them. 'Why don't you sit comfortably, Papa?' he chided him, and then looked at the beautiful receptionist and stared with a smile. He was staring at the beautiful receptionist with an expression across his face which one gets if one mixes the feeling of 'what can I do, he is my dad' with 'you are beautiful'.

The young man is also staring at his watch impatiently and feeling frustrated. Perhaps, he had to be somewhere and he was being delayed here. His face has a more pained look than Hippocrates'. 'How long will it be?' he asked the gorgeous girl sitting at the reception desk.

'It's your turn after them,' she replied, smiling.

And at that very moment, Hippocrates scornfully spat on people sitting underneath his portrait.

Thank God that the old man saw him spitting at the last minute, otherwise he and his son would have been sprayed with his spittle. The old man suddenly jumped from his seat and while he was jumping, he shoved his son sideways, saving him from Hippocrates' spittle too.

'What are you doing!?' the young man screamed, stumbling towards the receptionist's glass table.

'That...that old fella was spitting on you,' the old man pointed his finger at the portrait hung on the wall next to the oath.

Enraged, the young man started staring at his father and then kept on staring. The old man cowered and sat down. The young man angrily looked at his father as if he wanted to devour him alive, and then apologised to the receptionist and said, 'He does these wacky things all day long!'

The girl smiled and nodded at him, empathising with his predicament.

'Now, just sit tight quietly, okay? Not a peep out of your mouth! It is our turn next,' the young man said to his father while helping him ease into a sofa.

Looking at the old man, the other crazies also started smiling. Some were already smiling without any reason before all of this happened, lost in their thought—because, after all, they were insane, right!

This was such a time that it was only crazies who could smile.

# There Was Water Everywhere. This Was The Time Of Water Sports During A Flood

The suburbs were flooding.

The Bazaar was everywhere. Quite an embarrassing time this was.

It was a flood. Life was surrounded by the Bazaar, everywhere. It was the Bazaar that was flowing everywhere. Laughter, conversation, day-to-day dealings among people, literature, culture, folk, religion, thought, and music—everything was flowing with the flow of the Bazaar.

Since this was a flood, the suburbs should have been scared, right? People should have gathered everything they could find and moved on to a safer place, right? But such was the bizarre nature of these times that instead of panicking and getting scared, people in the suburbs were celebrating the flooding. The Bazaar kept on expanding. Flooding works on this principle. When it spreads, it swallows everything that comes in its way. The Bazaar had spread so far and so fast that the places which didn't even have a market were under its sway now. But nobody was concerned with this. Rather, suburbs were enjoying all of this, and everybody was happy.

The Bazaar had barged into the suburbs, which were flooding. Everybody in the suburbs was cheering and enjoying this from the sidelines, thinking that this was just another dog and pony show. And then the Bazaar rose higher. The floodwaters started rising faster and faster. The first ones to fall prey were the innocent bystanders to all of this. Then, the streets fell; and soon, neighbourhoods, too, fell prey to that. The suburbs were next to go. Roads. Doorsteps. Doors. If somebody could see this from a satellite in space, he would have been scared to see all of this happening. Everything was getting flooded. Everywhere, it was the Bazaar and only the Bazaar. Houses were getting flooded. Personal relationships were the first to dissolve. Friendships found themselves neck-deep in the muddy waters. The sludge of billboards, hoardings and advertisements had seeped into every house. Houses had lost their identity. Wherever you looked, you only saw the Bazaar.

The waves were sky-high. When they came, everybody would be ecstatic to see them. And man! in the beginning, this was an attraction in itself for lots of people!

The common folks in the suburbs also thought of this as a new game. In the beginning, they sloshed and ran around a lot, playing in the floods' rising waters. They started organising water sports in these waters. They started celebrating the flood. Some elders were alarmed; and they cautioned, saying that these waters are not to be played in or played with. When it starts flooding, the first thing to do is to head for the hills. Save your houses and homes. Save yourself. But people didn't listen. They started making fun of these elders. They started making and sharing jokes and funny memes about the elders on WhatsApp, Facebook, and other social media, which went viral. And then this, too, happened that others started advising these thinker types to let go of worries about flooding and, in fact, told them to change themselves and start going with the flow and not worry about the flood. Everybody started convincing everybody else in favour of the flood. They said that it was the Bazaar's magnificent arrangement that now things are sold to you right at your doorstep. 'All you have to do is whisper and they will deliver things to you at your doorstep, and that too at a significant discount—what else does one need? See, now we don't have to go to a riverbank to get water. The river has come to our doorsteps…and here you are, crying foul about the flooding! Tell me, have things been so easy in the world ever before? Go, on!'

But gradually, when this ankle-deep water started rising and became waist-deep, then few other folks—who were celebrating this spectacle until now—were concerned. But others cornered these people as well, and allayed their fears by saying that this wasn't a grave danger. Especially if one learns to swim and float with the tide, things become a lot easier and navigable. So there is nothing to lose one's sleep over. But while this was going on, the flood water had risen to such a level that it was now in people's homes. Everybody's home was looking like a makeshift shop. The home itself was homeless now.

And then, with time, floodwater rose higher and higher. People started climbing onto rooftops. Market-friendly folks still soothed everybody's fears by saying that if only one could get accustomed to this minor discomfort of living on the roofs, this barging in of the Bazaar into our lives would eventually turn out to be a good thing overall. Nobody dared to ask these wise market-friendly folks what would happen to the suburbs if the waters rose higher than the rooftops.

So—when everybody was already on rooftops and every single household was now in the grips of the Bazaar—this is a story of those times. This is the story of the world completely drowning in the Bazaar.

# God Was On The Bazaar's Side Because He Wasn't Insane

In the same psychiatrist's same clinic, there is a lovely small shrine for God.

In front of a tiny idol, there are lightbulbs illuminating the shrine imitating earthen lamps. God sits here with a needless smile. He watches everything with such an air of indifference as if this is not the same world that He created. Or perhaps, this is a world that is not under his control anymore!

Right now, the clinic is full. It always is.

'What happened to him?' a middle-aged woman with a child waiting for her turn spoke. It was she who inquired of—as if to kill time—the woman sitting next to her, who was accompanying an old man.

The old man is yawning. He is yawning sitting on the couch, awaiting his turn, or he is sleepy because he is under the influence of the medicines prescribed by the psychiatrist…it's hard to say. His wife is sitting next to him, and looking at him with an expression of deep concern on her face, when the woman with the child asked her about the old man.

On the other side, the kid is sitting quietly. Once in a while, he would start smiling, blankly staring straight ahead and not looking at anybody in particular. A couple of times, when he would burst into laughter, the woman who came with him would tell him to keep quiet. The kid's smile and his laughter aren't child-like, and the disturbing thing is that nobody seems to be disturbed by this.

What a time it is that even kids are going insane, and everybody thinks that this is quite normal.

'What happened to him?' she asks again.

'I don't know! He is spooked by something, and is frightened all the time,' the old woman replied, looking at the old man with a worried look.

'Why? What is he afraid of?'

'Something. He doesn't sleep. Nor does he sit still in any place. He walks around the house anxiously...startled, hearing the slightest sound in the house. He spends the whole night sitting on his bed, vigilant and scared.' When somebody was empathising with the old woman, she couldn't help but let it all out.

'What does he say? What spooks him?'

'How should I tell? I am too embarrassed to say anything... all childish things.'

'Like?'

'He says that we are used goods now. We are like old junk in the house. He is worried that one of these days our children might sell us on OLX. That is a website where people sell old and used stuff, right? Yeah, on that website. This is eating him alive. He says again and again that whenever our children would get a reasonable price for us, they will surely sell us online.'

'How so?'

'Haven't you seen that ad? All you have to do is take a photo and upload it on OLX. Somebody will surely buy it. Even old things get decent prices these days.'

'Yeah, that is true. But why is he thinking like that?'

'I don't know, it started just like that. He was sitting in his armchair on the porch one day. Our son had bought a new cell phone that day. He showed him his new phone and with the new phone, he snapped a photo of my husband. He showed it to his father and said, "Papa, what a great photo this is!" That did it. Since that day, he is in a panic. He says, "He thinks that we are fools and we will not understand his trick. But I saw through his trickery. He has taken a great photo so that he can upload it on OLX and sell me to the highest bidder, once the bidder likes what he sees." Since that moment, he is towing the same line day in and day out. My son pleaded with him again and again. Others, too, talked to him. But he just doesn't listen.

Nowadays, even the slightest sound startles him, even when the postman rings a bell, he starts running around the house thinking it must be the buyer!'

The old woman was brought to tears narrating this.

The woman who came with the kid patiently listened to all of this. Once in a while she would look at the old man too, who was cowering on the couch as the old woman was telling her story.

The old woman sat silently after pouring her heart out.

The other woman, too, was silent after listening to all of this.

Then she leaned towards the old woman and whispered in her ear, 'Who knows, maybe he is right?'

'What!?' the old woman replied, stunned.

'Yeah. It's possible that he isn't insane. What if, if what he is saying is true? What if, he is scared for the right reason? Then?'

'What nonsense!'

'See, whenever anything in the world happens for the first time, it feels strange in the beginning.'

'So, you also think that our son thinks of us as old junk and he is going to sell us online?'

'Yeah. Why can't he do that? Tell me. And it's just not him, many other children think like that. Although, your son's idea of selling parents online as used goods is quite new.'

'He doesn't have any idea like that, okay!'

The old woman was getting angry now.

'Please calm down. God forbid he has any idea like that. But how do you know for sure that something like this isn't cooking in his mind? It's also quite possible that he might be thinking about it. Why can't he have an idea like that? Or maybe it's possible that your husband has seen through him and you are the one who is being blindsided?'

'What cheap rubbish this is?'

'There is nothing rubbish in this, Aunty. It's not cheap either. Think for a second. Why…it seems possible the more I think about it. Who knows that there might be a lucrative scheme going on in the market where somebody can go and sell their old parents for a reasonable price? These days anything can be sold in the market. Happens every day. Heck, when there are ongoing schemes to buy people's trash, then why can't there be a scheme for this?'

'Have you, too, gone crazy?'

'Please think calmly and try to understand the situation. There is nothing wrong with exploring a possibility. All I am saying is that it's possible that uncle is not insane. And it is also quite possible that the reason your son sent you here…'

'Why did he send me here?!'

The old woman was now seething with anger.

'He might have sent you here, perhaps, because uncle would remain drowsy at home under the influence of medicines prescribed here, and then he can be packed and shipped easily to any buyer without any hassle or resistance. It will be difficult to ship him if he is wide awake. That's why. If he is awake, he can start screaming, he can call neighbours for help—who know what else he might do. That will surely turn off the buyer. The Bazaar thinks that no matter what happens, a customer shouldn't be angered. Customer is king, you know…'

'Do you have any idea what you are blabbering about?'

'I only shared a possibility with you. Times have changed, aunty. Be careful, and take care of him properly is what I am saying. Whatever he is saying, please pay attention to it and try to understand what he is going through. It might be possible that he was right all along.'

The old woman stared at her and then scooted over to the other side of the couch, putting some distance between herself and the other woman.

Has this woman gone crazy? She must have lost her mind. What if she has come here for a check-up? Sometimes in an asylum, it is difficult to decide whether the person you just met is an inmate or a caretaker of an inmate, or an employee working there.

The kid who came with the woman was gawking at the old woman.

Then he started smiling, looking at her in such a way as if he knew what was going through the old woman's mind. Then he started laughing.

The woman accompanying her kept her hand on his shoulder, as if to soothe him, and said, 'Kiddo, please don't laugh like that. It is bothering everybody.'

But the kid was laughing.

The old man was sitting still, and quietly.

The kid was still laughing while staring at the old woman. The old woman, feeling uncomfortable with all of this, was now looking at the tiny idol of God in the shrine.

God was also needlessly smiling. Perhaps, this was the time when God decided to side with the Bazaar. Perhaps, only this was best for God.

# Power Is Always With Them. Or, Perhaps, They Are Always In Power

Here, the reader might ask a few questions. For example, where was the government when the Bazaar was taking over everything else?

Why didn't it stop this disaster from happening?

What happened to the Constitution? What happened to the people who took an oath to protect and serve the Constitution? Why don't we see them anymore these days? How come the leash which was supposed to be on the Bazaar is now seen on them? Does the power in this place really lie with the government? Why did this happen, that when the Bazaar's tsunami came, law, rules, civil rights, the Constitution, religion, social sciences, and every other system was swept away? People were either trying to surf these waves or they were just drowning.

It is true that the government wasn't dissolved. The government was big, and it wasn't easy to drown it either. It survived the Bazaar's onslaught. It just kept on bobbing up and down in the floodwater. It knew every trick in the book to run itself. The government knew this. It had grudgingly accepted the truth that the Bazaar was much more powerful than itself. It then decided that it would use the Bazaar's power for its survival, and for staying in power. This was as if somebody decides to utilise a tsunami to generate electricity, and then congratulates oneself for this stupidity. And after this thought, the government decided to give up all of its welfare schemes and handed them over to the Bazaar. It publicly convinced itself that the only way for the nation's progress is through markets and malls. Once you hand over the country to the tsunami, then the tsunami will have no choice but to carry the country forward—that's what the government believed.

Such was the government's naiveté, meanness or shrewdness; nobody knows, but at least this much was clear that now the government was in cahoots with the Bazaar.

And this is how it became an unbelievable and terrifying time. The Bazaar's and the government's power had amalgamated into each other so thoroughly that it became difficult to identify where the market ended and where administrative offices began. The government announcements were dictated by the Bazaar. Parliamentary bills resembled a serpent's coil. Every honorable person present within the halls of that august body agreed with the consensus that now the Bazaar would be officially granted the designation of God.

They wanted that any questions or concerns about the piety of the Bazaar should be treated as a punishable offense, akin to defiling a place of religious interest.

Now, the Bazaar had the first rights for everything on every inch of this planet. And then, any leftover land could be used for agriculture, rivers could be allowed to flow, and grass could be allowed to grow. And whatever was left after this could be used for people to live on, or if he so wished, could be used for burial. Sky, water, air and sunshine, natural rights for all these things should be granted to the Bazaar—and this should be codified into law. Honorable members of the august body would feverishly discuss such thought-provoking matters in the esteemed chambers of the building. The Bazaar had dutifully, through media, converted these discussions into an entertainment channel.

This was the same time when man was completely lonely.

This was the same time when anybody who wasn't siding with the Bazaar was declared insane.

The Bazaar was redefining madness, and many people were on board with it. Stalwart intellectuals were busy with the Bazaar in coming up with this definition. A strange madness had taken over the world, where so many crazies were busy trying to redefine madness.

***

Around this time, some people decided that they will somehow escape the clutches of the Bazaar, no matter what. These were a *different* type of insane.

This story is the story of this bizarre time, and this different strain of insanity.

## He Was Digging A Tunnel To Escape From A Blind Tunnel

Eventually, he decided that it would be best to escape from here.

He had resolved to escape the Bazaar and its onslaught.

This was a fairly difficult decision. He didn't even know where he would go after escaping. Is it even possible to run away from the world which had so deeply fallen for the Bazaar? He didn't even have the slightest idea about this. Is there any place on this earth that was really left untouched by the Bazaar? He didn't even know that. All he knew was that he had resolved to go far, far away from all this. He also knew, all too well, that the Bazaar would not let him go far from itself that easily. Every person in the world is a valuable customer. The Bazaar can't let a client leave just like that.

Then?

How will he escape from this all too powerful Bazaar? What was his plan?

How will he escape? Every road in this world is under the Bazaar's authority. If he escaped using these routes, he would be caught immediately. If he really wants to escape, he would have to find a new way. A path that has evaded the Bazaar's watchful eyes till now. It was then, while thinking about such a path, that he thought of digging a tunnel. Yeah, that can be done. A tunnel can be dug, concealed from the Bazaar. He would do just that. He thought of escaping by digging a tunnel.

Now, he would dig a tunnel every day, little by little. If a tunnel is dug every day, little by little, then a long tunnel would give way, eventually. He would dig this tunnel alone. There was a risk of the Bazaar knowing about the tunnel if he worked with somebody else. No, nobody should know about this. Not even his family. When the tunnel is complete, only then he would tell his family about it—and escape with them. Not now. Now is not the time to let anybody get any whiff of this.

The first challenge he faced was to decide where to begin digging his tunnel so that nobody gets any clue about it. After all, where should he dig, hiding from everybody?

After some contemplation, he decided on a place for digging which was right behind the Bazaar's back. Right behind the market's glitter was a junkyard. It was pitch-dark there. This was a place where people threw their trash; it was filthy, and only trash-pickers wandered there. This was the trash that came from the Bazaar, and to which the Bazaar never paid any attention. 'Thats it!' he thought, and started digging there. When everybody in the house would fall asleep, he would come out of his house, cloaked. The Bazaar, too, would be half-asleep due to nighttime. He would walk behind the market to his chosen spot, clear out the day's trash that was thrown there, and uncover the hidden mouth of the tunnel. He would feel his way through the trash in the darkness and enter the tunnel. And then he would start digging. He would continue digging all through the night. He would be soaked in sweat doing this, but he wouldn't stop to even catch his breath. He kept on digging. The tunnel, too, would be drowned in total darkness. He would keep on digging in the dark. Though he did keep a torch with him, he would seldom turn it on. He was scared. He was cautious. The Bazaar is a mentalist; it has magical powers. It wouldn't be a surprise if it has the magical powers to detect light in the underground tunnels, despite remaining on the ground itself. If a torch is lit, he would be caught. He would only turn it on to check his watch. He would leave the tunnel just before the break of dawn. He would come back home and crawl into his bed, just like habitual morning-walkers. He would hide his tools, next to the tunnel's mouth, and would come back and fall asleep so fast and so deep that even his family wouldn't suspect a thing.

Yeah…and then he would wake up late. His folks would say, 'Babu ji's routine has been disturbed since he retired from his job. He sleeps throughout the day…'

## Even Though You Wouldn't Believe It, I Am Alright!

'What's wrong with him?' The psychiatrist, after looking closely at him, asked.

Well, actually he was caught red-handed one day. After digging the tunnel in the wee hours of the dawn, dust-covered, and after stealthily entering the house, he was changing clothes in his house under the bed when his wife saw him. And she started questioning what he was doing under the bed. He, too, was surprised to see his wife there. How in hell did she come there? He couldn't lie to her. He told her…he had to. He told her everything about the tunnel and the escape plan—he had to. She didn't understand a thing. She was dumbfounded. He didn't make any sense. She broke down and started crying hysterically. She started wailing. His son came running from the other room. His daughter-in-law, too, came in tow. And, his five-year-old grandson trailed behind the two, scared. The kid couldn't come near him. The daughter-in-law stopped the kid midway, pulling him close to her and putting her arms around him. Looks like father-in-law has gone nuts. It's better to keep the kid away from him must have been her immediate thought.

And since then, he answered every question by talking about escaping through a tunnel. It was obvious now that he had lost it. It took a lot of talking and calming him down before he agreed to see the doctor. They finally brought him to the clinic.

The psychiatrist's clinic was so grand and glitzy that he was even more scared after coming inside. The doctor sat on an imperial, throne-like revolving chair behind a huge shimmering glass table. The window was covered with thick, grand curtains. The wall was covered with half-hidden, half-exposed lights. The doctor was wearing expensive clothes. The carpet was luxurious. The whole office was oozing affluence—complete opulence was flowing through the whole space. When one entered the doctor's office, one's run-of-the-mill knees would be wading knee-deep in the affluence. He cautiously walked into the office. Gingerly, pulling his pants up to his ankles. Even now, he was sitting with his legs slightly up in the air!

'What exactly is his problem?' the psychiatrist asked, intently looking at his feet, which were still up in the air. He could tell a lot just by reading a patient's body language. Quite an experienced doctor he was.

The son narrated the whole story.

'My mother woke up this morning. It was still dark. She saw Papa wasn't in his bed. She started worrying. Then she heard a noise coming from underneath the bed. She found him there. He crawled out when she called him. Soaked in sweat, clothes covered in dirt and dishevelled hair. He was worried, as if he was caught stealing red-handed. He took Maa's hand in his, and made her swear not to tell this to anybody. He said that if the word came out, everybody would know about our tunnel. Poor thing…she couldn't understand a word of what he was talking about. She, too, was worried sick. She said that he was continuously talking about some tunnel that he was digging, hidden from everybody. That was the only thing he talked about. Then she started wailing. When I heard her cry, I came running to the room. He was still talking about some tunnel. And since then, he is just mumbling about this tunnel, the Bazaar, running away and whatnot. It took a lot of effort to bring him here…'

The son told his father's case history.

The father kept on listening to his son quietly.

'Why? What is he saying, sir?' the psychiatrist started probing.

What could he say? Telling his family about the tunnel was a different matter altogether, but how could he tell this doctor? It is a secret. My wife and son don't understand a single thing. If I tell the doctor, it will be out soon. And if it's out, in no time the Bazaar, too, will know about it. He would have to be cautious in answering the doctor's questions. He should prevent the doctor from having any inkling about the truth of the matter. Anyway, he looks mean.

'Oh! No, nothing. Hardly anything. I am perfectly alright, Doctor!' he said, and started smiling.

'And what about what these folks are telling me?' the doctor asked.

'Crazy, I know,' he responded, and started laughing hysterically. He winked, too, so it should become clear that the thing was said in jest.

'What's this thing of digging a tunnel, sir?'

'What?! There isn't any tunnel!' He lied with such confidence that he, too, was surprised…even proud of it. Bravo!

The son was listening to everything. He was agitated. He said, 'Why? How come there isn't any matter? Why don't you tell doctor sahab everything? Why don't you share your plan for the tunnel with him, too? You couldn't stop harping about it at home. What happened now? Did a cat get your tongue?'

He sat down quietly and kept on looking at his son.

The son continued. He said to the doctor, 'He said that since all of you now know about the tunnel, you all should give me a hand in digging, too. He said that we all would have to get away from this as far as possible. He even got scared, quite a few times, while telling us about this. He went to the window four times to check. Four times. He said that he was just checking to see if somebody was eavesdropping on us, you know.'

'Who is going to eavesdrop on you?' the doctor asked, looking at the old man.

He kept mum.

'He says that the Bazaar's folks are spying on people; and if anybody gets even a word, they will know about the tunnel. That's it. Things like that...' the son clarified. The doctor listened to everything as if he understood perfectly what the matter was.

The old man, though, was quietly laughing at the doctor in his mind. 'I wont let you know a single thing!' he was thinking to himself.

'Which tunnel are you digging? How far will it go?' the doctor asked.

The old man began staring at the doctor.

It seems like this doctor, too, is in cahoots with the Bazaar. He will have to be very cautious in answering his questions, or the doctor will tell the Bazaar about the tunnel. He will have to bluff.

'I ain't digging any tunnel, Doctor sahab,' he said, smiling.

'But what about what these people are saying?'

'Oh! Here, take a look…take a look at my hands. Do they look like the hands of a tunnel digger? Do you see calluses on my palms? No, right? Then?' he said, and started laughing.

The doctor kept on staring at him quietly. He then turned towards his wife and son, and started asking them lots of other questions.

'How well does he sleep? If he is asleep all day, then what does he do at night? How well does he eat? How is his appetite? Does he become violent now and then? Does he talk nonsense apart from talking about the tunnel? Has he been an atheist or a believer? When you saw him scared, did you guys ever ask him why he was scared?'

They answered as best as they could.

The doctor took notes in between all of this on his notepad.

The old man silently watched and listened to everything that was happening there. He kept on smiling at the doctor while looking at him.

Why was he smiling?

In reality, he was trying to show the doctor that he was perfectly alright. And this baloney about the tunnel is, well, just baloney.

## To Live Without Dreams

That night, when the whole neighbourhood was fast asleep, he was awake. The room was lit by the faint glow of a night lamp. Mosquito-net. Pillows. Pleasant weather outside. It was drizzling. Everybody was asleep. He was the one who was awake. His wife was lightly snoring, lying next to him, and he was sitting with his eyes wide open, resting his back on the two pillows against the headboard. Staring blankly, unblinking, and looking nowhere in particular. Wide awake. He lay down on the bed to sleep. The wife had fallen asleep long ago. He, too, waited to fall asleep for some time. Restlessly. Somewhat anxious, too. Then he felt uneasy. And he sat upright.

Right now, only God knows for how long he has been sitting like this, upright and leaning against the headboard for some time. Don't know how much of the night has passed and how much more remains. He was sitting silently, leaning against the pillows, thinking something.

And then, suddenly, his wife woke up. She turned around and saw him sitting like that. Seeing him sitting like that in the lonely solitude of the night, she got worried.

Outside, the rain had turned from a drizzle into a downpour.

'What happened?' she asked anxiously.

'Nothing,' he mumbled.

'Then why are you sitting like this? Why don't you sleep?' the wife asked.

'I just couldn't fall asleep,' he responded in the tone of someone who was somewhat lost.

'You okay?'

'Why, what's wrong with me?'

'Then?'

'I was just drifting to sleep when something flashed in my mind, and then I couldn't fall asleep. It's bugging me since then,' he told her.

She, too, was sitting upright now.

'What happened?' she asked.

'It just came to me that these days I don't dream in my sleep anymore. I haven't had a single dream in months!' he started explaining.

'So? What's there to worry about?' she asked.

'Why? You don't think that this is something to worry about?' he asked, surprised.

'Yeah. It's nothing. If you don't dream, you don't dream,' she replied callously.

'I am talking about dreams. Dreams,' he repeated himself.

'Yeah, yeah, I got you. I am also talking about dreams. I am not deaf,' she seemed annoyed now.

'I said that I have stopped dreaming and you are...'

'That's what I am saying. It's nothing to worry about. If you don't dream in sleep, so what?' she said.

'Are you out of your mind?'

'Who? Me or you?'

'I can't dream in my sleep and you are like...'

'Why are you talking crazy? Go back to sleep. It's already late in the night,' she said, and laid down on the bed again.

Though he remained the way he was.

'Oh! Come on now. Lie down. You'll fall asleep only if you lie down,' she said, and turned on her side. He sat there silently.

'Enough!' she said, lying down.

'Yeah, yeah...'

'Neither are you sleeping, nor letting me sleep,' she mumbled.

He, too, lay down...with his eyes wide open. And with the sound of soft snoring, it became clear that his wife was falling deep into sleep.

Antsy, he sat up again after some time. The bed creaked, and his wife mumbled again in sleep.

'Please, sleep...'

'What if I won't be able to dream in sleep anymore?' he started asking.

'Please, sleep. Why are you whining about dreams at two in the night?' she mumbled.

He didn't say a word.

'If you don't dream, you don't dream. No big deal,' she said, and tried to sleep again.

'But then, what's the point of this life without dreams?' he asked.

She didn't hear him anymore; she was already asleep.

After a while she screamed, half-asleep, 'Go to sleep, Maharaj! Worry about the dreams tomorrow!'

He lay down again. He couldn't fall asleep but he stayed there still. He thought about dreams throughout the night. It felt as if this night would never end, but it did.

The sun rose.

His wife had forgotten the whole thing about dreams by now; she usually has a thousand things to take care of in the morning. He peeked into the kitchen and saw that she was busy preparing lunch boxes for him and the kids.

He started getting ready to go to the office. He didn't feel like going but he thought that if he discussed this thing about dreams with his friends, they might be able to find a way out. He had been through such a disaster, and his wife didn't understand anything about it. Friends will surely understand.

After brushing his teeth, he started washing his face. When he was splashing water on his face, he suddenly saw his eyes. And he started screaming hysterically. Both his kids came running to him.

'Papa! What happened?'

The wife, too, came running from the kitchen.

'What happened?'

'My eyes...'

'What happened to your eyes? Show me...' she asked, concerned.

He turned his face towards her. The kids also started looking into his eyes. His wife pulled the lower eyelids to see.

'Looks fine to me. What happened?'

'They look fine to you?' he asked, excitedly.

'Yeah, they look redder than normal. That's all. Because you haven't slept properly, that's why...' she said.

'Look closely! I have just checked them in the mirror...' He was agitated now.

Seeing his father so worried, the adolescent son glanced at his mother with concern. His daughter was still a child; she still didn't understand many things. It had rained through the night. It was still cloudy outside. There were dark clouds in the sky. It was slightly dark inside. His wife turned on the lights in the bathroom.

'There's nothing. Why are you worried?' The wife checked his eyes once again in the light of the bulb.

'Yeah, Papa, there is nothing there,' his son, too, looked into his eyes to check and said with reassurance.

'Can you look closely? Really closely.'

'Look at what?' his wife responded, annoyed.

'See…don't my eyes look completely empty to you?' he asked anxiously.

'Empty?'

'Yeah. Totally empty!'

'What do you mean by empty? They look fine to me. Right son?' she asked her son. She didn't understand what he was saying.

'Yeah, Papa. They look fine to me,' his son said as well.

Seeing her father's pale face, the younger daughter hid behind her mother and wrapped her hands around her. Both the kids were in their school uniform, half-ready. They were getting ready to go to school when they had heard their father's scream. Now, everybody's eyes were also on the clock hanging above the bathroom mirror, except him. They had to keep in mind the school bus. His eyes, though, were fixed on the mirror. He was staring into his own eyes in the reflection.

'Wow! There is so much emptiness in my eyes, and you guys can't see it?' he said.

'Maa, what is Papa saying?' The boy couldn't understand what was going on. The wife was slowly getting it now. She was recalling what he had said last night.

'Beta, you guys should hurry and get ready for school. Your lunchbox is ready. I'll look after him...' she said to the kids.

She turned towards him after sending the kids away.

'Your eyes are perfectly fine. What's this clownery you are up to since last night?' she chided him.

'Yaar, my eyes are completely empty, and you think that is clownery?'

'You can see things fine? Right?'

'Yes, but...'

'Are they hurting?'

'No. Nothing like...'

'Yaar, then what's your problem? Why are you so worried? And why are you making me worried?' she asked, exasperated.

'See! My eyes are completely empty. I just saw them again.'

He tried explaining to her once again.

'What?'

'They are empty, as if somebody picked up everything and cleaned it good...'

'I don't know what you are saying.'

'As if somebody totally cleans the house, same as that. Nobody lives in them anymore. They are empty, like an empty house...'

'Empty house? So, who was living there that left?' she was irritated, and scared too, by his kooky thoughts. What's going on with him?

'Now I get it...while talking to you. My eyes don't have dreams anymore. There were dreams which lived in my eyes. They are gone now. Left it vacant. Empty. That's it. That's the thing! Anybody who doesn't have dreams will have vacant eyes, right?' he spoke, as if he was talking to himself now.

'Have you lost your mind?' her voice was both stern and scared now.

'Why? Why are you saying that?'

'You started that dream thing again! What has happened to you since last night?'

'Yaar, I can't dream in my sleep. Shouldn't I be worried about that?'

'You aren't dreaming at night. It's not like the sky is falling, is it?'

'I don't have dreams left in my eyes anymore and you say that there is nothing to worry about?' He was perplexed by how lightly she was taking this whole dream thing.

'Yeah, I got thousand other things to worry about. Should I bicker about them or should I cry my eyes out for your dreams?' She went back to the kitchen, muttering.

He was left standing there. Quiet, he kept on looking at himself in the mirror for a long time. The man in the mirror was looking so pitiful, lonely and empty that he was now pitying himself.

He was worried, and a bit surprised too, that his wife couldn't understand such a simple thing. As for kids, well, they are just kids; they won't understand anything.

He slowly started getting ready to go to the office, half-heartedly. He didn't feel like shaving. He took a quick shower and picked up something to wear. Took big bites of his breakfast and swallowed them. And then he remained quiet. He didn't say anything anymore to his wife on this topic. She, too, remained quiet. The kids said their byes and left. He, too, picked up his bag and left for the office.

'You okay?' His wife asked him as he was walking out.

'Yeah. I am fine,' he said in a trailing voice and walked out of the door without even looking at her once. But when he reached the office, everybody noted that he wasn't looking okay.

A sleepless night. Red eyes. Unshaven, long face. His whole demeanor was tense. His colleagues were concerned.

'Hey, what happened to you? Are you okay?' Somebody asked.

He didn't say a word. He kept himself occupied, rearranging things on his table. He kept on thinking whether he should discuss the dream issue with them; it was continuously playing in his mind, in a loop. Still. Non-stop.

'Are you feeling fine?' Somebody asked again.

He then decided that it was better to ask them too.

'Yaar, I am worried about one thing. Tell me something, do you guys dream while sleeping or not?' he asked, hesitating.

His co-workers didn't understand his question.

'What weird question is this?'

'Weird or not. I want to know.'

'But why do you want to know?'

'Because I am worried.'

'By this question?'

'Yeah…'

'What are you worried about?' they asked.

'I want to know.' He asked with such anxiety that, seeing his face, all of them were worried for him.

'Why are you asking about all of this?' they asked.

He remained silent for a few minutes. His long face became further drawn out. Then, in a shaky and tearful voice, he told his friends that he had stopped dreaming during sleep for months.

'So?' They didn't think of what he said as worry-worthy.

'So... I am worried.'

'You are worried about this!?' They couldn't believe him.

'Yeah…'

'Why?'

'I keep thinking about dreams.'

'What?'

'I keep thinking where they might have gone?'

All of them kept on looking at him with their mouths agape. What was he talking about? Has he lost his mind?

'What might have happened to them?' he asked with such intense concern that no one knew what to say.

'That's it?' one of them said, and started laughing.

'What do you mean "that's it"?'

'That's it means that you are sweating over such a small thing. Why?'

'Is it a small thing?'

His colleagues started staring at him closely now. One of them stopped laughing and asked, 'Dude, why are you losing sleep over such a trivial thing?'

He didn't say a word but just kept on looking at him blankly.

'Yaar, I am talking about dreams. Do you get it? Dreams...'

'Yeah, we get it.'

'I don't have any dreams left, you know. I haven't had a dream in months. I am worried sick. And you guys are laughing at it?' he said.

His colleagues tried to console him that it was no big deal that he was not dreaming at night. That, in fact, it was better to not have any type of dream these days as they were an unnecessary disturbance in sleep.

'What else! Truth be told, you are the lucky one who got rid of them,' one of them said.

He pretended not to hear what they said and asked the same question again, 'I want to know, do you guys dream or not?'

'Yaar, we don't remember, nor do we care. Actually, we don't even have time to think about this, you know…' they replied.

'You guys don't care about your dreams?' he asked, surprised.

'What's there to be surprised about?' his colleague retorted back.

Couple of them even advised him that these were not good times. It was so bad that some people were getting nightmares. 'These are the times of nightmares. You should be happy that you don't dream anymore. It is better not to dream than to have nightmares,' they said, unequivocally.

He was dumbfounded, absolutely and utterly dumbfounded to hear what his colleagues were telling him. What were they talking about?

'It is the ability to dream which makes us truly human, guys. Have you ever seen a dog or a cat dreaming?' he gave his final argument.

They were snickering now… 'Dude, what a load of bull' type of laugh, to be precise.

'And yaar, how do you know? Who knows, maybe they dream little doggy dreams? A little kitty dream!' one of them said, laughing.

'Then, won't this be even more dangerous, that we don't dream at all? Have we become worse than animals?'

His colleagues kept on looking at him in disbelief. He, too, looked back at them in disbelief.

What to say now? What could he say now?

And then for the rest of the day, he quietly worked in the office. He just sealed his lips. If anybody asked anything, he just grunted a nod or mumbled a monosyllabic reply. But after that day, it was as if his world changed completely. He changed completely. He would remain quiet, and keep to himself. Thinking something…he wouldn't sleep. He rode the bus in complete silence. If somebody sitting next to him on the bus inquired about the Ramnagar stop, he would reply saying that he didn't dream in sleep anymore, and asked of them if it had ever happened to them.

Gradually, the news spread everywhere that he had gone off the deep end. That he was worried about some random dreams so much that who's to tell; talked crazy these days, 24X7. People started avoiding him. He, too, started feeling good seeing that people were avoiding him now. He also avoided everybody.

And this is how, by avoiding everybody and far from everybody, he could quietly think about his dreams in peace.

Day-in and day-out, he was in the grips of this single thought: why couldn't he dream at night these days? If he was not dreaming dreams in the night, then where were his dreams? Where had they gone?

Now, he wouldn't shave for days on end. His wife would try to talk to him but he'd continue to wear the same clothes; he wouldn't change them even after two, three days. His hair would be disheveled all the time, so much so that a couple of times his boss asked for him in the office, and talked to him asking if he was having any trouble.

Everybody empathised with him though. He had always been an honest, conscientious, simple and responsible person. Folks were even whispering around that perhaps he had lost it because of these weaknesses. The times which we live in aren't the times to be conscientious, simple and honest. Everybody knows this and agrees upon this.

And then one day, he found a clue to his dreams being stolen while watching TV at home.

No, there wasn't any breaking news about this on TV. What happened, really, was that one day he saw his dreams being used in the advertisements being shown on TV! His jaw dropped. Stolen goods were there, right in front of his eyes. The thief was always around, somewhere near. It was he who couldn't see the thief who stole his dreams. Actually, he was so alone that he had stopped talking to his family members long ago; he had stopped shooting the breeze—sitting with his legs comfortably spread and head leaning back on a chair—with his family.

And due to this, he had stopped watching TV, too. Well, he was forced to watch it that day. He was sitting alone in the room when his son walked in and switched on the TV. He got up and was leaving when his son became angry and asked him to sit with him. He said, 'Papa why are you so quiet these days? You should watch some TV now and then. It will lighten your mood a bit.'

So, he walked back and plopped down on the sofa in front of the TV screen.

...And then, it was as if a miracle occurred. Suddenly in the middle of the TV show, he could see ads on the screen and as it goes, they kept on coming. He sat uninterested in the beginning; and then he was suddenly wide awake, startled. And then after that, he watched every ad closely.

He found that on TV, there were his dreams which were dressed anew and differently, and then presented in front of the world. Yeah, they were his dreams. Really.

There were Bazaar's ads on TV. The Bazaar had employed those dreams to sell things; it had mixed up dreams and things into each other so much so that a person would start dreaming about things.

He saw all of his dreams serving the Bazaar by working as ads on TV that day. All of his dreams, every single one of them. Truth, honesty, love, success, brotherhood, democracy, affection, goodness, beauty, health, peaceful sleep, unity, equality—every single dream of his had been abducted by the Bazaar and employed.

He silently watched all of this unfolding in front of his eyes on TV from his own two eyes, and then he silently got up.

So, that's the thing…he kept thinking, lying on his bed. His dreams had been abducted by the Bazaar!

What should he do now? He kept on mulling over, tossing and turning in his bed. But he couldn't come to something which he could do.

He was yawning now, after thinking so much.

And it happened after so many days, that he fell asleep. True!

And after so many days this miracle, too, happened that he saw a dream. Yeah, he dreamt in his sleep.

But it was a nightmare.

He saw that the Bazaar had imprisoned, chained and shackled all of his dreams. It intended to kill each one of them. The Bazaar had a steely sharp knife of Capital in its hands. And it was seen working on a big project of cloning every dream which was chained there. Eventually, it will use these dreams for itself, and will slaughter the real dreams. Right now, it was draining their blood to make clones. He saw his dreams soaked in blood and yelping, in his nightmare.

He woke up from his dream, sweating, and sat upright on his bed.

And then he couldn't fall asleep again.

He sat there motionless on his bed all through the night.

This meant that his dreams were in grave danger. He knew about the thief that stole his dreams. The thief, sooner or later, would eventually kill his dreams—this, too, was clear to him.

Then?

What should he do? It was meaningless to tell any of this to anybody at home. They would only get angry with him. They'll say that once again he has started talking about the same thing: his dreams. No, it won't do any good. There is no point in telling them anything. And friends? Colleagues? They, too, would laugh at him after hearing everything, and they'll say, 'Dude, seriously, get a grip on yourself. That's it. Nobody was going to understand the danger his dreams were in. Then, he thought of going to the police. The country was still under the rule of law; everybody falls under this rule of law. Even the Bazaar. He would go and lodge a complaint at the police station. The whole matter was crystal clear. Police would surely get his dreams back to him. Yeah, that's good.

He explained everything to his best buddy and begged him to come with him to the police station. His friend just kept on staring at him with his mouth agape and eyes wide open. So, is what his other friends say true? Has this man truly gone crazy?

His friend cautioned him that he should not even think about going to the police station, not even casually. Advised him to just banish that thought. He told him that it was not good to trust the law so blindly because even the law didn't trust the rule of law one iota these days. 'It's quite possible that they might blame you and ensnare you in this case about your dreams. And who knows...they could even beat you good and make you write up a confession,' he said.

His friend refused to go with him, point-blank.

His friend, again and again, cautioned him to not even think about going to the cops.

He somehow spent a few days in a haze.

And then he walked up to a police station to lodge his complaint. To complain about the kidnapping of his dreams.

## And Somewhere I Will Find A Different World

The night hadn't ended yet, and the dawn had dawned like an illusion. It was dark everywhere, but there was an illusion of light on the horizon.

These were some moments just before sunrise.

And at this very moment, he was standing next to a manhole, somewhat alert.

He was inspecting the manhole. And once in a while, he was also inspecting his surroundings.

The streetlights were off. A winter night. If darkness could be dissolved in the wintry fog, and then if one threw in a fistful of the glow of early morning descending on the horizon, the whole scene was appearing illusory like that. This long road was somewhat desolate—not a soul to be found.

He was bending and trying to lift the manhole cover.

Then, at this moment, far away he saw somebody walking on this same street; but he was walking slowly, and was quite far, for sure. By the time this guy would come close, he'd have definitely done his deed.

It was good that it was still dark. These days, one can hardly see anything. He, too, was looking like a phantom.

He was now completely bent over the manhole. He was about to touch its cover when, suddenly, all the streetlights lit up! The electricity supply to the lampposts was restored.

The bulb right above the manhole was now brightly lit and shining. He had now been completely exposed to the surroundings. All of his details were there for everybody to see. He was in tatters. Reed-thin. Disheveled hair. Balding head. Age around forty or forty-five years. Unshaven face, as if the last he shaved was at least four-five days ago. His two front teeth were missing. After seeing his face, one could say with certainty that he must have lost them somewhere in a losing street brawl. Old T-shirt. When he bent, the streetlight unveiled him from behind. His pants had holes in two places on the hip area.

All in all, his attire and appearance was such that any urbanite with open eyes could tell that he was a resident of a shitty slum of the city, who was trying to steal the manhole cover. These covers do get stolen now and then. But right now, all the responsible citizens of this city were busy getting some shut-eye. Yeah, someone was surely walking slowly towards this side, though he was quite far still.

He continued his efforts to lift the manhole cover despite the now brightly-lit street.

The manhole cover was quite heavy for him. Still, the reed-thin guy had managed to lift it. It even slipped out of his hands once as he was trying to hoist it on his shoulders. The cover had hit the road with a loud bang, and was now rolling off to a stop. He looked around cautiously after the bang. Had anybody seen him? The guy walking from in the distance had perhaps heard the bang. That's why he had stopped, and was trying to peer through the distance toward this side of the road. The rest of the road was empty. Puddles of light and darkness were scattered everywhere till far in the distance. Far out on the horizon, morning light was also rising somewhat slowly—as if taking stock of the situation, by peeking above the parapet of the horizon, before scattering all over. The manhole was open in front of him now. The cover was lying nearby upside down. No, nobody had seen him.

Now, he was standing upright and gawking at the open manhole from a few feet away and thinking about something. There, on the other side of the road, the man who was walking had now increased his pace. Soon, he would be here, next to the manhole. So whatever he wanted to do, he had to do it quickly. He had to do it now! He slowly squatted next to the manhole; and he looked inside while sitting like that. It was dark in there. Pitch black. Now, he was sitting at the edge of the manhole with his feet hanging in the void. He was sitting at the mouth of the manhole, as if somebody was sitting at the parapet wall of their roof with their feet dangling in mid-air. Now, he was trying to slip inside the manhole.

The door to a new world was wide-open in front of him. The world of sewage lines. He truly intended to go into this world. The portal to that world was right in front of him. The manhole was beckoning him. He was about to jump into it.

In reality, the world of sewage lines underneath the manhole had been beckoning him for quite some time. And when he left home, he was certain about everything. He was going to run away from the world on the ground and go to this new world whose door he had just opened by removing the manhole cover. The world that resided in the sewage lines.

He slowly started to descend into the manhole.

But how can somebody even think about doing something like this?

The world of filth and feces flows in the sewage pipes.

And this nutty desire to go and live in that world!

And this desire was such a strong one that it was irrepressible.

He had been thinking about doing this since last year.

But why would somebody want to go and jump into a manhole to live in the suffocating world of filth flowing in the underground pipes…was he mad? Sure, the world would say the same. And the world even told him that—that he had gone mad to even think of doing something like this.

But he had his own set of arguments…and quite compelling ones at that.

He said that he was already a resident of a world filled with faeces, dirt, flowing sewage and suffocating air, crammed with darkness. That he lived in a slum in this city, somehow keeping his knees close to his chest and keeping his head down. He was so used to the stench, mosquitoes, insects and murk that he couldn't imagine his life without them. He was tired of living in this world. He wanted to go and live in a new world. No, he didn't want that glittering, clean, spick and span, and fragrant world which was settled right next to the slums where he lived. He knew, and knew very well, that that world was not meant for him. Now, even if he imagined a new world, he imagined it with murk, stench and filth, but still, it will be very different from the world of his slums. There, he will have a bit of freedom, slightly less slavery, a bit of air to call his own, a bit of his own life, a bit of room to hold his head high, a bit of…something which he doesn't get here anymore, and there wasn't any hope of getting it anyway.

He had been out of work for many years. He hadn't had a full-square meal in ages. He hadn't lived, truly lived, in decades. He hadn't died, but he hadn't lived either. He was living in some strange condition, that was it. Once in a while, he came out of the slum and visited that world which was filled with light, which was awash with glitter, and which had shops crammed with so much stuff that they were spilling. It was not like he hadn't tried getting into that glittering world. But they quickly recognised him. Don't know how, but they recognised him. Even if he tried to go there under disguise, who knows, they might still sniff him out. Perhaps, they do sniff out people like him. Perhaps, he reeks of sewage. Don't know. And why, not just him, but his whole slum had tried to go there at least once. They still try. But that glittering world had drawn a line. They only allowed folks like him to come up to the point where there were furnaces that kept that place lit. Furnaces need fuel. The residents of slums are the fuel for that glitz and glitter and light. He, too, used to do that once upon a time. He, too, simmered and burnt for them. But now, he was tired. He knew this system of lights inside out. He now knew about himself. In this system, he was allowed to generate that light but he couldn't use it for himself. He had been granted the ownership of those darknesses which had been borne out of these lights. He was allowed to only stand in those darknesses. From there, he could watch that spectacle of light that had been produced by using him.

From the moment he took his first breath, he had been working as a fuel for the light of that world. Kept on working. Kept on being used up. Then he was exhausted. Then he stopped going to work. He would sit quietly at the doorstep in front of his shack. He would quietly look at the people walking up and down the drain-like street. People would laugh at him. They would say that he was living it up on his wife's earnings. Though he didn't really understand the meaning of living it up. Yeah, he would get drunk once in a while though. Perhaps, this is what these people called 'living it up'.

He would sit on a wooden board in front of his shack. All-day long, idling. He would take stock of the life of his neighbourhood sitting there. The more he saw things with his eyes wide open, the more his anxiety increased. What is this world of his? Is his whole life going to be spent just like that? Why don't these people find a new world? One can always go someplace new and start a whole new world altogether, right? He would think all of that, sitting there.

He would just sit there. He would just think. He would be found sitting everywhere. Always pondering something.

Often on that board, otherwise here and there. Folks from the neighbourhood would see him while going about their daily lives. There were folks who were going to their jobs. Don't know what type of jobs and don't know whose purpose they served. Components of a capital-generating machine, these people didn't know that the trash generated by this machine was what was being disposed of in their neighbourhood. It was this trash that was rotting in their neighbourhood. This poverty, this misery, this slime, diseases, hunger—all this trash was the by-product of that same machine. It was only now that he was able to understand the whole story. Otherwise, he had gone to work like this for years too. Sometimes as a watchman, sometimes as a guard, sometimes as a labourer, sometimes as a waiter, sometimes as a street vendor, sometimes as a vegetable seller, sometimes as a servant, sometimes as a juggler, sometimes as a courier boy, sometimes as a clerk, sometimes as a mason, sometimes as a carpenter—he had been going to their world in so many disguises. He knew all too well that he was a faceless person in that world. He also knew all too well that the Bazaar's world had something of an incurable attraction. Like a high. An illusion. On the surface, it seemed as if, if somehow you could please that world then your world would change too. His friends, too, told him the same thing. Folks in his neighbourhood, too, would gleefully tell him that since the Bazaar had expanded a lot now, they were getting a lot of work as well. And the same way, their lives, too, will change someday. Someday, they will be a part of that glittering world—that's what everybody thought. But entry into that world was strictly prohibited; when he would ask them this cruel question, they wouldn't be able to answer anything. All they could come up with in response was, 'Yaar, why do you talk crazy? Come to work with us.' He would never reply. Sitting on his board, he would smile a quiet smile. Folks from the neighbourhood would tell his wife that he had lost his mind, and to have him exorcised or something.

Though, gradually, people stopped listening to him at all. Instead, they started laugh at him. People hadn't started stoning him or slapping him yet, but with the speed with which the news of him going kooky was spreading in the neighbourhood, it wouldn't have been a surprise if that would happen someday. Folks around the neighbourhood called him crazy. His wife, though, had brought an amulet from a shrine and tied it on his arm. That shrine was quite revered amongst the residents of this neighbourhood.

One day, he was customarily sitting by the roadside. In front of him, a guy from his neighbourhood had gone down the manhole to clean it. When that guy came out of the manhole, he saw him sitting there.

He walked up to him, laughing. He, too, was from the same neighbourhood. He knew that this guy was crazy. Let's have some fun, he thought.

'How come you are sitting here?' he asked, presenting a *beedi*.

'Nothing,' he said while taking the *beedi*.

'So, what are you up to these days? Huh?'

'Nothing. Nothing much.'

'Tell me, would you like to work? The contractor needs a couple of extra hands. Pronto.'

'What for?'

'For this. You'll have to go down the manhole, though. You have to check sewage and all. That's it. Some cleaning, clearing the blockages. You'll make decent money in it too. So? Are you in? What do you say?'

He didn't say a word. He quietly kept on looking at the manhole. The manhole cover was lying on the side next to the opening. A mound of filth and dirt was piled up next to the road, waiting its turn to be soon taken to the garbage truck parked next to it.

'Don't you feel suffocated when you are down there?' he asked casually after a long pause.

'Nah. Everything is fine and dandy down there.'

'Everything is fine down there?'

'Swell!'

'Don't you feel jittery in the sewage pipes?'

'What for?'

'It must be pitch-dark down there?'

'Yeah. It is. But it's no biggy. Once you get down even in the pitch-dark, you start seeing everything after some time.'

'And filth? Stench?'

'It is the same as our neighbourhood. Same filth, same stench.'

'Really? That's it?'

'True. See it this way...it's as if our neighbourhood is like an open sewage...pipes down there have the same filth as our neighbourhood. That's all.'

He kept on sitting quietly, thinking something. His buddy took a puff or two of his *beedi*.

'So, it's the same down below as what's up here? Just like our neighbourhood, right?'

'Yeah. Something like that.'

'Then, somebody, if one wants, he can live down there. Right?'

'Yaar, why would somebody want to go and live down there?' he started laughing, hearing his crazy-talk.

'But suppose that if somebody is already living down there, then?'

'Yaar, stop talking like a crazy man.'

'You just tell me this…one can live down there, right?'

'But why would somebody go and live down there?'

'What do you mean why? That's the thing with humans. They can live anywhere. Don't you see them living everywhere, every day?'

'Yaar… You are such a…'

He kept on looking at the manhole, unblinking.

'Okay, tell me this…have you ever seen a neighbourhood down there?' he asked abruptly, just like that.

'What!? What did you just say?' he asked, astonished.

'I was thinking that there could there be a whole neighbourhood down there. Suppose people live in those pipes down there, then?'

'Yaar, you have really gone nuts. People are right.'

'Why? What about when people start living in pipes up here? Same way, even there, they could...'

'Get yourself checked. You are losing your mind. No, really. You are going insane.'

'What's so crazy about this? The whole city has miles of pipes laid underneath. Who knows a whole neighbourhood might have settled there? People might be living there..'

'Yaar...I have got a job to do. I already have a lot to do. That mound of filth has to be loaded onto the truck. In chatting with you...'

'Tell me the truth, you've never seen any settlement there?' he became restless and grabbed the guy's wrist.

'My bad...forgive me and let me go. I made a mistake when I sat down and started chatting with a nut like you.' He pulled his hand back and got up from there.

That man walked towards the garbage truck. He, though, was left sitting there. And then he kept sitting there on the roadside till late at night. Staring non-stop at the manhole. The guy from the neighbourhood, too, eventually put the cover back on the manhole and left. He shouted as he was leaving, 'Go home! Are you going to just sit here or what?'

It was as if he didn't hear anything. He was in deep thought. During the night his wife, too, came there looking for him, and eventually found him. Accompanying her were some folks from the neighbourhood. They managed to take him back somehow.

It was quite late in the night.

He lay down half-heartedly after eating something.

His wife sat next to him, worried.

His wife, too, had started to think that he had gone insane. How many times had she taken him to Babas and Sadhus? Brought in an amulet or something every other day. Even had a special puja performed in the shack. She remained quiet a lot these days as well. She was scared. Even before today, he had talked to his wife about discovering, and starting a new world. She started sobbing hearing that, and started telling him that he shouldn't think like that. He tried explaining it to her but she didn't understand. She didn't know that he was aiming at settling in a new world. He was ready to live in the world of sewers, dirt, filth, and insects—provided he had freedom. He had to build a new world.

The only thing he couldn't think of till now was where he should settle this new world of his, that's all.

It was not possible to evade them. Wherever you will go, there they will be. They will use you. It doesn't matter where you go. On a mountain. In a cave. In the sea. In a forest. If you go tribal in a forest, they will create a spectacle out of you and use you. If you become a sadhu and sit in a cave, they will find you and come to you posing as disciples and set up a shop at your pretense… No…you won't be able to build a new world according to your design here.

He was troubled for such a long time about where he could go…where they won't be able to reach him at all.

He found that place today after seeing the manhole. Today, he found the solution to his problem.

There were miles and miles of unoccupied land beneath this. Pipes, miles-long, had already been laid down underneath this.

Ah! What an idiot he had been for so many days. Why didn't he think of this place before? He kept wandering overground. The thought of the sewage pipes underground didn't even occur to him. Why not settle a new world in them?

That's the only place where they hadn't reached yet. Perhaps, they won't reach there anytime soon. They were so busy making money on the surface that they won't have time to go underground and capture that world.

Yes, that's where he will go.

There was only an iron cover on the mouth of this new world. He would open that portal and enter that new world. When everybody in the shack would be asleep, he would slowly get out. And then he would lift that manhole cover and exit this world.

A world filled with possibilities was waiting for him.

He was sitting, dangling his feet in the manhole with the cover removed.

Slowly sliding down.

And in a few moments, he would jump down.

By now the morning's faint light had spread everywhere.

The man coming from afar was now very close to him.

But before he could jump down, that man recognised him.

And that man was now running towards him. He was screaming, trying to stop him from jumping.

'What the hell are you doing Ramesh!? You'll fall!'

The man had come close now and grabbed his hand.

'Do you want to die?' he said, pulling his hand.

It was dawn.

## There Is A Psychiatric Clinic In The Open Grounds Too

One who comes disappointed from everywhere is the one who comes here, or is brought here. It is quite revered, this place, even in faraway places. The shrine has been here for years but it didn't have the splendour of today. Then, some ten years ago a somewhat eccentric fakir materialised there, don't know from where. Slowly, his spiritual fragrance wafted everywhere. The folks living nearby recognised that the Baba was miraculous. Even if he cursed anybody, that person's problem was solved. And if he kicked somebody, then it was as if that person's fate was getting a makeover. He was always staring at his worshippers, suddenly getting excited for no reason, and if and when his heart was over the moon, he started dancing in the crowd too. He lost his temper seeing a woman. Women were not allowed to enter this place; although he cured women too. If there was a problem related to a woman, one was required to bring a piece of her clothing to the durbar. If he even touched that piece of cloth or slapped the person bringing the cloth, that itself was considered his blessing.

Women came with family members but they didn't enter the shrine. They waited outside, sitting on the ground, praying and asking for blessings.

Lunatics from the world over were brought here. The cure here was cheap, and its curing power was almost guaranteed—or that's what was credited. The treatment of the mentally ill was so expensive otherwise that if you went for complete treatment, you would go insane yourself. Surely, it wasn't for the poor. The middle class also wasn't that crazy. The patient was taken to the psychiatrist's clinic in the expensive healthcare market maybe once or twice, and then the patient took those same medicines later in bits and pieces. These were difficult times. It was a form of extravagance to be a 'mental patient' these days. You could afford a psychiatrist only if you had a fat wallet. For other patients, there were shrines like these scattered everywhere, and the kicks and curses of eccentric fakirs and babas was the treatment. Although this, too, wasn't that cheap. This, too, had a market of its own. It was a different kind of bazaar around these shrines and temples. It was quite lively in this desolate area, far from the city.

There were lots of shops outside the shrine. It was a long continuum of shops on either side of the road. And then in the courtyard built in front of the shrine, people were selling things and whatnot too. Prasad, big or small, laced or simple, velvety spreads for the shrine—to each according to his faith and might—frankincense, photos of the shrine, fans made of peacock feathers, and brooms made of peacock feathers too. And then street food shops. Sometimes it took hours for a patient to have his turn to see the fakir. Till then, only these shops gave respite. Mentally ill patients waited for their turn, sitting or lying down on the mats spread here and there in the courtyard. There was an arrangement to see the fakir out of turn as well. Baba ji's trusted disciples could have that arranged for a small fee. They could sniff out the customer with the might to cough up the money. Even now, they were roaming around the courtyard trying to sniff out such a customer in the crowd.

'What has happened to Babu ji?' one such minion had just asked while pointing at the gentleman sitting on a mat nearby.

'Don't know what to say. He is always depressed. That's all,' the concerned woman sitting next to the man on the mat replied.

'Aunty, only depressed and despondent come here. What exactly has happened to him?' he asked again.

People sitting nearby, too, had turned towards their conversation to kill time.

'Oh! He is anxious all the time. Twenty-four seven. He wakes up in the middle of the night,' the woman started telling.

'He is looking anxious even now. Why is he so worried? Does he say anything?' There was extra dash of cordiality dripping from the disciple's voice; so much so that it was soaking the mat on the ground.

'He says that someone has seized his dreams.'

'Huh! Why would somebody seize someone else's dreams? And what will he do with them after seizing them?' the disciple replied while looking at the crowd sitting nearby, pulling them into the conversation as well.

The gentleman was staring into the sky sitting quietly.

'Uncle, why?' the minion asked him directly.

He raised his head.

'Have you lost your dreams?'

He sat there mute.

'You'll find every single one of them with the fakir's blessings, don't you worry. It will be alright. You will find your dreams back. Definitely. People even get their kids who were lost a decade ago back. Don't you worry.'

'I haven't lost my dreams,' he spoke eventually.

'Then?'

'They were seized.'

'Who in their right mind would seize dreams?'

'Bazaar. The Bazaar keeps an eye on everybody's dreams. It has seized my dreams.'

'Well. Everybody has to be careful these days in a market, uncle. There, anybody can take anything of yours. People pickpocket. They can take anything in a blink of an eye if you lose sight of it even for a moment.'

'No. They haven't just taken away my dreams.'

'Then?'

'The Bazaar confiscated my dreams from me.'

'Oh! Talk about hooliganism these days…'

'The Bazaar took away my dreams from me…' And he suddenly started screaming, saying 'My dreams, my dreams'.

'There, there…get a grip on yourself. Have faith. Everything will be fine. All you need is Fakir Baba's blessings once…'

'But there was a baba also amongst the ones who took away my dreams…'

'That must have been some charlatan. There are hardly true seers left in this country anymore,' the minion said.

'Please don't cry. You will get your dreams back,' another minion chimed in.

'Didn't you file a complaint somewhere?' an innocent-looking gentleman standing nearby asked.

Everybody broke into a burst of laughter upon hearing his question.

'Yeah. We did. He went all the way up to the police station,' the woman said.

'And then?' somebody asked.

'Why did you go there? God forbid, one is so crazy that he goes to the police station on his own,' a certain alert gentleman quipped.

'I told the inspector that they had taken my dreams away,' he started recounting.

'So...'

'So what? He beat me black and blue and sent me back,' he said, and started whimpering.

'And also tell them how much money they took from you before letting you go,' the woman added.

'Anyway, you would have had to spend some money if you went to the police station,' somebody said.

'By the way, how were your dreams?'

'They were shiny ones, my dreams!' he stopped crying, and was enthralled. Resigned, he started talking about his dreams.

'Such shining dreams they were, sahab! Our ancestors had nurtured them for ages. We thought that in the light of these dreams...'

Right behind this crowd, a man was lying down on the bare ground with his eyes closed. Somewhat poor; not in tatters, but not far from that either.

'I have seen your dreams…' he said lying down on the ground, and without even opening his eyes.

The man suddenly spun towards him.

'You've seen my dreams?' he anxiously started asking.

He opened his eyes now and turned towards the gentleman.

'Your dreams were somewhat shiny ones, right?' he asked.

'Good dreams have their characteristic true glitter,' he said.

'These dreams were emanating light, right? They could fill the whole world with light, they were that bright, right?'

'Yes, yes, that's right! They were just like that. Where have you seen these dreams? Tell me. Where did you see them?'

'I have seen them floating in a sewage pipe…' he said. Now, he was sitting completely upright and looking at him compassionately.

'In a sewage pipe? Why were you looking into a sewage pipe? Do you clean them or what?' people asked, scornfully.

Some folks even put some distance between them and him.

His wife started pleading with people.

'No, no. He doesn't work there. Please don't pay any attention to him. He has lost his mind.'

'Everybody who has come here is like that…' Somebody said in despair.

'So you've seen my dreams floating in a sewage pipe? Are you telling the truth?' When everybody had moved away from him, he had gone and sat down next to him.

'Why would I lie to you? Thats true, hand on my heart. Once I removed the manhole cover and took a peek inside...'

'If you don't work there then why were you removing the manhole cover, brother?' Somebody interrupted and asked him.

His wife once again pleaded with everybody.

'Don't listen to him, please. He doesn't know what he is talking about. He is out of his mind. He tries to go down the manhole now and then. He says that he wants to go and live down there in the pipes.'

'Down there!? In the filth of sewage? What the...?' Somebody said.

'Yaar, loonies of every make and model come here.' Somebody else added.

'Have you seen my dreams there?' He had taken him by his shoulders and was vigorously shaking him anxiously.

'Yeah, yeah. I have seen them. All the pipes below the manhole were suddenly filled with light. True. The corpses of your dreams were very bright.'

'Corpses?' He said swallowing a lump in his throat.

'Yeah. All of them didn't look dead. Some sure were, but others still had faint signs of life in them...'

'My dreams cant be dead. How would they shine if they were dead?'

'It is quite possible that all of them had some signs of life still left in them. The pipes were so filled with light, and dazzling so much that I had to shield my eyes… So I couldn't see clearly.'

'But, how did they reach there? My dreams?' he was excited and a bit worried too.

'How would I know? You probably would have a better idea. After all, they were your dreams. But, I've seen them there, that's for sure. Later, when I will start living in those pipes then I will try to look for your dreams,' the guy said.

He had grown quite restless.

'Surely, they must have killed my dreams and thrown their bodies down the manhole. Right, no?' he asked him.

'Yeah. It's possible. Haven't we heard such things happening in movies and stories?' somebody agreed.

He started trembling due to the peak in agitation. He suddenly stood up and started walking in circles around this guy.

'Will you be my eyewitness?' he asked, stopping midway while circling.

'Eyewitness?'

'Yeah. You've seen my dreams floating in the sewage pipes, haven't you? I will go to the police station once again. All you have to do is be a witness from my side. They will have to file a police complaint now.'

'Complaint against whom?' the guy asked.

'Against the Bazaar. It is the one that has…' he said.

Listening to him, that guy said, 'Who is going to believe

my testimony or what you have to say? It is quite a mighty presence against whom you want to go to the police.'

He broke into a sob.

'Forget about the cops. You know, you should come down with me. Look for your dreams in that world of pipes with me,' the guy said.

He kept on crying quietly.

The fakir's minion, too, got scared, seeing this scene. He hastily disappeared from there saying he had to go to try to arrange for the fakir's darshan for uncle quickly, and that he'd try to arrange for it for lesser amount.

'So nobody is going to listen to my complaint?' he asked another guy sitting nearby, still sobbing.

'He just babbles like this all day long,' the gentleman's wife said, looking at everybody with sorry eyes.

He had broken from sobbing into full-on crying.

'My dreams, my dreams,' he had started remembering his dreams while weeping too.

That guy, who had seen the dreams floating in the sewage, too, started slowly sliding closer towards him. He was crying loudly now. And then suddenly, that guy put his arms around him and started crying with him.

In the courtyard of Fakir Baba's shrine, two lunatics, with their arms around each other, were crying loudly and bitterly. They were mourning for dreams.

## They Are Coming For Eviction

When he sneaked back into the house like a thief, nobody had an inkling.

'When did you come back?' his wife saw him, and asked.

He didn't say anything. Only, quietly started locking the door.

First, the bottom latch. Then the latch on top. Interlock. He rapidly locked every single lock of the house.

And then he started running around the house bolting every single window in sight. He was sprinting as though if he got even slightly late, somebody would jump in from those windows.

'What are you doing?' Suddenly why was he locking down all the windows and doors? She couldn't understand.

But it was as if he just hadn't heard what his wife had asked. With haste and concentration, he drew the curtains in the room as well.

'Would you please tell me what's going on? What is this that you are doing?' Now his wife had gotten up from where she was sitting and came close to him.

She looked at his face while asking. Seeing his ashen face, she was worried about him. It was so white, as if somebody had drained every single drop of blood from it. Eyes, too, were vacant, but alert. Ears perked up. A worried, alert, scared, and watchful man was standing in front of her.

'Say something! What happened?' his wife grabbed his arm and gave him a good jerk.

He pulled back his hand, picked up the remote and switched off the TV as well.

Now for the first time, he said something.

'If you'll watch the TV with such loud volume, they'll know that somebody is in the house,' he said.

'Who will know?' the wife asked, stunned.

In between this little exchange, he had tip-toed to the window and peeked outside by raising a corner of the curtain.

'Who are you talking about? Who will come to know?' his wife yelled.

He said murmuring in a voice raising an alert, 'Speak softly. Very softly. They'll hear…'

'Who? Who will hear?'

'They are everywhere. They put an ear to everything. The walls are ours but it's their ears.'

'What are you talking about? Which walls? Whose ears?'

He was still trying to make an alert effort to take a peek outside by pulling a corner of the curtain aside.

The wife tried to pull the curtain and see what the matter was. Who was he trying to look for? He pushed his wife away in nervousness. She almost fell on the floor.

'Don't! Don't pull the curtain! They are circling outside!'

He was leaning back against the curtain and staring at his wife.

He was panting.

His wife was scared.

'Who? Who is outside?' she asked almost in a whisper.

He kept his finger on his lips, signaling her to keep quiet.

He was straining his ears, trying to listen to the sounds coming from outside.

There were sounds of cars and scooters passing through the neighbourhood. A few kids passed by, laughing. Sound of a bouncing ball. Perhaps, they were returning from a soccer game. Two dogs had started to fight. Then a few more dogs had joined in. The cacophony of barking was fading now. Perhaps, the dogs were going to a different street while barking. *Aarti* (prayers) had begun in the temple around the corner. He slowly left the window and came near her.

'Kids haven't come back?' he asked slowly.

'What are you talking about? It is only 7:00. It is 9:00 by the time they come home from coaching,' the wife muttered.

'It's only 7:00 now?' he asked, surprised.

'Why? You don't look at your watch these days?'

'Didn't get a chance. They were suddenly after me. They were chasing me. I wandered around trying to give them a slip and it took me a while to reach home. It wasn't easy to shake them off,' he started telling her, and once again mentioned them.

'After all, who is following you? What have you done?'

'Me? Why would I do something? I haven't done anything.'

'Then?'

'What do you mean by "then"?'

'Then why would somebody follow you?'

'It's not like they are following *me*. They are after everybody. Every citizen of this country is being followed around. What is he talking about? What is she doing? Everything, everything is recorded and noted down. Where does he live, even that is noted down…'

'I don't know what you are talking about. You are not making sense. All of this is beyond me.'

'See! That's the problem, right there. People are unable to understand that they are being followed. And by the time they will understand, it will be too late.'

Just then he heard some noise in the kitchen. He became so agitated that it was difficult to handle him.

'They are here! See! We sat here shutting the main gate and they came into the house through the backdoor!' He was pressed against the wall in fear.

'Ah! That might be the cat. Doesn't it come in sometimes when I leave the kitchen window open?' the wife reassured him.

'Don't you be so careless. They can come into the house in the disguise of a cat.'

He started pacing the room in a frenzy. His wife couldn't think of anything to do.

She ran inside and brought a glass of water for him. She forcibly sat him down on the sofa. Gave him water. Caressed his back. Touched his forehead.

'Here, take a sip. Calm down, make yourself comfortable and then tell me what's going on.'

'They are dangerous people.'

'We are simple people. What do they have to do anything with us?'

'They have to do everything with everybody. They want to evict us. They are going to evict everybody.'

'What are you talking about?'

'Why don't you understand? They incline to evict us from our homes.'

'How can they?' his wife asked.

'These people are on a mission to expel us from life itself and put the Bazaar there,' He tried to explain himself to her.

'How can anyone evict us just like that?' the wife said, her voice filled with disbelief, and also with worry about the nonsense he was talking about.

'Why? Why cant they?'

'Is it a joke or what? This eviction you talk about. How can anybody evict us just like that without any rhyme or reason? This is our house. We have a registry in our name for this. Isn't there something called law or not?'

He started smiling even in distress.

'Law is the biggest joke in itself.'

'What nonsense!'

'I am telling the truth. Law is a joke. You know, though I do feel like crying instead of laughing. If those people come, don't you start talking about the law in front of them.'

He remained restless after that, and kept looking into things around the house. Then the children, too, came back home. He opened the door only after thoroughly examining everything.

Then it was night. They didn't sleep. Wife, children—everybody was worried. And then he said that he will keep vigil on the roof because he thought they could come in the night and they would be caught sleeping.

By the time the children could understand a thing or two, he ran upstairs to the roof. He didn't want to come back. When somehow they managed to bring him downstairs, he kept on saying that he will go to the roof now and then to keep an eye out. Then through the whole night, he kept getting up and roaming around the house, repeatedly checked everything. He kept on going back to the roof, kept on looking at the street below, standing next to the parapet. If he heard even the slightest sound, he would jump off his bed and run in its direction. Neither did he sleep, nor did he let anybody else sleep.

And then, this became an everyday affair.

After that night, he became like that forever.

Now his days and nights passed just like that—in fear. He would be anxious, always. Always restless and constantly alert. He even stopped blinking, dreading the unexpected. He would walk around the house stony-eyed, in a daze. And even if he slept for a brief moment at his wife's coaxing, he would sleep under the bed with a thick pole close at hand. He would explain to his children and wife that they should always sleep keeping the chilli powder at hand at all times. He even stopped meeting anybody. Stopped going out of the house. Stopped going to work, and sent an application for a long leave.

It was best to stay at home and keep an eye on the enemy's activities. He will have to shoulder this responsibility himself. All the other members of the family were way too careless. He tried to explain to them but they still didn't understand. He ran around shutting the doors and windows around the house but those fools, his family, opened them again and again. He couldn't trust his house to these people. And that's why he didn't even get out of his house anymore. If somebody came to see him, he asked even them in whispers that they sure must have seen it, to tell him how far the Bazaar had reached and where else in the city was the eviction going on. And then his friends, too, stopped visiting him. Neighbours and acquaintances also started saying amongst themselves that these days Sharma ji had completely lost it.

And then, gradually, his condition worsened further. His fear increased more. Now, he would constantly be in fear. He'd be startled at the slightest sound. If somebody knocked on his door, he would run and hide under the bed in fear. And would remain there, would insist on staying there, always afraid that they will find him under that bed. He would intercept the government's secret messages, which they send through wireless, mid-air. And that's how he knew that the government was now hand in glove with the Bazaar. And that's why the government's agents, too, were looking for him. The government kept an eye on anybody who was against the Bazaar.

And then, the other day, it went too far. That day, he went to his bank. There, he filed an application to withdraw all his money from his savings account and sat down quietly, hidden, far from anybody's sight. And it just so happened that the bank employee was a family acquaintance. He, too ,had heard few things about him through the grapevine. He was suspicious. He told him to sit tight and had somebody phone his home. They all came running.

Somehow they managed to bring him back home.

'What was that you were trying to do, Papa?' he asked, scolding him after coming back home. It was as if the adolescent son has matured overnight. Father's mental condition had increased his wisdom and understanding by years.

'They were going to confiscate our money.'

'Nobody can do anything like that, Papa'

'They are going to issue an order with the help of the government, saying that all the money deposited in the bank should be handed over to the Bazaar.'

'Oh! Come on! There is nothing like that,' his wife chimed in.

'It is like that. I know. I have intercepted their wireless messages.'

'Oh, my God!' she started crying.

'Why don't you take a rest for a while? Just a shut-eye for a few moments and you will feel...' his son tried to make him lie down forcibly.

'Shut-eye? Have you gone mad? This is the time to keep your eyes wide open. They can come here any minute. Those who are going to evict people have been sent for here.'

'Papa, nobody is coming here,' his son replied, irritated.

'They are coming. I know.'

'And our government? Won't it stop them?' his wife asked.

'They evict the governments first. They have already done that.'

'And the Parliament?'

'Don't even ask. It's better to keep that illusion alive.'

'And the Constitution?'

'They have forced so many amendments in the Constitution that every page in it is now in tatters. It is unreadable. And understanding it is almost impossible. Evicting us would be declared constitutional. They will come with the government's order in their hands. They will hand us a puny compensation. And even if they drag us out of our homes by the neck, all courts will say that we have been compensated for our discomfort.'

'How do you know all of this? Does nobody else talks like this?' the wife asked.

'I can see and hear things that nobody else can.'

'How?'

'I have Divine Vision. I have a direct link with God these days.'

'What!? What do you have with God these days?'

'Gods tell me every insider story every day by whispering it in my ears. Though, even He can't tell anything reliably these days.'

'Oh Lord!'

'What if they stopped talking to me for the fear of the Bazaar? If they won't tell me, how would I know?' he grew concerned while mumbling to himself.

The wife rested her head in her hands and started crying again.

'You know, I even told God that when He knows everything, why doesn't He stop these wicked people? Here, they are mercilessly evicting His worshippers and all He is doing is just watching this quietly, sitting and doing nothing?' he started mumbling again.

The wife kept on crying.

'God said that the Bazaar is beyond even us. It has become the Supreme God now.'

'You are making us crazy…' his son said, face-palming himself.

The man kept on mumbling.

'Even God can't fight the Bazaar now. When I asked Him, He said that our *puja* is in the Bazaar's hands now, so we are helpless. All we can do is whisper into somebody's ear now and then.'

The wife kept on crying; the son started consoling her.

## Who Am I?

'How may I help you, sir?' the Bazaar asked courteously. 'Yeah. Could you please tell me who am I?'

'Sir…!?'

'Yeah. My memory isn't serving me right. So much so that I can't even recall my name right now. What can I do? I have forgotten myself. And I don't know whom I should ask. Here, there, and everywhere, all I can see is you—so I am asking you. Please, help me! Who am I?' he asked the Bazaar.

The Bazaar smiled a market-friendly smile. It pressed a switch next to its lips and the smile increased manifold, without even emanating the slightest warmth. And along with the smile, the face also started expressing shades of politeness.

'So, what's the big deal? This is a very common concern these days. Please don't worry. We, as a matter of fact, know you quite well.'

'Oh! So, please tell me now!'

'You.Are.Our.Most.Valuable.Customer, sir,' the Bazaar said with a dramatic flair.

He was pleased.

At least he found somebody who knew him, as his memory wasn't serving him well these days. He forgot familiar routes. He didn't remember faces these days either. Now, just a few moments ago, he couldn't recall who he was. And that was too much. And in such a tricky situation, what a great relief it is to meet somebody who knows you well.

'Wait a second! You said you recognise me, right?' he asked, wanting to confirm.

'Yes. I know you very well. You are our important customer, sir.'

'Important?'

'See, every customer is very important to us, sir,' the Bazaar pressed another switch next to his neck with such sleight of hand that its head bowed in respect without feeling even a trace of respect. Such a lifesaver, this switch. Always comes in handy in sticky situations while delivering such lines—the Bazaar had been thoroughly trained in business etiquette.

'So, please tell me how can I help you?' the Bazaar asked again.

'That's about it. See if you can help me with this. These days I forget almost everything, my friend. Right now, I can't even recall who I am. I can't recall my name even. What do you think I should do?' he asked the Bazaar.

'But right now, you are recognising me, sir. Right?' the Bazaar asked.

'Who doesn't recognise you these days!'

'That's so nice of you to say. That's your graciousness,' the Bazaar pressed another switch to kick its politeness a notch higher.

'You recognised me, which means your memory is working well. Right, sir?'

'No, it's not like that. You are everywhere these days. It's impossible to forget you. But I still can't recall my name. I mean, I really can't. I am unable to,' he said.

'Sir, even if you can't recall your name, I am sure you can recall at least one of your many important ID numbers. You can tell me that. We can feed that number into any computer and retrieve your name,' the Bazaar suggested a way out of this.

He chuckled to himself, 'When I can't recall my own name, how would I be able to recall any ID number?!'

Still, there was no harm in making an effort to recall. He started thinking.

And the more he thought, the more surprised he became.

Slowly, and one-by-one, he was able to recall his PAN number, his two cell numbers, his job staff number at the place he worked, the PIN of his credit cad, and his driver's license number—all of them. What the…? I can recall so many numbers yet I can't recall my own name. How remarkable, he thought to himself.

'Have I been reduced to just an ID number now?' he asked.

'Beg your pardon?' the Bazaar couldn't understand his concern.

'I only ask this because I can recall all these ID numbers yet I can't recall my own name.'

'Ah! I see. Anyway, what's in a name, sir? Just make sure that you don't forget these ID numbers. You need them everywhere these days.'

'Still! My name…'

The Bazaar, seeing him getting worried, swiftly pressed another switch and also started looking worried without feeling the slightest trace of worry. How efficiently it could help this potential customer!

The Bazaar was 'deeply committed' to helping its customers. This helpfulness was an intimate part of its persona, its being. It didn't matter if it were truly being helpful or not—as long as one gave a feeling that the person was being helped in some way or the other, that itself sufficed. The Bazaar did exactly that.

'Sir, you have some type of card with you, don't you?' the Bazaar asked.

'Yeah, yeah. There are so many of them,' he started checking his pockets as he was finishing his sentence.

'Then there is hardly any problem, sir. You can take out any card and have a look at it. It will have your name on it.'

Duh!

Why didn't he think of such a trivial thing? The Bazaar was perfectly right. He should have checked his name already. Embarrassingly, he started taking out cards from his pocket. He started closely looking at the first card which he could find. The card had a name and a photo of a guy on it but he couldn't identify with him. Was that him or somebody else?

He showed the card to the Bazaar and asked, 'Is that me?'

'Yes, sir. That's you. It must be you. Who else could it be? If the card is yours, then it must be you on the card, right?'

'But how can you be so sure that this is *my* card?'

'I mean this came out of your pocket…so if this is not yours, then whose could it be?'

'But that doesn't mean anything. What if this is somebody else's card and it accidentally came into my pocket? Then?'

'Though I do think that this photo is yours,' the Bazaar responded after comparing the photo on the card with his face.

'Mine? But this doesn't look like me.'

'Why?'

'The man in the photo looks very happy. I haven't been that happy in years.'

'Well…look, sir, when a person has his photo taken he pretends that he is happy. They say that having one's photo taken this way, they turn out much better.'

'But I have never even pretended to be this happy.'

'Whatever, but this photo is yours,' the Bazaar looked at the photo and then at him, and said in a tone as if it was declaring a final verdict on the matter.

'But his nose is crooked,' he, too, looked at the photo closely and then objected.

'Please don't pay too much attention to the nose, sir. The new cards which are coming out these days for customers don't even have a nose on them. That's the latest trend these days, to have your nose removed from the photos. This is what customers like and want.' The Bazaar keeps an eye on the latest trends. Always.

'But, but a man without a nose!? That's like losing a part of your face,' he said, surprised.

'Yes. A person must be without a nose in the right fashion. These are the times when Time itself has lost face, so it becomes a necessity for a person to lose face in some way,' the Bazaar shared its world philosophy of losing face.

'But a man without a nose would look strange, no?'

'Just take a good, hard look around you one of these days, sir. Does anybody walking around here look strange to you? Take a look around. Everybody has lost face in one way or the other.'

'No, no. They all look fine to me,' he turned his head, took a good look all around and said.

'No, sir. They all have lost face,' the Bazaar explained.

'But their nose?'

'That's not their nose. It's an illusion. These days you can get a decent durable illusion at a discount and any face can be sold to anybody at a premium. People sell their noses but keep an illusion affixed. Everybody is comfortable with this.'

'Comfortable?'

'Yeah. Comfortable. At ease. The nose was quite an obstacle in many things, sir. Somebody would thumb their nose at something or somebody would keep their nose too much in the air. You know, things like that. And then what's the use of a nose when Time itself has lost its face? Wouldn't it be foolish to worry about the nose in such trendy times? Right, sir?'

After hearing about Time so many times, suddenly he thought of time too. What time was it? He had been wandering in the market for quite some time now. Folks at home might be worried about him.

He glanced at his wristwatch.

What time must it be? He looked at it closely.

And he was stunned.

The watch was firmly on his wrist, the way it is supposed to be but Time had disappeared from there.

The watch was telling the time correctly when he had left home. Then? What happened between now and then? Where did his time go? As soon as he stepped out of his house, it was the Bazaar's territory. Could it be that his time fell off of his wrist and in the market somewhere? And now he was just left walking with an empty wristwatch.

'I have lost my time somewhere,' he said.

'It must still be there, somewhere in that watch. With you. Please carefully double-check again. See, how the times are changing at such a fast pace that people can hardly recognise it. Please check again.' The Bazaar understands Time well.

He looked at his watch closely once again.

The hands of the wristwatch were so bent out of shape, as if somebody had wrung it out of the watch by twisting Time's wrist; nor could one see the digits on the dial. In reality, the dial's face was flat and empty. The watch was looking quite alarming.

'These are alarming times,' he mumbled to himself.

The Bazaar kept on looking at him compassionately.

'What has happened to you, sir? Be positive, think positive.'

He stayed silent. He was caressing his face, especially his nose. Was this his nose still? Or was it an illusion? He also closely looked at the photo on the card.

'Say, what exactly is my real face?' he said, mumbling.

'What does it matter, sir?'

'No. I mean still.'

'You would have had at least some memory of that, right?'

'Had I remembered that clearly I wouldn't have been in this pickle now, would I?'

'What pickle?'

'The same pickle that one gets into when one loses all of their memories. It is necessary to take care of one's memories. Memories should be cherished—by man, and by society too.'

Don't know this customer is talking all gibberish. Making such a big deal out of losing a teeny bit of memory, the Bazaar thought to itself and kept on closely looking at him.

'You would have remembered at least traces of your face, correct?'

'Why?'

'Well, if you won't remember anything then how will you identify your photo? How will you confirm?'

He, too, started thinking. It made sense.

'I trust myself. I will be able to recognise myself when I'll see myself.'

'But weren't you saying moments ago that you forget a lot these days?'

'But I haven't forgotten myself yet,' he broke into a smile, hearing his own thought.

'Then this is a piece of cake. Why don't you take a look in the mirror there? They have huge mirrors in the washroom. You can find them when you take a left turn next to the footwear showrooms. You can go there and compare your face to the photo. It's also quite possible that by doing this exercise you might get your memory back. Go, have a look,' the Bazaar said, wanting to get rid of this customer by any means necessary.

The Bazaar thanked him and as it was turning to address other customers; he, too, ended up thanking Bazaar.

And then he ambled his way to the washroom.

He had a card in his hand. The card had a photo which, as was told to him, was his.

There were huge mirrors on one of the walls of the washroom. The frame of the mirror itself was so ornate that he couldn't gather the courage to look at such a luxurious mirror. He was a bit afraid. What if he was about to take a look in the mirror and somebody walked in, grabbed him by his neck and threw him out saying how he could be so idiotic as to commit the folly of looking into such a precious mirror?

He stood there in front of the mirror but without looking into it for a while.

And then, slowly, he raised his head and looked into the mirror.

He saw a person standing in the mirror. Staring at him.

Who is this man? Is that him? If that's him then why can't he recognise himself in the mirror?

Has he changed? Has he become now what he looks like in the mirror? He tried to remember his old face. Nothing concrete came to his mind. Though he still remembered the fact that if one stood in front of a mirror, they will see their image in it.

So, according to that, the man standing in the mirror must be him. He took another close look at the man in the mirror. So this is me, he thought to himself. But I haven't seen this person before. Then? What is going on? Could it be that this mirror itself is playing tricks on me? One can't just randomly trust the mirrors hanging in a market. No matter how ornate and fancy a frame might be, the thing which will matter the most is how the mirror is. What if the Bazaar had some other person altogether and had him stand in this mirror, then? Who knows, the Bazaar might have had somebody stand within the mirror who was more favourable to it. An exact person of its liking, just the way the Bazaar wanted to shape you. And if you saw that person day in and day out, you would become like that person who is in the mirror and forget yourself too. The image which you are seeing in the mirror, thinking that it is you is, in fact, the one that has been fixed by the Bazaar. You are not *you* anymore. You do look into the mirror but what you see is that guy. Could it be that seeing one's reflections in the Bazaar's mirrors, the world itself was forgetting its true self? Aren't we shaping ourselves the way the Bazaar wants us to be shaped? Isn't our reflection in the mirror being manipulated? Could the mirror be photoshopping us? Could it be the reason that the Bazaar sent that guy here so that now I start seeing myself like him? And stop searching for my forgotten self?

He kept on staring at the man in the mirror.

The man in the mirror, standing, was also staring at him.

Suddenly, the man in the mirror winked at him. Did he? Or did he not? Or maybe his eye was twitching?

No, the man in the mirror was even smirking after winking.

He suddenly became nervous seeing this scene. And in that nervousness, he moved away from the mirror. And doubling his pace, he walked out of the washroom.

Outside, the Bazaar was brimming over.

Outside there were waves. Escalators were going up and down. The surf was floating. The crowd was flowing. Deep whirlpools would form and the customers would disappear into them. Flood-like anarchy was everywhere in the market. He came further out, following the arrows pointing towards the exit. The road was in front of him now.

He sure had lost his memories, but thank God, he knew his way home.

# They Have Barged Into Every Mirror

He hadn't hit the crowbar so hard but it had still gone deep into the earth. Perhaps, the ground underneath must have been hollow. One doesn't know about the ground beforehand these days. It appears solid on the surface and then turns out to be hollow. He was digging, furthering the tunnel. Then this mishap occurred. Suddenly, lots of soil came crashing down. The tunnel's roof had a big hole now. It was now filled with light coming from the hole.

Where did his tunnel open up to?

And so much bright shining light outside?

He started staring outside through the newly-created hole in his tunnel.

What to do now?

Should I try to close this hole? But this is too big of a hole to patch up. And it's impossible to patch it up quickly right now. And then people outside, too, might have seen this hole by now. There is no point in closing it. The tunnel would be found out now. And he, with it. So, would it be better to run back within the tunnel? And then out from there?

This way he might be able to escape but his tunnel would be found behind his back.

But then he observed something surprising. Something strange. Such a big hole was suddenly created in the ground but it was as if nobody paid any attention to it. Perhaps, nobody was surprised either. Nor did anybody come towards this hole—as if nobody cared in the world! So what to do now? Should he run back? Or should he climb outside and check?

He decided to climb out and assess the situation himself. Who knows, maybe outside nobody would pay any attention to him either.

He climbed out of the hole on his elbows.

The tunnel had opened up into a plush waiting room.

What is this place? He couldn't figure it out. This story's reader, though, recognises this place all too well. The reader is aware that this tunnel has opened up into the clinic of that psychiatrist. It is the same waiting room. The same girl at the reception, sofas, lights, Hippocrates' oath, a crowd of mental patients, and their kith and kin.

He stepped to one side of the hole after coming out of it. Nobody had paid any attention, neither to him nor to the hole in the ground. Dust was stuck all over his hair and elbows. He slowly brushed away that dust with his hands.

A man was sitting in a corner, lost in his thoughts. He kept looking at him. Should I ask him? And just then, that guy's eyes met his. He, too, looked at him. And then that guy suddenly got up and started walking towards him quite carelessly. He was afraid. The hole was right there in his path.

The way that guy was walking towards him, unaware; he sure was going to fall into that hole.

The guy coming towards him was now at the edge of the hole.

'Watch out!'

He could shout only this much when that guy raised his foot in the air.

Hearing his instruction, he merely smiled. Didn't stop. Didn't hesitate. And brought his foot, which was mid-air, down—smack in the center of the hole.

And he was stunned to see what happened next. The guy continued walking on that hole. He didn't fall into it. He was walking on air. Something like magic was occurring in front of him. It was such a big hole. It was still in front of him. But it was as if that guy just wasn't seeing the hole. In fact, nobody here was seeing that hole. Why wasn't somebody seeing that hole? He climbed out of it just moments ago. That means that nobody saw him coming out of the hole either. And now this guy was mightily stepping on that hole and walking towards him. How on earth? Why didn't he fall into the hole? Why couldn't anybody see this hole? That guy crossed the hole, came near him and stopped.

'So, you can walk on air?' he just blurted out without thinking.

'Why? Why do you say that?'

'I don't know. After seeing you walk I felt that you probably could walk even on air.'

'I've never tried it, sir. And even if I did walk on air in the past, I can't think of it now when I did it.'

'You would have remembered it if you did it.'

'That's true. If one has learned to walk on air, he shouldn't forget it. If somebody were to suddenly forget walking on air, in the middle of an actual act of walking on air, he sure was going to fall hard.'

'Anyway, I felt as if…'

'And I don't have a memory of walking on air or anything like that, sir. My memory isn't helping me out these days. It is also quite possible that I might have had the ability to walk on air once. Who knows?'

He kept on looking at him with questioning eyes.

'Do you recognise me by any chance?' that guy asked.

'No, not at all!' he said.

'Oh! I am sorry. My bad. I came to you with so much hope,' he said.

'What do you mean?'

'The way you were looking at me, I felt you surely must have known me.'

'No, I don't know you.'

'That's a bigger quagmire.'

'What quagmire?'

'I was sitting there. And suddenly, I tried to recall but I couldn't recall my name. I was worried sick. If I can't recall who am I then what should I do? What would I say if somebody asks me who am I? Where would I go if I can't recall my own name? I was worried thinking all this, and then I saw you.'

'Oh!'

'The way you were looking at me, I thought you sure would be able to tell me my identity.'

'Oh! I am sorry, but I don't know you.'

'Then who am I?' he muttered as if he was asking himself.

He was looking at him in disbelief.

What an oddball. And if he is so confused himself, how on earth will he be able to guide me?

Then the other guy spoke.

'But the way you were looking at me was as if you know me well.'

'Sorry, I am troubled myself. I have lost my way. I have come here but I can't figure out where I am now. And that's why I was looking at you that way. I saw you sitting idle so I thought I should ask you what this place is.'

The guy was stupefied.

'You don't know!? Where you are, you don't know?'

'Yup.'

'How can that be?'

'What?'

'That which you are saying, that you don't know where you are.'

'But that's the thing.'

He minutely scrutinised him.

'Can you recall anything?'

'What do you mean by anything?'

'Because I, too, can't remember anything. I don't have a memory anymore. Why, see, I can't even recall my own name right now.'

'Why, what happened to your memory?'

'Oh! Where do I begin…let's just say that nothing of it is left anymore. Though, I think it is somebody's conspiracy. My memories are being removed from my brain under a well-thought-out plan. They are knowingly emptying my brain. Slowly, bit-by-bit.'

'Emptying it?'

'Yeah, they are emptying my brain. Every day, a tiny chunk of my memory is removed.'

'How can somebody do that?'

'They very well can. They have the latest technology.

They can, through the internet, by riding the airwaves, by dissolving in our breath, and they are making their way into our brains by burglarising our senses. They are the ones who abduct our memories.'

'Why would somebody in their right mind do this?'

'They, those who want to fill my brain with their useless things, they are doing it. They want to fill everybody's brains with their junk. And that's why they need empty spaces in our brains. You see, they want to possess our minds. That's why they are emptying everybody's brain. You'll see, eventually, every citizen will wander around just like me—without an identity. Everybody is going to lose their memory. You'll see, one day you'll lose it too…'

He stood there babbling.

'No, my memory is quite alright…' he said.

'Great! Be careful though, my friend. They keep an eye on everybody. You too. Everyone. Remember that. One day they will empty everyone's brain. Everyone. And then we all will wander around aimlessly. Just like me. Door-to-door. You can't fathom now how lonely a person becomes from within when he is devoid of his memories. I am like an empty house, sir. Totally empty. There are cobwebs everywhere, in every corner. Whenever I try to think of anything, I hear echoes. Be careful. Save yourself from their conspiracy.'

He stood there next to him muttering whatnot.

'Calm down, sir,' he said.

He started sobbing.

'There...there, please don't worry. Everything will be alright...' he started consoling him, forgetting his own worries.

But he kept on sobbing.

He started soothing him by caressing his back. Slowly, he stabilised.

And then a long silence. Meanwhile, many more people had walked over that hole; nobody fell into it, and nobody paid any attention to it either.

And then that guy spoke.

'Why do people think that I have gone crazy?'

'What?'

'Yeah. People think of me as insane.'

'Who thinks like that?'

'My family.'

He was silent. What could he say?

'Do I look crazy to you?'

'No, no. Not really...'

'Then why do they bring me here again and again?'

'Here? Where?' he cautiously asked. That's precisely what he wanted to know since he climbed out of that hole—what this place was.

'What is this place?' he asked.

'Why, don't you know?'

'No, I don't.'

'This is a Madhouse.'

'A Madhouse?'

'Yes. A psychiatrist's clinic.'

Now, he started closely examining his surroundings.

'You didn't really know this place, did you?'

'No, I didn't.'

'Then how did you end up here?'

'Oh! That. Just like that.'

What could he say? How could he talk about the tunnel?

'It's okay. If you don't want to tell me, it's fine. But nobody comes here on their own.'

'But I did come on my own.'

'On your own?'

'Yes. On my own.'

'Then you are a lot crazier than me.'

'Why?'

'Because people are generally brought here. Who the hell comes on his own!'

'So, who brought you here?'

'My son. Didn't I tell you, they don't believe a word of what I say? He thinks that what I say is craziness.'

'But you are losing your memory...he, too, must be seeing that. No?'

'He thinks that, too, is a sign of my craziness.'

Both of them stood in silence for a few moments.

'Um...you do recognise your son, right?' he said after pondering for a while.

He smiled for the first time.

'It hasn't worsened that much...' he said, still smiling.

'Then what's the problem? Why don't you ask him your name?'

His smile widened on his face. If you happen to mix some sadness into a smile and the resulting smile would be the ashen smile—he smiled that smile.

'If I end up asking him that, then he won't take me back home. He will just have me admitted here. He already says that I unnecessarily bother everybody at home. After all, how long can one tolerate a madman?'

He couldn't figure out what to say seeing his sad smile. He kept quiet for some time. And then he thought it best to leave this place.

'I guess I will take your leave. It was nice meeting you.'

'Sure, sure. Though, feeling nice after meeting an insane is also a sign of insanity,' he said this, started laughing and shook his hand. And then that person also walked somewhere else.

He started looking all over. Where is the exit here? Or shouldn't he just climb back down into his tunnel?

And anyway, nobody was paying any attention to him here. Nobody had paid any attention to him even when he was climbing out of his tunnel. Moreover, nobody had even seen that huge hole created on the floor. Everybody was crazy here. That's why it was a good thing that this hole opened up amongst the crazies. Had it opened up anywhere else, it would have caused a big problem. Hard work of many months would have gone down the drain. Then, perhaps, it would be better to climb back down into the tunnel.

He turned back in the direction of the hole. And seeing what he saw he couldn't help but rub his eyes in disbelief. There wasn't any hole anywhere anymore. He was flabbergasted.

Wow! Where did that hole go?

And the tunnel? That too?

Right now, all he could see instead of a hole and a tunnel was a fabulous marble floor there. That was it.

The hole had disappeared.

What's this madness? If I told anyone about the hole right now, who is going to believe me? Everybody is going to think that I am crazy.

He was perplexed.

Now what?

I guess, let's get out through the clinic's exit. He started walking towards the exit. As he was walking, his attention drifted toward the other guy once again. Now he was standing in front of a huge mirror. There was a huge mirror on one of the clinic's walls. Huge mirrors give an illusion of huge spaces.

He stopped and started watching him.

He was talking to his reflection in the mirror. He was standing in front of the mirror, agitated. Very angry. Suddenly, he shook his fist at the mirror. His reflection, too, shook its fist. He made faces. The reflection also made faces and taunted him.

He was very outraged now. Livid. Now, he was threateningly looking at the mirror. Muttering whatnot as he was doing this. His muttering was increasing in volume. Now, he had started screaming. People came running towards him. He was feverishly punching his reflection. People were trying to stop him, pulling him away. But he was beyond their control. It was complete chaos in the waiting room. He was raining blows on his reflection. A young man ran towards him and tightly embraced him in a futile effort to stop him. It was quite clear that the young man must be his son. The son was trying to stop him but God knows from where that guy had gotten tremendous strength in him. He had wrangled himself free from his son's embrace and managed to land a big blow on the mirror.

The whole mirror had shattered into pieces now, with shards falling every which way. Some of them had even lodged themselves deep into his palms, which were bleeding now.

The reflection had disappeared due to the shattering of the mirror. Now, nobody was there with whom he could fight. Slowly and eventually, he calmed down. Blood was still dripping on the floor from his palms.

'Bastard ran away in fear...' he said, seeing the now-empty frame of the mirror.

'What have you done, Papa?' his son was holding his palm pressed in his hand.

'What else could I have done, Son? He, too, was one of those rascals. He was the one in the market too. He has ousted me from my own mirror. And it's just him in the mirror now. I am nowhere. And if these people will take away all the space everywhere, then where will I go? It is necessary to teach them a lesson, Son. They are very cowardly, these bastards. Did you see that? One perfect blow and he disappeared in a flash.'

He had started laughing at his own deed.

A guy was standing within the shards of the broken mirror and laughing.

Spilled blood was all around him. His palm is dripping blood.

The nurse had brought cotton and a bandage, and now his wound was being dressed. Everybody's attention in the room was on him at this moment.

He started walking towards the door discreetly. It was better to get out of this place. He was leaving. And right then, somebody's hand rested on his shoulder from behind. Standing behind him were his son and his wife.

'Where are you going, Papa? It's our turn now. They are calling. Be quick. It's our turn to see the doctor now.'

He stood there befuddled, and in incertitude for a few moments. And then, with his wife and son, he slowly started walking towards the psychiatrist's cabin.

## He Is Not Alone

A thud.

And the second one.

And the third one.

And some more…and more…and more and more.

He kept on listening to those sounds coming from that direction with bated breath.

He, slowly and without a sound, let go of the crowbar in his hand on the floor of the tunnel.

And then he slowly slid down, eventually crouching on the tunnel floor with his back leaning against the wall. He sat there. He was still sitting there with his ears perked up, listening to the sounds coming from the other side of the tunnel's wall.

Can't say he was afraid but he sure was alert. Though, he was afraid too.

Who is that? Who is digging along with his tunnel right now?

So, was there someone else there who was also digging a tunnel here apart from him?

The sound of the blows of the crowbar coming from the other side of the tunnel wall definitely gave this impression. But, who was that? Who was there? Right next to his tunnel. On the other side. Was there anyone there to apprehend him? Has the Bazaar become aware of this tunnel? Are these the Bazaar's posse? He tried listening to the sounds with complete attention.

Right now, the sound had stopped coming from the other side.

Was the person digging on the other side also trying to get a reading on him?

After all, he was digging a while ago as well. Perhaps, the person on the other side, too, must have heard the sound of the blows of his crowbar from this side.

He was absorbed too much in digging his own tunnel when he felt something was not right. He could barely hit his crowbar when the sound of the crowbar landing on the ground would be heard coming from the other side. What was going on? Was there somebody else who was also digging a tunnel or were his ears tricking him after continuously listening to the sound of his own crowbar? Or, perhaps, was he really going crazy as his doctor suspected?

Somebody was digging there again. The sound of blows of the crowbar was coming again. No, this was not his illusion. There *was* someone there.

One. Two. Three. Four... Somebody was digging there. His crowbar was lying on the floor. He was sitting crouched on the floor in the confines of his tunnel, with his ears next to the wall of his tunnel, dumbfounded.

And the sounds were dwindling now.

Now what?

He sat there, speechless. Sat there. Just sat there. Don't know for how long. And while sitting there, his hand fell on his crowbar on the ground lying next to him. Cold iron. And he inadvertently started caressing his crowbar.

His hand reached the tip.

He started running his fingers on the tip of the crowbar.

Had his crowbar become more piercing these days?

That's why it was suddenly lodged in the tunnel while digging yesterday. It went through the roof. And it even created a big hole in the psychiatrist's clinic above. It was good that nobody found out about the tunnel. Till today, he couldn't figure out what had happened to that hole, or why the tunnel couldn't be found.

Today, if he dug some more and the crowbar went through the neighbouring tunnel, then? No, he was not going to dig anymore now.

He was going to investigate.

Till the dust about the neighbouring tunnel settles, it was better to sit tight.

## The One Who Is Digging The Tunnel Alongside

He was a famous fat-cat in the city. Rather wealthy, actually.

He had so much money…what could one say? He had heard such a jingle of coins all his life that his ears had never heard any other note. So many currency bills, such a huge stack, and the rustling of bills everywhere was the only breath of fresh air for him. The zephyr. So much money, and then minting more money from money, more and more money, money, money everywhere, money piles all around, so many and so high that he never saw anything else in his life from behind these mounds of money.

But he was very scared these days.

Scared because what if someday somebody steals all of this money from him, or what if he loses all of his money in the market in losses, or what if the government forfeits everything, then? These were strange times. Anything could happen. He minted a lot of money all of his life. But the more it came, the more it raised his fear.

These days he was frantic about the safety of his money. 'In the middle of a decent normal conversation, Papa starts babbling mumbo-jumbo these days,' his son had noticed his frantic behaviour in the last few days.

All of his business was handled by his son these days.

Though he still visited his factory now and then, it was just for the sake of showing his face; and that too, not very often. He got to see his son only at night; and not always. His son would come home late, by which time he would already be in bed.

Even today, his son came home very late at night. But he wasn't asleep today. He was found waiting for him.

As soon as the son walked in, he earnestly grabbed his arm. Even before the son could regain his balance, he started pulling him toward his bedroom.

'What happened, Papa?' his son jerked his hand back in irritation.

He pressed his finger on his lips, signalling him to keep quiet. He then leaned in towards his ear and whispered slowly, 'Come to my bedroom. I want to tell you something.'

The son stopped and took a step back, and started examining his father's face closely. He appeared quite sapped, spooked and suspicious.

'What happened, Papa? You didn't go to bed even until now?' he asked.

'Not here, Son. Let's chat inside,' he said.

The son was perturbed. What was the matter? He followed him to his bedroom.

Now, both of them were in his bedroom. He slowly closed his bedroom door, walked to his son and started talking in whispers.

'Yaar, can you be louder, Papa? I can't understand a thing of what you are saying,' the son said, annoyed.

'How can I be louder, Son? Even the walls have ears these days,' he amped up a bit.

'What are you talking about? What's the matter with you?' The son's voice had a dash of concern and a bit of annoyance.

He started whispering again. His son walked near him, thinking to at least hear what his Papa had to say.

He was whispering:

'Remember son, every wall has an ear in it.'

'Yaar, can you cut this whole wall and ear thing out? Don't get too hung up on it. Okay? Tell me something else,' he was annoyed furthermore.

'No matter how thick a plaster is on the walls you have, even if you erect a stone wall or paint it to camouflage it, their ears can't be sealed shut,' he kept on whispering.

'Did you drag me all the way here to tell me this bullshit?' the son yelled loudly without having the slightest concern for the ears-in-the-wall thing.

'Lower your voice because…'

'Because walls, too, have ears. Is that it?'

'Spot on!'

'Okay, I got it. What's next?' the son was fed up with his theatricals.

He came closer even more, almost right next to his ear, and started whispering in an even lower voice. The gist of what he said in whispers was that the times were changing and they had to be extremely cautious in terms of their money. Anybody could deceive them. They could incur losses in any deal. Anybody could forfeit on the slightest, and even fake pretense of some obscure rule or law. That their home could be burglarised. That the market could tank anytime. The money invested in the market could suddenly disappear anytime...

The son, interrupting him mid-way, said, 'Why are you telling all this nonsense to me?'

He came even closer, and whispered, 'Because it's about time I told you what my plan is…'

'Plan?'

'Yeah. Plan.' He looked at him with a mysterious smile on his lips.

'What plan?' the son asked.

'Well, the thing is that we don't have to worry about our money anymore,' he said, his voice lowered to a whisper again.

'Who should we be afraid of?'

'Anybody. Now our money is going to be extremely safe,' the words were barely audible.

'What?'

'I am telling you that from now on you don't have to worry even slightly. Our money is going to be totally safe.'

Even his smile seemed like a whisper, and then he started chuckling, as if he had such a secret to tell that once he let it out, his son would be stunned to hear it; he kept on chuckling, looking at him with those eyes.

'What are you saying?' the son had his head in between his hands. 'Nothing of what you are saying is making any sense to me.'

'Listen,' he said, taking another step closer to his son. He was now almost glued to his son's ear. His voice was now only made up of sounds passing through his lips, vaguely sounding like actual words.

'I am digging a tunnel,' he said in a rock-bottom voice.

His son couldn't make out anything of what he said.

'Tunnel? What's this new tunnel thing?' he asked.

'Whoa! Whoa! Slow down. Quietly. Speak quietly. They will know if you speak loudly,' he said in a way as if he was speaking in a confessional booth.

'Who will know?'

'They. Those who have installed their ears in our walls and we didn't even know.'

Now the son was irate. He started shaking in agitation. He started staring at his father menacingly and violently.

'Papa, I've been running errands the whole day. I am exhausted now. And you're talking like this…'

'Sorry,' he said.

Then he stayed silent for a few moments.

His son looked at him with questioning eyes. His anxiety was increasing. If he isn't told the truth, the whole truth and nothing but the truth right now, then and there, he might just snap and do anything.

'I am digging a tunnel,' he spoke slowly.

'Tunnel?' the son couldn't understand.

'Yes, a tunnel,' he said, and smiled again as if he was enjoying a moment after pulling a prank on someone.

'Where? What tunnel? And where is that tunnel?'

'I'll show you. I'll show you that too. I'll even take you inside it with me so you can see it for yourself.'

'But why a tunnel? What will you do with it?'

He kept on smiling. Stayed silent. Making faces as if he was chew-sucking something sweet. And then he spoke in a manner as if he was revealing a big secret.

'Even you couldn't understand it, could you now? I knew that. Nobody can even think of it. My idea of digging a tunnel and stashing all of our money in it is just like that. Pure gold.'

'Money in a tunnel?'

'Yeah, we will keep all of our money hidden in that tunnel. Nobody will come to know. It is totally a secret tunnel. It is so secret that if I didn't know about it and I came across it, even I won't be able to see it. It's like that.'

'But won't those labourers would already know about it?'

'What labourers?'

'The ones whom you must have employed in digging the tunnel.'

'I didn't employ any labourer in digging the tunnel. I dug it myself. All alone. Single-handedly. It's been six months since I started digging. I dig it every day, discreetly. Nobody knows about this,' he kept on spilling his secret.

What the heck was this man talking about, yaar? The son was not able to figure out what should he say, what should he do. Papa was hallucinating—this was clear as daylight. He will have to take him to a psychiatrist first thing in the morning, for sure.

'You are thinking that this man has gone crazy, right?' he said, pointing at himself as if he had read his son's mind.

The son kept on looking at his face.

It was better to keep mum on such kooky talk. Better yet, it was best to just walk out of this room. He started to make his way towards the door.

'May I leave if you are done?' he said to his father as he started walking towards the door.

He had sat down on the bed while talking. When he heard his son's desire to leave, he sprang to his feet and stood in front of him, squarely facing him.

'You don't believe me, do you?'

'How can I? Forget me, how can anybody else believe you either?'

'I am not talking about anybody else. They can't even think about this.'

'What can't they think about?'

'Forget them, nobody can think about this. Nobody.'

'What?'

'Okay, you tell me…'

'Tell you what?'

'Tell me, would you have ever thought that I would have dug such a tunnel that would have its mouth in this bedroom? No, right? That's the thing. Son, the mouth of the tunnel is in this bedroom but you won't be able to find it.'

'Our apartment is on the third floor. Papa, you are aware of that, aren't you?'

'So?'

'So what?'

'So how can one dig a tunnel till here?'

He smirked.

'That's the thing…'

'What thing?'

'See, everybody would be fooled. Our tunnel opens up straight into the air from my bedroom.'

'Into the air?'

'Yes. This end of the tunnel is in the air. Thats the trick with this tunnel. Tunnel in the air. In plain sight.'

'You think bizarre things these days.'

'Not bizarre. Totally true things. That's the truth. I've done this to keep them guessing.'

'Them, who?'

The son was looking at his father in utter disbelief.

'They can't even imagine seeing any tunnel like this…'

'Who cant imagine?'

'Those who are waiting for a chance to forfeit our money.'

'Who is waiting for a chance? Who are they?'

'They are invisible, but they are everywhere all the time.'

'If they are there, then they would be visible. Won't they?'

'No, no. It's not like that. They are everywhere in the world. Just that nobody can know about them. They have their eyes set on our capital; in fact, on everybody's capital.'

'I don't know what you are talking about?'

'See, that's the thing. Even you won't understand for now. This is the thing which nobody seems to understand.'

'And you understood it perfectly. How come?'

'Son, I figured it out somehow. But I want you to understand, too, that our money is in grave danger. Everybody's money is in great danger. The whole world is in great danger. There are a few people in this world who would slowly take everybody's money. Eventually, everybody's capital would be concentrated just in a few hands. We'll have to hide our money before they can reach us. Discreetly, unbeknownst to them. They are shrewd. And cruel too. The clock is ticking…'

He started pacing in the room while voicing his worries.

He was also muttering things, but he was doing so in whispers so that nothing reached the ears within the walls.

'I am going to go, Papa,' his son opened the bedroom door and walked out.

He stopped pacing and ran after him.

'Wait! Stop. I brought you here to show you my tunnel. You should see it at least once,' he ran and caught hold of his arm.

'You have lost your mind. Nothing else,' the son said, stopping.

'That's not your fault. Forget you, anybody would think like that. But what if, what if I took you with me and showed you my tunnel right now? You would believe me then, wouldn't you? Come with me and see for yourself. Let this tunnel be completed once, we will keep all of our money safely there then. Once and for all. Alright?'

He grabbed his son's arm and once again brought him back into his bedroom.

It was as if somehow he had the devil's strength in him. The son tried to free his arm from his father's grip, but his grip on his arm was so firm and strong that in the end he simply gave up. He came back into the bedroom with him.

And then he brought his son to one of the windows in the bedroom, his arm still firmly in his iron grip.

He let go of his son's arm after reaching the window.

The son didn't run away; he just stood there.

He closely started looking for something on the window pane. And then he gently placed his fingers on the glass. Then he started tapping his fingertips here and there on the windowpane as if he was punching numbers on the keypad of a cell phone.

He had a code for this tunnel.

'And this is not some window, Son. This window is just a façade to fool them. In reality, this is the door to the tunnel…a secret door. The door opens by punching in a secret code. And I just punched in the digits of that secret code. The door only opens when the correct code is punched in...' he was describing things in detail.

He tapped his fingers on the windowpane once again.

'You have to punch in the code twice,' he let him in on the secret.

Now, he was standing next to the window, waiting for the tunnel door to open up. His son was standing right behind him, thinking, let's see what theatrics he displays now.

Street light was falling into the room through the window; this window opened up towards the road down below. Suddenly, he swung open the latch of the window and pushed its panes outwards. There wasn't any grill in the window.

'See!'

'What?'

'The door to the tunnel has swung open!' he said, pointing at the now-opened panes of the window.

'And that tunnel of yours?' the son asked sarcastically.

'This is it! Right in front of you,' he was pointing outside the window.

'Here? Where?'

It was clear that there was nothing there. It was an empty sky outside the window.

He started laughing.

Right then a burst of mischievous breeze jumped into the room through the window; and after slapping the son's face, hid somewhere in the room.

The son was further annoyed seeing him laugh like that.

'Why are you laughing like that?' he asked his old man.

'I was laughing at myself. That's true. How would you see it? This is a tunnel in the air. That's why. You cant see the air. Right?'

He came closer to the window and started looking out of it.

'Nobody can see air, that's the good thing about it. Come on, let me show you everything. See! So this is the tunnel door. Whatever is visible from here till that small bridge on the road—that, in reality, is the tunnel. Tunnel in the air. It's not visible but it is there. Just like air, which is not visible but is still there. And I dug it using such a technique that even if they pass through our road, they won't be able to see it,' he started explaining.

'Neither will they be able to see it, nor us,' the son said, mocking him.

'Nobody can see this tunnel through naked eyes. Not even I can do that. You'll have to have special glasses for it. Really, a special pair of it. Then, and only then will you be able to see it. I'll show it to you; I have special glasses.'

He skipped over to the other side of the room, opened a drawer and took out two pairs of goggles, and showed them to his son. He donned one and gave the other one to his son.

'Wear this. You will see the tunnel clearly. Go on! Put it on.'

He started pleading with him to wear the black glasses.

The son flat-out refused to wear them. He started pleading with him again and again to wear them.

By this time, the son was completely exasperated. He pushed his father's hand. But he didn't listen.

'Son, how will you see the tunnel if you don't wear these special glasses?'

He took a step closer and forcibly tried to put them on his son's face.

The son was livid by now.

He snatched the pair of glasses from his hand and threw them out of the open window.

It went flying out of the window, and made a soft landing upside down on the green grass next to the road.

'You don't believe me, right?' he was asking him, standing, holding the windowpane, and looking at the goggles below on the ground.

His son looked at him with anguish and disgust, and then walked away.

He was watching him walk away.

'Oh! So, you don't believe me!? Okay, fine. I'll show you. Watch. Watch me. The tunnel is here. Definitely. I'll show you by climbing down into it,' he said, grabbing hold of the two window panes and standing up on the ledge, facing outside. He donned the goggles.

His son had stopped mid-way.

What the hell is he going to do?

He turned around.

'I am not alone. Other people, too, are digging tunnels. I know that. Yesterday, somebody else was also digging alongside our tunnel. I am in contact with them,' he was telling his son, stepping onto the windowsill as he did so.

And other people were digging tunnels too. They knew. Yesterday, somebody else was also digging right next to his tunnel. He heard the sound and, as a precautionary measure, stopped digging and came back home. There, other people were busy digging tunnels, and here his son was not ready to believe him—that was too much even for him.

He was now sitting on the windowsill with his feet hanging outside the window. He was ready to jump any moment now. Quite a dangerous moment it was. He could fall down the window at any moment.

His son ran towards him, grabbed his hand and started pulling him back inside. His father's body was somewhat okay, and somewhat on the heavier side. When he pulled, the body didn't budge an inch.

And then, the night watchman standing on the road, too, saw him hanging mid-air from the windowsill. He started screaming from the road itself.

Here, the son was trying to bring him in by pulling on his arm. Hearing all the commotion, a crowd was gathering on the road under the window.

Neighbours, too, were in this crowd. Everybody knew him. He was a famous rich man in this city. People were calling his name, trying to stop him from jumping. 'Watch out!', 'Be careful!', 'He is going to fall.', 'What are you doing, Chopra Ji?'—such calls could be heard coming from the crowd.

The noise from the road could be heard all the way up—up to the bedroom here.

But it was as if he wasn't willing to listen to anybody. He was still sitting on the windowsill, mid-air, with his feet hanging in the air-tunnel, eager to climb down his tunnel. He knew that his air-tunnel was completely safe. Ah! After all, he goes in and out through this route every day.

The son was trying to pull him in, screaming his lungs out.

There, on the other side, some folks were banging loudly on the door of their apartment as well.

House servants and other family members, too, had come to the bedroom hearing the kerfuffle. Everybody had joined hands and somehow pulled him in from the windowsill.

And this was how he had made quite a spectacle of himself. The whole city came to know about this within a day.

Everybody knew that such a wealthy man of this city had gone insane. If the family members hadn't caught him in time, he would have almost committed suicide by jumping out of the window!

## The Sound Of His Footsteps From Under The Ground

These were the days of winter. Extreme winter.

It was around 10 o' clock at night. The moon looked down on the earth from the sky, and was surprised. He saw something strange happening there. He turned to the moonlight and asked 'Did you see that?' Before the moonlight could take a good look at what was going on, or the moon could figure the matter out, a floating cloud half-covered the moon. The moon was annoyed. 'Seriously!? Couldn't you find any other time?' The clouds acted as if they didn't hear him. They were surfing the wind. By the time the moon could gather himself, the clouds covered it completely.

Although one could say it was a moonlit night, right now it was dark on earth.

And then the fog was dense too.

That deserted road that runs along the big pond was also shrouded in dense fog. It was on this road that the moon saw something, and was surprised—and right then, it went dark. When the moon hadn't been veiled by the clouds, even then the weak moonlight had mixed with dense fog in such a way as if a shimmering and somewhat transparent curtain was hanging between the earth and the sky. A slight illusion of visibility, and a feeling of invisibility too. Till just a few moments ago, one could see the full moon in the sky. Round. Just like the manhole cover on the road. Like a shining manhole cover on the sky's black road. The moment when the moon was being veiled by the clouds, right at that moment the moon's eyes were fixed on the actions of that man who, for a long time, was standing next to the manhole on the side of the road, staring at the manhole cover. The moment the moon was covered completely, right then that man squatted down and started lifting the manhole cover.

Why was this man lifting the manhole cover at this hour of the night, in shivering cold and dense fog? What exactly were his intentions? By the time the moon could make sense of all of this, the deserted road was covered in complete darkness.

Right now, neither the moon nor the moonlight could make sense of things. That piece of cloud was big and grey. Although, apart from the moon, another man was also watching the actions of this guy. This was somebody who is unemployed and wanders around the city, hiding from himself. Right now, he was sitting on a bench in a small park next to the road. Just like that. Idling. 'What would I do even if

I went home', thinking these kind of thoughts, he was sitting in the park when he saw this guy who was circling the manhole cover. What's the matter? What is he going to do? Is he some kind of manhole cover thief or what?

The moon, the moonlight and the man sitting in the park, everybody was watching him when it went dark. All three of them were worried, thinking of what that guy must be doing now.

Although the manhole cover was also watching that guy for quite some time, thinking, 'Why, why is he standing here and staring at me for some time? Why doesn't he pick me up if he intends on stealing me? Pick me up and let's go.' The manhole cover didn't care. It didn't have any commitment to the manhole. A manhole cover's life is worthless. It doesn't matter to it if it is stolen and sold or just lies there on the manhole. But this guy wasn't doing anything. He was just standing next to it, staring at it for quite some time. Either he was scanning his surroundings or staring at the manhole cover. Without a word. With a thoughtless face. Empty, vacant eyes that appear watery when the moonlight is reflected in them. After all, what was he going to do? The manhole cover, too, was guessing. What the heck was going on in this guy's mind?

The streetlights, too, were gone for some time.

Lights were off from the clouds, fog and the cluster of trees next to the road—all in all, it was so dark on the road that it was difficult for anybody to say what that man was doing standing next to the manhole.

'Then?' the friend asked.

It was like a soirée of the unemployed on the small bridge.

The unemployed were on the rise in the city. These days, every bridge in the city was falling short. Every once in a while a new member joined a bridge-club. Now and then, somewhere or the other, labourers were laid off. The Bazaar was on the rise but unemployment was rampant. Every other day, a factory was shuttered down. Every day, somebody or the other was handed a fortnight's or a month's salary in an envelope and thrown out of the door.

The bridge was running out of space.

Right now that same unemployed young man, who was sitting on the bench in the darkness of the park and watching that man circling the manhole, was telling the story of that night to his idle friends.

'So, I got up from the bench to see what was going on, what this man was doing here. The moment I got up, the streetlights came back and I could see everything.'

'So, what did you see?' somebody else asked.

He stayed silent for a few moments. He was somewhat stressed about answering this question. His face was showing signs of anxiety too. His voice was quivering while telling the story. It was as if on that night, on that road, he saw something, the mere thought of which was still scaring him!

'... saw that man held the manhole cover to a side with both of his hands...'

'Must be some manhole cover thief, yaar. You went on and on, only to tell this!' somebody started snickering.

'No, no. That man had held the cover to his side, and was sitting at the edge of the manhole with his feet dangling down.'

'What?'

'Yeah. In a posture as if he was about to jump into it.'

'Have you gone mad? Whatever comes to your mind...huh!?'

'I am telling the truth, I swear! He was sitting with his feet dangling in the manhole, steadying its cover on one side with his hand. He was startled because of the sudden glare when the streetlights came back on. He turned around. And for a second, I saw his face when he turned around. I could only catch a glimpse. Perhaps he, too, might have seen me. Perhaps, he smiled too. Perhaps, even our eyes met. But only for a brief second. I saw him for a second or two. That's all.'

'And then?'

Then what. He suddenly let go of the manhole cover and...

The manhole cover had been watching him in astonishment.

That man had lifted the manhole cover with both of his hands. And then, after steadying the manhole cover on its side, and leaning it against one side of the circumference of the mouth of the manhole, he had squatted down then and there. He kept on peering inside the manhole, squatting at the edge. Manhole was darker than the outside. And then, he slid closer to the edge. He sat down and spread his legs. And then he dangled his spread legs inside the manhole and sat down. He sat there with his feet dangling. His hands were still holding onto the manhole cover while his feet were dangling in the manhole. When the cover was lifted, it was as if the darkness from underneath boiled over and spilled out, and mixing with the darkness outside, was now flowing on the ground and the sky.

'What was it he was about to do, yaar?'

If that manhole cover slipped from his hands and fell back on the mouth of the manhole, both of his legs would have broken immediately. It was a heavy iron lid. The cover knows how heavy it is. For a while, this scene continued. The man, with his feet dangling in the manhole, steadying the manhole cover on its edge with his hands on the side of the mouth, sat quiet and motionless in the utter darkness. Right then, even the manhole cover couldn't figure out what this man was is going to do next. And then, two things happened simultaneously.

Rather, three things.

The cloud, floating in the sky, floated away from its previous position and the moon came out bright and shiny. The moon shone brighter. The road was somewhat lit now.

And right then, streetlights came back as well. Everything was basking in the light.

And after that, in the next few moments, the man let go of the manhole cover mid-air. It fell back on the mouth of the manhole with a loud bang. The loud bang of the heavy cover falling back on the mouth shattered the pervading silence of the night.

But his legs didn't break. Because that man wasn't there anymore.

By the time the lid fell back on the manhole, the man had already jumped inside it. The manhole was shut again. Tightly. The manhole cover was firmly back in its place, and the manhole shut. Everything was spick and span, and back in its place—just like before. Yeah, the man sure was underground now.

And suddenly, the streetlights started flickering.

The manhole cover was frightened, as if saying to itself, 'what's happening, my God!'.

'And then that man jumped into the manhole...' he was telling that night's anecdote.

'Into the manhole??'

'Yup. That's right. He let the lid go, and bang! He jumped into the manhole. The cover, too, fell back behind him with a loud noise. It was such a loud bang that even the streetlights started flickering.'

'You weren't scared?' a friend asked just to get a kick out of it. Nobody believed a word of what he said, that much was clear.

'Scared? I was so terrified that I almost peed in my pants.'

'You should have!' somebody said, snickering.

'True that. You should have. Who was going to see you in that darkness anyway?' another added.

'And even if somebody saw you, it wasn't as if he was witnessing you committing murder or something. Is peeing a crime these days or what?' the first one added further.

He just watched them with his jaw dropped.

'You don't believe a word of what I say, right?' he started asking.

'Oh! No, no. Nothing like that. Quite an interesting story this is. Go on,' everybody said.

He went silent.

'Then? What happened after that?'

He started telling furthermore when everybody pleaded with him.

'And then I went to the manhole, nervous and scared. The cover was shut and so perfectly in its place as if nothing had happened,' he started moving the story ahead.

'Didn't the manhole cover tell you anything?' somebody once again needled him to get a kick out of him.

But he didn't catch on the jest.

'What would the cover say? The one who had jumped had already jumped inside.'

'Oh! I thought perhaps the manhole cover might have told you something. Anything can happen these days in the darkest of nights,' somebody egged on to further the fun.

'How could it say? It was so frightened that it almost choked on its tongue.'

'Tongue? Manhole cover's?' two friends asked in unison.

'Yup. Covers. Actually, the manhole cover was spooked too. When I reached it, the manhole cover was shaking like a leaf in fear. Loudly. So loudly that all you could hear was the sound of its clanging. And then streetlights were flickering too.'

'And you?'

'Me? I was so scared that I just ran after that and kept on running, and only took a breath when I reached home,' he started trembling while recounting this as if he had high temperature.

'Yaar, enough of that. He needs to be consoled. See how he is trembling in fear,' they signalled each other.

All the friends empathised with him; one started caressing his back. Another one took his hand in his, and started consoling him, 'Yaar, don't think too much. Do you know what your problem is? You have started overthinking things, yaar. That's all. Nothing else.'

'Take a chill pill. Don't overthink things. Once you start doing that, you'll start seeing things,' a third one said.

'So you think that there wasn't anybody there and I am making things up, and that I have lost it altogether?' he asked, irked.

'Why would I think that about you? No, that's not the point. But this is also true that you have started thinking too much these days. True. Everybody says the same thing about you these days.'

'Yaar, not everybody can handle being laid off like that. It's stressful,' somebody else chimed in.

'But you shouldn't worry too much. You'll find work somewhere else. It happens...people get laid off. Sometimes a job is terminated. They let us go just like that, telling us not to come back to work tomorrow. Happens to the best of us. These days whose job is permanent, yaar? Even the best and the brightest are shown the door any minute. Don't you read it in the newspapers?' a friend tried to soothe him.

Everybody believed that he hadn't been able to handle the trauma of being laid off well, and was slowly losing it.

'Yaar, it isn't like that. I am not stressing over it. I swear!'

'Okay, not a problem. It's good that you aren't stressed out. You shouldn't be.'

'Yaar, I am telling the truth. I saw that, all of that with my own two eyes. True.'

'Fine. Now let it go. Forget about what you saw last night and don't even think about it anymore.'

'How can I let it go? A man disappeared underground in front of me and I shouldn't even think about it? What about the man who went underground? I shouldn't think about him either?' he started asking.

His friends felt as if they were banging their heads against a wall. Yaar…enough is enough.

'Oh, come on! Let it go!'

'How can I? Yaar, I can still hear the sound of his footsteps from under the ground. Tell me, what should I do?' he said, exasperated.

'The sound of his footsteps?'

'What else? I can hear them.'

'From under the ground?'

'Yes, from under the ground.'

'Yaar, even if somebody jumped down there, he would have been dead in those sewage pipes by now. Then how can you hear the sound of his footsteps all the way up here?'

'He isn't dead. Who knows he might have started living in the pipes buried deep under the ground?' he said, pondering.

'Yaar, can anybody live in those filthy pipes? They have the whole city's filth flowing through them! How can one live there?' someone tried to talk sense to him.

Now, everybody was worried about him. He really was losing his mind.

'It's the same amount of filth outside here too. But aren't we all living here anyway?' he asked.

'Yaar, those pipes are carrying the whole city's urine, faeces and whatnot in them. Who can live in that stench and sludge of filth?'

'But doesn't this earth too has the same amount of filth? Don't we live here? And what filth do we see? Hardly any?'

'Yaar, you should go home and get some sleep. Everything will be alright,' somebody grabbed his arm and stood up.

A friend had tagged along with him. He would walk him home.

As he was leaving, he turned around and stopped, and started closely listening to something.

And then he cupped his hands next to his ears and said, 'Listen…listen. Quiet down a bit and listen. If you keep on talking, how will you listen? Listen. I can hear the sound of his footsteps from underneath the ground.'

These were complex times.

It was getting difficult to decide who was crazy.

Are all of these insane? Or it is just these wise ones who are left, and the rest of the world has gone crazy?

The time, after some time, will surely decide; but the Bazaar had already decided who was crazy and who was not.

## The Bazaar Was Keeping An Eye On Everybody, Especially The Crazies

The Time was in the tight, vice-like grip of the Bazaar but it wasn't floundering to free itself from its grip.

The Bazaar had possessed Time.

Time was now learning to flow according to the the Bazaar because it, too, had accepted that these were the times of the Bazaar.

The Bazaar made ample time for the crazies too; after all, the crazies were its clients too. It made time for every client. It firmly believed that even crazies were useful people. Who knows, it was quite possible that tomorrow a product could be launched exclusively for the crazies, what then? Won't you need crazies for it then?

Yes, the Bazaar did keep an eye on the crazies for sure. The times were bad. Some crazies had gone against the Bazaar, it was heard. So it strictly kept an eye on them. Although the Bazaar kept an eye on those people who were with the Bazaar too. It kept an eye on *everybody*.

But it was getting difficult even for the Bazaar to keep an eye on everybody like that. It was getting difficult to spot the difference between a regular man and a crazy. This difference was getting finer with every passing day. It was getting difficult to figure out who was sane and who was insane. The whole citizenry was living with such a fine difference that even they couldn't convincingly say what they were exactly. And that's why the wise were being labelled crazy and the crazies were suddenly being declared geniuses. Then? Then how was the Bazaar able to keep an eye on such crazies? This, after all, was a difficult task. But the Bazaar had invented a very simple formula for this as well. You see, the Bazaar, after all, placed huge merit on efficiency. According to this formula, the wise ones were those who were with the Bazaar in every black and white with their eyes wide shut, and the rest were crazies who refused to side with it.

The Bazaar was quite an illusionist. It had already invented an illusion to manage the wise and the crazy simultaneously. It didn't matter if one became very wise or very crazy—Bazaar could make do with both of them.

It wasn't afraid of the crazies. It just remained cautious of them.

# A Dream Within A Dream, And Blood On The Palms

He would cry in solitude for his lost dreams. Long streaks of tears had formed on his face while crying. If a streak of water flows for a long time on rocks, it leaves its mark even on stones. This had happened here too. Day by day, the streaks of tears were deepening on his face further and further; so much so, that despite thoroughly washing his face and applying a lot of cream on it, streaks remained as they were. His face had become permanently tearful.

His wife worried about him.

'What are these streaks on your face?' she would ask. Often.

'Streaks?' he would try to feign ignorance.

'Do you cry in hiding?' his wife once asked him, point-blank.

'No, why? Have you ever seen me crying?' he denied it point-blank as well.

'You shouldn't cry,' his wife advised again.

'But I don't cry.'

'But these streaks on your face? They look like tear streaks. Why don't you take a close look in the mirror?' the wife said.

'Oh! I never paid any attention,' he lied to her.

'Alright, let's go and see a dermatologist then…'

'How will a dermatologist erase tear-marks?'

'But weren't you saying moments ago that these are not tear-marks?'

'Yes, but weren't you saying that these are tear-marks?'

'I said that these tear-marks like…'

'There is nothing else which is tear-mark like… the only thing tear-mark like is the tear-mark itself,' he said.

'Oh! The things you say are beyond my understanding,' the wife said.

'When I, myself, am unable to understand what I say these days, how will you understand what I say?' he said.

His wife shut up.

The truth of the matter was that he cried for his dreams. He sobbed for them, alone, in complete solitude. A somewhat sense of guilt and sadness surrounded him—all the time. Where would his dreams have gone? Why didn't he see any dreams nowadays? After all, what happened to his innate capability of seeing dreams?

Could it be that the whole of mankind had altogether stopped dreaming? Where he once used to dream with open eyes...now, he didn't even have a single dream. Now, there were only dreams of the Bazaar—and a bazaar of dreams, everywhere. He considered himself equally guilty. Why did he fall for the Bazaar's trap in the beginning? Why did he become a part of this Bazaar himself? Why did he use all of his might once for the Bazaar that he eventually lost his capability to dream? He didn't even realise this for a long time. The Bazaar had taken him to such a world of illusory dreams that it was as if he had forgotten the real dreams of life... And now, when he opened his eyes and returned to the world of reality from the illusory dream,- it had been quite late. And then, he never found his dreams. He could never dream. His dreams were stolen.

But, after all, where would have his dreams been kept after stealing? What would the Bazaar have done with his dreams? If he came to know that, at least he would try to bring them back.

And then one day, a huge miracle happened in the midst of all this.

One night, he had a dream. And in this dream, he saw his lost dreams.

In his dream, he saw a faceless man. In the place of his facial features was something flat, something emotionless. That faceless man had a bunch of hidden dreams on his motorcycle. On his bike, these dreams were hanging, tied in a bunch. Who knows how many dreams he had tied on the handle and carrier of his motorcycle, taking them who knows where. The dreams were hanging upside down; they were fluttering. The dreams were alive, but they were in trouble. He felt the scene to be familiar. He had seen the same scene somewhere else before. Yes, he had seen roosters hanging upside down on a scooter, just like that. The scooter was going towards the butcher's shop. Yes, there was a difference though. The roosters hung calmly. They didn't flutter. They hung silently, as if they weren't aware that they were going to be slaughtered.

That faceless man was speeding with his motorcycle, with the dreams hanging. The dreams were fluttering. He had tied the dreams here and there on the bike. Handlebar, carrier, grill, bumper, number plate—he had tied the dreams everywhere…The dreams were being taken to the slaughterhouse, even the onlookers knew this, and the passersby knew as well; and perhaps, even the dreams were aware of this…which is why they must have been fluttering. He ran after the motorcycle. The faceless man was speeding. Still, he ran after him. Kept on running. Suddenly, he had gotten so much strength in him to run after the motorcycle to save his dreams. He sprinted so fast that he almost reached his dreams. And while running, he caught hold of the carrier of the motorcycle from behind. He was hanging from the back of the speeding bike. He was dragged for some distance but he didn't let go. His knees were bruised.

He didn't let go of the motorcycle despite getting bloodied. He was dragging with the bike. The faceless man increased the speed further. Now, the motorcycle was on those roads which were being widened. Gravel, stones, coal tar…

The road here was unpaved, and full of potholes.

The motorcycle was speeding, bouncing over these potholes. Now, he was getting exhausted as well; his grip was weakening. The dreams were slowly slipping away from his grasp. He gave it a last try. And gathering the strength of all of his body, he tightly hugged his hanging dreams. His nails dug into the wrists of the dreams. His dreams were bloodied now. His palms had become wet with the blood of his dreams. The blood of his dreams had now started trickling onto his wrists. And as the palms became wet and slick, his grip loosened…

His grip was lost, eventually. At one pothole, he fell into it with a jerk.

And the motorcycle carrying his dreams sped away towards the horizon. The horizon was turning red. Was the slaughterhouse of his dreams there? Who knows.

He started crying, lying on the ground. And kept on crying.

And the sound of his sobbing in sleep was filling the silence of the night with anxiety. His wife woke up from her sleep. She shook him and woke him up too.

'What happened?'

He woke up but was still half-asleep. Lying on his bed, he kept on crying.

'Arre, what happened?'

He gathered himself. He remembered that he was in his bedroom.

He quieted down, and stopped crying. He didn't say anything. Though he did open his eyes and kept on staring at the roof.

His wife caressed his hand.

'Why are you crying?' she asked.

'I had a nightmare just now... Evil...' And he started sobbing again as he said this.

'But, didn't you stop dreaming in sleep altogether, no? And you were worried about that too,' his wife said.

'Yes, but I just had a bad dream...'

'See, you should be happy now! Whatever it may be, at least you had a dream!'

'But this was such a nightmare...'

'You had a nightmare now, who knows you can have a good one tomorrow. Why don't you think this way that at least you had a dream...you'll have many more once again.'

'No, I won't have dreams anymore.'

'What are you talking about?'

'Truth. I am telling you the truth. Absolute truth. I have had a dream that now I won't be able to dream anymore.'

His wife kept on staring at him.

Had this man gone completely insane?

'What are you talking about? I cant make any sense of it.'

'Not just you, perhaps, nobody would be able to make sense of it.'

'Why? What bizarre dream did you have?'

He sat still and silent for a few moments, thinking. And then, after a while, he haltingly spoke,

'They are going to slaughter my dreams.'

'They, who?'

'Those people, those who have abducted my dreams. My dreams, they had hung them upside down...'

'Hung them upside down? Where?'

'On their motorcycle! Just like roosters! I even ran after them. And I caught them too...but in the end, they took them away. They threw me on the ground and they took my dreams away,' he started sobbing once again.

'How do you know that they were your dreams?'

'Because...because I can recognise my dreams anywhere...'

'You say that they were hanging upside down? If they were hanging upside down, could it be that you mistakenly recognised them as your dreams?'

'No, they were my dreams. Upside down or right side up, I can recognise my dreams in any condition. They were mine. And they were hanging upside down. And they were imploringly gawking at me.'

'Look, don't you worry. After all, whatever you saw was a dream, wasn't it? It can be a false dream too.'

'No, I've seen them. As clearly as one can. This can't be a false dream. They surely will slaughter my dreams. Definitely.'

'How can you be so sure?'

'When you see a butcher on the road taking roosters just like that with their feet tied together in a bunch and hanging upside down, aren't you sure then or not? Barring roosters, everybody is sure that they soon will be slaughtered.'

His wife fell silent.

He too fell silent.

He lay down again.

'You should get back to sleep now. And don't ponder things unnecessarily.'

'When did pondering about one's dreams become unnecessary?'

'Good heavens! I just said that because if you think bad thoughts, you will dream bad dreams. And you keep on pondering over bizarre things all day long. And then whatever you think about the whole day, you have a dream about that at night. That's what people say.'

'So, you mean I should just stop thinking?'

'That, too, wouldn't be a bad thing either. In fact, you are right. You should just stop thinking. All hell is broken loose with a person's thinking.'

'But you do know that the only difference between being dead or alive is that of thinking. Corpses don't think.'

'You are wrong. Not only corpses but even the wise don't think.'

'And if you want to think of this as being alive then you are free to do so but I don't consider such people to be alive!'

'Alright, fine! Keep on thinking. Who is stopping you from thinking? Think to your heart's content. But, at least think positive?'

'For example?'

'For example, for example,… Yaar, you can think a lot many positive things…'

'For example? Arre, at least give me one good example?'

When the wife started thinking, she couldn't come up with even a single good example. She was flustered.

'Alright, even if you don't think positive, at least don't think negative, okay?'

'You know what, I can't explain it to you.'

'That's right. These days what you talk about is so bizarre, how can one understand any of it?'

'That's the face of the truth these days. Now you tell me, what can I do?'

'Don't do anything. Just go to sleep properly. Go to sleep and let me sleep too.'

She lay down, flustered.

He, too, remained lying down with his eyes closed.

Both of them kept on turning on their sides. Both of them had lost their sleep.

The wife was worried that he was becoming mentally unstable.

And he?

His only concern were his dreams…

## There Is Hardly Any Lock Like That

That shop was the most famous shop for locks in the city. One could get locks of any brand, any make, and any configuration in there.

In fact, they had the best of the best locks for you to buy.

They also had locks of which they claimed that nobody could make a duplicate key for them. And if somehow, someone did succeed in making a duplicate key, the lock itself would recognise this duplicity and decide to remain locked. Their locks worked with artificial intelligence. They identified the lock owners' fingerprints and if they matched, then and only then could the key be inserted into the lock. They could even read the intention of the person trying to open the lock. The lock could keep itself shut if it detected the faintest of vibes of a desire to steal. The shop also had some locks which would have to be broken if the lock owner lost its original key. And there were some locks that would explode if one tried to forcefully open them. They had such a variety of locks for sale that it would be impossible to even get into a house if one locked his house with all the locks bought from this shop.

It is in this shop he was standing, hesitant. Would he be able to find such a lock in this shop which when used once, wouldn't allow those who wanted to evict him to enter the house?

He was looking around in the shop for some time now. He had examined so many locks closely. Along with locks, one could also find a card with claims of their reliability affixed next to them. He was closely reading them. So, did he settle on any lock? No. Right now, he was still standing there, confused. Will any lock, out of dozens displayed here, be able to stop them from entering his house? Would it happen that when they come to seize his house and see a strong secure lock protecting the house, they'd leave disappointed and empty-handed, thinking it impossible to open a lock like that? No lock of that sort was displayed here.

What to do then?

He was awkwardly standing there perplexed when a young salesman walked up to him.

'May I help you, sir?' he courteously asked.

'Are these locks really that strong? How strong are they exactly? Strong. The way they have been advertised?'

'Sure. They are even stronger than that, sir. We guarantee their strength.'

'But what's the guarantee of your guarantee?'

'That was a good one!'

'No. I am not kidding.'

'We totally guarantee their strength, sir.'

'But break-ins do happen in the city despite that, right?'

'What can we do, sir? What can we… Not everybody buys locks from us. And how can we guarantee somebody else's locks? And then people are careless too. They even forget to lock their doors. They lose the keys. They misplace keys and then forget about them. There are many reasons for a break-in,' he answered, smiling a customer-friendly smile.

'I think you should go for this one, sir…' he showed him a lock.

'But this one doesn't look very strong, why?' he asked, examining the lock handed to him.

'It looks fragile, but it is very strong.'

'So what's the point of looking fragile?'

'Because fragile looks are the latest trend, sir. That's why.'

'Nope. Show me something else. Anybody would be tempted to evict me after seeing this lock.'

'Evict!?'

'You won't understand.'

'What type of lock will you need?'

'I don't need it. My house does.'

'One and the same thing.'

'Show me something strong and hardy,' he said.

'Well, whatever we sell here is strong and sturdy. You can take anyone you want. See this one. This is so strong that…'

'Show me something so strong that nobody else should be able to open it…'

'Sure, why not?'

'Nobody should be able to break it.'

'Yeah. Sure.'

'Nobody should be able to unlock it,' he repeated himself.

'You do want to unlock it, right? You don't want something which you yourself can't…' he smirked. He was customer-friendly.

But he didn't laugh at the salesman's joke.

He walked up to him, leaned towards him, and whispered in his ears, 'It's fine, even if I am not able to open it. Just show me a lock which neither the government nor the Bazaar could open…'

The salesman laughed. Perhaps, he is replying to my joke with a joke of his own, the salesman thought.

'We'll give you something like that, sir ji. Don't worry.' He said sorting through some locks.

'Why shouldn't I worry?' he asked suspiciously.

'Go ahead, but don't go overboard.'

'Then how should I worry?'

'Well, why don't you let our locks worry for you? That's all.'

'Your locks worry too?'

'These days everybody worries, sir.'

'Yeah, that's true, for sure.'

'You can pick one from these, sir. See! Not even a hammer can do anything to it.'

The salesman demonstrated this by hitting a lock with a hammer.

He wasn't impressed.

'Why don't you show me a big, huge lock?'

'How big?'

'So big that anybody who wants to break it breaks into a sweat just by seeing it. Nobody dares try breaking it if he sees it on the door.'

'Do you want to set a lock on the door or set a bomb?'

'Why would I set a bomb?' he said, startled.

The salesman started laughing. 'I am just joking,' he said.

'But how could you joke about a bomb? If you are playing with it and it explodes, it can blow a man into a million pieces. You know that, right?'

'Where is a bomb here, sir? I was only…'

'Then why talk about it, if it ain't here.'

'Sorry, sir.'

'These are tough times. You should think twice before joking like that.'

'Yes, sir. Where do you want to set a lock on?'

'On the door. Where else?'

'One can set it anywhere if one so wishes, sir.'

'Okay, suppose I put a lock on everything, then?'

'Your wish. Why not?'

'What would you recommend for this, though?'

'Well, that's the problem with locks, sir. You can slap one on every place if you like but then keep in mind that once you do that, you will have to remember to open them up too. Better to think twice before doing this.'

He started thinking. The salesman was right.

'Suppose I put one everywhere and never open it ever again, then?'

Now the salesman was looking at him closely. Why do I get all the weirdo customers? He'll probably buy only one lock but looks like he is going to empty his safe of personal philosophy right here, right now, he thought to himself.

The salesman quietly picked one lock and handed it to him.

'Sir, you should take this one.'

'Is it strong?'

'Yes, very strong. Lock it and forget about it.'

'Why should I forget about it?' he was doubtful again.

'When did I tell you to forget about it?'

'You said that just now! You said, Lock it and forget about it. Didn't you say that?'

'That's the tagline, sir.'

'Very funny. Either you are joking or you are speaking in taglines. Why are you doing that?'

'Sorry, sir.'

'How could you tell me to lock something up and then forget about it?' he was getting irked.

'I already apologised, sir. What more do you want me to do?'

'How could I forget something after locking it up?'

'That was just a tagline, sir! Please don't take that seriously,' he pleaded.

'Why shouldn't I take that seriously? It's a serious matter to lock something up, right? And that's why you have this shop here. Why don't you just sell locks and forget about the taglines?' he was getting even more irritated now.

The salesman was quiet. The only way to deal with this wacko is to keep your mouth shut, he thought.

The man then started looking around him. There were locks everywhere.

'What type of lock do you use?' he asked the salesman.

'For my home?'

'No, for this shop.'

'This shop's door has an in-built lock.'

'Why don't you use your lock here? The one that comes with a guarantee.'

'I don't know anything about that. Please forgive me. Perhaps the owner would be able to better tell you about that.'

'Suppose I install such a door in my home, then? Then nobody would be able to break into it, right?'

'Sir, I don't think anybody would be able to break-in with this. It's next to impossible.'

'And what about the government?'

'What?!'

'Can the government be kept out by installing this door?'

'Who can stop the government, sir? They will make you open the door. They can even break the door.'

'Oh!'

'But why will the government come after you? And people lock their houses against theft.'

'What's the difference between the government and a thief?'

'You are going to get us killed, sir.'

'Can you show me a lock that will stop the government from evicting me?'

'You are not making sense, sir.'

'Why am I not making sense? They want to evict us and I am asking you if you have a lock that can prevent them from doing that!'

'I think you are getting afraid for no reason. No lock can stop the fear.'

'I am not afraid. I just know that they are coming.'

'What?!'

'That's why, show me a lock which, when set on my main gate, would stop anybody from evicting me.'

'No lock can stop an eviction, sir…'

'Why? If the door is locked, how will they evict me?'

'Who told you this, uncle?'

He switched to addressing him as 'uncle' now.

'Why? If I lock my door, how will they come in? And if they can't get in, they wont be able to evict me, right?'

'These days you can be evicted without them coming into your house.'

'How?'

'They bulldoze houses.'

'How can they bulldoze a house? After all, there is something called the rule of law…'

'Rules and regulations can be amended.'

'How?'

'Every lock fails in comparison to the key of amendments in the Constitution,' he said, laughing.

'Suppose I lock my house and stay inside, then?'

'You want to stop a bulldozer by locking yourself in?'

'No. But how can they bulldoze a house if I am inside?'

'They can bulldoze your house with locks and all. Will you get it then?' he said in disgust, and started gathering all his locks.

'Why are you taking away these locks? I am not done yet!' he said.

While gathering all his locks, he sarcastically smiled and quipped, 'I can't show you any more locks, uncle.'

'But, why?'

'I've been told not to.'

'Who told you that?'

'It's a government order. An order is issued that uncle shouldn't be shown any locks. Whosoever does that will be arrested immediately,' he was toying with him now.

'But moments ago you showed so many of them to me, then?'

'The order wasn't issued then.'

'And now?'

'It came just now. The government just emailed me. I checked it on my cell phone.'

'What does it say?'

'It says, "Beware if anybody sold any locks to uncle. Anybody found doing so would be reprimanded".'

'Oh!'

'What else? Who would have thought that the government would issue such an order!'

'Who is going to stop the government, uncle? Suppose they send an order right now to take uncle's pants off and install a lock in its fly. Then we'll have to comply, right?' he said, meaningfully looking at him.

'But I am not wearing anything underneath that. If I take my pants off, I will be naked!'

'The government can take anybody's clothes off.'

'You work for them, right?' he asked, taking a step back after suddenly recognising him.

'Everybody works for them these days.' The salesman didn't understand the question but he did answer.

His face turned pale due to fear. Ashen.

'You are not looking well, sir. You are talking baloney. You should go home.' The salesman was worried, seeing his face turn pale.

He kept on stepping backward.

This salesman must be one of them. He must be trying to coax things out of me by pretending to be a salesman. I wont say a word to him, the man thought to himself.

He quietly kept on distancing himself from the salesman.

Suddenly, he glanced at the ceiling and saw CCTV cameras installed there.

They must have recorded everything; he shuddered at the thought of this.

Now they have seen me, and they can track me and reach my home.

He broke into a sweat thinking this.

His hands started trembling and his mouth went dry. His face was turning white. He covered his face with both of his hands to hide from surveillance cameras. He quickly turned around, with his face covered with his hands, and briskly walked out of the store. He started running as soon as he stepped out and started running faster and faster.

He felt as if somebody was following him, so he broke into a sprint.

He was close to his home now. The street which had his home was right in front of him but he went into a different street. No, he didn't lose his way. He was just trying to shake off the person who was following him.

## Everybody's Hands Are Stained With The Blood Of Dreams

He was continuously crying.

The tears were flowing along with the deep marks etched on his cheeks.

The doctor kept on looking at him while he was crying. He didn't say anything.

'He is crying like that since four in the morning…' the wife told the doctor in a concerned voice while caressing her husband's back.

The doctor feigned as if he was understanding everything in depth.

'Did he ever cry like this before too?' he asked.

'Not in front of me, but he must have. Why, see the streaks of tears which are on his cheeks. Though when you ask him, he never agrees to that. He keeps applying facial cream on them just to show us. He says that the cream is prescribed by a doctor, that it is some type of skin disease. That's what he keeps on saying. But he must surely be crying. Definitely…' the wife said, as if talking to herself.

And he was just crying on and on. Still.

And the doctor, too, was silently looking at him, continuously.

'Just this morning, he woke up with a scream and has been crying since then.'

'Does he say or tell anything else or…' the doctor asked.

'Only, "My dreams, oh! My dreams!" He continuously keeps on saying this. Saying just this and crying.'

In the meanwhile, his crying had slowed down. Now, he was just sobbing, again and again, while looking at his palms.

'What are you looking at in your palms?' So much sweetness was oozing from the doctor's voice that all the ants of Creation were looking this way, startled.

He raised his head while sobbing and stopped crying, and started staring at the doctor.

'Can't you see? Look…' And he spread his palms in front of the doctor.

The doctor lovingly caressed his back with his tender hand. And along with that, he spoke with such sweetness that the doctor himself felt something sugar syrup-like floating on his tongue. One needs a lot of sweetness in this business of being a doctor nowadays too. It has become a somewhat of a sweetshop type matter these days.

'Your hands look good to me. Don't you worry… Don't cry,' the doctor said.

But he started crying again. Bitterly. And repeating only one thing again and again—'My dreams, my dreams!'

'See, just like that…' the wife said.

He kept on crying. The doctor addressed the wife, leaving him crying like that.

'Could you please explain the whole thing in detail to me? For how long has this been going on? Or is this the first time this is happening?'

The wife told the doctor the whole matter.

First, he was restless for last many months. And kept on saying, again and again, that he can't dream anymore these days. And then later, he even stopped sleeping properly because of this concern of his. I tried to explain to him a thousand times that he has plenty of things to worry about already, and when he doesn't sleep properly, how will he dream... But he doesn't listen to me. He says that I was in the habit of dreaming with my eyes wide open. He says that he doesn't dream anymore these days because somebody has stolen his dreams.

'Then? So, does he cry like this for his dreams?' the doctor asked.

'No... He has cried just today.'

'So, did something new happen today or very recently?'

'Yes, yes! It did! Seven days ago, he had a dream…and since then he has been dreaming that dream, again and again, and wakes up in anxiety.'

'Did he cry every day, too?'

'No, he never cried the way he cried today.'

'What dream has he been dreaming for the last seven days?'

'He says that he sees somebody taking his dreams, hanging them upside down, towards a butcher's shop. Every. Single. Day.'

'Who is taking them to a butcher's shop?'

'He says that there is some faceless man…'

'How does he know that the faceless man is taking them to a butcher's shop and not somewhere else?'

'He says things are taken only to a butcher's shop if they are hanging them upside down…'

'How so?'

'He says that roosters, too, are taken the same way to a butcher's shop, ' the wife said.

'Interesting case…' the doctor muttered to himself.

'The roosters have a different case, sir! Please don't compare your dreams with roosters. Your dreams aren't going to go anywhere. You shouldn't worry at all,' the doctor tried to console him in his way.

He kept on sobbing.

'Just because they are hung upside down doesn't mean that they will be killed. Have that dream one more time tonight. They can even hang them right-side up in tonight's dream. Be positive,' the doctor kept on trying to console him. He stopped crying. He raised his head and looked at the doctor.

He suddenly stopped crying and started staring at the doctor.

His eyes were so unrestrained that even the doctor was scared.

'How do you know?' he questioned the doctor while staring at him.

'How do I know what?' the doctor asked.

'Who told you that they are going to transport my dreams by hanging them right-side up?'

'Nobody...'

'Then how could you say that with so much certainty?'

'I said just like that...'

'Liar! You know everything beforehand, don't you? You know everything, don't you?'

'What do I know?'

'You are hand-in-glove with them, aren't you?'

Now the wife interjected. She started scolding him loudly.

'Should you talk to a reputed doctor like that?' she yelled, placing her hand on his back and stopping him.

He jerked her hand away and yelled, 'Arre, he is one of them. Recognise him!'

'He is one of who? What are you talking about?' the wife grabbed his shoulder and shook him.

'Them. Otherwise how would he know that they sometimes take the dreams away by hanging them right-side up? He, too, is an agent of those assassins. True...' he said, and started getting up from his chair.

The wife caught hold of him and forcibly made him sit down. And then turned towards the doctor and apologised to him, saying that his mental condition was such that...

The doctor started smiling.

He asked her not to apologise to him. 'When a man goes insane, he can start thinking anything, start saying anything,' he said.

'I want to go home. Please let me go...' he got up and joined his hands in front of him.

'Oh, sure! You can go at any time, but please give us some company too. What will you do at home anyway?' the doctor said with business-friendly cordiality.

'I might have to perform the last rites of my dreams after reaching home. They would have murdered my dreams by now,' he said, and started crying again.

'After all, why would somebody kill your dreams?'

'Because...because I had refused to pay the ransom... that's it. That's why they would have killed my dreams...' he said, sobbing.

'Who would have killed...' the doctor asked.

'The Bazaar. Who else is going to kill them?'

'Bazaar?'

'Yes, the Bazaar is the one who had abducted my dreams. It wanted a large ransom. I refused.'

'What ransom?'

'It used to say that I should write all of my life in its name. My everything…my every moment, my every breath! Now you tell me, how could I have done that?' he said.

'Really?' the doctor asked with plastic curiosity.

'Yup! The Bazaar now wants that every person in the world should hand themselves over to it.'

'But the Bazaar didn't say anything like that to me, ever.'

'Because you have already handed yourself over to him long ago. You are one of them, Doctor.'

The doctor didn't mind what he said.

Once you consider the other person insane, things get a lot easier from thereon. Then, even the truth uttered by a person can be taken as a joke.

'What you did was right…' the doctor said.

'What?'

'…that you didn't agree to its demand for ransom.'

'But what if they killed my dreams, then? They do this to anybody who refuses to pay the ransom.'

'No, no. They won't do anything like that,' the doctor consoled him.

'Why won't they do that? How are you saying that with certainty?' his suspicion was increasing.

'Yaar, why would somebody kill your dreams?'

'Some, they have already killed! Just tonight in a dream, I saw the dead bodies of some of my dreams. There was a designer dagger being stabbed into their chest. They were bleeding. My dreams died, dragging their feet, asking for help. Right in front of me...and I couldn't do anything,' he said, and started bitterly crying once again.

'He has been crying just like that since this morning...' the wife said.

'Please don't cry. I am sure you've had some misunderstanding. All of your dreams are alive,' the doctor soothed him while caressing his back.

'No, I am not under any misunderstanding. Please look at my palms. They are coloured with the blood of my dreams, aren't they? Here...have a look!' he spread his palms in front of the doctor. The doctor started pretending to look, inspecting his outstretched palms.

He kept on staring at the doctor.

The doctor caressed his palms with his fingers and looked closely at the outstretched fingers. And then while letting go of his fingers, the doctor smilingly said with certainty, 'Your palms are completely clean...there is not a single blotch of blood on them anywhere.'

'Please look at them carefully, Doctor Sahab! There is blood on them. Arre, my hands are getting sticky with drying blood,' he once again jerked his palms and stretched them in front of the doctor.

'Don't look for red colour, Doctor. The blood, when it dries, turns black. See...here, it is everywhere...' he said once again.

His palms were outstretched in front of the doctor.

The doctor pretended to examine his palms once again and declared one more time, 'No, your palms are totally clean. There isn't any blood anywhere.'

'And what are these?' he pushed his palms further toward the doctor's eyes.

'These? These are your fortune lines. See, how clear they are! How would they be so clear had they been covered in blood?' the doctor explained to him.

'The fortune lines of the likes of us float on blood. Don't show all of this to me, Doctor. My life has been spent gawking at my fortune lines,' he muttered.

The doctor smiled. He then extended his own clean, spotless open palms and placed them next to his. Now, he leaned forward and started explaining to him, 'Okay, look at my palms...they are clean, aren't they? Go, on. Take a close look. See, your palms are clean just like mine. Match your palms with mine and see for yourself. Go on.'

He started closely examining the doctor's palms.

And then he gently caressed the doctor's outstretched palm with his fingers. He pinched two fingers in a way as if something sticky had gotten onto them.

Now, he grabbed the doctor's wrists forcefully.

'Bastard...how did you get the blood of my dreams on your palms! Tell me?'

His grip on the doctor's wrists was so strong that his nails were digging into the skin. The doctor didn't squirm but he sure became nervous.

'No...' the doctor said while trying to wrestle his wrist free.

'Look, you better come clean,' he had tightened his grip on the doctor's wrists so much now that they started dripping blood. The shirt's sleeve started getting soaked.

'You, too, are among the assassins of my dreams, you evil one! What did you think, that I won't be able to recognise you? Why?' he pulled the doctor towards himself by his wrists so strongly that the doctor almost fell out of his chair.

The doctor's ribs collided with the corner of the table in front of him. He yelped.

'Despite being a doctor you ended up joining these murderers, didn't you?' he was asking the doctor as he was twisting his wrists.

The blood from the doctor's wrists started dripping on the floor.

'Your sleeve is stained with the blood of our dreams. People will never forgive you,' he was screaming.

The doctor screamed and called for his staff.

In the meanwhile, he had dragged the doctor from his chair almost on the ground.

An insane man musters a lot of strength. He held the doctor with all of his strength.

The doctors table, too, had slid from its spot. The paperweight kept on the table had fallen on the ground loudly.

The doctor was stuck between his table and the chair. On the other side, he was screaming. Announcing loudly that he had caught the murderer and he won't let him get away at any cost. Meanwhile, hearing the noise, the clinic staff and other people, too, barged into the tight room.

His wife was so scared that she was shaking, standing in a corner of the room. And from there, pleading her husband to immediately let go of the doctors hands.

The people who had barged into the room tried to grab him and pull him back. The doctor's arm was pulled some more due to this. And because of the pulling of his arm, his collar with the tie around it was pulled in such a way that he started getting strangled.

The doctor's face started turning blue and he screamed amidst gagging sounds, 'Nurse, give him sedation! Give him an injection!'

The doctor managed to free himself after a lot of difficulties. On the other side, he was now in the grip of the people who had barged in. They had even slapped him a couple of times.

The doctor was still under stress, and quite disturbed too. His shirt was all dishevelled. Blood was dripping from his wrists. The doctor was quite scared. The nurse had run and brought the injection.

The doctor yelled, 'Hold him tightly. The patient is becoming psychotic. Quickly, give him a shot!'

He was given a shot.

He calmed down sometime after receiving the shot.

And then slumped and fell asleep.

He was still in the grip of the hospital staff. He fell asleep, swinging in their arms. A strong sedative had been given to him, perhaps. He was asleep now.

Did he see a nightmare even in this sleep? Who knows?

## The Tunnel Was Found And He Didn't Even Know

And one night, his tunnel was eventually found.

He didn't come to know about it though. At that time, he was inside the tunnel, busy digging it; and just then, outside, his tunnel was found.

He had made all the arrangements for his tunnel to remain hidden from the outside. And that's why he was digging the tunnel in a totally desolate area, drowned in darkness and filled with trash. And anyway, nobody came to this region. This was a densely dark area right behind the glimmering market. The more glimmering the market became, the more darkness underneath it—and behind it—deepened. It was this area he had chosen to dig his tunnel; this was a problem-free place to dig it. Nobody even bothered to peek here. The Bazaar didn't have time from its dazzling lights that it would ever come here and take a peek at these darknesses…and he had started digging his tunnel right from here. He would come here daily, and start digging. Every day, after the digging was done at the end of the day's work, he would cover the mouth of the tunnel with trash and return home.

But it was this tunnel that was found out that night.

Well, what happened was that night the Bazaar suddenly thought about darkness. It suddenly felt a churning within its stomach, thinking about its social responsibility. And in the name of corporate social responsibility, it went to see the darkness behind it, which it had created itself. This was the quintessential quality of the Bazaar. It created darkness itself, and then it worried about these darknesses as well. And it also seemed to be dispelling the darkness created and nurtured by it. The Bazaar took a vow to remove these darknesses, and also arranged for fireflies to do that. It even placed wick-less candles in these darknesses. It sponsored conferences and organized discussions that expressed their profound concerns about these darknesses. And to decide a definition of these darknesses, it invited those scholars who sang odes to it.

So the Bazaar, that night, had gone out to investigate the darknesses which were its own. Minions accompanied him. It brought dazzle along with it as well. It went and stopped at every dark corner it could find. That night, it moved every mound of trash and looked under it. While expressing deep concerns about the darknesses pervading the whole world, it kept roaming amidst the mound of trash within its backyard. Minions recorded the concerns it expressed. They were collecting data on the pervading darknesses. The Bazaar kept on surveying the darkness; its minions gravely noted down every aspect of the darkness in their record books. They updated the list of all the dark corners. Lots of light was shown in the darkness to understand them in depth.

And right then, the Bazaar saw that tunnel.

The mouth of the tunnel, carefully covered and hidden under a mound of trash, was in front of it. It would have been difficult to see the mouth of the tunnel unless somebody looked closely though. But the Bazaar had quite a sharp eyesight. It saw the tunnel in an instant. Its minions, too, saw the mouth of the tunnel; they also saw the changing expressions on the Bazaar's face.

The Bazaar glowered at its minions.

'What's this?' Bazaar asked.

Minions were taken aback. The Bazaar's eyes were conveying that stern action would be taken against somebody after ascertaining the responsibility of this deed. The Bazaar was very cruel in this matter. It didn't forgive anybody who made a mistake. Who will lose their jobs because of this tunnel, this fear started crawling on the backs of the minions like ants.

'What's that all about?' the Bazaar growled while shining light on the mouth of the tunnel.

Minions quietly lowered their heads.

The Bazaar was shining a light on every bowed head, one by one, and stared at them; the heads remained bowed.

'A tunnel was being dug behind our backs, right in our backyard and none of you saw this thing?'

The heads remained bowed.

'What's the meaning of this tunnel?'

They remained silent.

'Speak up… what could be the meaning of this?'

Now somebody will have to speak up and say something.

'We should climb down this tunnel and properly investigate it. To see how deep it goes, you know…' one of them spoke.

'We should catch the guy who has dug this thing…and from him, we can know more about this,' another one said, cutting the first midway.

'And what are your thoughts on this?' the Bazaar sarcastically asked the third minion while shining light on his face.

'I think that somebody is trying to escape from the Bazaar. You know the way prisoners dig a tunnel in an attempt to escape from prison? This seems something similar to that,' the third minion said.

'But how can anybody even think of running away from the Bazaar? Doesn't he know such a simple thing that wherever this tunnel will open, he will find Bazaar there as well?' the fourth minion chimed in.

'But suppose if this man has gone crazy, then? And suppose in his craziness, he thinks that he will succeed in escaping, then what?' the third minion held firm on his argument.

The Bazaar agreed with him, and was worried too.

'This man is right! Someone crazy is surely trying to escape from the Bazaar. This is the truth. Otherwise why would somebody dig a tunnel?'

The Bazaar stood there thinking for some time.

'Sir, what's the point of thinking about a crazy man?' a minion tried to make light of the situation.

The Bazaar sternly rebuked him.

'What nonsense are you talking about? Arre, if the path on which one crazy man is going today, tomorrow everybody else can walk the same path too. It has happened in the world... so many times a crazy man has shown the way, and millions started following him. We shouldn't take crazies lightly. Today, one man is trying to escape, tomorrow it will be everybody. The Bazaar would be drowned forever...'

The Bazaar's face turned red in anger. Seeing his face, his minions became alert.

'After all, who could this man be? Is this man alone or are there other people with him? Where does he plan to reach by digging a tunnel?' the Bazaar kept on pondering while muttering to itself.

'Can any person escape from ME?' Though the Bazaar didn't have any expectation of any independent thought from his minions, still, he asked.

And that's exactly what happened. All of them started saying no in their own way.

'Then what should we do with him?' the Bazaar asked.

'We should climb down the tunnel, catch him right now and bring him here,' all the minions said in unison. They started competing with each other as to who should climb down the tunnel. They started pushing and shoving each other. A couple of them even took off their pants to show their readiness. Everybody wanted to impress the boss with their loyalty.

The Bazaar kept on looking at this jousting of theirs and then suddenly yelled, 'It's not a matter of catching him and bringing him here, you imbeciles! Yes, he can be nabbed right now. This is true. Perhaps, he might be found inside. That's not the point, and that's not what I am worried about. I am worried about something else. Why is that man running away from the Bazaar? Why is he trying to escape? Where has our marketing strategy gone wrong? Are the marketing boys slacking off and freeloading? Why did this happen? Why is a customer thinking that there could be any option other than the market? And if even a single customer is trying to escape from us, then this is a failure of ours.'

All of them listened to his scolding with their heads down. The marketing minions almost burrowed themselves into the ground with shame.

'You understand the meaning of this tunnel, don't you?' the Bazaar asked in a harsh tone.

The heads bowed so much that they almost disappeared.

The Bazaar continued.

'I'll tell you. I'll tell you, you idiots! This tunnel means only one thing. And it means that some people are still under the illusion that they can have a world outside of consumerism. Only crazies who think like that can dig a tunnel. This tunnel also means that we haven't been able to reach everybody as of yet. Why haven't we been able to do that? And then, what do you bastards do all day long? After all, what are your responsibilities? The market should have established control even on the breaths of people by now. The life-force is in the Bazaar's grip, and the heart should seek the Bazaar's permission before doing anything—isn't this the plan which I had prepared and gave to you? Then? Then how come this tunnel is here? There is somebody there who isn't under my spell. And if even a single person like this exists somewhere, then this means that all of you bastards are useless imbeciles and are mooching on me...'

The heads remained bowed.

One or two, with their heads down, agreed in a loud voice, 'Yes sir, we turned out to be completely useless but we should be shown mercy, and given at least one more chance.' Many of them quickly prostrated and started apologising by rubbing their noses on the ground.

A minion did commit the stupidity of trying to make the situation lighter, 'Sir, the whole world is already with us. If one or two dimwits do try to escape from us, we shouldn't be bothered about them.'

This minion was the Bazaar's sycophant, and used to think that he is the boss, the right-hand man.

'Who is this idiot?' the Bazaar signalled toward that minion and asked the executive who was walking along with it.

'Sir?' the executive asked.

'Sir, I was…' the minion tried to save the situation.

The Bazaar brushed both of them off with a wave of his hand.

'Yes, I asked who this dimwit bastard is, who thinks that a consumer is an idiot. He doesn't care about the consumer and he's still working in the market. Clearly, he doesn't understand the fundamentals of the market,' the Bazaar looked at the minion with disdain.

'Sir, I am sorry but…' the minion tried again.

'Oh! Come on! Will somebody please tell me who this idiot is? Remove him from here. Give him a month's salary and send him packing. Pronto!' the Bazaar ordered.

The minion could barely let out a squeak.

The executive always kept the termination letter with him.

By the time the minion was yelping his apologies, his termination letter was typed up and handed to him. He was terminated right then and there, in the darkness. And then when and where he was lost in the pervading darkness behind the Bazaar, nobody knew. Nobody even tried to look toward him. Everyone was concerned about themselves. There was dead silence between the minions. The beams of light in the darkness were wavering. And the sky which was leaning on them, too, was wavering.

The minions were standing silently.

The heads were down and the ears perked up.

The Bazaar warned everybody thus:

'We will have to get to the bottom of this. We will have to find out. And all of this would have to be done quietly, in hush-hush. Nobody should have even an inkling of what is going on. And most definitely, not the man who is digging this tunnel. Let him continue digging. Let's see what he does. Yes, we do have to find out who this person is, after all. Is he alone or is he part of a group...'

The Bazaar paused and took a deep breath.

In a threatening tone, it further, explained:

'Nobody should get even a whiff of this incident. If the word leaked out from here that somebody is thinking about escaping from the Bazaar, it would gravely hurt the market sentiments. And if the Sensex fell, it would be difficult to say how many of you would die getting crushed under it. When the Sensex falls, many people die, getting crushed under the market's debris. You know that, don't you?'

Everybody swore that not a word of this would leak outside. But one of them rightly asked what would happen if somebody else ended up seeing this tunnel.

The Bazaar, too, agreed that as being a valid point. Something would have to be done about this. But, what?

The Bazaar stood there contemplating. The Bazaar was in the darkness and enlightened. All around it was the darkness borne out of illusory radiance.

Two of his minions had torches in their hands. Right now, the torches were facing downwards. The circles of light, after getting absorbed in the mounds of trash and junk, were becoming a part of the darkness. A bizarre light was in the hands of the Bazaar's minions, who themselves were in the dark and were creating more darkness.

After pondering for a while, the Bazaar spoke, 'Cover the mouth of the tunnel the way it was found.'

'Yes, sir. I think that would be best. Let's cover it. Bastard won't be able to come out,' one of them said.

'He will die on his own inside,' a second minion said.

The Bazaar stared at them in anger.

'We don't have to make this his grave here. Only cover the mouth of it. Just keep a plank on top of it, that's all,' the Bazaar said.

The Bazaar was worried why its minions still couldn't think like it.

'We don't have to kill him. He is our respected customer,' the Bazaar further explained.

'Respected?'

'Yes, for us, he is still respected. It's us who have somewhere made a mistake in properly explaining our point of view to this customer...' the Bazaar said.

'But he'll be able to come out easily by removing the plank,' one of them said.

'Then?'

'And he is going to come back, again and again, and continue to dig the tunnel,' the same minion said.

'So?'

The moon shone brighter. The darkness was illuminated somewhat.

Now, the minions could see the Bazaar somewhat clearly.

They saw it had a dagger of Sensex in his hand. If one explains anything while holding a dagger in hand, everybody understands everything quickly. The Bazaar explained, 'Look, sooner or later he is going to remove the plank and come out. A person from marketing should keep an eye on him from afar. That's it. Wherever he goes after coming out of the tunnel, he should be followed. Who is he? What does he do? Who are the people he hangs out with, and spends time with? Get the whole thing. And then, we will have to sit down and do a proper analysis of this case, as to why he is doing this.'

Everybody loudly said, 'Sir, yes, sir.'

The Bazaar stood there for some more time, staring at the mouth of the tunnel. For a while, nobody uttered a single word.

And then, the Bazaar directed the beam of his torch at the face of one of the minions and asked, 'Why does a man run away from the market?'

The minion didn't say a word at first.

'Because he has legs,' the minion gathered some courage and responded.

'That's all fine. He has legs and that's why he can run. I didn't ask that. Don't talk baloney...' the Bazaar reproached.

'Because he has brains, sir,' another one said.

The Bazaar liked this a lot.

'The most dangerous thing is that a man can think. He has brains. He reasons before he runs away. Even a dog has legs but we aren't bothered by the running away of a dog. We are concerned about the man because he can think,' the Bazaar said.

'Yes, sir,' everybody said in unison.

'Why does a man think?' the Bazaar asked, as if to itself.

'Yes, sir. That's the biggest fault with him.'

'I think the time has come, and we should do something so that man stops thinking altogether. Because if he kept on thinking like this, he would be bothered by such useless thoughts as the ones about digging a tunnel...'

'Yes, sir. That's alright.'

'The task of thinking should only be done by the Bazaar now. That's it. Only, the Bazaar should think. If a man thinks the same way as the Bazaar, then we don't have any issues,' the Bazaar said, thinking.

'You think so well, sir,' one of the minions chimed in.

'Think, how dangerous it is that people are still thinking. We should try to make it such that a customer is entangled with the Bazaar 24X7 in such a way that he doesn't get time to think about anything else. And that's why the market will have to expand some more. Till you have complete control over life, a man will continue to think useless thoughts. A man's cry, laughter, sitting, walking, thinking, doing—everything should be in the hands of the Bazaar. Till the time that golden day arrives, we will have to remain alert. We will have to investigate such tunnel-diggers, and we will have to nab every single man who thinks like this and convert them. Buy them. Word, thought, thinking, culture, meditation, philosophy—whatever it may be, everything should be in the hands of the Bazaar. Do you understand?' the Bazaar asked.

A thought ran through one of the minions' head, that he should blurt the truth out right now—that this can never happen, but he remained quiet. Had he said a word, everybody would have thought that he was working with the tunnel-digger.

# He, The One Who Jumped Into A Manhole

Did somebody really jump into a manhole?

Yes. He did. Or we can say he was mulling over it with his feet dangling in the hole of the manhole; thinking hard on whether he should jump…and just then, he slipped into it.

That night, he had removed the cover of the manhole with the intent of looking for a different world to settle in underground. The night was chilly. It was moonlit but the moon was going behind the cover of clouds. The street light was off. He was sitting in the darkness, somehow balancing his buttocks on the slippery edge of the manhole. He took one last look at the world that he was about to leave. For good.

And just then, the clouds moved and the moon came out. He closely started looking at the moon, and kept on looking.

Somewhere in that new world, there would be a moon, right? He started thinking. And just then, the street lights came on. The voltage surge was high. The bulb of the street light flashed brightly for a second.

It was such a bright flash that he was startled and blinded for a second.

And because of this, his attention wavered for a second and his buttocks slid from the edge of the manhole.

He crashed into the sewage pipe.

And as he was falling, the iron lid, too, slipped from his hands. The lid fell back on the manhole. There was a loud bang and the manhole was sealed shut. And with the loud bang of the lid, first, the voltage dropped and then the street lights started to flicker. Amidst the moonlight, the fog and the flickering street lights, the manhole cover was lying on the mouth of the manhole as if nothing had happened there!

He had regained his balance as he was falling, otherwise he would have fallen flat on his face.

And still, he fell into the fast-flowing sewage down below.

Now, he was lodged knee-deep into the sludge of urine and faeces flowing underground. It was pitch-dark inside the sewage pipe.

The loud bang of the lid and the noise from his fall agitated the quiet and still underworld of the sewage pipe. The noise reverberated for a while into that stillness. The insects floating on the surface of the sludge and sitting on the surface of the sewage pipe were startled, and they started buzzing in the confined atmosphere of the sewage pipe. These insects were now colliding with his body, sitting on his clothes, getting entangled in his hair and sticking to his face.

He was left standing in the sewage pipe, stupefied. He stood in one place for a while. Around his feet and underneath them, slimy sludge was flowing continuously. There was a strange buzzing in the air; the insects were flying all around.

Winged insects were also fluttering all around him. The sound of wings fluttering—insects' own note. The buzzing was all around. All other sounds were also continuous. The stream of open gutters was falling into the sewage pipe incessantly. The continuous sound of streams falling was also there. And then, the flowing sewage stream, too, had its own faint sound. All in all, he was surrounded by unbroken streams of sounds from everywhere while he stood there, stupefied.

It was as if the world underground had put the whole of its orchestra in his welcome, and he was standing there mesmerised in the dark solitude of the sewage pipe.

# The Man Hidden Behind The Plank

When the plank was being kept on the mouth of the tunnel as per the orders from the Bazaar, he was somewhere there...inside the tunnel.

With the crowbar in his hand, he was drenched in sweat; he had continuously been working the crowbar.

Sweat. Mud. Darkness. Muddy streaks were flowing on his body. The dim light of the torch surrounded him. He was digging the tunnel, lost in his thoughts. He didn't know that in the world outside, his tunnel had been found.

Here, the ground was hollow. Even if he struck lightly with his crowbar, it got lodged deep into the ground. This time when he hit the crowbar on the ground, it went and lodged itself in too deep. When he made a strong effort to pull the crowbar out, a lot of dirt came along with it.

A wide hole opened up in the wall of the tunnel. He peered through the hole. He shone a beam of light from the torch into it.

He found out that a tunnel parallel to his was being dug simultaneously!

He was stunned.

This meant that he was not alone in doing this. There was somebody else who was also digging a tunnel. It was quite possible that right now that person might be in his tunnel as well. Or, could it be that the Bazaar itself had started digging tunnels now? Some underground project of the Bazaar which the world hadn't got an inkling of as of yet?

He gathered all the soil in anxiety. And then kept on filling the hole with the gathered soil for a long time. The person digging the tunnel adjoining mine shouldn't know about the existence of my tunnel, he thought.

After properly closing the newly-dug hole, he sat down in a corner, leaning against the wall of the tunnel. He sat there pondering for a long time:

What tunnel is that? Right alongside my tunnel. Could there be more tunnels like these? So, how many people are digging tunnels to run far away from the Bazaar? When so many people are digging tunnels all around me, then why does my family think of me as crazy? He was flummoxed thinking all of this.

He once again patted the soil which he used to close the hole for a long time. The hole should be properly sealed, he thought.

The hole was closed, for now. But the time had come for him to take this task of tunnel digging to its conclusion now, otherwise somebody could reach his tunnel just like this, anytime.

He picked up his crowbar once again…and then he stopped. Not anymore today. I will be back tomorrow and work my butt off. Today is not a good day, he thought.

The torch was lying next to him, on the ground, leaning on two clods of soil. The tunnel was lost in a faint light for some distance, and then there was dense darkness. He rested the crowbar on the ground, extended his hand and picked up the torch. He had turned it off now.

So, let's go. Let's go home. He started crawling in the tunnel to get back home. He crawled, and crawled some more, and kept on crawling. Towards the mouth of the tunnel.

He was anticipating seeing the faint light as he came closer to the mouth of the tunnel. With the torch turned off, he was crawling in the dark towards the mouth of the tunnel. When it was nearby, a faint light started to descend. The reflected light of the lights outside.

But, right now, he couldn't see any light anywhere.

What happened? Had the lights outside been turned off? But this couldn't be possible. The lights were always on in the market. There was no dearth of light there. It was that light that came all the way to the back where the mouth of the tunnel was. So, then?

When he crawled some more, he found out that the tunnel had ended.

He turned the torch on. His heart skipped a beat. The mouth of the tunnel was closed. He turned his torch towards the mouth of the tunnel. There was a plank covering it. Somebody had closed the tunnel from the outside. His heart sank. Somebody had closed the mouth of his tunnel.

Who would have closed the mouth of the tunnel? Who kept the plank here? Perhaps, some kind-hearted man saw the mouth of the tunnel and covered it with a plank so that some stray person doesn't fall into it. But such kind-hearted people were in madhouses these days, or in some hole themselves. No…this was someone else's doing. But whose? Could it be that a whole new market was being built behind this market? Could it be that the construction material of that market had been dumped here, which then closed the mouth of the tunnel? It didn't occur to him that his tunnel could have been found!

He sat there in the tunnel underneath the plank with which it was closed shut. What to do now?

He tried to move the plank. It moved a little. If he applied some more force, he could've easily dislodged it. But would it be wise to do that right now? Or should he wait for some time? But how long? The tunnel was closed at both ends! He was feeling suffocated. His chest was feeling heavy, and his heart started beating faster and faster.

Suppose he got a heart attack right here, right now, in this closed tunnel…then? What if he died right here, then? Outside, nobody would know. His children will wander around from police station to police station trying to have a report filed for him having gone missing. His children will search for a good photo of him to be published in the newspapers in the missing person ads!

And then a strange thought crossed his mind. What reward will they settle on for the information of his whereabouts? He had seen a lot of reward posters asking for information about a missing loved one and offering rewards for it. What reward would be set for him? What was his price? And suppose if they didn't keep any reward then? Then why would somebody be interested in looking for him? Arre, if you don't get anything in return, what's the point of doing anything like that? Rather, people will laugh at that.

And it was as if he stabilised in the tunnel itself while thinking all of this. Neither did he have that initial restlessness, nor the anxiety or the fear of being left behind, trapped in this. He had no eagerness to get out of the tunnel either.

Suppose, if I spent the rest of my life here in this closed tunnel, then? He started smiling at this anarchic thought of his.

So, right now, a smiling man was sitting squatting in a dark, closed tunnel. If one considered him crazy then he was crazy; otherwise, he wasn't that crazy.

## He Lost His Mind, And His Memories

He had been walking in the market for a long time. From this showroom to that showroom. Inside. Outside. Walking. Strolling. Stopping. Looking and inspecting things.

He seemed to be searching for something. There was something that he was looking for but couldn't find.

'What are you looking for, sir? May I show you something?' a salesman politely asked him. The salesman wasn't showing him respect though. This was in-built in his manner of speaking.

He didn't say a single word for a few moments.

And then he responded, saying, 'I am looking for my memories.'

'Sorry, I didn't get you, sir,' the salesman responded.

'I, myself haven't understood this thing completely as of yet. How can I explain it to you?' he said and walked away.

The salesman was left gawking at him. You get one of each kind in the market, Sahab! With whom and how many can I butt my head? But the salesman wasn't saying anything wrong.

And the poor man, he wasn't able to understand himself... What had happened to him? His memories had disappeared. He couldn't remember things these days.

Although the incident of losing his memory was grave, it had been building over a period. Gradually. Over the years.

It went something like this:

He was an alright middle-class man. Content with himself. Small family life. Office. Kids. Job. Music. Literature. Poetry... And such an aficionado of folk music that he would forcibly get into a soirée and play it. He somewhat dabbled in painting as well. A voracious reader. Organised Ram Leela. Attended poetry recitals. Watched movies. Sang ghazals. All in all, a fabulous man. And then what happened was that a new car came into the country. Though cars had already been in the country, this new car turned out to be somewhat magical. The citizens of the country were outdoing each other in trying to buy it. This was a new technology and a new culture. And soon this car became the metric to measure each other's capability, progressiveness or backwardness. And that's where the incident began. He belonged to the common middle-class. Neither had he the wish, nor the capability to buy such a car. But he saw that people like him, people with him, people who were his neighbours, whosoever had this car had become divine in their totality—important, and a different type of human...

Suddenly, he and his family fell under an inferiority complex.

Gradually, he started being stressed and worried. He started walking around the neighbourhood with his head down. His family members started looking at him with complaining eyes. Wherever he walked, the road—even lampposts—laughed at him. Just a small car had derailed his heart and mind. And then he found out that this car could be bought by taking a loan in easy installments. His family members, too, started goading him. A loan was taken. The car was bought. The installments began. Along with the car, the path to buying many more things by taking a loan, too, was paved. Now he started living just so that he could buy random things from the market on loan and pay their installments.

Soon it became difficult to keep paying the installments, and he kept on taking more and more debt to make ends meet. Now, he had taken on a whole new lifestyle, where taking a loan wasn't a thing of shame, and a man's worth was evaluated on the basis of how much clutter he had accumulated. And then somebody advised him that the most effective way to pay off all the debt was to invest in the market. 'If you invest you'll get three-four folds in return', he was told. And he took a plunge into the share market. The car was changed. Many more things came into the house. More and more. Loss, profit, market, buying and selling, goods, market—these were the only things he was worried about now. He thought about this all the time. That was all he remembered. The Bazaar had pervaded his memories. A market had opened up in all the corridors of his memories. Now, he only lived engrossed in the market. He lived only with the Bazaar. The Bazaar, too, had started living with him. And in all of this, a new problem began. The family members noted that he had started forgetting.

These days, his memory wouldn't serve him. He would often forget. This memory defect, too, was bizarre. He would remember the complete accounting details of the shares but forget the names of his friends. Poetry, literature, folk, ancestors, relationships—the memories of all of these had already been wasted away but nobody paid any attention to any of that. And he never became aware that his memories had been evicted by the Bazaar. He had forgotten about friendship, society, literature, culture, values—everything. He had started thinking only about the Bazaar. He had started living and breathing the Bazaar, and he didn't feel anything bizarre about that. When he started forgetting even the smallest things, it was then that he was startled. And this was the point when even the family members paid attention to this problem of his.

Nowadays, he would forget if he ate or not. He would be lost while coming back home. He would go to the bathroom to pee and forget why was he there. He would be left standing there, flummoxed. If he went to take a shower, he would find himself sitting idly with the shower on and wondering what was he doing there. How a belt is buckled around the waist, he wouldn't be able to figure that out. He would work up a sweat trying to fit both of his feet in one sleeve of the pajama. And sometimes, he wouldn't be able to recognise his family members, and occasionally end up asking his son, 'Who are you? And how come you are roaming in our house?' He would catch a reflection of himself in the mirror and would struggle to recall where he had seen this man before.

His family members tried to explain to him that since he had lost his memory, he should stay at home. He couldn't believe what he heard. How so? Alright, I have lost my memories, but wouldn't I be able to find them if I went looking for them? And one has to go out to look for the memories, isn't it? Had they been lost within the house, wouldn't I have found them by now? And he would walk out in search of lost memories, after thinking all of this to himself. But where should he go? Where should he look? He would try to recall but his memory wouldn't serve him. Where did his memories go? He would try to recall but it was the memory itself that was faltering. Whenever he tried to think of something, all he could think of was the Bazaar. That was all. He couldn't think of anything else. His family members had advised him to leave the house with a card in his pocket which had the home address and phone number. And gradually, the situation kept on deteriorating, but he didn't stop going out to look for his memories whenever he got a chance. Countless times, he would be found roaming the streets and the markets, and friends and acquaintances would safely bring him back home.

He was troubled by the loss of his memories. He wanted to find out where his memories had gone after all. The more he tried to contemplate this, the more he could recall only the Bazaar.

He realised that his memories went as far as the market, but then why couldn't he remember anything else beyond that? Could it be that he lost his memories somewhere in the market? The more he analysed this, the more his belief strengthened, that surely there was a strong connection between the loss of his memories and the Bazaar. Did he lose his memories somewhere in the market? Did they fall there and somebody picked them up? And even if somebody found them lying on the ground, what if that person threw them in the trash, treating them like garbage? The more he pondered this, the more he concluded that he should look for his lost memories in the market. And that's why he left his home every day, bright and early, and roamed the streets of the market—looking for his memories, all over the place. And at first glance, it seemed as if he was window shopping. He loitered near or within the shops for hours on end.

He was loitering just like that on that day as well.

A salesman had been eyeing him for quite some time.

He would go from one shelf to the other. Stand there. He would just stand there gawking at the merchandise kept on the shelf. And then, without picking anything up, he would walk away and stand somewhere else. This had been going on for a while.

'May I help you, sir?' the salesman asked after walking near him. His attention was disturbed.

'Yes?' he asked.

'Are you looking for anything, sir?'

'I don't know,' he said absent-mindedly.

'May I help you?' the salesman asked again.

'How?' he asked back.

'Please tell me what are you looking for, and I will try my level best to find something of your liking and give it to you,' he said respectfully.

'What can I say? I can't recall why I came here…'

He was suffering from a memory lapse. His eyes had so much emptiness in them that had the salesman peered into them, he would have been perturbed. But the salesman was looking at the clothes. He assessed the customer by the glitz of the clothes they wore.

'Well, please try to recall… or you can call home and ask your wife. Perhaps, you came here to buy something for her?'

He tried to recall.

Suddenly, something flashed in his mind. He spoke

excitedly, 'Yes, I just remembered what I am looking for in the market…'

The salesman smiled.

'I knew it, sir…' the salesman said for the sake of saying.

He was startled and said, 'How do you know?' He started looking at him suspiciously.

'What?' the salesman didn't understand anything.

'How do you know?'

'How do I know what?'

'But, didn't you say just now? Didn't you say just now that you know?'

Now, the salesman looked at him with suspicion for the first time. Is this man in his right mind? And for the first time, the salesman peered into his eyes as well. There was so much emptiness in those eyes till far in the distance, just like the vast expanse of a desert…and it felt as if sand was pouring out of his eyes.

'Oh! I said just like that. I knew that you will surely remember. Please tell me, what are you looking for? May I help you?' the salesman asked again.

He kept staring at the salesman. Silently. As if thinking, should I tell him or not? And after reaching a certain conclusion, he eventually said, 'I want my memories. That's what I was looking for.'

The salesman couldn't understand. What the heck is he

asking for, yaar, he thought to himself.

'What?'

'Memories…I am searching for my memories,' he repeated.

'I don't understand, sir. What have you come to buy?' he asked again.

'I am talking about my memories.'

'Sorry, sir. This is not a showroom of memories.'

'But I only want memories.'

'Sir, to the best of my knowledge, there is no showroom of memories here that would sell memories. If I had even an inkling about such a showroom, I would have surely guided you in its direction. By the way, why are you looking to purchase memories?' he wanted to know, and started laughing.

The man said, 'No, no. I am not looking to buy memories. Memories aren't bought and sold.'

'That's exactly what I was telling you. Memories aren't bought and sold in a market.'

'That I am very well aware of,' he said, thinking something.

'Then?'

'But they will be found here. That's for sure,' he was saying confidently.

'How so?'

'They were my memories. I know that.'

'If they were yours, then why don't you go home and look

for them? They must be there somewhere.'

'No, no. They were lost somewhere here in the market.'

'But why did you come to the market with memories? You are supposed to come here with an empty mind,' he said.

'Could it be that somebody stole my memories?' he said, pondering something.

'Look, sir, the customer is responsible for their belongings, and the Bazaar can't be held responsible for any kind of theft or loss. We have such warnings written and displayed all over. Now if people don't pay any attention to such warnings then what are we to do?' the salesman started muttering.

'I am not complaining about you. I am telling you. Here, in this market, my memories have been stolen,' he started telling him.

'It's quite possible you might be right. One has to be very careful when out and about in a market, sir. Thieves, pickpockets—people of all kinds are in a market,' the salesman agreed with him.

'Why would somebody steal my memories though?' he asked the salesman lost in his thought.

'Yes, that's a valid point,' the salesman, too, agreed. He was agreeing to everything he was saying. Actually, the salesman was convinced that this uncle's mind was not in the right place. Now, he was playing with him. Now, not a customer but a crazy man was standing in front of him.

'Okay, tell me one thing…' he walked close to the salesman and started asking in a whisper.

'Sure. Why not? We are sitting and twiddling our thumbs here anyway. The market is slow these days. There's hardly any work to do. Ask away!'

'Could it be that the Bazaar itself would have stolen my memories?' he asked almost in a whisper.

The salesman faced him squarely and started looking at him, stupefied.

'Why in the world would the Bazaar steal your memories?'

'But suppose for a second that the Bazaar has stolen my memories, then?'

'What makes you think it is like that?'

'Because the more and more the Bazaar intruded in my life, the more and more my memories started to disappear…'

'Do memories even have value, sir? Come on, even if the Bazaar stole them, for how much would it have been able to sell them for?'

'No, it's not the point of selling.'

'Then? Arre, why would the Bazaar be interested in something which can't be sold?'

'They were priceless to me.'

'What's the big deal about your memories?'

'Memories are the earnings of life. A life without memories

is lonely and bottomless. As if somebody has pulled the ground from under somebody's feet...'

'Oh! Yeah!'

'Yes, sir! It is these memories that make a human, human. Otherwise what is a man without these memories? Just a mechanical robot.'

'What are these memories which you are talking about?'

'There were so many! Memories of my ancestors, of society, of history, of folklife. It had folk music. It had stories. It had poetry... Who knows what else was in there? All of it vanished suddenly. I can't recall anything. *Anything*. I got so busy in the Bazaar that when these memories of mine vanished, I didn't even know. When I gained my senses back I saw that nothing was left of my memories. There was only the Bazaar. Everywhere. As long as the memories went, the Bazaar went as far as that, and talks about the Bazaar pervaded my mind.'

The salesman started smiling. What gibberish is this oldster spouting?

'Your memories were priceless, weren't they?'

'Absolutely! They were priceless!'

'So if they were priceless, as you say, then you definitely must have insured them?'

'Memories aren't insured anywhere.'

'The heck priceless they are then!'

'Why?'

'Rather, they aren't even worth two bits, your memories!'

'Why, why do you say so?'

'What I say is an absolute truth. Whichever thing that has even a teeny bit of value is also insured these days. There is a huge market for insurance, sir.'

He went silent. And started looking pitiful.

The salesman took pity on him. Expressing so would be considered against the sales principles because the Bazaar, basically is against pity though. Yes, he had to help a customer for sure, but only so a customer stayed in the market, continuously.

'You should go right away and file this complaint of yours in the Customer Care of this mall,' the salesman lent a 'helping hand'.

'Why would the Bazaar file my complaint against itself? Wouldn't this be crazy?'

'It will surely do it! At least give it a shot.'

'Is the Bazaar crazy?'

'No, it isn't crazy'

'Then? Then why would somebody file a complaint against itself? This would be craziness, wouldn't it?'

'Many things which the Bazaar does when seen from above look crazy but they aren't.'

'Sorry, I don't get it.'

'Look, this is the Bazaar's characteristic. On the surface, it will appear to you that this is pure craziness. If something is selling you any product at eighty per cent, how is it doing that? If it is giving you three items free for the purchase of one, but how so? Surely that entity is crazy! But it is not crazy. This is the math of its wisdom.'

'But what could be the math of filing a complaint against itself?'

'Yes, that, too, has math which you, perhaps, wouldn't be able to understand.'

'You are right. Anyway, I've been weak in math always.'

'And then this math is quite different, Uncle. Here the problems of arithmetic are solved with the formulas of algebra. Here, everything goes…'

'Oh!' he said dejectedly.

'Though, you must have checked all the trash cans of the market, haven't you?'

'Trash cans? Why trash cans?'

'Let's assume that your memories slipped from you and fell somewhere in the market, then? And if somebody even saw them lying on the ground, he either would have walked away trampling them or picked them up and threw them in the nearest trash can. An alert citizen throws such trash into trash cans these days. This is in vogue these days.'

'But my memories aren't some trash. And they haven't

fallen somewhere; they've been stolen.'

'What would someone do by stealing something like that?'

'What something?'

'The thing which you are describing. And even if somebody picked it up, they would eventually throw it somewhere. That's why I was saying, that you should check out the trash cans.'

He stood there silently, gawking here and there.

'You should definitely file a complaint with the Customer Care.'

'Will they bring my memories back to me?'

'Well, that's quite difficult to say.'

'Then?'

'But they will address you "yes sir, yes sir" so many times, they will file your complaint with so much patience that you will end up having a good time; and just for the sake of it, you will have some hope. And don't be surprised if now and then they even sprinkle a few "sorry sir" in the middle of the conversation as well…'

'But how is all this going to benefit me? I wont get my memories back!'

'But you will feel good after going through this whole process. You will feel satisfaction. Your trust in the Bazaar will increase, that whatever the way things might be here, at least the system they have here is fantastic.'

'Quite a bizarre system this is that it is fantastic but of no use whatsoever!'

'But why don't you thank heavens, they at least have a system! Suppose if they didn't have any system at all, then?'

He was rendered speechless.

Perhaps, whatever the salesman was saying was true.

'Alright, son. Then I will go and check it out…' he left saying this.

'Please have a look. You will feel better,' the salesman said with a namaste, smiling. The man walked away without turning back.

And when he walked out all the way, it was then that the salesman turned around. He ran to his senior standing right in front of him.

'What a weird customer he was, sir,' the salesman started telling him.

Even before he could say anything more, his senior started laughing.

'I know him. Everyone knows him here. You are a newbie, that's why. You, too, will come to know him eventually,' the senior said laughing.

'Arre!'

'He is quite a weirdo! He has lost his mind completely. I can't tell you how many times his family members have come here looking for him. They enquire if he came by the showroom because he hasn't reached home still.'

'Poor Uncle!'

'He has completely lost his memories and talks crazy. He looks fine though.'

'One can't figure out the first time if a crazy appears absolutely fine,' the salesman said.

'Yup. That's the thing. These days, not even the crazies walk around in tattered clothes. They can even be found in a three-piece suit!' his senior said.

'So then everybody should be assumed crazy here?' he joked.

'The Bazaar, too, does this these days. It deals with everybody as if all of them are crazy,' the Senior started laughing.

The salesman, too, started laughing.

And though this wasn't a joke, neither of them knew that.

## The Rubble Of Dreams

'Doctor Sahab, he has a lot of relief now…' his wife was thanking the psychiatrist.

'How is his restlessness these days? Does he still cry for his dreams? Does he even sleep or…' the doctor asked.

'Like a baby! He sleeps like a baby, and doesn't even mention dreams,' his wife told the doctor in a chirpy tone.

The wife was telling the doctor that his medicines were working efficiently.

And he was sitting there, smiling. Quietly listening to their conversation. The funny thing was that everything which was spoken about him was wrong, and he was listening to it sitting silently.

'And how are you, sir?' now the psychiatrist was addressing him.

He smiled more freely, and laughed after looking directly into the eyes of the psychiatrist.

'I am perfectly alright. Madam is already telling you my condition…' he said.

Satisfaction scattered across the psychiatrist's face.

'Very good…' he said, as if to himself. He started revising the prescription he wrote earlier.

The man kept on gazing at the psychiatrist while sitting there. And kept on smiling too.

He was happy that he didn't have to tell the truth either to his wife or to the psychiatrist. If they were happy with the fact that he was not talking about his dreams these days, then he thought it best to let them remain happy. And as far as the truth was concerned, it was him alone who knew the truth.

When nobody believes what he says, then why should he share with anybody how much progress he has made in his search for the Truth?

And in this search of his, this psychiatrist's medicines had helped him in a different way altogether. Just for this one thing, the psychiatrist deserved his gratitude.

'Thank you, Doctor,' he said.

Looking at him, the doctor smiled. He, too, was sitting and smiling.

Only he knew what the truth was.

The truth was that in the beginning, he was sternly against taking any type of medicine. He knew that he was not an insane. And if that was so, then why should he take these medicines?

After a lot of pleading, and after surreptitiously mixing them in his tea or milk, or simply forcing him—that is to say, his family members tried every trick in the book and eventually gave up because he kept on refusing to take the medicines prescribed by the psychiatrist. Opposed them vehemently. He would be agitated at the mere sight of the medicines, and would clench his teeth. And if someone, somehow, forcibly put them in his mouth, he would just keep them in there; he wouldn't swallow. His family members would have to struggle a lot…and then after such theatrics, he would eventually swallow them. The psychiatrist believed that mental patients do behave this way. It was his opinion that if they get violent, then they should be dealt with tactfully and administered the medicine. There was no other way. The insane…you know! His family members somehow gave him those medicines. But after taking the medicines for three-four days, it was as if a miracle happened. He started sleeping soundly.

And on the third day itself, he had a very deep sleep.

Otherwise, he hadn't slept properly for months. When he slept, he felt quite a relief. The next day when he woke up, he wasn't feeling agitated. He was able to ponder over his dreams with peace of mind.

And then he started taking his medicines regularly. And then one day, a miracle happened: in deep sleep, he had a dream. And in that dream, he ventured into the world of dreams while searching for his dreams.

And from then on, he would have a sound sleep, daily. He would dream on daily basis, and he would venture to look for his lost dreams in his dream.

He would wander the whole city in his dream. It was easy to wander around the city in the dream. He could fly in his dream. His stride would lengthen in his dream. He would cross the whole wide bridge just in a single stride. If he wanted to run, he could run faster than cars. He would get a lot of strength. He wouldn't fear even his enemies. He would topple buildings with just a single punch; he would punch and break boulders into pieces. He would take a peek inside the whole house without even opening a single window or door. He would even understand the language of birds. Forget birds, he could even talk to the electricity poles. He would even interrogate the electricity flowing in the electrical wires, saying to them, 'You have access to bathrooms and bedrooms of every house and if you ever see my dreams there, then please, please come and inform me'. He would say to everybody that if they ever found out anything about his dreams, then they must tell him. He went there every day in his dreams. And then, in a single breath, he would describe the looks of his lost dreams to everyone. *Everyone*. Anybody who crossed his path in his dreams, he would describe his lost dreams to them. This happened to such an extent that even the people whom he met regularly in his dreams began smiling whenever they heard him talk. How long could people listen to that same talk every single day!? And that's why, when he asked a flying bird about his dreams the other day, the bird carelessly replied, 'We haven't seen such dreams even in our own dreams, especially the type of ones which you describe! Surely you must be having some misunderstanding.' And like that, even the citizens of the world of dreams had started thinking of him as insane. But he didn't let go of his efforts.

At least this much was certain that the last time he saw his dreams, it was in his dream. The chance to meet them again would once again be in a dream only. He would have to burrow inside his dreams to look for his dreams. Every day he would wait for bedtime. He would make plans for his upcoming dream at night, all day long. He would make a list of neighbourhoods to scout for his dreams that night; he would work out search and rescue strategies for his hunt. And as soon as the night would fall, he would eagerly take his sleep medicines.

Here his family members would get happy seeing that he had stopped dithering in taking his medicines nowadays. 'In fact, he asks for them…' they would talk amongst themselves. He hardly mentioned his dreams anymore…They didn't know that he was already on his secret project. He was searching for his dreams, in his dream. He would fall asleep because of the medication. He would then dream in his sleep. And each night, he would enter a dream as if he was opening some portal, and would get busy in the task of searching for his dreams. Nobody would get even a whiff, and he would look for his kidnapped dreams all night long. This arrangement of his search for his lost dreams was convenient for everybody. The Bazaar called such situations a 'win-win'. His family members weren't getting disturbed. He, too, was able to comfortably look for his dreams at night. He would get into his dream and he would methodically and meticulously search every nook and corner of every neighbourhood at night.

So many of these nights, he had passed awoke in his dream. He hadn't felt tired a bit. If a person believes in his dreams, he never tires. He knew that he would surely find his dreams. One day. Or one night. For sure. They must have imprisoned his dreams somewhere. He would be able to recognise them from afar. So glittery, so golden and so beautiful were his dreams that he would recognise them even with his eyes shut. He wandered around all night in his dream, looking for his dreams. Searched every street in the city. On the road. On the side of the road. In every home. In every corner. Behind every lock.

Sometimes he started to get disappointed though.

Could it be that they might have assassinated his dreams in reality? So then, it didn't matter if he searched for them on heaven or earth, they wouldn't be found anymore! He had fallen asleep thinking all of this when a miracle happened. He found his dreams. The way they were found, the condition they were found in—that was a different story altogether. But at least he found them. After getting into his dream, he was roaming in a new neighbourhood in the city. This was an ultra-posh neighbourhood. Huge buildings. Very wide roads. The price of one square foot of land was so much that if one were to buy only underwear for 10 lakh poor people with the money, they would still be left with lakhs of rupees. That's where he found his kidnapped dreams.

A new road was being constructed there. Some new technology was being used in the construction of that road. There were a few heaps of gravel, mounds of sand and drums of coal tar on the road.

The rubble of dreams of the whole world was scattered on the entire road. They were pounding this rubble of dreams with the engine which is used in pounding the gravel. The dreams were scattered on the road like gravel. They had scattered the shattered dreams on the whole road and were pounding it hard. The trucks laden with shattered dreams were coming and unloading the rubble on the road which was under construction. The road roller was compacting this rubble from the other side of the road.

The mounds of shards of glittery dreams, pieces of those dreams and dust were scattered on the road everywhere. They had so much glitter left in them that even after shattering into pieces, there was hardly a possibility of any suspicion left anywhere. Yes, it was the rubble of his dreams which they had crushed and turned into rubble, and used to construct the road. For a long time, he had been reading in the newspapers and hearing in the news that from now on, using new technology, such glittery roads would be paved that there wouldn't be any need for any street light or any other light next to the road. These roads would be filled with such a glittery mix that its shine would last a lifetime.

Today, when he saw this road under construction, the whole thing became crystal clear to him. So, these people were naming their conspiracy of shattering glittery dreams and burying them within roads as new technology. Such a time had come that you could hoodwink anybody with anything as long as you named it 'new technology'. They were making solid arrangements for crushing the dreams daily, after burying them on the road. People would participate in crushing their own dreams—such was the finesse of the technique. He was speechless.

As far as the eye could see in distance in front of him, he could see the rubble of his dreams—and other dreams like his—spread on the road.

He started crying loudly in his dream.

And while crying, he started running on the road which was under construction. He kept on running. On the rubble of dreams. Dreams which had been broken here and there. He would gaze at every single piece of his dreams. He would cry. He would sob. He ran and started gathering the shards of his dreams. He started filling them in his pockets. And kept on stuffing his pockets more and more. Irritated, he kept on picking up the pieces of the scattered rubble from here and there. All around him were so many pieces of his dreams, scattered every which way. How many could he pick up? He kept on gathering them, kept on running and kept on crying. The shards of his dreams were lodged into the soles of his feet. The soles of his feet were now coloured with blood. The labourers working there, the driver of the rubble truck, and the passersby came running to stop him.

'Have you gone mad?' a labourer grabbed his hand and asked him.

'Why are you running barefoot on the rubble like that? And why are you filling your pockets with this trash? Why are you crying?' people started asking.

What could he reply? How could he explain to them? If he said a word, these citizens of the world of dreams, too, would start calling him crazy. He stood up, sobbing. People gathered around him in a circle to see the spectacle. And then suddenly, he screamed and started rolling on the shards lying on the road. And he kept on wailing while rolling on the road. The shards of the dreams lodged themselves in his body all over. He was bathing in the pool of his own blood. Somehow and with a lot of difficulties, people were able to stop him. He sat down right there, in the middle of the road, and started sobbing, burying his head in between his knees. Clenching the shards of his dreams in his fists.

The shards had lodged themselves in his palms, his hips, and the whole of his body here and there. And he was walking while crying and screaming, 'My dreams, Oh! My dreams!'

## This Was The Time To Lift The Plank

He looked at his watch, and was startled.

A hand from his watch was missing, and the other one was bent. As if somebody had twisted the arms of Time… It was a watch alright, but it was incapable of telling time… Or could it be that his watch itself didn't want to tell him the time? Could it be that they even had his watch on their side?

He had ended up sleeping in the tunnel for a long time. Lost in sleep, right underneath the plank that somebody had left on the mouth of the tunnel. Before falling asleep, he had stayed within the tunnel in the dilemma of whether he should get out or stay within. He had been thinking who knows what, leaning and half reclining against the wall of his tunnel. Getting out in such a condition had its own dangers. It was quite possible that those people might have found out about him and his tunnel. If he lifted that plank and got out, and he might have found somebody waiting for him right at the mouth of the tunnel. So he thought that he should get out only late at night. Perhaps, he won't find anybody then. And thinking this, he had even checked his watch, half-reclining. The watch had even shown the correct time at that time. Five hours were left, for that span of time late at night. He stayed there, half-reclined, lazing and waiting. And as to when he fell asleep, even he didn't know.

And now, when he had suddenly woken up from his slumber, the tunnel was pitch dark. What time would it be now? How long had he been sleeping? That was when he had checked his watch, and he was startled to look at it.

The watch had refused to tell the time. He felt around the watch in the dark. Could it be that the watch came under him while in sleep and the glass cracked? Even the hands of a watch can break when crushed… But the glass was intact. The hands did look bent though. The small hand was missing; the big one was so bent that it was difficult for it to move even with a limping motion. It was dragging itself. And the second hand, it was as if it was scared and alert, but was moving aimlessly…

Time was out of the clutches of the watch now.

Time was in the tunnel, and wasn't in the tunnel at the same time.

Now what?

Now what should he do?

Who knows what time it was now? And if he got out of the tunnel now, would he be able to find his Time there or not? Suppose while he was in the tunnel, Time had now completely gone under the clutches of the Bazaar, then? Suppose that he lifted the plank and comes out, and finds out that now there was not even a single moment left that belonged to him, then? What if his Time had left him as an orphan and gone with the Bazaar? Then?

He was sitting under the plank, squatting.

What should he do?

But he must take a chance.

Whatever it may be, he will get out.

He tried lifting the plank with utmost caution. He had thought that they surely must have kept the plank under something heavy. But it didn't turn out to be like that. The plank gave way with the slightest of effort.

He thought one more time and then pushed away the whole plank.

# If You Wear The Shoes On Your Head, The Feet Are Left Bare

Both of his feet were bandaged.

There were bruises on his palms, here and there. It was as if they were bruised when he slid and fell somewhere. The face had dark lines of tears on it. Huge swollen bags under his eyes. As if he didn't sleep all night, such was the look on his face. He was staring unblinkingly in who knows which direction. Such an empty stare, like a desolate place.

He was sitting there in a way as if he was there but he was not there. He was sitting in front of the doctor right now though. He was silent. His son was standing next to him; he was the one who was telling everything to the doctor. The doctor was listening to everything with professional interest. His son was talking about him, but he was listening to him talk with such raptured attention—as if he was telling a story about somebody else.

'Doctor Sahab, this time something new has happened in his case. That's the reason I came along,' the son said.

'Yes, before your mother used to accompany him. In the beginning, he would wake up in the middle of his sleep and start crying. He had big issues with his dreams. I remember the whole case,' the doctor spoke while throwing a cursory glance on his writing on the prescription note that he had written.

'Yes, yes. Exactly...' the son said.

'Once, he even became violent in my clinic, and had attacked me. I remember it all.'

'Yes, yes. Sorry, sir!'

He sat there. Stone-faced. Calm. Untouched. Listened to everything which was being spoken about him.

'But wasn't he getting better lately? I think that's what your mother had said on the last visit.'

'Yes, he did improve somewhat. He slept well and wasn't worried about his dreams either.'

'Yup. That's it,' the doctor nodded.

'When he came last time, his wife had said that he was alright now. I had even revised a few of his medicines then,' the doctor was speaking as if he was talking to himself while perusing his notes.

'We, too, were under this illusion until yesterday, but...' the son continued.

Before his son could continue further, the man started narrating the whole thing himself.

'Nothing, Doctor… I hit my toe a little. That's it. And these people got worried and brought me here. Just a tiny thing…'

Actually, he was trying to suppress the whole thing. He was sternly against bringing in the doctor when it came to his dreams. And that's why he had previously stopped raising the matter of his dreams. He had total suspicion of this doctor. Rather, he believed completely that the doctor, too, was siding with the enemies. Hence, he shouldn't know anything. This man was not right. Although he was a doctor, he was still a minion of the Bazaar.

'Alright, why don't you tell the whole thing then? Please tell Doctor Sahab how you got this wound. Go on. Come on, tell him…' the son said, irritated.

He went silent.

'I'll tell you the whole thing, sir…' the son said.

And whatever he told, the gist of it is as follows:

There is a posh colony at some distance from the house. There is a road under construction in that colony these days. Gravel, sand, coal tar, everything is scattered all over the place. It was early in the morning. The son was returning after the night shift at the factory. One had to cut across that posh colony to reach home. When he passed that colony in the morning, he saw quite a strange scene unfolding there. The construction work on the road, perhaps, had gone on all night long. Coal tar, gravel, sand, trucks, the engines to pound the road, labourers, supervisor—the whole works—which are required in the construction of a road were present there.

On that road, a man was running barefoot and out of breath from here to there aimlessly, like a madman. He was falling all over the place. Sometimes, he would sit on the mound of gravel and fill his palms with gravel. And then, he would run on the gravel, and sit down again. Roll on it. And then start running again. His bare feet were badly wounded. The bizarre thing about that man who was running with bloodied feet was that he looked so familiar to the son, that he was completely resembling his father.

At that time, the son's motorcycle was slowly moving on the ground next to the road. And suddenly, that man plopped down on the ground and started crying. Bitterly. The workers ran towards him. Everybody had surrounded him. He kept on crying bitterly. Even amidst the sound of the motorcycle, the son recognised the sound of his father's wailing. And then that man started screaming, 'My dreams, my dreams' in the middle of his wailing, so there was hardly any possibility of suspicion left.

This was his father who was wailing while rolling in the coal tar, sand and gravel scattered on the road which was under construction, and was mourning over his dreams. He got off his motorcycle, parked it and ran towards him. And he consoled his father with great difficulty. Three people grabbed him and made him sit on his son's motorcycle. He came home crying all the way, glued to the back of his son on the motorcycle.

When he reached home his wife, seeing his condition, started crying too. The son chided his mother. He said, 'Stop crying, Maa. I can't handle two crazies simultaneously.' He then went next door and brought a compounder with him. But he wasn't even eager to show the compounder his wounds; he refused to have his wounded feet bandaged. He said, 'Beware! If anybody even touched the shards of my dreams lodged in my feet…' He wasn't agreeing to have the feet cleaned off of the gravel and sand lodged deep in the soles of his feet. Finally, after a lot of hassle, they were able to clean the wounds and have his feet bandaged. When the mother stabilised somewhat, she said to her son, 'It's quite a surprise! How did he manage to get out of the house? And you've returned now, the house was locked from inside until then.'

She was surprised. The house was still completely locked from the inside. Then how did he get out of the house, and when? He was sleeping there, on the bed, right next to her at night. So then, when did he get out of the house and reach that road? And after all, how did he get out of the locked house? The latch was locked at two places from the inside. So, how?

When he was asked about that, he said, 'What's so odd in this? Anybody can get out of a locked house. Arre, it's no big deal. The house was locked. So from there, from the locked house I went directly into my dream, and then walking in my dream I reached that road, that's it. What's there to be surprised about?'

'Getting into the dream? How does one get into the dream? What nonsense is this?' the wife had asked.

He had smirked at this question of hers despite having wounded feet.

'If you start seeing real dreams, this can happen too,' he had said, smirking.

And then after looking at the face of his son, he said, 'You won't understand. If ever you ended up dreaming like me, then only you'll be able to comprehend what I say.'

He continued further.

'If a man is truly, madly and deeply in love with his dreams, then the world of dreams and this world merge. Then, a man can come and go from one world to the other quite easily. In reality, these two worlds are parallel to each other, and there are already 50 bridges built between the two. A bridge opens up in every house. Whether a house is locked or open, it doesn't matter. Through the bridge, one can get into the dream, and from there one can go anywhere. He continued to blabber who knows what else. All nonsense.

'Sir, with so much difficulty we were able to bandage his feet, and then I was able to bring him here,' the son said.

The doctor listened to this whole incident with a lot of interest.

He, too, listened to this incident about himself that was being narrated to the doctor with a lot of interest. He was sitting quietly right now, with both his feet and knees bandaged.

'Why, sir? How are you?' the doctor asked.

He smiled silently. What could he say!

'What is it that your son is telling about you?'

He still remained silent.

'So, if the house was locked from inside, how did you manage to get out?' the doctor asked.

'It was easy. My dream had an opening in my house. That was it—from the house to the dream. From the dream to the road. You, too, can go. Anybody can go.'

'But...'

'But what? The problem with you people, Doctor, is that you folks have stopped seeing those types of dreams which can only be seen by getting into them.'

'Meaning?'

'You won't understand.'

'Please explain it to me. Please make us understand. Why won't we understand? We, too, have dreams.'

'I am not talking about those dreams...'

'Which dreams?'

'Your dreams are different. The dreams I am talking about are something else altogether...'

'How are my dreams different from your dreams?'

'Okay, let me tell you. For example, you must be dreaming every day that the whole world has gone insane and everybody is now your patient. Right?'

The doctor didn't feel embarrassed at this but he surely was surprised as to how this man knew about his dreams.

The son scolded his father and said sorry to the doctor.

'He has been talking all this nonsense, sir,' the son said.

The doctor was looking at the bandages on his feet.

'So, how did you get this injury?'

'Please don't call this injury, Doctor Sahab.'

'So, what's this then?'

'These are my dreams. When they shattered in my heart, they ended up getting lodged in the soles of my feet.'

'Come again?'

'I don't know what your medical science calls shattered dreams but in my experience, the dreams are shattered within the heart but their shards get stuck in the soles of the feet…and in the heart too.'

'Oh!'

'Yes, why don't you put this stethoscope of yours next to my chest and see for yourself, no? Please listen to my heartbeats for a moment. There are more shards stuck in my heart than there are in my feet.'

The doctor looked at him as if he was looking at an innocent boy. He would have to be entertained. The doctor placed the stethoscope on his chest for his satisfaction, and pretended to attentively listen to his heartbeats for a long time.

'No, your heart seems alright. Hardly a shard or two anywhere,' the doctor offered silly assurance.

He smiled at the doctor's playacting.

'You lack the ears to hear the voices and understand my dreams, Doctor... You don't even try; you won't hear a thing. The cacophony of the Bazaar is so loud in your ears that you won't hear the sobs of my dreams even with your stethoscope,' he scoffed.

'The cacophony of the Bazaar? This chamber of mine is soundproof, sir! Not a single sound can penetrate this,' the doctor retorted with a pride-mixed smirk.

'Such soundproof chambers are quite dangerous, Doctor. In these, gradually one stops hearing one's own voice. Be careful,' he said in a cautionary tone.

The doctor kept on smiling.

'Don't you worry. My ears are okay...' the doctor said.

'It doesn't matter how fine one's hearing is, one can stop hearing their own voice even then,' he said.

'I am not that deaf.'

'God forbid, anybody goes so deaf that he stops hearing the voice of his own soul,' he said.

The doctor didn't let the conversations with an insane go too far beyond the limit. He was aware of his limits in dealing with the illusions and delusions of new patients every day.

'So, you weren't wearing any shoes?' he asked, changing the topic of the conversation.

'Yes, I was wearing them.'

The son interjected and said that he was found barefoot, that he was running barefoot on the gravel.

'But your son is saying that you weren't wearing any shoes?'

'When did he say that?'

'Why? Didn't he just say that you were barefoot...'

'What do feet have got to do with shoes?' he said.

'Had you been wearing shoes, you wouldn't have been barefoot then? And you wouldn't have gotten this injury either...' the doctor said.

'But what do shoes have to do with the feet?'

'Why? The shoes are worn on the feet, aren't they?'

'Who says that?'

'So?'

'I was wearing my shoes on my head. Whenever I go through the market, I wear my shoes on my head.'

The shoes on the head? Although he was a doctor for the insane and often heard such nonsense all the time, this statement had taken even him by surprise.

'Yes...wearing shoes on my head. Why, can't one wear

shoes on their head? What's so odd about it?' he asked, inquiring in such a way as if wearing one's shoes on the head was a common occurrence.

The son went livid hearing his father's arguments. He jumped into the conversation between the doctor and his father, and addressed the doctor, 'Did you hear that? That's why I was saying that you should hear for yourself—right from the horse's mouth—what all he is saying. He says "you don't know, I take out the shoes and wear them on my head as soon as I step out of the house". He continues to spout such nonsense,' the son explained.

For a psychiatrist, it was nothing new to hear such baloney. Mental patients always suffer from hallucinations and delusions. They may have any illogical beliefs and they can see or hear anything.

'Why, Sahab, aren't the shoes made to be worn on feet? Then?' the doctor asked. Perhaps, he might get into the psyche of the mental patient through this shoe-talk, he thought.

'No, Doctor. It isn't like that. The Bazaar has many shoes out in the market which fit on people's heads too. If you wear them on your feet, they will be tight and you'll end up with blisters. The Bazaar has the measurements of everybody's head with him these days,' he started explaining.

'Why would the Bazaar make shoes fitting the size of somebody's head?'

'Because the Bazaar is bothered by a person's head. It knows that there are quite a few crack-brained folks out there who don't recognise the Bazaar's power.'

'What do you mean?'

'Anybody who isn't with the Bazaar is a "crackpot".'

'So?'

'We are considered crackpots, crack-brained. Our brains run backward. If we won't wear a shoe on our head, it would become very difficult for us to move.'

The doctor continued to listen with his eyes closed. Quite an interesting case this is turning into, he thought.

'Quite an interesting point you have…' the doctor said, and started laughing.

'Please don't laugh, Doctor. I was only explaining to you why my feet were bare. If one has to wear shoes on their head, the feet are bound to remain bare.'

'I wasn't laughing,' the doctor said.

'Those are the people who have sided with the Bazaar.'

'Okay!'

'Just understand this much that every wise man these days wears his shoes on his head the moment he steps out of his house. You can't keep your head uncovered these days. If the head remains uncovered, the Bazaar will keep its shoes on it,' he explained.

'But I wear my shoes on my feet. Am I not wise?' the doctor asked.

'No, you are more than wise.'

'Sorry?'

'Those who are more than wise have stopped keeping their head on their shoulders,' he looked at the doctor's face as he said this.

His son quickly jumped in for mediation, 'Please don't take offense, Doctor. He says anything to anybody these days.'

The doctor had gone silent, and was looking at him. It was difficult to understand if this man was really insane or just eccentric! The doctor eventually concluded something.

'I am altering his medication. One pill, four times a day…' the doctor started scribbling the prescription on his pad.

He was gazing at the doctor with amused interest. A man without a head wearing a white coat is playacting to be a doctor. A man, if he removed his head from his shoulders, how easy would things become… But tragic too, he thought.

# Every Refuge Is Of Trash

The son knocked at the door. Somebody opened the door. 'Is uncle at home?' he asked.

The person who opened the door was in a hurry. Perhaps he was going to open the door and leave for somewhere even before there was a knock on the door, and right then the son knocked.

'He is at home. Where else will he go?' he called out, saying, 'Papa, Mahinder is here.' And saying this, he hurried out. And while he was leaving, he said, 'Yaar, I am in a hurry. I'll see you later boss!'

The uncle came. The son told him the whole thing.

He told him that his father wasn't home since the morning. Nobody knew where he had gone. He had gone out for a walk in the morning, and didn't return…

'When did he leave in the morning?'

'Don't know… He leaves at daybreak every morning. Actually, we only get to see him on his return…'

'Then how can you say that he leaves at daybreak? Who knows, he might have left for somewhere at night itself?'

'Yes, it is possible,' the son agreed.

It was noon now and everybody was worried. Kith and kin were contacted on the phone. Nobody could tell anything. Everybody said the same thing: that it had been months since they last saw him.

'But we couldn't get you on the phone, so I decided to come and ask you myself... Did you check with his other friends, lad?'

'Everybody said this, Uncle...that he hadn't met us since who knows when...'

'They are right. Who has the time for friendships these days, lad? A lot of time is wasted on friendship, Brother, and nobody has any time these days...'

'Yes, Uncle. Everybody only said that they hadn't seen him for quite some time... And then I went and looked for him at the market, the park, the emergency room of the hospital—everywhere; he was nowhere to be found...'

'Did you try his phone?'

'It's continuously out of reach. It was getting dark. I looked for him everywhere, he couldn't be found anywhere still.'

'You were the only one with whom I couldn't check. I thought...'

'Lad, these days even I don't get to meet him that often. Sometimes I didn't get time due to my business; and the last five-six times we did meet, your father had been talking all nonsense. Even on the phone, it has been jabberwocky. He has become bizarre, lad. He has changed. Why, just ten days ago he was asking me if I had made arrangements for the escape. Now you tell me! I even asked, "Where are we escaping to, bhai? Where do we have to run, and from who?" He didn't say a word. Then he spoke on his own and said that he was just making conversation! The other day he was asking if it was better to use a crowbar to dig a tunnel or if somebody can buy a machine for that nowadays! Always some gobbledygook like that. To tell you the truth, the last time I talked to him I feared he was becoming insane. I had even thought of discussing this with you but, bloody hell, these days I hardly get any time! What can I do? You've filed a complaint at the police station, right?'

The son told him that he was just thinking of filing a complaint at the police station but thought of asking him first. 'And then if you agree, I will ask you to come with me to the police station,' he added.

'Lad, why did you come so late? The folks in the station will say that the person is missing since the night and…'

'Not since night, he left early in the morning…'

'You didn't see him in the morning, now did you, lad? The last time you saw him was in the night, right? Then? The police will consider him missing since the night. They will see something dodgy in having a complaint filed so late. You see, they will be suspicious of you.'

'Then? Then what should we do?'

'Then what? Let's go and file a complaint at the police station. We'll have to do that anyway. Let's go. I have to go to the market, so I'll just go from there after we are done at the station.'

'But if they ask why we took so long to report, then?' the lad was getting nervous.

'Just say that he left for a walk in the morning, that this you saw yourself. That's it...'

This uncle had spent a lifetime lying. He was very much aware of the need to lie on such delicate occasions.

And then after thinking something, uncle spoke on his own, 'Yaar, you should just say night. Yes, suppose if something happened to him in the night itself which we find about it later, you'll be caught unnecessarily. Just say night.'

'We can wait some more if you say so. Suppose he doesn't return even by tonight, then we can go and file a complaint,' the son was getting scared of the police now.

'Lad, have the complaint filed. These are awful times. People are murdered for 20-50 rupees. You should have the complaint filed. I agree that the police just won't embark on a search for him right away. Where does it have time to look for a crazy old man? Forgive me for calling him crazy. These days, he had been talking crazy…I don't know if you observed that or not. Well, it's not your fault either. Many times, when the person living with you is going crazy, those living with him hardly seem to realise. A man often goes crazy quite slowly, that's why…'

The son wanted to tell that his father was being treated for that already. That his father *was* a mental patient. He knew that already. But how could he tell his uncle that his father was insane?

The son quietly sat with him in the car. Now they were driving towards the police station.

'God forbid if something untoward happened with him, the police will come and catch you first. If he disappeared, then why didn't you file a complaint? We should have a complaint filed,' uncle was explaining to him while sitting next to him in the car.

'Let's do this too, Uncle,' the son was driving the car. They had almost reached the police station.

Suddenly, the uncle screamed and told him to stop the car. The son anxiously slammed the brakes, and the car suddenly came to a screeching halt. The car behind their car came within inches of slamming into them. The man coming from behind drove from the sides, giving them a caustic stare. If he had cussed at them, there wouldn't be any surprise either. They couldn't find out because the windows were rolled up.

'Stop the car at the curb for a minute...' the uncle said.

'What happened?' the son started asking, while slowly stopping the car next to the curb.

'I saw your father just now!' the uncle excitedly said while getting out of the car.

The police station was only a few paces ahead.

There, right next to the mound of trash was a huge dumpster. Lots of trash was in that dumpster, and more of it was scattered around it. A tall mound of trash it was. Dogs were sniffing and investigating this mound here and there. Two cows were sitting there too. Mosquitoes and flies were already there. He to was found there.

It was behind that mound of trash, that he was found, sitting and hiding. The uncle had seen him sitting there from the moving car while looking outside, and had stopped the car. These people reached him, jumping over the trash. Seeing them walk this way, the dogs were startled and moved away. The cows didn't even bother to look towards them. When the trash under their feet was crushed and moved from its place, the insects crawling underneath it came out and started crawling away quickly. Seeing his friend and son walk towards him, he slid out from behind the dumpster and slowly made an effort to stand up.

'Papa, what are you doing sitting in this trash?' the son asked.

'What am I doing?'

'Yes, here.'

'I am sitting here hiding from them. I was saved by a whisker…otherwise, they had almost caught me.'

'They who?'

'They. They who had covered the mouth of my tunnel with a plank.'

The son looked towards the uncle; the uncle cast a glance of consolation towards him.

'Come on, yaar, come and get in the car. Now nobody is going to catch you. We are here. Don't you worry.'

Now he was in the car, half-reclining. He was recalling the whole sequence of the events:

On finding the tunnel covered with a plank, he was startled at first but then he slowly gained his composure back. Right there, underneath the plank, he lay down and pondered. Then, he fell asleep. He slept for long. And he had woken up suddenly… Then he slowly slid the plank and climbed out of the tunnel. It was sunny outside. Quite bright. He was dazzled by the brightness. The bright light had pulled a curtain of darkness around his eyes, which had been accustomed to the darkness by now. For some time, he couldn't see a thing. It was afternoon outside. But the sunlight was bright. He stood there blinking his eyes in the bright sunlight, in the middle of the trash and junk scattered behind the market.

And then, gradually, his eyes started seeing properly. And just then, he saw that person. Right in front of him, standing at some distance from him.

He was pretending to be closely looking at a mound of trash. But as soon as he saw him, he recognised that person. That person was standing for him. With complete patience.

It was obvious from his demeanor that he could stand there for centuries with this patience.

After keeping the plank back on the mouth of the tunnel, he looked at that person again. That person was staring at him with the pretense of staring at the mound of trash. The man had averted his eyes and started looking at the mound of trash again as soon as their eyes had met.

He started walking on one side while keeping his eyes fixed on the man. Let's see, what this man does now. That man, too, started walking behind him. He hadn't turned around, and wasn't looking at him but knew well that the man was right behind him. He could sense that the man was following him. On the nape of his neck, he could feel the hot spot of that man's intense gaze.

He was now on the main road. All around it, there was a market everywhere. He kept on walking on the main road for a while. Then he saw a street branching off from the main road. He turned into the street. Till now he hadn't turned around and looked back even once, but he knew full well that he was still being followed. The hot spot on his neck was still there. And then he suddenly stopped. Alright, let's turn around and see for once.

He stopped and turned. Looked back. The person who was following him quickly turned around in the middle of his walk and started looking in the direction of the market, which was left behind on the main road. He, too, stood there.

After turning around, he started reading a poster pasted on a wall in the street.

He stopped and kept on observing him. He thought even this: suppose he were to go right now and ask that man why is he following them, then? What reply would he give? Perhaps, he would deny it completely. He might say why 'would I be following you, Mister? Is that what is left for me to do? Is somebody else not allowed to walk on this road? Is there a new law in effect that says that if you walk on a street, the street behind you should be left empty?' Or, suppose he agreed that he *was* following him, then? What if he said that the Bazaar was following everybody these days and society had accepted it, then what was his objection? On the contrary, he might allege that he was the one who was being antisocial, then? What if he started talking about the freedom to follow somebody in a democracy, then?

And if he said 'yes', then he would stammer, rebutting his arguments. Democracy, freedom, the right to privacy, duty—

that person could render him speechless using any such words. Every word with beautiful meaning was under the possession of the Bazaar nowadays. It now had the technique to render every decent word hollow. It used these words in its own ways now. Democracy, honesty, love, affection, brotherhood—every word was now under the Bazaar's possession, and the words weren't even writhing...

No, it wouldn't be right to approach this man right now. Nor would it be right to ask any question. It would be better to give him a slip while walking. There was no point in having any argument with him. The man would have to be deceived to get rid of him. He would continue to walk and suddenly somewhere in some street, he would hide behind something... and he will continue to take refuge there until this person would leave after giving up.

He stood there for some more time.

He stopped for so long that the man following him got nervous. He couldn't figure out what else to do while standing on the road. He had turned around furthermore, and now his back was towards him. This was it, this was the chance.

He suddenly sprinted.

He ran towards the nearest alley, and then from that alley he went into another alley. And then, he kept on running. He ran so fast that even he was surprised at his own speed. The alley ahead was turning. Here, he had to slow down the pace of his running because a few dogs in the alley were suspicious of his running. He stopped running and started walking instead. Yes, he kept his pace fast; and kept on walking. The dogs followed him for some distance and then went back. He went from one alley to another, walking at a breakneck pace. And for a while, creating some sort of a labyrinth from his walking, he turned around to assess the situation eventually.

No, now nobody was behind him. So, he did succeed in giving a slip to the Bazaar's minion.

He started walking leisurely now. He guessed which part of the city he was in, and in which direction he should head home. After guessing for a while, he started walking in one direction. From here, he would reach another road and from there, he would get the road that will take him home. He even reached that road after getting out of the alley.

Just for precaution, he turned around and looked back to check once. No, still nobody was following him.

This road was basically part of a huge market. The market was on either side of it. The Bazaar was swinging on the road, mounting it, standing in attention at every step of the way, was alert, and in searching mode—everywhere. The Bazaar was present there simultaneously in many gestures.

It was here that he saw the same person again. By the time he took stock of the situation, he saw many other people just like that person. All of them were each other's lookalike. All of them fit. All of them were ready as if they were about to hunt. All of them had a peculiar mix of politeness and shrewdness on their faces. All of them smiled, bent, stood erect, walked and sat the same way. It was as if the Bazaar had cloned itself in the form of its minions. The person who was following him, too, had gone and mixed somewhere in this crowd. Or, perhaps, that person might not be here even. But what if that person took his photo and sent it to all the minions? Then every one of the clones would know who he was. All of them would have their eyes on him.

He became anxious just thinking that.

He ran breathlessly on the road.

He was almost run over by two cars.

The road was crowded anyway. There was a lot of hustle-bustle there. Everybody was in a hurry. Everybody was running, who knows where. Amidst these running people, he ran as well. Nobody paid any attention to his running. People run all the time. Who is running, why he is running; who is dying, why he is dying; who is and why he is, and who is there and who isn't there—all these questions in front of the crowd of the market were excess. Nobody had either the time to ask these questions, or was looking for answers to such questions.

But he ran. Terrified. He was afraid that the person following him would catch him anytime. He kept on running.

And just then, he saw the building of this police station. He felt relief. He took a deep breath and started running towards that building.

Who isn't afraid of the law and the police? If he enters the premises of the police station once, the Bazaar would have to think a hundred times before trying to catch him. The world doesn't have that much anarchy as of yet. There is still a rule of law in the country, and this thing is not just a rumour.

So he started running towards the police station.

There, right outside the police station, two constables were chatting.

He went towards the main gate of the police station, and started walking slowly. And as he was walking, his gaze went to the constables' faces. He stopped anxiously as if somebody had slammed breaks on his feet. His heart skipped a beat. He was stunned. Speechless. At least the constables hadn't seen him, which was good. They were busy amongst themselves; their attention wasn't on him. If they had glanced towards him, it would have been a disaster… Actually, as he reached the gate, he had closely looked at the faces of the two constables… Alas! They were the same—exactly the same. Bazaar's men. Exactly the same face. They appeared to be policemen but in reality, they had become the minions of the Bazaar. The face of the law had metamorphosed into the face of the Bazaar.

So, there was no point in going to the police station now.

Rather, if the police had seen him, he would have been caught.

He slowly turned around and, slowly sliding backward, came to the edge of the road. It was there that he saw this big box for trash. This dumpster. He, avoiding the line of sight of the policemen, jumped behind the dumpster.

And now he was going to hide behind it and wait for an opportune moment to go home.

'Uncle, you'll have to have a cup of tea at least,' the son insisted.

The uncle sat down again. The drawing room was as it is often found in middle-class homes; all three of them were sitting there.

He was sitting right in front of his friend. On the sofa. In his own home, like a stranger. A muddy shade wafted over his face. Salt and peppery beard. His hair was a tangled mess on his head. Crumpled clothes. He was gawking at the wall in front of him. There was a clock hanging on that wall. He was looking at the Time in the clock sitting on that wall. The Time was riding on the hands of the clock. Right underneath the clock was a calendar. For the last two months, not even a single page had been changed in it. Time's corpse was lying on the spent pages of the calendar. What a bizarre Time this was, it was dead but it was also running.

There was a Time in the room which was standing, restlessly waiting for tea as well.

'Please talk some sense to him, Uncle. Perhaps, he might listen to you,' the son said.

Here, he was unblinkingly and completely silently gazing at the wall, smiling.

'What were you doing behind that mound of trash, yaar?' his friend asked as if to start a dialogue. Upon hearing the question, he started smiling some more. He still didn't speak, and kept on looking at the wall.

'Why were you hiding behind the mound of trash? Uncle is asking something. Please answer him…' his son asked, irritated.

'If I had gone and hid behind anything, I would have eventually been found behind a mound of trash,' he spoke while still looking at the wall.

'What do you mean?' the friend asked.

'Did you hear that? He just talks like that!' the son complained.

'I mean one can't hide from them. Every refuge would be useless, eventually. Totally useless. For them, every refuge is trash. The Bazaar would have caught me,' he said.

'Arre, who is going to catch whom, yaar?' his friend asked, surprised.

'It has let its men out. You can't hide from them…' he spoke in despair.

'Did you see, Uncle? He just keeps spewing such nonsense, sitting all day long. The whole family is fed up of him...' the son got up, complaining. He was going to the kitchen to get tea that his mother had prepared.

By the time tea came, he restlessly tossed and turned on the sofa. He was thinking about something while gazing at the wall. What if Time, which was imprisoned in the wall clock, stopped riding the hands of the clock and came down? Or if Time, which was riding the hour hand, started riding the minute hand of the clock? If the hour's, minute's, and second's hands entangled with each other, what would happen to this Time? He was in a conundrum regarding Time at this point, but it wouldn't be right to talk to these people about this conundrum right now. These people were already considering him insane.

His son brought the tea. While drinking tea, his friend eventually asked, 'Didn't you feel stench there? Behind the dumpster?'

Now he answered, moving his attention from the clock.

'Okay, tell me of a place that doesn't have a stench. Even places where you feel a fragrance, is nothing but an illusion of fragrance.'

'Really!'

'Yes, sir! These days, whenever that stench becomes too much, they spray a fragrance over it; the fragrance is an illusion. The stench is the reality. In reality, it is the stench that is everywhere,' he said.

'So, all you smell everywhere is stench?'

'Of course! Why, don't you smell it?'

'No, not at all.'

'Yaar, try taking in the smells around you for once. An intense stench is reeking from the Bazaar and wafting over the whole world.'

'But we don't smell any stench. Why, lad?' the friend said, looking at the son.

'Sniff properly, yaar. Only then will you be to detect it.'

'How does one properly sniff, My Lord? Right now, all I can smell is the aroma of the tea prepared by Bhabhi. Am I right, lad?' he looked towards the son and laughed.

'Uncle, didn't you see just now? He talks such nonsense all day long,' the son said.

'But how will you guys sniff properly? All of you keep the handkerchief given by the Bazaar on your nose.'

'Bazaar's handkerchief?'

'The Bazaar has kept the handkerchief of its fragrance on every nose.'

'Yaar, all I have is the handkerchief given to me by the wife!' the friend broke into a burst of laughter.

'You think that I am joking?'

'Yaar, whatever you are saying sounds like a joke. Anybody will laugh hearing them,' the friend said.

'If you take something as a joke, then soon the joke will be on you,' he said.

'What are you talking about, Papa? Sorry, Uncle! These days, he talks such…' the son didn't even finish his sentence.

'I get it, lad,' uncle said, nodding his head.

'Yaar, are you really not understanding anything? I feel that this whole world is getting used to this stench in such a way that from tomorrow onwards it will start to believe that this stench is a fragrance. You'll see, this whole world is going to turn into a mound of trash one day. The world filled with useless clinky trinkets where there won't be a place left for you to even stand,' he said.

'Yaar, we will continue to sit here on this sofa. This will be my seat. You shouldn't worry unnecessarily, Bhai…' his friend said, finishing his tea and placing the cup on the table.

He started smiling upon hearing the response.

'You are still thinking of this as a joke, right?'

'Okay, what else should this be taken as? You tell me.'

'Yaar, you people will never understand,' he said in a tone of despair.

'Alright, suppose we are idiots. We don't get anything. But why don't you explain to me right now where you disappeared to from the last night? We were going to the police station to file a missing person complaint. Arre, if a man leaves for somewhere, shouldn't he at least tell his family members where he is headed? Do you know how worried the children were?'

'What does he care about someone getting worried!' the son said, irritated.

'Where were you for so long?' the friend asked again.

'Yaar, I was stuck in the tunnel...' he blurted out but became nervous too. The tunnel was his secret mission. Until now, he had told the plan of the tunnel only to the family members, and even they didn't believe him.

'Tunnel?' the friend asked, all confused.

'What's this pickle of a tunnel you've gotten yourself into?' he turned towards the son.

'Don't even get me started. That's a whole different pickle altogether,' the son said.

'Yaar, get him treated properly. If the illness increased, it will be trouble for everybody,' the uncle said while looking at his friend with a concerned face.

'He is getting treatment. The doctor says it will take time...' the son spoke slowly.

'Bloody doctors say this sentence all the time these days... It's all a trick to keep the patient hooked. Doctors, too, are running shops...' the uncle started muttering.

'It's the Bazaar. Till wherever it spreads, it will create shops. Then won't the doctor, too, run a shop? You couldn't stop the

Bazaar, and you are blaming the doctors…' he said. He had found his favourite topic.

His friend said laughingly, 'Yaar, why do you bring the Bazaar into every conversation?'

He, too, responded laughingly, 'What can one do? These days hardly any conversation is complete without mentioning the Bazaar. You tell me, what can one do in such a situation?'

'What you can do is tell me about your tunnel. Which tunnel were you stuck in?' the friend asked just like that, taking the whole problem as a big joke.

'There is a tunnel…' he said, not wanting for the tunnel to be identified.

'How were you stuck in it?'

'How could I not? I was inside and they brought a plank and covered it from the outside. They covered the mouth. I was stuck.'

'Who brought the…what?'

'They. Those who are closing our every escape route.'

'Escape to where?'

'Escape to a different direction from their way of thinking…'

'I don't know what all you are saying, yaar!'

'Yaar, you won't understand.'

'We surely will understand if you explain it to us. Why, wouldn't we?'

The son was listening to the whole conversation quietly. He was seething.

He said, 'Tell him! Come on, tell him the whole incident of your tunnel!'

He was left gawking at his son's face. He even tried signalling to him that it wouldn't be appropriate to talk about such things in front of outsiders. The secret of the tunnel wasn't to be made public just like that.

His son was even more incensed now.

'See! Did you see that? Did you see how he was signalling to me? He tells us every day that he is digging some tunnel somewhere. He says that as soon as that tunnel is finished, we will safely escape. You tell me! The whole house is in trouble and he doesn't care!' the son started narrating his deeds with actions and gestures.

'Lad, keep an eye on him. You live on the third floor. Who knows, he might end up digging the floor of the apartment itself. The roof of the apartment below would sink…' the friend, said and started laughing now. How long can one control one's laughter at their friend's crazy theatrics after all?

'No, Uncle. He doesn't dig. He just talks about digging…' the son was telling him the whole thing. The father was instantly enraged by this false allegation.

'So you think that I am not digging? That there is no tunnel anywhere? If there is no tunnel, then where did they keep their plank? Arre, there is a tunnel, that's why they kept a plank there…' he said.

'You talk hooey, Papa.'

'What's hooey in this?'

His son started scolding him, but he didn't listen.

He said, 'But why did they cover it? They could have reached inside the tunnel and pulled me out. Their arms are longer than the law…then, why didn't they catch me?' he asked, as if questioning himself.

'If they had caught you, they would be crying now.'

He was startled. What's this that his son was saying?

'Why would they have cried?' he asked.

'Because of listening to you talk, what else! If they had caught you, they would have sent you home by nightfall. They would have said that this man belongs in the tunnel.'

'Okay. But just for the sake of it, what do you think? Why would somebody cover that tunnel?' the friend asked, teasing him.

'Yaar, you don't know them. They can do anything.'

'Who?'

'The Bazaar's men. They can do anything. Many times, their actions are incomprehensible. For example, even when they are giving something for free, they can make money out of it. How? Do you know? No, right? Nobody knows.'

'Then you shouldn't think about these things, okay? When it is so difficult to find out, then why do you keep thinking?' his son said.

'Yaar, you shouldn't think so much…' the friend advised again.

'But somebody has to think about these things…'

'Why does somebody have to think about these things? Arre, why do you even think? Look, you shouldn't think so much! Rather, you shouldn't think anything at all. Just enjoy life!'

His friend was trying to advise him in his own way.

He was speechless hearing his friend. He was looking at him in disbelief. What is the advice he is giving me? Could it be that even my friend has joined them? He is talking in their language. Doesn't the Bazaar, too, tell everybody not to think? The Bazaar wants to evict thoughts from a person's mind. But how could this be possible? A man thinks, that's why he is a man. If he doesn't think, then wouldn't he become a thing? Just like a piece of furniture in a home or a shop. Wherever and whichever way you keep it, it will stay that way. Keep it on its head. Keep it in a corner. Sit on its handle. Turn it towards the right side. Turn it south. Turn it left. Cover it. Leave it to gather dust. Let it sit forever to become junk. How scary this thought is that one day everybody will become junk. The man who will turn into junk without thought wouldn't even be aware of this thing because the junk doesn't know that it has turned into junk. All these thoughts were racing through his mind.

'Why do you think that thought has died?' he asked his friend. How could anyone bid him not to think?

His friend couldn't understand the context of such a question.

His son, too, shook his head with such restlessness, as if to say that he was incurable now.

'Eh! What is all this you are talking about?' his friend asked.

'I am asking: has anybody seen Thought's dead body somewhere?'

'I don't know. I don't understand a word of what you are saying. What is he talking about?' the friend said, desperately confused.

'Has the Bazaar issued a postmortem report of Thought?'

'Lad, you better have him treated properly. This looks like a serious matter to me.'

His son stayed silent.

But he didn't. He kept on saying, 'When a man has to stop thinking altogether, then why shouldn't we perform the last rites of Thought? I mourn, would you come and attend the final rites?' he grabbed his friend's hand and insisted.

The friend got uneasy and got up. But he held on to his hand. Somehow his son managed to get the uncle's hand free.

'Let go of his hand, Uncle has to leave…'

As soon as his hand was freed, the friend sprang up and moved to the side, some distance from him. He, too, began standing up but his son forced him to sit down.

'Please sit! Uncle's two hours have already been spoiled because of your disappearance. Uncle, please come this way...'

The son came to see the uncle off till the main gate.

'Yaar, keep an eye on him. These days, people have been disappearing in the city a lot anyways. The city is peppered with missing persons' posters. You should snap the latest photo of him. If the need to have his photo printed on a poster comes, at least the face would be visible properly...otherwise, every photo on a missing person's poster looks the same to me...' the uncle was giving instructions as he was leaving.

And then he left.

After closing the door, when the son returned to the drawing room, he was startled.

His father had disappeared from the drawing room. He wasn't seen anywhere in the room.

'Papa?' his son called out, worried.

'Yes?' his voice came from inside the toilet.

The son cursed himself. Had he too started thinking like a crazy? But suppose, if Papa was found gone once again, then? Suppose, if somehow he had gone back to his tunnel again, then? Yaar, what's this that you are thinking? The son slapped his head.

And there he was, standing inside, peeking outside from the toilet window.

He was scanning the road down below, hiding in the toilet. What if somebody following him came all the way to his home?

Just then, he saw something.

Yes, there was someone there. He was standing outside. On the road. Leaning against the electricity pole. He was looking towards their apartment…

He moved away from the window, scared…

## There Is Somebody Down There

Time, sometime after noon.

A busy-ish road of the city.

There on the road, towards one side, a garbage truck was parked. Two men were standing there. Next to them was an open manhole. The lid of the manhole was lying there on the side of the road. The upper half of the ladder descending into the manhole was visible as well. Both men were in the uniform of sanitary workers.

It was clear, the work of cleaning the manhole was going on here.

One man had a rolled-up newspaper in his hand. The other one was smoking a *beedi*. Both of them were in the demeanour of joking.

Right then, a breathless man stepping up the ladder in the manhole came out staggering and fell on his face upon reaching the road. Almost unconscious. Breathing heavily.

Both of them looked at him, startled, and ran toward him.

He was drenched in sweat. On the road, on his face. Both of them quickly turned him on his back. They were gobsmacked to see him. Their companion's face was turning pale, as if somebody had drained all the blood from it.

One of them ran and brought some water. Some passersby, too, stopped there. The traffic had halted as well. They splashed water on his face. They fanned him with the newspaper. They shook him and asked how he was doing.

The cars passing on the road, scooters and autorickshaws slowly started moving from the leftover narrow space on the road. A couple of car drivers even rolled down their windows and instructed, 'Yaar, do this circus at the side of the road!' Some left muttering that these people get so drunk even in the morning, exclaiming, 'What the…!?'

Slowly, he was regaining consciousness. He looked awfully scared.

'What happened?' the first man lightly slapped his cheek, and asked.

He didn't say a word but slowly sat upright.

Even when he sat upright, he stayed silent. He kept looking at both the men with vacant eyes. Unblinking.

'Arre, at least tell us something?' the second man asked.

Some passersby lingered on. The rest of the folks, on finding out that he hadn't died and seeing that nothing exciting was happening, left—somewhat disappointed.

'Yaar, what happened? Is your chest congested? Are you having trouble breathing? Say something?' he was asked again.

He pointed at the manhole with quivering fingers and stammered, 'There…is…somebody…down…there…'

'Down there? Somebody? What are you talking about, yaar?'

'Down where?' the second man asked.

'There, down there…' he pointed once again towards the manhole.

'Who is there?'

'When I climbed down the pipe, I found a man sitting there…' he shuddered while saying those words.

'Down there? In the sewage pipe? A man!?' the first one asked in surprise.

'Yaar, who is going to go and sit inside a sewage pipe…' the second man said, finding it hard to believe it either.

'But he was there. I saw him myself. There is somebody down there…'

He was still nervous but was slowly gaining his composure back.

'Yaar, think for yourself how dark it is inside the pipe. Your mind must have tricked you in the darkness. Don't you worry…'

'No, I don't have any illusions. There was somebody there for sure. He even talked to me…'

'Talked to you?'

'Yes, he started saying...'

'..that come on in Bhumanideen. You are welcome?' the first one started laughing. He was finding it hard to believe anything.

'Don't laugh. This is nothing to make fun of. Somebody was sitting inside the sewage pipe. When he saw me, he signalled me to come to him...and said, "Come and sit next to me. Come and comfortably take a seat".'

'He was sitting inside the pipe?'

'Yes, he was sitting leaning against the wall of the pipe. When I climbed down the manhole, he was already sitting there.'

'There in the middle of the faeces and sewage!?' the first one asked.

'*In* the pipe?' the second one wanted to confirm.

'Yes, there. Down there. When he saw me he got up and said, "Come. Let's go inside". And then he got up and started walking further down the pipe. He said that he knew that other people from the outside world will come here.'

'Other people?'

'Yes, he said that the world down below is fabulous.'

'Yaar, you are babbling who knows what,' the first one said. He couldn't believe what he heard.

'Well, you told this to us, but don't tell this to anybody else. Everybody will think that you've gone crazy,' the second man advised him.

'But there is a man down there... Arre, I've seen him with my own two eyes, Brother!'

'Okay, then you tell me. How can somebody stay alive in those pipes down there?'

'Brother, at least don't say this about a man. A man can survive anywhere...' the first one said to the other.

'Yaar, how can we believe anything as it is? Why would somebody start living within a sewage pipe?' the second man said.

'Yaar, the whole world is going through a tough time right now. Anything can happen these days.' The first one didn't believe a word of his story but it was not as if he was losing money in throwing an argument.

'Yaar, anything, eh!' the second one protested.

The first man was still caressing the man's back.

The second one, too, was still fanning him with the rolled-up newspaper. He slid the newspaper under his arm and said, 'Yaar, you are getting worried unnecessarily... Look, I've spent the whole of my life getting in and out of manholes. Arre, had somebody been there, he would have bumped into me by now at least once.'

He was still sitting silent.

'Could it be that he might have seen a corpse or something?' the first one said.

'Corpse?'

'Yes. Somebody must have murdered someone and thrown the dead body in the sewage. That body must have gotten stuck here, floating through the pipes. And that's how the corpse must have acquired a sitting position. This could have happened, couldn't it?'

'But how will the corpse talk?'

'Arre, he must have gotten scared seeing the corpse, and in that state of fear he must have heard something.'

'Arre, what I am saying is that there is nobody there... What corpse. He saw something in fear, heard something in fear...that's it,' the second one said.

'But there was someone there. Down there. There is someone there for sure,' he said again.

'Yaar, you should hang tight for some time. Calmly. Take a rest. Have a *beedi* or two. And when you feel better, then you'll go down there again...' the first one said, patting his back.

'Go where?' he stood up, startled and alarmed.

'Down below. Where else? To work,' the first one said.

'I...Am...Not...Going...Down...There...' he said.

'But isn't that our job?'

'I am not going down...' he said, shaking his head vigorously.

'Yaar, that's strange...'

'Well, so why don't you go down?' he said.

'But isn't it your turn right now?'

'Down below? I ain't going there.'

'And what if the supervisor sahab came right now and chewed us out yelling why all three of us are standing outside?!'

'So why don't you go down below then? Go and see for yourself if somebody is there or not...' he said.

'Yaar, perhaps, he is telling the truth. Suppose somebody is really there, then?' the second one said.

'Yaar, who is going to be down there?'

'You people believe it or not, but I have seen it myself. There is somebody down there. For sure,' he started muttering.

'Yaar, could it be some occurrence of a ghost or something?' the first one suggested.

'Yes, yes. That could be true. That's the truest thing you've said,' the second one said.

'Because ghosts can be found anywhere...' the first one said.

'Somebody must have killed someone some time ago and thrown the dead body in the sewage...and now, his soul is wandering in these pipes... You are right,' the second one said.

'Yaar, it wasn't a ghost. It was totally a real man,' he said.

'Brother, what can one say about a ghost? A ghost can turn into a man at any time. A ghost can take any form,' the second one said; he absolutely believed in ghosts.

'Then?' the first one asked.

'So, Brother, now nobody is going to climb down. We aren't putting our lives in danger. It's a matter of ghosts...' the second one said in a decisive tone.

All three of them agreed that they won't go down right now. After deciding this, they went and sat at the side of the road. They started talking about the man who was seen down below.

'But if we don't go down below, then...'

'So, what?'

'Yaar, we will be herded out of the job. Our job is to go down a manhole.'

'Brother, the contractor pays us to clean, not to pick a fight with ghosts and ghouls.'

'Still...'

'Still, what?'

'You should think at least once...if not twice.'

'Alright, then you tell me. I ask that if somebody agrees to pay you—double the salary even—would you still be willing to go down there right now?'

Everybody went silent on this question. He was right.

Just then, the supervisor arrived there.

'What's going on?' he spewed, livid, when he saw all three of them sitting outside, idling.

'Sir?'

'If all three of you beauties are royally sitting here, then who is working down below? Whose turn was it to go down?'

'It was his. He was down there. He climbed out just now.'

'Why? Are you tired, My Lord?' the supervisor asked sarcastically.

'No, it isn't like that…' he tried telling.

'Then what's the matter, My Lord? Please do enlighten us.'

'Sir, he ran for his life from there…'

'Ran for his life?'

'Yes, sir. There is a danger there. There is somebody there…'

'What did you say?'

'He met someone down below who was sitting in the pipe…'

'Down below? In the sewage pipe?'

'Yes. There.'

'Who is going to be sitting there?'

'That's the thing. But somebody was there…'

'Are you guys out of your mind?'

'No, sir. We think it might have something to do with ghosts…'

'Yaar, don't make useless excuses for idling. If the contractor…'

'No, sir. There is someone there for sure. I've seen him with my own two eyes. He was sitting in the pipe…' he started telling the supervisor.

'Have you gone nuts?'

'It ain't about going nuts... He has seen the man himself,' the second one said.

The supervisor kept looking at the three of them with mixed expressions of anger and uncertainty.

'How can somebody be there?'

'That's what we are troubled by too...'

'Hey, why don't you speak up?'

'What can I say, sir...the truth is that I've seen him. Down there, somebody was sitting there...' he narrated the whole story again of how somebody was sitting in the pipe leaning against its wall, and how he was calling him and asking him to come near.

'So, you did go near him?'

'How could I?'

'Why?'

'I didn't go. I was afraid.'

'You didn't go because nobody was there. You got scared for no reason.'

'No, sir. There was somebody there.'

The supervisor now lost his temper completely.

'So, shall we do some work now? You know it, don't you? We have to clean all the manholes by the tenth of this month. Enough with the excuses. Enough with taking a rest. Enough with fun and frolicking. Now, go and get some work done… Come on, go now, and climb down!' the supervisor ordered him.

'I won't go down, sir…' he took a few paces backwards in nervousness.

'Why?'

'I just told you. There is somebody there down there…'

'There is nobody there down there, Mister!' the supervisor screamed.

'No, sir. There is somebody there…' he went further back.

'Then you have to go and tell this thing to the contractor yourself. Let's go, folks. Leave this nutcase here. Hey, you. You should climb down,' he said, gesturing at the other guy to climb down the manhole.

'I won't climb down, sir. When he is not doing it, I won't either. I, too, love my life,' he said.

'Eh! Who the hell is telling you to give your life?'

'Who knows who or what is down there, and what he might do to us.'

'Who is going to do what to you, yaar?'

'He can do anything…'

'There is nobody down there!'

'Suppose, if there is somebody there, then?'

'It's nothing but his illusion…'

'But, what if somebody is there? We are family men too, sir.'

The second one went farther back from the manhole and stood there. The supervisor was irritated with this insubordination.

He turned towards the first one and said, 'And you?'

'I won't climb down either…'

'Alright, do this. Just climb down and see if someone is really there or not.'

'Are you trying to make an eyewitness out of me, sir?'

'Our contractor won't need an eyewitness to declare his verdict, son…' the supervisor threatened.

'What's the contractor going to do in this, sir?'

'If the work isn't done, the contractor will kick you and me out of the job. Get it?'

'But who is going to put his life in danger? If he keeps us employed or kicks us out, who is knowingly going to walk into the mouth of death?' the first one said, and went and stood far from the manhole.

'What the… Who the hell is shoving you into the mouth of death?'

'This is like going into the mouth of death.'

The supervisor stared at all three of them for a long time. All three of them stood there with their heads bowed.

'Arre, this one has gone nuts, but why are both of you putting your jobs in danger?'

'Our job is to clean the manholes. Our job isn't to fight ghosts.'

'You really properly know what your job and what my job is, don't you?'

'Whatever...'

'It's not the matter of whatever, son. It's a matter of keeping it in mind. Remember that your only job is to do whatever the contractor says... He says jump, you shouldn't ask "why", instead you should ask, "how high?"'

'Is the contractor God, sir?'

'He isn't less either...'

'Look, sir, please don't force us. If all the sanitary workers gathered here, then...'

'Oh! So, you are trying to act like a leader?'

'This is not acting like a leader, sir. He has seen somebody down there. Tell me, how can we climb down in such a case?'

'No, sir. There is somebody down there for sure. I've seen him with my very own eyes,' he said again.

'Okay, sir. Please climb down with us and see for yourself what the truth is,' the first one suggested.

The supervisor was further enraged.

'Don't get me down there...If I went down there and really found somebody, then...'

'Then?'

'Then, I will offer him the job right then and there, saying that since you already live here why not clean this as well... Then you guys should go and sit at home. Have fun.'

'Sir, don't threaten us about our job in a roundabout way every now and then.'

'I am not saying this in a roundabout way, I am telling you directly. Either climb down or don't show up for work tomorrow,' the supervisor said, as if declaring a final verdict.

And just then, he fainted. He once again rolled over and lay down next to the road. His two companions started fanning him again with the rolled-up newspaper, staring at the supervisor in anger. The supervisor, too, became nervous...

And then a sequence initiated...

A few other sanitary workers gathered on the spot from here and there. The contractor, too, reached there. Then some other people came there as well. Then somebody posted this whole matter on social media. The matter took wings. The news flew like trash. It went viral. Thumbs, touch screens, cameras, newspapers, discussions—all of them came. 'If somebody is there down there, then what he can shove and where'—many jokes and memes started showing up on this matter. A horde of emojis was let loose. That sludge started floating on social media, the cover for whose manhole hadn't even been invented yet. The news spread in the whole world, that there was somebody down there! That somebody had gone and started living in the sewage system of the city; this was hugely sensational news. In the media market, this was an arrangement for a couple of days of splendour.

He, unaware of all this activity, was regally wandering in the world of the sewage pipes, settled underground! There was somebody surely down there—this, nobody else knew better than him!

## How Can You Fall Asleep?

More than half of the night had passed.

He was sitting on the rooftop, totally alert, squatting. Right next to the parapet of the roof.

He was on a watch.

From the roof of the third floor of his house, he was intensely keeping an eye on the street down below…

A narrow street, when seen from above, looked even further narrower. There was a series of houses on either side. The street opened up at the main road further ahead, where there was the Bazaar all around. It was on the lookout to stretch in this street and capture their colony…this, he knew. And it was because of this fear that he wouldn't sleep. The people of this colony still didn't know… Oh, how they were sleeping so soundly and carefree.

But how could he fall asleep? *Somebody* had to stay awake and keep a watch.

He had been staying awake day and night for the last many months. The children had taken him to the doctor…

He couldn't fall asleep. Neither during the day nor at night. He remained quite restless, pacing here and there in the whole house. He kept making rounds everywhere around the house. He wouldn't sit still in any place. These days, he didn't even blink…

'Sir, these days his eyes are wide and strained. He says, "What if they captured us during the blinking, then?" He is worried about some capture, day and night. Who knows, he is scared of which capture…"—he listened to these conversations of his children. He didn't say anything. What could he say? The children won't understand a thing.

The family didn't even consider the threat which he could see exactly right in front of him.

The world, too, wasn't able to understand this threat.

It felt as if it was only he who was aware of it.

He knew that the Bazaar was out on a mission to capture everything. It was out to seize peoples' lives. It was out as a guerrilla warrior. It had even captured smaller fronts, and people didn't even know it. By winning smaller fronts, one after the other, it had already seized a larger area of life. A huge part of our mind was now in the Bazaar's possession. But the Bazaar was now performing the *Rajsuya Yagya*, and how soon the *Ashwamedha* horse let loose by him would come to these streets and declare total capture, nobody knew. Its hoofbeats could be heard. Don't know why, but it was only he who could hear those hoofbeats. Nobody else in the neighbourhood was hearing anything.

He knew that the Bazaar's platoons were ready. They were on the march. From every direction. *In* every direction. Something whirlwind-like was seen rising on the horizon. It was coming closer every day. Like a storm. That's why he remained so alert these days. He kept an eye all around. He was on guard. The house was three-storied, and quite big. He was always afraid, and he made sure that the house wasn't left open from anywhere. And that's why, he didn't sit still in any place. The members of his family were bothered by him. 'Why don't you comfortably sit, Papa? Why do you go up and down?'... How naïve were his family members...they didn't understand anything.

At night, he was on guard at the rooftop.

He was on the rooftop even right now. On guard. But suppose he did see the enemy coming from the rooftop, then? What were his preparations for a fight?

He wasn't prepared at all.

And in any case, it was not possible to fight alone. Even if he saw them coming, what would he be able to do? He would be able to wake the neighbourhood up, that's for sure, but that was about it. He would make a ruckus and wake the whole neighbourhood up. He had even left a drum on the roof, hiding it away from his family members. If the opportunity came, he would loudly sound the drumbeats. And he would beat it in such a way that everybody would wake up and face the enemy in the street. On the rooftop, he had even left piles of stones and bricks in a corner. He would throw them at the enemy entering the street.

When the world sleeps, it was he who continued to stay awake.

He was often inspecting every latch, every bolt and every lock of the house at night. Totally silently. Not a peep. If there was even a peep, the family members got angry. 'Neither do you sleep, nor do you let us sleep', they'd tell him. The son even told the doctor, 'He doesn't sleep. All night long. He keeps walking in the house restlessly.' The doctor had given him sleep medication. He would tell his family members that he had taken them, but he never actually took them. He knew. He knew that the doctor was in cahoots with the enemy; he wanted the only alert citizen of this neighbourhood to fall asleep too, so the enemy could easily come here and capture it.

'Yaar, he has troubled the whole house. He doesn't sleep. He sits on the rooftop at night. He says that he is keeping an eye on the enemy. Such nonsense! All night and all day, he continues to talk hooey. Sometimes he just talks to himself, and when asked who he was talking to just now, he says that he has a direct connection with God. He says that God talks to him. That God keep warning him, saying, "Don't you fall asleep."

Sometimes he stands in deep concentration and quietly tries to listen to something. He says that he has acquired some divine power. That he is standing and catching those cryptic sound signals wandering in the air that the enemies are sending to each other. He is suspicious of every stranger. He says that people who lay a siege can come in any form. That the Bazaar can come even in the form of a saint, or in the form of a beggar. That's what he says. Yaar, we've had him treated at fifty different places. Even black magic. But instead of reducing, his problem is only increasing. I don't understand what to do. After all, he is my father. Had this been somebody else, he could have been treated with two good slaps…' his son was narrating the whole sob story on the phone to his friend.

One day, he woke the family members up at the break of dawn. The other day he was on the rooftop all night long. There, he got a fantastic idea. He got excited. Suddenly, he came running down from the roof. Woke everybody up. Woke up the son who was still rubbing his eyes, and said, 'Why don't we dig a bunker in our own home? Suppose they were sighted coming in the street, we could quickly get inside our bunker.' His son, well…he didn't beat him because it isn't considered appropriate to beat one's father but he did forcibly shove him aside without even getting up from his bed. He said, 'Let that bloody siege happen now. We are ready for it. Just let us sleep peacefully for some time, Oh, Lord!'

This was a hundred per cent true that God regularly talked to him though.

Generally, this conversation was only one-sided. Only God talked. When he was standing on the roof, God kept cautioning him even through the voices from heaven. God continuously expressed his concerns. God told him that there was a conspiracy against God carried out in the *mrityulok*, the mortal world. They say that the Bazaar was on the lookout to capture even God. One could sense God's nervousness through his voices. And here, it was him who had a lot of hopes from God. Whenever he was in trouble, he always remembered him. Even now, he had said many times, 'Oh, God! Please save us! If they are marching to capture us, then please save us! I have spent the whole of my life in worshipping you, now the occasion has come, so please at least save this devotee of yours.' God never answered this prayer of his.

It was only once when God surely did answer his prayers.

He had prayed to Him for his safety. He definitely prayed for his safety every time he heard the voices from heaven. He did the same that day too. This time, an answer came from God.

God said, 'Dear Child, our job is only to caution you. Now, you should defend yourself. We have birthed you with the power of intelligence and strength, haven't we? Then? Why don't you fight your own battle?'

He realised instantly. God was making an excuse.

'You are Omnipotent! Oh, Lord! Save me!' That was all he could say. He couldn't complain even to God. Alleging God of making an excuse would have been called infidelity.

The other day, even the doctor had asked if he heard voices.

He had retorted and asked the doctor if he didn't hear any voices himself at all.

He was quite surprised. When voices are coming from heaven, why isn't everybody able to hear them? Has the Bazaar done some arrangements, that even if God says anything against the Bazaar, nobody would be able to hear it, he thought to himself.

These days, he didn't tell anybody what God told him. He used to reveal that stuff in the beginning. Everybody would laugh hearing it. So now, this time when even the doctor asked, he told him that he didn't hear voices these days. The doctor had told the son, expressing his happiness, that the medicine was having its effect, and that his auditory hallucinations had ended. The doctor termed these voices as hallucinations…

The night was passing. The dawn was breaking. He, right now, was lying down next to the parapet wall of the rooftop.

Far in the distance, the coming and going of vehicles on the main road had started. Somebody had just passed on the street, running in sports gear. He kept looking at him till far in the distance. The enemy could come on the street in the name of jogging too.

He caught the sound waves floating in the atmosphere, all night long.

The enemies had been sending messages to each other in cryptic language, after making plans all night long. He was concerned.

He had slowly come down from the roof.

Without a peep.

The whole family below was still sleeping.

He went to the lower half of the house like a cat. The bedroom was dark. Even after so much precaution, his foot collided with something. The water jug sitting on the stool rolled and fell on the marble floor with a loud noise. There was a huge bang!

His wife woke up, scared.

'Who's that?' she asked.

'It's me...' he said.

'Neither do you sleep, nor let others sleep. Why don't you sleep for a while?' his wife said, and fell asleep again, muttering.

He didn't lie down even after coming into the room. There was hardly any time to lie down. He softly walked towards the window and slowly slid the curtain. The street lights were off.

The street outside was still desolate.

No activity was seen in any house.

Everybody was sleeping soundly.

Even outside.

And within his own home too.

It was only him who was hanging by the window like a ghost.

He was astonished.

How could one sleep in these dread-filled troubling times?

## Did You Also Dig A Tunnel, Sir?

That same psychiatric clinic. That same psychiatrist. That same beautiful receptionist.

That same business-like ambiance. So much so, that even the insane are the same as well.

Those same crazies…

There was a huge crowd of patients in the clinic. All the chairs in the waiting room were occupied. Some insane were standing; everybody was waiting for their turn. The crowd was dreadful. So, had the number of crazies increased so much in this world? Could it be that even the wise ones were being brought here, assumed to be insane? Could it be that they had decided to come up with a new definition of insane from the scratch? Could it be that the healthcare market had changed the metric of deciding insanity according to itself?

In this crowd, they had come and sat on the adjacent chairs out of sheer coincidence. Both of them weren't familiar with each other at all.

But we should tell you here that both of them had been brought here due to their passion for digging tunnels. Their hands had developed calluses from so much digging. Any wise person could take a look at their palms and know that they surely must have been digging something.

Right away, he saw the same calluses as his on the hands of the person sitting next to him. He was startled. So, was this person also preparing to escape somewhere like him? But, could it be that he was digging something else somewhere? Suppose he was a grave digger? Or a foundation digger? Or buried corpses? Or somebody's roots? If a man decides to dig, he can dig anything. He can dig up anything.

He kept his palms hidden, always. He feared that the calluses on his palms might let his secret out.

But the person sitting next to him didn't appear that cautious. Rather, he had extended his palms and done something like a deep inspection of them. Perhaps, he was reading his own fortune lines.

Anyhow, the calluses on the person sitting next to him were quite visible. This person, too, might surely be digging a tunnel like him—his sixth sense was informing him.

So, should I probe something in this regard, he thought to himself.

Why should he probe?

Because it was quite possible that apart from him, many other people might be digging tunnels to escape from the Bazaar as well. Alone, on their own. He should seek out such people. If he could find a few of them, how easy would it become to dig a tunnel! Everybody would get together and dig just one tunnel, and go beyond the limits of the Bazaar. Right now, he was doing this all alone and he was called insane for it. Alone, he was going to be considered insane. But if many joined him in this endeavour, then this would be called a movement, a new revolutionary thought! He smiled. Every revolutionary thought in the loneliness of the beginning is nothing but madness.

From today onwards, he would search for people around him who had calluses on their hands. Let's start this from the person sitting next to me, he thought.

'What are you looking at on the palm of your hands for so long?' he asked the person sitting next to him.

The man stared at him. He didn't say a word. After staring at him for some time, he started inspecting his palms once again.

And then, while keeping his sights fixed on his palms, he answered as if he was addressing himself, 'Looking at the lines of my palms, sir...'

He didn't raise his head even after speaking; he kept on looking at his palms.

He had had unfathomable faith on the lines of his palms. All life long. His fortune was always strong. Wherever he struck, he struck gold. When he was born, some astrologer had said the same thing after preparing his horoscope that wherever this boy will strike, he will strike gold, his mother would reveal. And that's exactly what happened too. He spent his whole life striking gold. A lot of wealth he had now was all thanks to his stars, his fate. If one has too much wealth, that also makes one fearful though. The fear of losing all that wealth becomes strong. He had so much wealth and, with that, so much fear. Now, he wanted to hide all of his wealth somewhere safe. And it was to keep this very wealth safe somewhere that he was digging a tunnel. Naïve family members thought of him as crazy! 'Now you tell me!', while looking at the lines of his palms, this was all that he was thinking of.

His fortune line on the palm of his hand was quite long and deep, from top to bottom.

And here, since last few days, he had found out that this fortune line of his was deepening further. Every day, deepening further and further. That's why he was becoming richer and richer every day. The properties bought by him became more and more expensive by the day. The shares bought by him increased in their value. But, suppose if this line deepened further then? Could it happen that the palm of his hand would cleave into two along the fortune line?

'Do you believe in the lines of your palm?' he asked for no reason other than to further the conversation.

'Yes, I do. And you?'

Hearing the question, he started laughing.

'Why did you laugh?'

'And what else should I do?'

'Why?'

'I don't have any lines in the palm of my hand, sir. What can I say?' he said.

'How can that be possible? You must have at least a line or two? Is anybody even born without a fortune line?'

'That's not necessary…'

'It's necessary, Bhaisahab. The lines on the palm exist. Yes, this can happen that your fortune lines might be very bad, but they surely will be there. Your fortune might be bad, but it will be there.'

'Okay! Suppose, there are no lines on the palm of my hand, then? Does a person like that not have any fortune?'

'It's impossible not to have a fortune. Everybody is born along with their fortune.'

'No, these days, people without fortune are born too.'

'If there is no fortune, then who is going to decide the fate and life of a man, Bhaisahab?'

'These days, this job is performed by the Bazaar, Mister.'

'How come? You are saying whatever comes to your mouth. So, is my life going to be decided by the Bazaar?'

'The Bazaar is already doing that. It's just that you aren't aware of it yet. The Bazaar, just like the fortune and without becoming visible to you, decides the direction of your life.'

'I don't know. Whatever you say sounds so strange!'

'Because I am crazy, that's why,' he said this and started laughing.

He started looking at him. Looked at him closely. Perhaps, he might actually be insane. Anybody who is sitting here nearby could be insane. So, should I look at his palm right now? We can find out right now if he is talking crazy or if his palms really are flat, he thought to himself.

'Could you please extend your palm a little?'

He extended his palms in front of him. He was startled to see them.

Truly, his palms were flat. Yes, one could surely see calluses here and there.

'Arre, how's that possible? Really! Your palms really don't have any lines!'

'There were lines… Once they used to have a lot of lines… my palms, too, used to teem with a lot of lines.'

'Then?'

'And then I woke up one day. Woke up and started washing my hands and my face, and my attention drifted on to my palms—they had become flat overnight. The fortune lines of my palm had vanished overnight.'

'Arre! Then?'

'And then I went to the doctor. He said that I was not the only one. That these days, this illness was on the rise. People were walking into the clinic every day with this issue. And the doctor also said that there might have been thousands who didn't come to him; they must have thought of this as their fate.'

'Then?'

'Then, nothing. Nowadays, many people are living without fortune lines.'

'Amazing! It's hard to believe.'

'But it has happened. I just showed you my hand. Many are like that. Just like me.'

'This is a bad omen, then. To live without lines in one's palms is a bad omen.'

'Bad omens are occurring everywhere, but people don't believe in them these days.'

'Then?'

'Then, what? I am just trying to escape from this place of bad omens.'

'You are doing right. There's wisdom that lies in it… But where will you go?'

Both of them went silent. The answer didn't lie with either of them.

He felt he should tell him that not everybody's lines are disappearing; that for some, the lines were deepening further and further.

Should I show my deepening fortune lines to this man? He should be aware of this too, that it's not like everybody's lines are vanishing. When the lines in the hands of many are vanishing, the lines in the hands of few are deepening.

'Have you seen the palm of my hand?' he suddenly asked.

'I just…' he said.

'Then why don't you look at it properly? Just look at the palm of my hand. Look closely.'

He extended his open palm in front of him.

'Do you see that? Look at my fortune line, how deep it is!'

When he looked at the line, he couldn't take his eyes off it. A deep line had captured the whole of his palm. On his palm, it looked like a deep wound.

'What is this wound-like thing?'

'This is my fortune line.'

'So deep?'

'Yes, sir, and it is getting deeper and deeper every day,' he said. He was left gawking at his face and then, after a few moments, he said, 'The times are like that. Those whose fortune lines were deeper, they are getting deeper further and further.'

'But I am afraid of this, these days.'

'Why?'

‘I am scared of this further and further deepening fortune line.’

‘What’s there to be afraid of? Your fortune line is getting stronger. You should be happy. And you look like somebody who believes in fortune lines.’

‘I hope it doesn’t cleave my palm in two, as it is getting deeper and deeper every day.’

To a certain extent, this was true. His concern was valid. And the other man agreed.

‘What you’ve said has a ring of truth to it. When the fortune line turns into a wound, a man should get afraid. Be really afraid,’ he said.

‘Yup. That’s it. The line keeps getting deeper and deeper, and if its bottom falls out then my fortune will fall too. Why, sir?’

He kept on thinking. What should he say in response? He didn’t know too much about palmistry either.

Suddenly, it was as if something flashed in his mind.

‘Could it be that somebody is digging a tunnel in your palm?’ he asked.

‘Tunnel?’

‘Yes, tunnel. These days, there is a trend everywhere of digging tunnels,’ he said. He wanted to bring up the topic of the tunnel in any way possible.

‘If somebody were digging a tunnel in my palm, wouldn’t I know about it? What a strange thing to say!’ he said, and became alert at the mention of the word 'tunnel'. No, this person isn't crazy either. This could be an investigator sent by the government. He wants to subtly push me to reveal any information about my tunnel by chatting me up. But I am not the one to get easily trapped in somebody's conversational trap, he thought.

'Sahab, many a times even the hand doesn't know... Isn't there a saying that what the right-hand doeth, not even the left-hand knoweth?'

'Yaar, what's the meaning of this saying in this context?' he asked.

'Please do remember, many meaningless things do have some meaning, Mister! If one tries to understand, then any meaningless thing can have some meaning,' he signalled. He wanted this man to understand the signal he was indicating by raising the point of a tunnel.

'I don't know, what do you mean by this? This humble servant of yours isn't able to understand a single thing of what you are saying,' he deflected despite understanding fully well.

'Look, I just said one thing after looking at your palms. I thought about why your fortune line is getting deeper and deeper. It wouldn't deepen on its own, right? So, who knows, if somebody might be digging it? Plain and simple.'

'Yaar, you think something would be occurring on my hand, and I won't be able to notice it?'

'Noticing is not completely necessary, Sahab. Just take my case, for example. They stole the lines of my palm overnight, didn't they? Did I notice? These days, they work so cleanly and efficiently that one hardly notices anything. So, no. It's not necessary for you to notice...'

Both of them sat silently for a while.

In the meanwhile, the son came and informed the father that it was going to be their turn soon so, hang tight.

He didn't reply. He was quietly gawking at his son.

'Where else does he need to go, son? Where is he going to go?' he said while sitting next to his father.

The son shifted his gaze from the father and on to him. Looked closely. He appears to be completely normal...but he, too is insane because, after all, he is sitting in the queue for patients. These days, even the crazy look so normal, yaar, the son thought.

'You don't know him. He disappears suddenly these days. When asked, he says that he was in the tunnel... You know? That's why I came to tell him,' the son responded to the man .

He just sat there without a word. It was better not to reply to whatever his son had said. He unnecessarily mentions my tunnel in any conversation. He just doesn't understand the gravity of the matter, he thought to himself.

His son went back again.

Both of them once again sat there silently for a while.

'What's this tunnel matter, Sahab?' he asked. Luckily, it was his own son who had raised the point of the tunnel now.

'Which tunnel?' he stammered while answering the question.

'The one where you disappear often?'

'Arre, my son talks crazy sometimes…' he tried to deflect once again.

'Talks like crazy?'

'What else! All this talking is insane, isn't it?'

'But aren't we the ones who are insane, and not him?'

'No, we are not insane.'

'But, aren't we the ones who have been brought here for treatment?'

'Only you would know about yourself, but I am not insane.'

'That's what every insane person thinks.'

He went silent.

Meanwhile, some mad man started wailing loudly. His companion was consoling him. Another crazy sitting in another corner was continuously talking to himself. A cockroach, running on the grill of the air conditioner, had disappeared somewhere.

'Which crowbar is good, big or small?' he suddenly asked.

'Crowbar?'

'Yes, crowbar…a tool somewhat like a pickaxe, right? The crowbar is sometimes used for digging too.'

'Bhaisahab, how would I know anything about this?'

'I don't know why I felt that you would surely know about it somehow.'

'But why are you talking about a crowbar?'

'I, too, dig a tunnel, that's why.'

'Well, you speak for yourself. I don't dig anything.'

Both of them sat there with their heads down.

Both of them were lost in their thoughts.

For a long time, both of them remained silent.

'What are you thinking, Bhaisahab?'

'I was thinking that if someone were to dig a tunnel somewhere, he shouldn't tell anybody. Not even to his family members. Folks unnecessarily start to think of him as insane,' he said.

'Digging a tunnel is not insanity in my view though.'

'Why?'

'It's quite possible if I have to escape from somewhere, then?'

'So? Arre, there are so many ways to get out, no?'

'And if all the escape routes are closed, then?'

'But where are the escape routes closed?'

'When have you ever gone and seen some? Try going out sometime. All of them are closed. Every route, these days, reaches a market and ends there. No route goes beyond the Bazaar.'

'So? Where else do you want to go beyond the Bazaar?'

'Suppose, I don't want to go to the Bazaar?'

'Where else will you go other than the Bazaar, yaar?'

'Is the Bazaar our last and ultimate destination?'

'Bhaisahab, I am not getting any of what you are saying.'

'I am crazy, that's why. How will you understand what a madman is saying.'

'You are not insane but whatever you are saying is quite obtuse.'

'I haven't said anything that difficult. All I wanted to say was that if seen from a different point of view, a tunnel, after all, is another route. Why, what do you say, Sahab?'

'I don't know. I have never dug a tunnel,' he lied.

'Must have seen one?'

'Why would I see one?'

'If you've ever been to an old fort or so, the guide there surely informs that there used to be a tunnel here which…'

'…which opened at a hundred miles from here. Isn't that what you are saying?'

'Yes, exactly. At least you must have seen that?'

'Where do they ever show that tunnel? They just say that there is a tunnel like that.

'That's what I am saying too. Even in those times, a king would have a tunnel made to escape, no? So, just like that, if one has to escape, wouldn't a man take refuge in a tunnel? If you look closely, the world hasn't changed much. Even today, if one has to escape one has to dig a tunnel.'

'I don't know all these things, Bhaisahab.'

'But your son was saying that you are in a tunnel…'

'Oh, come on! And you believe the bloke? Seriously?'

'But king…'

'Whatever the kings used to do, what do we have to do with it?'

'That's right. Fair and square. The kings would even dig a tunnel and hide their treasure in it.' He just said that. Out loud, for no reason.

He was startled.

What is this man pointing at, after all? Does he have an inkling that I am digging a tunnel to hide away all of my wealth? But how does he know? He had been working so surreptitiously that nobody could have the slightest hint.

Just then, his son returned, walking fast.

'Okay, let's go, Papa. It's our turn next…'

He got up.

'It was nice meeting you…' he said to the man while getting up.

'Pleasure is mine.'

'Even the crazies should meet with each other from time to time,' he said, smiling.

This last thing he said so that his son hears it, who was unnecessarily hell-bent on making him insane. Arre, even if he is thinking of digging a tunnel to hide the wealth, you tell me, what's so crazy about that, he thought to himself.

'Sure thing. We'll meet again.'

'See you later,' he stood up and said.

'Take care.'

'Yes. Definitely. And we have the doctor to take care of the rest!' he winked mischievously.

'Oh, come on, Daddy! Let's go!' his son said.

'In a minute. Let's go...' he said, and followed his son towards the psychiatrist's chamber.

As he was leaving, he turned around one more time. Their eyes met. Both of them broke into a smile.

He left, but the seat vacated by him didn't remain empty even for half a minute. The very next moment, another patient came and sat on that chair. Certainly, he must have been a madman but he looked so wise that he couldn't gather the courage to ask anything of him.

## Dreams Only Hurt

The soles of his feet had been so badly bruised from running on gravel that for the next several weeks they were dressed up in bandage.

These days, he walked around with his feet wrapped in bandages. Limping throughout the whole city.

'Your wounds are slowly healing,' the compounder assured him.

'Soon, everything is going to be alright...' the doctor chimed in.

But he knows. The shards of dreams make deep wounds.

Seeing the bandages, people did end up asking. If he ran into acquaintances, they expressed their concern, 'What happened, Sharma ji?' He wouldn't reply. He'd just smile and stay silent. 'Nothing, just something happened...nothing to worry about,' he uttered just this much and deflected. He didn't tell the true story behind it to anybody. If ever he ended up telling this thing of the shards of his broken dreams getting lodged in his feet to somebody, people would start to call him crazy too. Even mentioning such dreams was utter craziness these days. Once, he had talked about the dream of everybody's welfare and the right of equality of rich and poor getting fulfilled, and his neighbour had started laughing loudly to his face.

The neighbour had said, 'These days this is called a joke, not a dream, Sharma ji.' And he was left gawking at his face.

These days, he wandered quietly—through the whole city.

With his feet wrapped in bandages. Like a wounded, unarmed warrior.

On the other hand, he had been seeing a new thing in the city these days.

He saw that many people, here and there, who had bandages on their feet—just like him.

Bandages wrapped around their feet, limping, sad and somewhat anxious people. There was another thing he had observed in these people. The face of most these people resembled his own face quite a lot. Just like identical twins. Do people look alike after having broken dreams, he wondered. One day, he came across a man with so much resemblance to him that he suddenly felt as if he had looked into a mirror. Just. Like. Him. But that man wasn't startled. Did that man see his face differently? So, was he just a one-sided doppelganger of his?

Are all these people the ones who have been wounded by broken dreams?

Should I talk to these people to unite them with me?

He even tried talking to one or two folks but they gave him a blank stare as soon as he talked about the shards of broken dreams.

'You shouldn't think so much. These days, if you think too much you might end up needing to see a psychiatrist,' that person told him as he left, laughing.

Since then, he had been wandering completely alone.

He wandered around carrying a black bag with him. Searching for something on the roads here and there, and then he wandering around, gathering them in his bag. He collected the shards of his broken dreams scattered on the roads. If he collected them now, he would be able to rebuild all of his dreams if and when an opportunity arises in the future.

Someday, this world would surely come out of the clutches of the Bazaar, money, capital, profit, etcetera. Then this bag of broken dreams would come in handy. Till then, he will have to be the custodian of this bag.

He picked up trash from the road and filled his bag with it, all day long. The world considered broken dreams as trash. He would hide the bag upon reaching home. His wife had seen this bag of his once. She had chided him a lot, 'What all gravel and stones have you gathered and brought home?'

After that, he had taken precautions; he kept his bag hidden.

These days, this bag was his biggest treasure. He would have to preserve the pieces and shards of his broken dreams. One day, all the dreams would come back to life again.

He had observed a hopeful thing. Many people with bandaged feet were seen wandering in the city, collecting trash. Certainly, they were collecting their broken dreams; that's what he believed.

And this filled him with hope. But these days, he was also filled with fear a lot. He remained concerned, day and night, for the safety of his bag. He kept the bag hidden in the house, though he took it out only at night. Often. To make sure that everything was alright. Fear has taken shelter in his heart, and he was afraid that those people must have seen him collecting his dreams, that they could snatch his bag anytime.

And amidst this fear of his, he saw a terrifying nightmare. In the nightmare, a huge mob of armed people was chasing a man. And even though the assassins were chasing that man with a ferocious intensity, they weren't able to catch him. That man was completely unarmed. Weak even. But right now that weak man was running at full tilt. All of his life force was in his feet in a way. As if all the storms of the world had become a part of his breath.

In the hands of the mob, those weapons made in the old way were certainly there; there were some weapons that he hadn't even seen in his life before this dream. He was unable to identify these weapons. The assassins were armed with weapons made out of the pages of history and the *Puranas*. Many of their weapons didn't even resemble traditional ones. Many attackers in the crowd were running with bouquets and garlands in their hands. And after coming into their hands, even bouquets, politeness, prayer and odes seemed like piercing weapons. They could make a weapon out of anything. They could even kill a man without murdering him.

The assassins had vulture-like patience in them. They kept running after that unarmed man. They were going to tire him out and catch him; they were making him run right now. He was running from them with the distance of just a thread in between them.

The dream was filled with running footfalls.

And just then, a strange thing happened. He found out that though he was dreaming, instead of being in the dream, he was running with it—parallel to the dream.

He saw himself running next to the dream in the dream itself. Right alongside this armed mob, parallel to it, on a running track next to the dream he, too, was running with it. He was within the dream and he wasn't within it either. He tried to identify these assassins while running. After all, who were these people? Why were they following this man like that? He would have to understand that. He was running on the track alongside the murderers but nobody saw him. This was the advantage of being in the dream. There was neither logic nor science here.

The whole dream was filled with the rumbling of the fast footsteps of the running legs, and the reverberations of quick and intense breathing that it seemed as if the whole dream was running. He tried to identify these men chasing him again and again while running. These murderers looked like humans but they had souls of wolves in them. They were running like a pack of cunning hunting dogs, growling, and with their tongues lolling out. They had the infinite patience of vultures. The sockets of their eyes had eagle's eyes in them. Their faces had the cunning of a fox painted on them. Their teeth were sharp. Their tongue was so big that their whole persona had transformed into a tongue. Yes, they didn't have anything which resembled a lion. They were not lions either.

He was running with the attacking mob, in the dream, alongside the track made next to the dream. The dream had become narrow further ahead. The track was thin. Many times, he almost fell out of his own dream while running on the track.

He tried a lot to identify the faces of attackers. He couldn't find anything which would help him identify, as that mob was a mob of ghosts. They had something mask-like on their faces but in reality, there wasn't any mask there. Their faces had turned into masks or, perhaps, they might have worn a mask once but it was stuck to their faces in such a way that now it had become a part of their facial skin. Faces like masks. Neither any identification nor any expression. Flat, expressionless faces. Totally empty eyes. Even their running had something mechanical about it. They were running very mechanically, like a robot controlled by a remote control. In one set form, at a set speed. As if somebody had programmed them and let them loose for chasing.

On the track left between the running mob and the border of the dream, he was running with them. This was the benefit of a dream. One could do anything easily. He suddenly increased his speed. The man whom this fast-running mob wasn't able to catch suddenly reached right behind him.

And while running, he cast a glance at the back of the man whom the mob was chasing.

He was surprised. The man who was running was wearing a similar sweater as his; why, yes, that's the exact sweater he was wearing. The same design. The same measure. Same loose-fitting. So much so that this man's sweater was also coming undone at those exact two places where his sweater was coming undone. No, this sweater isn't like his sweater...rather, it was his sweater. So, who was this person who was wearing his sweater and running away breathlessly like this from that murderous mob? Was just the sweater his, or even the back of that man was his? He looked closely at the back of the running man.

He was startled. This back was his. Although he had never looked at his back, he recognised his own spine quite well. It's this spine that had put him into trouble the whole of his life. In places where the world would bow and prostrate, his spine never bent. How could he forget that?

He started running faster at that narrow track left on the side of the dream. On this side of the track, the dream was happening and the other side was the edge of waking up. He had now reached almost parallel to the person who was running so fast. Now, he was running neck-to-neck with him. He wanted to see who, after all, this person was!

By now, he had reached very near to him, and was running with him; and while running, he turned his neck to see the other person's face. He was stunned to see what he saw. His face was exactly like his own face. The same facial features, just like his… It was as if this running person had stolen his whole persona. Or, perhaps, was he chasing himself? Was he seeing himself running in the dream? Was it him who was running away from the assassins? But, why were these murderers chasing his doppelganger? Why did he have to run? He would surely save his doppelganger from these murderers. But what if the assassins' attention went toward him instead of his doppelganger, then? Then both of them would be killed.

He looked closely at his doppelganger who was running breathlessly in the dream.

His doppelganger had that same black bag in his hand in which he had been saving the shards of his dreams. Wow! Amazing! My dreams are being chased, here, in a dream too, he thought. The assassins were after his dreams during waking time as well as in the dream. These assassins must surely be running after this bag. They want to completely annihilate his dreams. They didn't want to leave even the shards of the dreams. He started running faster on that narrow track.

His doppelganger, too, was taking strides. Right next to him.

The assassins, too, had come close. He was running with the bag of dreams clutched to his chest when a mountain came in front of him. He jumped over the mountain in one stride… and now, he faced an ocean. He started flying above the ocean… and now, a desert came in front of him. His feet started sinking in the sand. Sandy storms started blowing over. But he didn't lose courage. He had boundless strength in him. If one runs to save their dreams, one is bound to get boundless strength. He was running, flying, swimming, doing summersaults in the air, putting distance between assassins and himself. He was speeding through the sky like a jet with his bag clutched to his chest. But those who were chasing him weren't less either. They too, just like him, were crossing the mountains, rivers and the sky, and came chasing after him.

And why just the assassins, he was running in the air, right next to himself on the narrow track next to the dream too.

'Bravo!' he said to his doppelganger while running next to him. The dream had reached quite an exciting phase. What's going to happen to his doppelganger? He had an intense curiosity to witness that. He had started slamming his hands and feet on the bed in his sleep. He was getting restless. What's going to happen to him, and his bag?

He recognised his bag of dreams quite well.

'You are running to save my dreams, my friend! But be careful!' he called from outside the dream to his doppelganger who was running within the dream.

When the running doppelganger heard his voice, he looked in his direction too, startled.'These are our shared dreams. These are not only yours, but they are my dreams too… Some dreams belong to everybody. That bag of yours is mine too. This bag of yours belongs to the whole world… Dreams belong to everybody, Bhaisahab…' he said while running.

'Be careful…be very careful!' he cautioned his doppelganger again while running parallel on the sidelines of the dream.

By now, even the mob of attackers had levelled up with them.

The assassins were now in front, back, left, and right—all around the doppelganger.

The assassins were now running on even the sidelines of the dream. He, too, was running there. What if an assassin bumped into him? He had started running, moving further to the edge in the dream. What if they shoved him over the edge while running? He was getting worried in his sleep. He was scared. And while still asleep, he was loudly slamming his feet and hands on the bed. Perhaps, that man was going to be murdered in front of him.

But the good thing was that the mob hadn't paid any attention to him till then. Perhaps, he was beyond the circle of the dream, and that's why he wasn't of any concern. By now, some of the attackers had gone farther than his doppelganger and stopped on the way. They had come right in front, squarely facing him. The attackers who had come in front put their heels forward and blocked the doppelganger's path.

He had now clutched the bag to his chest even tighter, and was facing his attackers. He was surrounded by the attackers. From the front and from the back.

The chase was over.

The chief of the attackers was now squarely facing him. In the threat-filled ominous voice, he said to the doppelganger, 'Look, sir. We have no intention of harming you in any way whatsoever. You are our customer too. You are very important to us. In our world of marketing, there is no place for beating, violence or looting. Although we agree that if we wanted to do that, we could have easily done that as well. We have deadly weapons at our disposal too. If we were to decide to, we could even kill you. We've taken care of many before you, if you catch my drift. But, basically, we don't believe in killing anybody till the water reaches our eyeballs. We have realised that there is no need to kill a person if his dreams are taken away from him. This is more than sufficient in itself. A man without dreams is almost cadaver-like. Or, perhaps, even more harmless than that. You, too, should just hand over your dreams to us. We won't do anything to you after that. Just hand over your dreams to us, that's it. We'll let you go alive. Don't worry!'

He was listening to all of this, standing on the sidelines of his dream. He screamed from there, 'Don't you hand over your dreams to them, my friend! What meaning would then be left of our life without the dreams?'

His voice this time, apart from his doppelganger, reached the attackers as well. They never cared for the people on the sidelines though. They consider the sidelines to be the trash cans. They assign every disagreement to the sidelines. Thinkers, writers, philosophers and naïve intellectuals have already been assigned to the sidelines by them. But he had shouted so loudly that they had to reply to him.

'Yaar, you should keep your mouth shut! He is the one who has the sack of dreams, right? Then? Let us deal with him, okay!' one of the attackers told him.

There on the other side, his doppelganger had clutched that bag of dreams more tightly to his chest. So much so that his knuckles were turning white.

'Just give this bag of dreams to us. Say your price. We will give you whatever you ask! All you have to do is hand over the bag of dreams to us…' their leader said while extending his hand towards the bag of dreams.

The mob had come closer and surrounded him in a tight circle. Almost up, close and personal. But he, too, was stubborn. He tightly embraced the bag to his chest and sat down on the ground, squatting, with his knees pulled towards his chest.

'Don't be afraid!. You just name the price of these dreams,' the leader of the attackers consoled him in quite a soft, sweet and affectionate voice. His politeness was quite terrifying!

It was getting impossible for him to remain a silent spectator on the sidelines of the dream like that. He wished to jump into his own dream and at least lend a helping hand to his own doppelganger who was now surrounded on all sides.

He screamed from the outside of the dream, 'You bastards! You don't have the guts to price these dreams! Do dreams even have a price? Dreams aren't for sale, Mister!'

The leader of the attackers turned around and glowered at him. His eyes had such an expression of threat emanating from them that despite being outside the dream, a chill ran through his spine. His dream came inches close to getting shattered!

He was babbling in his sleep, and tossing and turning on his bed. His wife lightly kept her hand on his shoulder in her sleep. He worries for no reason these days, she thought, half-asleep.

The attacker growled, looking out in the direction of the sidelines of the dream, and threatened, 'Don't unnecessarily interfere in the dream, standing on the sidelines, Uncle! Otherwise you'll be in trouble!... And shut this ridiculous talk of yours, will ya? What's this nonsense? Of which era you are rambling about, Uncle? These days, everything is for sale! On sale is every particle of this Creation! Go to a mall sometime. You'll find a rate list for every item there, and that rate list is updated all the time.'

'But the dreams…' he said getting restless.

'Shut the f…!' somebody screamed.

'So, yes. Come on, tell a price!' the attackers asked surrounding the person squatting on the ground.

He shook his head, raising his face ashen with fear. He was saying no.

'Bravo!' he shouted again from the outside to boost the morale of his doppelganger. 'Thats the spirit! Bravo!'

'Shut that piehole!' somebody screamed again.

'You will be better off if you hand them over quietly… Otherwise we will snatch them from you. Think about that for a second.' The attackers had come closer and tightened the circle furthermore. They were extending their hands towards that bag of dreams.

He was ready to jump into his dream now. He won't let his dreams be robbed just like that at the hands of these assassins.

On the other side, his doppelganger was lying facedown on the ground with the bag of dreams glued to his chest. He had covered the dreams with his body.

The mob of attackers was now jostling with him. They had grabbed him, and were trying to turn him over. All of them were pulling and tugging from here and there at the bag of dreams which was underneath him. That moment wasn't too far when they would snatch the bag away from him.

Now, it was fundamentally wrong to silently stand on the sidelines just like that. So he leaped from the sidelines and jumped into the dream. He went straight for the attackers.

Now, he grabbed the bag from one end too. Now, in his dream, there was quite a tug-of-war for the bag which had his dreams.

And just then, the mouth of the bag opened up.

The pieces of dreams were now falling from the bag and scattering everywhere. The shards of his broken dreams were now flying every which way on the road. And then, in this tug-of-war, suddenly the half-opened bag was thrown in the air. The bag went in the air and turned upside down.

The pieces of broken dreams were scattered far into the distance in the sky, and started slowly falling to the ground. He now jumped on the road to collect his dreams. His dream was now filled with restlessness.

He started throwing his hands and feet on the bed with so much restlessness that his wife was completely awake now. She sat upright anxiously.

On the other hand, in his dream, his dreams fell to the ground and were scattered till far in the distance. The shards of the broken dreams shot out like arrows and struck his eyes. He wailed in pain. He started rolling on the ground while rubbing both of his eyes with his hands. He had also started crying loudly.

When his wife shook him, grabbing his shoulders, he woke from his sleep.

He woke from his sleep wailing loudly.

Restless. Anxious. Caressing both of his eyes. Wailing loudly. He was in agony while sitting on his bed. His eyes were in excruciating pain. Something was piercing them, from everywhere. His eyes were moist. Something was flowing out of them. His hands were getting wet.

And just then, his wife got up and turned the lights on in the bedroom.

He took his hands away from his eyes and looked at them, extending his palms in front of him. His palms were drenched with blood. The shards of his dreams, perhaps, had lodged deep within his eyes. The blood was flowing from his eyes.

'Blood, blood…it is blood!' he extended his palms and showed them to his wife.

'Where? There is nothing there,' his wife said, touching his hands.

'Arre, look at my eyes…blood is coming out of them!' he screamed.

His wife looked into his eyes. There were only tears there. And apart from the tears, there was nothing else there. But he was writhing in pain, rubbing his eyes.

'My eyes, my eyes' he cried.

Tears were rolling down his cheeks like a waterfall. He was wiping his cheeks with wet palms and looking at his palms in wide-eyed surprise.

'Blood…it is blood! What else is this? Look, look again!' he was squatting on the bed with his open palms outstretched in front of his wife. More than half of the night had passed.

A car had gone speeding, right next to the house. A stray dog ran after the car, barking loudly. The sound of loud barking was slowly fading away.

'Arre, this isn't blood. These are your tears, nothing else. Don't worry,' his wife assured him, caressing his back.

His sobbing sounded scary in the silence of the night.

'You don't understand. These are tears of blood. When the shards of dreams are lodged in the eyes, then one cries tears of blood,' he was babbling while crying.

He was looking at his hands with a lot of concern. If he could clearly see it, then why couldn't somebody else see this blood?

His palms were soaked with blood. Blood was oozing out of his eyes…nobody was willing to see this.

## He Is At The Gates, Beware!

More than half of the night had passed.

The stars were yawning while twinkling. The moon, too, was somewhat sleepy. The sky was lying with its face covered with a dark quilt. The street was almost pitch dark. If one were to look at the street from the roof, they wouldn't see anything. The lights of the verandahs which were spilling into the street, too, had been extinguished a while ago. Yes, that mall built at the mouth of the street was glittering in some type of divine light.

And amidst all of this, he was on the roof, habitually. On guard.

When the whole world was lying with a quilt over its head, he was awake. The night watch was quite difficult and challenging. The eyes were on the watch but the eyelids were eager to deceive.

He wasn't the one to get caught in the deceit of his eyelids though. He was alert. His life was at stake. One couldn't take the risk of even blinking. Those who evict could come at any time. Any moment. From any direction. At any hour. No direction was forbidden to them. Every hour was favourable to them. He will have to remain alert, and he was alert. He was behind the parapet wall, in position. But the problem with him was that the enemy didn't have a set face. Nor was its cloak set. The enemy could be in the garb of a saint, have the demeanour of a revolutionary or appear like a serious scholar...or, perhaps, could even be like a punk. It was going to be quite difficult to identify him. He didn't have any scent. Nor sound. His facial features weren't set. All that was known was that he was out there, somewhere. The enemy was dissolved in the air. Even if a gust of breeze came from the direction of the Bazaar, he was frightened. He trusted his sixth sense completely though. He knew that he would recognise the Bazaar the moment he will see it. For sure. The enemy could come with as much camouflage as it could, he would still be able to recognise him. Every non- or anti-human face, despite being blindingly beautiful, is strangely slimy, afraid of itself and so familiar in its trick to appear scaringly congenial that it can be easily recognised. He will recognise it for sure.

And see! Today, he even recognised him.

After all, this daily nightly watch didn't go to waste. He sensed the enemy even before it could enter the street. He recognised it right at the gates of the street. Perhaps, even the enemy saw him standing on his roof. The enemy was so gargantuan that it could see him even on the roof of the third floor. It wasn't afraid even after seeing him. Nor did it try to hide, or run away. It stood there, at the mouth of the street, with complete daring. And it was from there that it was staring at the whole street.

He looked at the enemy closely. How fearless! How gargantuan! Almost kissing the sky! What glitzy clothes! The one with the thousand eyes. Scary yet beautiful. Horrifying beauty. Its whole personality was like a huge kick that was raised in the sky and was about to trample the street…

So, the enemy was here. The time for action was here.

He started sliding back, still lying on the roof. He wanted to climb down the roof without coming into the enemy's line of sight. His family would have to be woken up right away. It was necessary to warn everybody. People were left in slumber like that, and they wouldn't even realise that the enemy had captured them. And then people were forced to live like renters in their own lives. So many streets, so many houses, so many farms, so many villages, so many lives…the enemy's minions came from somewhere, and they grabbed the people by the neck and made them sit out of their own lives. The land was requisitioned. Many villages were submerged under the water of a dam. People were laid off. The shops were lost in floods. People's lives changed overnight. The enemy was quite cunning. It came in a way as if you were the one who had invited it. Even right now, the enemy was standing in the same way at the mouth of the street. Tomorrow, it will enter the street. Good thing that he was alert on his guard. He saw it.

He was crawling backward on his roof. Behind him was the staircase. He wanted to go down and wake his family up. He wanted to show everybody right now and say, 'See! See for yourself! Didn't I tell you before? He slowly slid all the way down the stairs. This spirit of a mere soldier who is posted on a front against a very powerful enemy was worth saluting. The eyes of sleepy stars were now wide open in surprise. The sleepy moon, too, was startled. The darkness looked at him in astonishment. He sprang up like a fit soldier and ran down the stairs. Even if his body had gone old, his knees creaked when he walked and his back was stiff all the time. But if only somebody saw him today. It was as if the whole world's gravitational force had come under his command. He was climbing down the stairs fast, pushing beyond his pain, stiffness and fear. He came down the stairs. Ran fast into the verandah. Opened the door and barged into his room.

His son's bedroom was adjoining his.

There was a door separating the two, and a wall too. He kicked open that door. Bam! His son, who was in deep sleep, woke up startled. He went into his son's room and struck his hand on all the switches on the wall as if he was striking the keys of a piano. All the lights in the room came on simultaneously. The room was suddenly dazzled. His son was sitting on the bed, rubbing and furiously blinking his eyes. He pulled the quilt away from his son and grabbed his hand.

He was soaked in sweat. He was agitated, and he was saying something while pointing towards the roof. His son knew that his father's mental condition was not stable but he hadn't seen him this excited ever before. He, too, was suddenly worried.

'They are here! They are here!' he was mumbling continuously.

His wife, too, had come into the room after hearing the noise.

'What happened? At least tell me something!' his wife was asking.

'They are finally here, you silly! They are here! Arre, go run and hide somewhere…' he shoved his wife away and started pulling his son towards the stairs. His son went along with him. No, he wasn't some ridiculous obedient son who would follow his father just like that but the way his father's face was ashen, he deemed it fitting to go with him and investigate. Surely, he must have some serious trouble on the roof. He went along. His wife's knees remained swollen. She could barely walk a few feet. But dragging herself, she followed him too.

'At least let go of my hand!' his son had his hand jerked free by the time they reached the stairs.

He started climbing the stairs very quickly. He was mumbling as he was climbing.

'You guys think that I am crazy, right? You...and that crazy doctor of yours? Come, come on now and see for yourself! The enemy is at the gate.'

His son also wanted to see what strange entity his father had seen! What had he seen which got him so excited? So late at night, who had come into the street that he was so scared and worried? Let's at least go and see, he thought. So he was also quickly climbing the stairs behind him.

Both of them were on the rooftop now. As soon as he reached the roof, he jumped and quickly lay down on the ground like a trained soldier, and took the position. He was alert after taking the position and, while in that position, insisted his son follow suit as well. He told his son that he should take the position too, so that the enemy doesn't see them.

'Why are you rolling on the ground?' his son asked, irritated.

He pulled at his son's pajamas while laying flat on the ground.

'Arre...you should take the position too... Otherwise the enemy will see us.'

He tugged at his son's pajamas so forcefully that he almost fell on the ground.

'Have you completely lost your mind!? Arre, who is going to see us?' his son yelled in anger.

'Speak softly, son! He will hear us,' he was trying to caution his son while holding his position.

'Who is going to hear us, Papa? Everybody is sleeping!'

'But he is awake. He will see us. He will hear us…'

'Who? Where is he?'

'He. He is there…' he gestured in the direction of the mouth of the street, still holding his position.

'Where? In which direction?'

'There…in that direction.'

'Who is there? There isn't anybody there.'

'There is somebody there. Look properly.'

'Oh! Come on! Just tell me who is there? There is nobody there. The whole street is empty!'

'Right outside the street. Look at the road. Arre, at least squat down a bit. Otherwise you will be in his sight.'

'I don't see anybody there. After all, what are you trying to show me?'

'Arre, why don't you try to see it for yourself? You thought I was going crazy, huh?'

'Oh, my God! Please forgive me! We are the ones who are crazy, okay?' his son was annoyed.

'Didn't I say that one day the enemy will evict us from this house? And all of you thought this to be my craziness, didn't you?'

'So?'

'So, see for yourself now. He is here. He is standing right outside your street. Look. Soon, he will enter our street and he will possess our homes.'

'Have you gone completely mad, Papa?'

'At least see for yourself, and then tell me who is crazy!'

'What should I look at?'

'Just look at there, will ya? He is already standing there,' he was gesturing while holding his position.

'Arre, I've seen enough. There is nobody there!'

'Look properly, son… And recognise him properly too… he is our enemy,' he said, squatting now and signalling in one direction. His son tried to look in that direction.

There, in that direction, there was a lot of light. A lot of dazzling. There was a huge mall there. The mouth of the street was lit with the light of that mall… Had anybody been standing there, he would have been visible right away.

'Theres nobody there either, Papa. Get up. Go downstairs and sleep, and let us sleep too!'

His son turned to leave, and just then the old woman came upstairs too, panting and moaning but somehow climbing the stairs.

'What happened, son?' she asked her son instead of her husband. His son stopped as he was climbing down the stairs.

'He wants to show who knows what! Ask him!' his son was getting aggravated.

He was listening to his son speaking with his mother.

'You'll see only if you look!' he, too, was getting annoyed.

'What were you showing him?' his wife asked.

'He says that the enemy is standing there. Seriously!' his son gestured toward the mouth of the street and said.

'He is standing there! See how tall and erect he is!' he said.

'There?... Next to the mall?' his wife asked.

He became excited. 'Yes, right there…'

'Who is there? There is nobody there.'

'There is… See! How he is staring in this direction!'

'There is nobody there!'

'He is there! So tall! His head is reaching the sky. He is standing erect! So shiny! Just look! Please look there! He is right in front of us! How come you people can't see him?' he was quite excited pointing in the direction of the mall.

His son was going back to the staircase, peeved; and while going back, he yelled, 'Go and sleep, and have some mercy on others too. It's already quite late at night. And there is nobody there. Neither an enemy nor a friend. And if they are there, they might be sleeping wherever they are.'

'Wait, wait…' he said in a pleading voice. His son stopped midway.

'Son, stop for a second and at least familiarise yourself with the enemy. He is standing there.'

'Arre, if he is standing there, then why isn't he visible to us?' his son said, annoyed.

'He is there. He is there right in front of us. In those glittery clothes. The one with a thousand shiny eyes. He is standing right in front of you,' he was pointing again. His finger was pointing towards the mall.

'There is nobody there for crying out loud!'

'He is there… So tall!'

'The only thing tall there is the mall, that's it!'

'Yes, yes. That's it!'

'So, you woke us up at this hour and brought us to the roof to show us that mall? Seriously, what the f…!?' the son yelled while looking at his mother, agitated. If he had his wish, he would have thrashed his father real good.

'It is the enemy. It has come here in the form of a mall and that's why you aren't able to recognise it.'

'And you recognised instantly?'

'I wouldn't have been able to recognise him either. It was his eyes. It was because of his eyes that I was able to recognise him.'

'His eyes?'

'Yes, eyes. Look! How he is staring at this street of ours! A thousand eyes, he has. A thousand. And his every eye is trained on us,' he was pointing at the lights of the mall.

'How can a building stare at somebody? Could you care to explain?' his son said.

'Son, that isn't just a building. That, in reality, is a group of enemies. And these are not just some shops in this building. That actually is a cluster of enemies that is standing there. They are biding time to capture us,' he was whispering in the manner of exposing a conspiracy.

'Yaar, don't give us this bullshit in the middle of the night, Papa!' his son went livid.

'Does anybody talk to their father in this language?' he said in disbelief and anguish.

'Well, then a father should also show some fatherly wisdom. If you wake us up in the middle of the night and show us some building as our enemy, then what else is one supposed to call this?'

'You are still thinking this to be a building? You have gone crazy and you tell me that I have gone...'

'So, according to you, this isn't some mall?'

'Yes, this is not a mall.'

'So, what the heck is this then? Could you please enlighten us? Let us crazies receive some pearls of wisdom from you!' his son said in a dramatic voice.

'Arre, this is the Bazaar. The Bazaar! It has come and stood at the gates of your street.'

'So? What's up with that?'

'Oh! Okay! So, there is nothing wrong with that?' he was dumbfounded at his son's stupidity.

'Yes. So, what's the problem with this?'

'Son, try to understand what I am saying with a cooler head. You are not understanding it properly. This isn't a mall, son. This is a gang of shops that have come here, sniffing for a chance. Quite clever, this group. The members of this gang will enter the street one by one. You will get out of the street and wonder, "Arre, there wasn't any shop in this house until yesterday, and today a shop has opened up!" And gradually, a shop will open up in every house. There won't be any homes left. Every home will convert into a shop. You will start living in a bazaar, not at a home. And that's how it will first capture the street, and then it will possess you…' he became breathless while explaining all this to his son.

'So?' his son asked.

He was stunned. What was he talking about? Is this his son or somebody else?

'Why don't you think of it in these terms, Papa, that the price of the houses in our street has increased tremendously because of the construction of this mall next to our street, and who knows how high the prices may go? Do you even know the current market value of our house these days?' his son asked.

He was stupefied! Who is this man who is standing in front of him? If this man is his son, then why isn't he able to recognise him right now? How strange this man is—the one standing in front of him... Why is his face so terrifying? His eyes... Oh! His eyes are exactly the same, the one through which the enemy is staring at us.

'Why are you staring at me like that, Papa?' his son started to feel uncomfortable.

Yes, this was the enemy. For sure. No, the enemy wasn't just outside the street. The enemy had already captured his house. Here, he kept a watch on his rooftop; and there, on the other side, the Bazaar had already converted his son to its side.

No, this is not his son.

This, too, was the enemy, standing in front of him on the roof. He started moving backwards in anxiety. While squatting on the roof, he started moving back towards the parapet wall of the roof.

He went and stuck close to the parapet wall.

'Papa, Papa...' seeing him go to the parapet wall, his son became nervous. What if he ended up doing something stupid? Who knows he might jump off the wall. His son slowly took a couple of paces toward him. And he became more nervous.

'Who are you?' he nervously asked from there. He was in shock.

'Who am I? Don't you know who I am?'

'Yes, perhaps, I don't know you,' now he was trying to stand up with the support of the parapet wall.

His son quickly moved forward anxiously.

'Don't come close to me...' he started warning him, getting afraid.

'Papa, this is me...me...' his son assured him and slowed down his pace considerably while continuing to move towards him. His son was afraid that his father might jump off the roof in his lunacy!

He was leaning against the parapet wall. He turned around once again and looked at the mouth of the street. There, at the gates, the enemy was still standing erect and staring at him. He was also sarcastically smiling, as if saying 'how about now'.

He turned in the direction of his son. He was moving towards him. The enemy was closing on him from both sides. He was surrounded. All of his maintaining a watch for so many days had become useless.

Suddenly, he jumped in his place and started climbing the parapet wall. He wasn't going to get captured by the enemy. His son ran towards him. His wife started crying loudly. Now he was on top of the parapet wall. The enemy was very close, and was about to pounce upon them. Just then, his son leaped with all of his might and swung, grabbing his feet from behind. He started struggling with his son. He was writhing to free himself from the grip of the enemy. On the parapet wall, the son was pulling his half-hanging father back on the roof.

## You Are Crying Even Though You Don't Know

The ophthalmologist deeply and extensively examined his eyes for a long time. He looked at his eyes from various angles, shone it from all over. Showed him charts. Asked questions. Gathered history. Measured the pressure in his eyes. Looked deep into his eyes through machines. Examined every single strand of his eyes. And after finishing his examination, he gazed at him with a huge and somewhat satisfactory smile. And then with complete confidence, he made as if an official announcement.

'His eyes are alright. There is no problem anywhere. Please don't worry.'

He stayed silent. Who is to argue with a doctor! If an ophthalmologist wants, he can give even a blind man a certificate of the pleasure of sight.

'Sir, then what has happened to him?' his son asked with concern.

'There is no need for any concern. His eyes are perfectly alright,' the doctor said again.

'But he has been worried since morning. His eyes are hurting. Something is piercing sharply in them. He has worn himself out rubbing his eyes since morning. Both of his eyes are watering…' his son explained.

'There is nothing there. Everything is alright,' the doctor said again, and said it with a lot of confidence.

'But so much water from his eyes?' the son asked again in a perplexed voice.

Here, on the other side, he was listening to all of this sitting silently.

'What's from the eyes?' the doctor hadn't been able to hear properly what the son had said.

'Water from his eyes…' his son repeated.

'No, these are only tears. When a man cries, tears are bound to flow, no? His eyes aren't bad. He is just crying, that's all…' the doctor said, as if giving the final verdict.

He couldn't stay silent anymore now.

'But I am not crying at all!' he said.

'No, you are not crying. Often, you yourself won't even know that you are crying. In fact, the truth of the matter is that you are crying.'

'Sir, I am not crying at all.'

'No, you are crying hard. Tears are flowing from your eyes. Even now. Look!'

'These aren't tears, Mister.'

'These are tears. I am a doctor. I know. You should at least believe the expert.'

He couldn't continue to argue further. Had the doctor said all of this in a court of law, even the court would have said that he was crying! He went silent. Rather, he ended up even doubting himself, thinking, who knows, the doctor might be telling the truth! Who knows that he might be actually crying and he isn't aware of it himself. Could it be that some change had occurred in his body, that a man had started crying unbeknownst to himself? These were dire times. Anything could happen these days.

He thought it to be appropriate to directly ask the doctor.

'Am I really crying, Doctor?' he asked.

'Yes, these are tears, after all,' the doctor responded with the authority of a specialist.

'And I didn't even come to know that I am crying?' he asked, astonished.

'It's quite possible. Yes, this can happen. When a man cries day and night, and continues to cry, he doesn't even know how one feels when crying…'

'So, do the tears pierce too?'

'What?'

'Sir, can the tears pierce, in the eyes?'

'What type of question is this?'

'Because something has been piercing my eyes. Continuously. That's the reason they are watering too...'

'But your eyes are perfectly alright...'

'Could you please examine my eyelids at least once, sir?'

'I've examined everything.'

'Could you please examine it one more time, sir?'

'What should I look for? Why don't you tell me?' the doctor said in a sarcastic manner.

'Actually, the shards of my dreams are stuck in my eyelids, Doctor Sahab. Please look closely. You'll surely be able to see them. See, they are piercing my eyes anyway...'

'The shards of your dreams! What's that? Yaar, what's this your father is talking about?' the doctor asked his son.

What could the son reply?

He had been advising his father since they left home to not start again with the story of shattered dreams at the doctor's clinic. He had instructed: just tell him your eye problems, that's it. It's not necessary that we tell the whole world that we've lost our minds. At that time, his father had even agreed to it. He had said, 'I will keep my mouth shut at the clinic. If the doctor prescribed some medicine after seeing my eyes, why would I unnecessarily say even a word about my dreams? I can be crazy but I am not that crazy.' But see, that's exactly what happened! Right now, that's exactly the thing he was talking about with the doctor.

The son said in an apologetic tone while making circles with his index finger next to his head, indicating that his father has lost his mind, 'Sir, please don't pay any attention to what he is saying. These days he goes astray. He is even under treatment from a psychiatrist.'

'Oh! No problem, then.'

'Doctor, it could very well be that I might be insane. But my eyes are still watering so much. So? This couldn't be madness, right? These are the shards of my dreams which have lodged into my eyes. Please believe me,' he was insisting with such graveness that even the doctor was ready to reconsider once.

'And what's the matter of these shards of dreams, sir?' the doctor asked with a lot of respect.

He started talking just like a schoolmaster, explaining the relation between the eye and dreams.

'Look, Doctor Sahab, these are not tears. In fact, I had a few precious dreams. They stole them. And then, they shattered even those dreams. They shattered my dreams. These are the shards of those shattered dreams which are lodged in my eyelids. And that's where this water is coming from...'

The doctor listened to him with interest, and earnestly.

'You sure must have had some misunderstanding. Anyway, the eyes can't have 'shards of dreams in them.'

'Why? Why cant they be there?'

'These days, dreams don't live in the eyes. The latest research in ophthalmology tells us that the dreams of human beings don't reside in the eyes. We have proven this after an intense examination of the eyes. So, if there aren't any dreams there to begin with, how come these shards of your dreams would be lodged there?' the doctor explained to him, referring to some latest scientific journals.

'But in my eyes...'

'Are your eyes different from other human beings' eyes, Mister?'

'This, too, is possible that I am the only one left with human-like eyes?'

'And the eyes of the rest of the world aren't human? They are fake?'

'Yes, why can't this happen?'

'So, are my eyes fake too? I am examining the real eyes of my patients with my fake eyes?'

'I am not talking about you, Doctor. You are different. But it is quite possible that they might have changed people's eyes in the world. Therefore, your science doesn't find dreams in their eyes.'

'You mention "they" again and again. Who are "they"? What's the meaning of they? They, who?'

'Those are the people who are out on the prowl to

steal dreams from everybody's eyes. The world isn't able to understand this.'

'And it's just you who has understood this?'

'Oh! It was that I caught them red-handed in my dream while they were stealing my dreams, that's why I am able to tell this to you.'

Now his son jumped in. He started chiding his father.

'Papa, you started with that useless talk once again even here too, didn't you? Didn't I tell you not to do that? The doctor doesn't have the time to listen to your useless gibberish…'

The doctor, too, stared at him. He shut up. Sat silently, rubbing his eyes. His eyes were still watering, continuously.

The doctor once again told his son in such a way so he, too, could hear it properly, 'His eyes are completely alright.'

'And this watering?' he started asking again.

'These are your tears. Didn't I tell you? You are crying…' the doctor said.

'I am not crying. I know that.'

'You are crying. For sure. I know. Trust me…' the doctor said.

'I know quite well what crying is. I have spent my whole life crying. I may not have the experience of laughing but I do have long experience of crying! It is for sure that I am not crying right now, Doctor Sahab!' he said. 'Whatever is piercing my eyes, it is because of that they are watering. Please have a look at it,' he added.

'I don't have any machine, Mister, which would take out the shards of your dreams from your eyes. Any machine like that doesn't exist. So, you tell me what to do?' the doctor was now getting annoyed.

'Doctor, medical science would have to invent such a machine sooner or later. And it will have to do that soon. A machine that would be able to pick and collect the shards of dreams from people's eyes. Many folks like me will start coming to you soon. There are so many dreams broken to pieces everywhere and all around that the shards of those dreams will be lodged into the eyes. How many will you be able to entertain by saying that their eyes are alright? No, Doctor, you folks will have to come up with a solution soon. Please do something.' He became breathless and agitated while speaking.

He was now sitting while tightly grabbing the doctor's hand. The tears were rolling down his cheeks like a waterfall. The doctor slowly freed his hand from his grip and signalled to his son to take him away. His son grabbed him and forcefully got him up. He kept on mumbling even while getting up.

'You aren't taking this to be a disease, are you, Doctor? But this is. This soon is going to spread everywhere like conjunctivitis. You should think of a name for this disease, Doctor...'

He got up and started going towards a wall.

'Not that way, Papa. Come this way...' his son turned him towards the direction of the door.

'I can't see properly, son. What can I do? The pieces of broken dreams are piercing my eyes...' he said while walking.

'You and your damn dreams!' his son erupted in frustration.

'What a strange man! He is crying but he isn't ready to believe that he is crying,' the doctor muttered under his breath.

The son stopped for a moment while taking his father outside, and returned leaving his father at the door. After coming near the doctor, he said while apologising, 'Please don't take it otherwise, Doctor Sahab. Papa has become a bit mental these days.'

The doctor replied, smiling, 'I understand. That's why he is crying and yet not believing that he is crying.' The doctor broke into a burst of laughter while explaining.

For a doctor, somebody's crying had become a matter of laughter.

# The Bazaar Has Sent A Proposal

Such a peculiar incident happened the other day. Peculiar in the sense that the Bazaar sent the 'Tunnel Uncle' a proposal for a project regarding the tunnel he was digging.

He had started to remain quiet these days though. He didn't even mention the word 'tunnel' to anybody—not even to his family members. These days, everybody was happy that he was getting better. This doctor was quite smart; any type of lunatic taken to him was eventually cured. He didn't let anybody get even a whiff of this, that he had hastened the job of digging the tunnel so much that the day was not far when his tunnel would open there, where the Bazaar didn't have its reach.

But even before that, the Bazaar itself came and met with him, and presented him with an attractive proposal regarding the tunnel.

He was already suspicious of the Bazaar. It was aware of the tunnel he was digging after all. In the beginning, he was completely worried. He didn't even go towards the tunnel for many days. Then, after a few days, he just passed by the tunnel once or twice. His tunnel was the way it was. Untouched. The plank, too, was as it was…on the tunnel's mouth. Untouched. It also didn't seem like anybody was nearby, keeping an eye on the tunnel. So, was all of this an illusion of his? Did someone random place the plank on the mouth of the tunnel so that somebody doesn't fall into the hole?

After some time, he began digging the tunnel again with double the enthusiasm. And taking even more precautions. He would continuously dig, all night long. He lazed away or slept in his bed all day long. His family members would think that he was probably sleeping a lot these days because of his psychiatric medicines. He, too, would say the same thing. He would never even mention the word tunnel by mistake. Let's get the job done, first. Let the tunnel complete. Then, suddenly, the news would be broken to the whole family. Then, everybody would come to know that he wasn't insane after all. He would smile to himself, thinking all of this!

One night, he had just climbed out of the tunnel after digging, and was just covering the mouth of the tunnel by sliding the plank when he was awfully startled…

The Bazaar was standing right in front of him. Smiling. A long, deep smile on its face, yet its eyes were staring deeply.

Lips stretched, but brows furrowed. A congenial expression of innocence but with such a shade of meanness that you wouldn't be able to figure out if this person was going to embrace you the very next moment or kill you!

He had just gotten out of the tunnel. Covered in dust, and soaked in sweat. Tired. Exhausted. His eyes were blinking rapidly with tiredness. He just wanted to reach home as soon as he could and sleep…

And that's when the Bazaar pounced upon him. He wiggled and squirmed, but any effort on his part to free himself would have been futile. Quite a customer-friendly pouncing this was! The Bazaar never pounced on anybody in that wild way—the imagery that the word 'pounce' generally evokes. The Bazaar had gone for higher education just to learn this magical pouncing: let the hold be fatal but it should still appear to be soft. Killing them softly…such fascinating management the Bazaar had learned.

The Bazaar's hold was so friendly that he couldn't dare to free himself or writhe strongly. He tried to use strategic means to get himself freed.

'Your suit will be ruined, sir. I am covered in dust. Please let me go,' he pleaded and, while speaking, he tried to wriggle himself free.

The Bazaar didn't let his hold relax, and doubled his politeness.

'Good evening, sir! How are you today?' it respectfully bowed a courteous bow to him while still maintaining its grip on him.

Even if you have to murder someone, respectfully bow to the person along with the knife before proceeding further! By doing that, the guilt of committing a crime is gone and the person who is dying, too, dies with gratification for having died a respectful death. This was the Bazaar's novel thinking.

'How am I?'

'Yes, how are you?'

'I am drenched in sweat. That's why I am saying that your suit would be ruined.'

'No, it won't. Please do remember, we make perfumes out of others' sweat. The sweat which reeks out of your body, that same sweat will waft off sweet fragrance later when applied to our clothes. Please don't worry...'

'But apart from sweat, my body is covered in dust as well... Please let me go.'

'Where have I held you, sir?'

'Well, I am in your clutches.'

'Oh! This? This is our embrace! The Bazaar is yours—that's all I am trying to show you. Please don't call this pouncing. And nothing will be spoilt with dust. Dust flies everywhere. After all, one needs dust to throw it in somebody's eyes, too, right?' the Bazaar broke into a guffaw, saying this so that it remained clear that the sentence was being uttered in jest.

Suddenly, the Bazaar loosened its hold and set him free. Now, it was standing in front of him with a lot of respect and courteousness. He closely looked at the Bazaar. Smart. Sucking the protruding gut in. Tie. Suit. Glitz. Glitter. Meanness. A twinkle in the eyes. Its form resembled an animal who is ready for a hunt and has patience in him, along with the eagerness-filled restlessness of jumping too.

The Bazaar was standing in front of him, blocking his way with so much politeness that he couldn't dare circumvent it.

'I have to go home. Ill talk to you later,' he tried deflecting and made a motion to leave.

'You are in the Bazaar. Please consider this as your home as well…'

'You can see that I am tired and exhausted. Covered in dust as well. I'll go home and shower.'

'The Bazaar has made fabulous arrangements for the tired and exhausted. We, too, yearn for the tired. Please give us a chance at least once…'

'If I go home and take a shower, my exhaustion will end anyway. May I leave?'

'Alright, then I will come to your home. Shall I call you in two hours?'

'I didn't give you my phone number. Where will you call me?'

'We have that for all of our customers. We have the horoscope of every customer with us. Please tell me the time, and I will be at your doorstep,' it said coolly, with quiet satisfaction. To remain cool, and to have vulture-like patience, these were the fine weapons at its disposal. The Bazaar knew. If somebody's throat has to be slit, a lot of patience is required for that.

'He started walking without giving a reply. The Bazaar, too, walked behind him. Almost like his shadow. He knew. It was difficult to get rid of one's shadow.'

'I'll sleep after taking a shower. I am very tired. Since I am tired, the sleep won't come easily,' he told the Bazaar, which was following him, as a maneuver to get rid of it.

'There are many things in the market for insomnia too. Some mattresses have been made by filling them with sleep. Lie down and sink into sleep! There are free apps with special lullabies too. There are accessories that will make your eyelids heavy as well,' the Bazaar told him, still following.

But he wasn't going to fall into the clutches of the Bazaar. He was alert. He said, 'No, I don't have any such trouble falling sleeping. Never had. I fall asleep as soon as I hit the bed. I sleep so soundly, like a log, that my wife gets exhausted in trying to wake me up every morning,' he said as he was walking. It was clear from his mannerisms that he was saying that he should be left alone.

The Bazaar said, 'If you can't wake up from sleep, then there are many services in the market for that as well. You can subscribe to anyone. Some are even available on monthly or quarterly subscription plans.'

'Services to wake somebody up from sleep?' he asked, astonished.

'Yes, the Bazaar wants to be able to serve its customers from waking them up to helping them fall asleep—in all of it,' it said.

'So, is there an intention to possess people's sleep?' he asked in disgust.

'I didn't say anything like that...'

'Many things are left unsaid...'

'No, it isn't like that.'

'What are the services in the market to wake somebody up though?' he asked, curious how far the Bazaar had entrenched itself in a man's life. He shivered just thinking this.

'There are many,' the Bazaar was telling him excitedly. It hadn't paid any attention to his surprise. 'There are many services. You are the one who has to choose. There are new types of alarms. All you have to do is say the magic word, and somebody from our team will come, knock on your door and wake you up. Or someone can come to your bed and wake you up by lovingly caressing you. This scheme also exists. All you have to do is tell the age of the person who would need the caressing, and other such minor details, that's it. There is a service to play the drum next to your bed to wake you up as well. The one who brings the drum can bring a sitar as well. There is a provision to kick you to wakefulness as well.'

He stopped mid-way. 'What will you take to leave me alone? Or is there going to be a service charge for that too?' he said gruffly.

'That was a good one! Nice sense of humour, sir!' the Bazaar praised him, ignoring his gruffness.

He started walking again. But the Bazaar stopped, staying behind. He didn't follow him.

'Please go home and rest for a while. Whenever you wake up, I'll be at your doorstep. Actually, I have a fabulous proposal regarding your tunnel,' the Bazaar said while standing there.

He was stunned, and froze midway in his tracks.

'Tunnel?'

'Yes, tunnel.'

'Which tunnel?'

'The one you are digging.'

'How do you know?'

'The Bazaar knows everything. It has to know everything. We know. You are digging a tunnel, aren't you?'

'Oh, that! That's just…that!'

'So, you are digging a tunnel to go where? Where are you going, sir?'

'Nowhere. It was just like that…'

The Bazaar kept talking while still staying where it was. He had returned and was now talking to him though, facing him.

'If you don't want to tell, don't tell. It's fine.'

'There is nothing to tell.'

'So, you are digging so much for no rhyme or reason?'

'Yes. For no rhyme or reason…'

'Alright! Let it be then…'

'This is the truth! The truth!'

'Alright! Agreed. But suppose if I got you some money for this hobby of yours of digging tunnels, then?'

'Money?'

'Yes, money. Look, you are already digging. You are already wearing yourself out. The Bazaar has seen your tunnel from the inside. All the way. And it has shown it too.'

'Who have you shown it to?'

'Some TV channels have expressed their interest in this. They have come and seen it from the inside. All the way. They were quite excited to know that one man is digging such a long tunnel just for the heck of it. They say that if this is marketed properly, then crores of viewers would like to watch how a man of your age is digging a deep tunnel owing to passion.'

'Why would people watch?'

'They would watch. They would surely watch. Arre, it is not like everybody is digging a tunnel. When a person like you digs such a long tunnel for the heck of it, why wouldn't people want to watch it? They will find it to be quite an interesting idea.'

'What's so interesting in that?'

'There is… That's man's temperament. If a child is born with two heads, don't you know how a crowd gathers to take a look at it? So it's the same mystique, if you will. You are digging a tunnel, now you may not find this to be interesting, but others may very well find it interesting. The Bazaar would make some money out of that. You will have your cut too.'

'What's there in digging a tunnel?'

'There must be. A child falls into a borewell. And we dig another well next to it to take that child out, people watch that digging, don't they? Your tunnel is going to be further interesting. Why is somebody digging a tunnel in this old age, after all? What does he want to do? What path is he making? Where does he want to go using that tunnel? This will become a sizzling hot issue, sir! You will get so busy with the TV that you won't even get time to dig your tunnel.'

He was stupefied. How easily the Bazaar could make everything saleable!

Here, on the other hand, a representative of the Bazaar was excited and started telling further.

'Once this tunnel becomes popular, we will bring a whole project of tunnel tourism. Tunnel Tourism, yes! Even the name sounds cool. People will buy a ticket and enter the tunnel, and they'll see you digging the tunnel—live! They will be able to take selfies with you. They will have your autograph. Who knows, we can even sell the tunnel dirt in pouches as a souvenir…'

'Please forgive me…'

'Arre, please at least try to understand?'

'I didn't know that the Bazaar would barge into the tunnel as well.'

'The Bazaar is expanding, sir. If it's expanding, it will come into the tunnel as well.'

'Is the Bazaar akin to a flood now?'

'You can think of it like a flood, sir. If the Bazaar expands like a flood, what's your problem with that?'

'A man drowns in flood. That's the problem I have.'

'But if a man sees flood ahead, why doesn't he turn into a fish?'

'What nonsense?'

'Why? Why is this nonsense?'

'Arre, man was a fish billions of years ago. He evolved from there over the millennia, and was able to become a man! Why do you want to turn this wheel back? A man should turn into fish again for the Bazaar! Really? Wow!'

'Why? After all, what did he achieve until today by being a man?' the Bazaar asked.

He was stunned at his response. Speechless too. What is this entity that is standing in front of him? It is against humanity, and it is neither afraid saying this nor embarrassed!

He took a few paces back, scared of him. Then, he suddenly dashed. He was tired but he ran headlong. He didn't know if he was being followed or not. He didn't even try to find out. He just ran, and kept on running. The Bazaar didn't run after him; it stood at its place. Just calmly looking at him until he disappeared around a bend.

The Bazaar, standing alone, just kept looking at him running. It smiled, and kept on smiling. The Bazaar's smile wasn't the Buddha's smile, that was for sure.

## There Is Somebody There

The city was surprised, and scared too.

How can this happen?

How can somebody live inside a manhole?

But on the other hand, many people also said that one is not truly able to fathom a man's will to live. That the conditions in many areas of the city weren't any better than hell but the man, after all, was comfortably living there, wasn't he? 'Alright, let's not call it comfortably…but at least he was alive, right,' they would say. Many others had started saying this too, that this seemed like some ghost or possession-type of affair. Some other folks believed that it wasn't anything like that; that it was all nothing but a prank circulated by these crazy, lazy sanitary workers. And that was it, there was nothing else to it. They are three sheets to the wind and once a person is inebriated so much, a man can see anything. They were not at fault either, that one descended into this hell only after getting drunk!

The market was hot with the talk of the man in the manhole.

People had many stories; and that too, of different types—and all of them were taken to be authentic. People had heard the sound of footfalls coming from underneath the ground. The watchmen doing their nightshift had heard such footfalls in the silence of the dead of the night, as if somebody was walking below, underground, in the mud, splashing.

Many people had heard similar sounds under their beds at night and they had woken up startled, screaming 'Thief, thief!'

Some people, late at night while returning home, had seen such shiny light seeping through the slit in the manhole on the road—the type which is shown in the pictures of the gods around their divine countenance. And some people from that group had even offered coconut and incense sticks to the manhole, considering it all to be a divine miracle.

Some people had seen a shadow-like entity climbing out of the manhole late at night, which would then merge into the night's darkness within moments of coming out, right in front of their eyes.

The news had reached the Bazaar as well. New game apps flooded the market quickly, which had become quite popular among children and adults alike. In one such game, the player was stuck in a sewage line. And then in this, many different levels had been provided to come out of the manhole, crossing many hurdles. In another game, there was a colony of aliens that had come from another planet and settled in the sewage pipes, and the player would be stuck in that colony. He would have to cover the distance to the manhole by killing these aliens. These rumours were on the rise and gaining strength in society that aliens were hiding in the sewage pipes underground, and were just waiting for an opportunity. That they could come out on the surface anytime and capture our earth. Some people had even seen flying saucers coming out of the manholes and flying away into space from there.

All around, there were talks of some mysterious being living in the sewage pipes underground.

But what was the reality, after all? He, who had climbed down the manhole sometime ago, where was he now? The readers could ask this question here. The answer is that nothing concrete was known about him. These footfalls have been heard even by the writer though.

It seems that that person was surely still living in the sewage pipes somewhere. He was alive. And If he had to become a vermin to stay alive, then he would have even become a vermin by now. If he lived there by becoming a vermin, then it shouldn't come as a surprise to anybody. Many people had already been living a vermin-like life above the ground already. So, in this, if a man became a vermin by going underground, then what was there to be surprised about?

But, had he truly become a vermin, how would this discussion continue—which was currently happening amongst the vermin crawling in the sewage pipes down below? The insects sitting on the pipe were shooting the breeze amongst themselves just for the heck of it. An insect had asked another insect, 'Yaar, where has that man who was wandering within these pipes gone? He isn't seen around these days. What happened to him?' the vermin were asking amongst themselves.

Amongst all these vermin, one vermin's face resembled that man's face quite a lot. It was listening to these conversations amongst the vermin, crawling. And that vermin had suddenly raised its front legs and kept them in such a way that his face was now hidden behind his paws… Was that vermin deliberately trying to hide his face? Could it be that this was the same man who had acquired citizenship of the sewage lines?

***

And then the crazies met the same fate which the crazies have been meeting ever since.

# The Cancer Has Reached The Brain

Gradually, the Bazaar expanded in such a way that wherever one stuck their hand in to look for life, they would get the Bazaar in their hand when they pulled out. Now, there was an insistence to consider the Bazaar as *life* itself. So much so that now only those values of life deserved credence which had a value in the market as well.

Sensex was such a value that was left. Every door had started opening into a shop; the Bazaar peeked out of every window, every latch was now knocked on by the Bazaar only, and every person had transformed into a customer.

Let's tell you about an incident from those days.

A very big capitalist had died. Needless to say, he died in a big five-star hospital.

The sources from the hospital informed folks that he died of cancer. He came to know about the illness at the very end of his life. The cancer had been living and thriving in his body for a long time. It had already been in the body, it was just that he wasn't aware of it. Cancer slowly spread in his body. He didn't understand. He was a great man. And in the efforts to become greater, he couldn't make time to understand his own cancer. Rather, he understood it to be completely opposite.

When his body swelled, he took that to be weight gain; and when his appetite declined, he rejoiced that this would help him control his weight. When the blood came in his vomit, he believed that his body was purifying, that bad blood was getting out. And when he became short of breath while climbing the stairs, he believed it to be only natural to be short of breath as one gained altitude. Here, on the other side, the Bazaar was expanding. In all of this, the poor capitalist didn't have time to think about anything else apart from money and the Bazaar.

And then one day, he had a bout of epilepsy. He was in the market when he experienced dizziness, and fell. For a while, people thought that he had fainted because of the trauma caused by the fallen Sensex. When they realised the truth later, they took him to the hospital. It was then he found out that the cancer had spread to his brain.

After the death of the capitalist, there were discussions regarding cancer in the media. Everybody agreed unanimously that if cancer was caught early on, then and only then could it be contained. If one didn't catch it in the beginning, it would spread in the whole body. The train had left the platform. And if cancer spread all the way to the brain, the situation would become dire. The disease then possessed a man's body, and possessed his thinking even.

All around, one could hear such highfalutin talks. Everybody agreed that it was necessary to make efforts to stop cancer at the beginning itself, and that cancer reaching the brain was quite a frightening and fatal eventuality.

These discussions went on for some days. Then they were left behind. By that time, it was Valentine's Day. Now, Valentine's Day would be on everybody's mind for a day or two.

This was the time when a man's mind had come under the possession of the Bazaar, and he wasn't even aware of it. Now, people talked about only those things which the Bazaar wanted them to talk about. It had spread to a man's mind but the man hadn't been able to detect that yet. Just in this one matter, the Bazaar was different from cancer—ahead of it even!

# The Spiritual End Of The Revolution

And then for three days, he didn't go to dig his tunnel. A fear had stricken his heart. He would get out of the house and the Bazaar's men would surely follow him. They could come into the tunnel and grab him. The Bazaar's men were definitely after him. They were keeping an eye on him; he had seen it himself. They often stood outside the house and maintained a rotation so they couldn't be identified.

He was looking outside the window and investigating right now. Checking if they were still there outside or not. It was an hour past midnight. The feeble glow of the streetlight was scattered on the road in front. A man, standing at some distance on the road, was gazing at their house just a while ago. In fact, there was nobody there for the last hour at first. The road was empty. Their watch had broken. It was quite possible that after some time, a new person might have come to watch in the place of the first one. There was a window of opportunity right now.

Right now, none of their men were on the watch. He looked at his watch. It was 2:00 o'clock at night.

He picked up his bag, which had the tools for digging the tunnel, from under his bed. Yes, that was the opportunity. He slowly got up, opened the door and cautiously went out. He looked in both directions on the road with alertness. There was nobody there right now. Yes, this was the chance. Perhaps, the last chance.

He hoisted the bag on his shoulder and ran. He dashed. Kept on running. Who knows from where he had gotten so much energy within him. He had never run so fast in his whole life. He kept on running. The night was deep and dark. Perhaps, it was the night of a new moon. On the roads, in the streets, it was darkness all around. There were a few patches of light, here and there, which he dodged. And eventually, he reached behind the Bazaar, running.

The plank covering the tunnel was right in front of him. He didn't let a single moment go to waste. He removed the plank and jumped into the tunnel.

This was the last day that anybody had seen him; that, too, if somebody even had seen him. After that, he was never found by his family members again. When they woke up the next day, he wasn't in his room. The door to the house was open. His family members searched for him everywhere. He wasn't found anywhere.

And then, he was never to be found again. Police, missing person's poster, the whole scramble—he wasn't found anywhere.

Where was he?

News spread throughout the whole neighbourhood that Ram Kumar ji had disappeared from his home. Ten different types of things were being said about him. One thing that was common among all of them was that the poor guy's mind had become unstable. Such people do often run away from their home—everybody agreed on that.

'Where do such people go?' somebody was curious.

'Yaar, who has the time to find all this out…' somebody else replied.

The world was very busy, so nobody knew when he went back into the tunnel again. His family members were worried for him and kept on looking though.

That night when he entered the tunnel, he never came out after that.

He didn't want to take any risk now. The Bazaar could enter his tunnel at any time. And before that, not only did he have to get away far from all this but, while going away, he had to close the other end of the tunnel in such a way that nobody could follow him… And the family? Once he reached the new place and properly made a shelter for himself which was away from the Bazaar, he could bring his family members in the second installment.

In the dark tunnel, he placed his torch to one side, and started digging. And he didn't stop. He kept digging. Continuously kept on digging, without getting tired. Without stopping. He kept on digging without any rest at all. Days passed. The nights went one after the other. He neither ate nor drank. There was only passion. He was soaked in sweat. If he felt hot, he took off his clothes. Only undergarments were left on his body. He just kept on digging. Crowbar and the tunnel. And his hands at it.

Who knows for how many days? Or, perhaps many months.

He neither ate anything nor drank. He just kept digging his tunnel. Dug it for miles, perhaps. He didn't remember. Only a single passion existed: that he had to get out by digging the tunnel. He was reduced to a skeleton. He grew a beard. His hair grew and became dreadlocks. The whole body was caked with dust…but he kept on digging!

His family members searched for him everywhere, but he was nowhere to be found. Months went by. Phone, advertisement, bus station, police station… all avenues were exhausted. When asked, the family members finally told the police that he talked about running away via some tunnel, and that a psychiatrist was treating him. The constable and the police inspector unanimously explained to the family members, 'Who can trust a crazy man, Sahab. Who knows where he might have gone? Who knows, he might have become a sadhu?

Or, he might just be wandering somewhere just like that.' The constable expressed even this suspicion, 'That tunnel thing which you people are talking about…could it be that he might have jumped into some well, thinking it to be some tunnel?'

And then with time, the search for him dwindled. Once in a while, here and there, when they would come to know about some enlightened fakir or an ascetic, his family members would surely visit them. But nobody could tell. Everybody said that he would surely return one day. But when? This, nobody could tell.

How could anybody tell when he himself didn't know how long he would continue to dig the tunnel, and when he would find that end from where he would find a way to get away from the Bazaar!

And then one day, it was as if he had woken up from a long unconsciousness, a deep slumber. He couldn't recall anything for some time.

It was as if he had seen himself for the first time. He stopped the digging and took stock of the tunnel. Otherwise, he had continued to dig until now, continuously. When exhausted from digging, he would roll off to one side and would start digging again as soon as he woke up. This long sequence that had been going on in a loop had finally broken today.

He found out that he was sitting within a very long, seemingly infinite tunnel. His beard was reaching his chest and his hair had grown all the way to his shoulders. And there was such a thick layer of dust on his skin that if he didn't move, he would totally feel like an earthen idol!

Today, for the first time, he was in the condition to think of something else apart from digging the tunnel.

He sat like that, with his back leaning against the wall of the tunnel, for quite some time. Pieces of gravel and heaps of dirt next to his feet. The dim light of the torch was getting reflected from the shiny surface of the sharp point of his crowbar, and had stabilised at one place on the tunnel's roof…

He was gazing at the roof of the tunnel with his eyes wide open. Right at that circle of light… Unblinking.

Enough, this tunnel journey ends *now*. Enough. He had come quite far. It was as if even God was signalling to him. He decided that he would start digging at the roof of the tunnel right at that spot in which the circle of reflected light was pointing. And he would get out of the tunnel by digging right at that spot.

He started digging at the roof of the tunnel, right at that spot. Kept digging. And just kept on digging.

And then, suddenly, his crowbar broke a stone, and it was as if went flying in the air. The way out of the tunnel was getting formed! Soon, he was squatting under a wide hole.

He half-climbed out of the hole and took a peek around to take stock of the situation. Where had his tunnel opened up?

But even outside the tunnel, it was pitch dark. Was he entering one darkness after getting out of another?

No, perhaps, it was night outside. It might be the darkness of the night. Some slight, somewhat dim light was there. There, in a corner, two lamps were lit, in front of an ancient idol of a deity. Their flames flickered for a moment. He climbed out of the tunnel and carefully sat down.

The stone underneath him was cold. Some of it was visible in the dim light of the lamps. He recognised it upon touching it—under him was a marble floor. Lamps, an idol of a deity, marble…he realised that the tunnel had opened up in the sanctum sanctorum of some temple. The doors of the sanctum sanctorum were closed right now.

Priests make even the deity sleep at night. The deity was lazing in the dim light of the lamp. He didn't know if the deity even noticed his climbing out of the tunnel by cracking open the floor of the sanctum sanctorum of the temple.

He was exhausted. He couldn't even sit properly on the floor. He was carrying the fatigue of so many months. Since the job was done, the entirety of immense fatigue had suddenly descended upon him.

He lay down on the marble floor. It seemed almost impossible to think of anything else right now …and within moments, he was in the grips of deep sleep. He hadn't slept in months. And then, he slept as if comatose until the morning.

And in the morning, the priests opened the locks of the sanctum sanctorum.

God was safe, but he was found unconscious-like, right next to the idol, on the stone floor. His mien was such that he could easily have been taken for a cunning criminal or an enlightened saint.

'Perhaps, he is a thief?' the priest mumbled, and kicked him with his feet to wake him up. He woke up, rubbing his eyes.

The dawn was breaking. The sun had risen outside moments ago. The sunshine from the outside was reaching the sanctum sanctorum by getting reflected from here and there. A yellowish light and the darkness seeping from the dark corners were mixing here in such a fashion that an illusory aura was pervading the sanctum sanctorum as well as emanating from it. The marble floor was slightly muddy. And then he, too, was sitting on that floor—covered in dust and dirt. The muddiness of the floor and dust covered him from top to bottom. Long overgrown beard. Long dreadlocks. Reddish eyes because of not having slept for months. Thin, skinny body. He wasn't saying a word. Just staring at everybody with his reddish eyes.

A young priest was moving forward in anger when the head priest stopped him. No, this couldn't be a thief, he thought.

Hardly anything had been disturbed in the sanctum sanctorum. The idol was untouched and safe. The ornaments and jewellery adorning the idol were just the way, as they were before. Even the doors were found locked from the outside. Untouched. And still, having found this person inside this way, it was like a miracle.

'How did you get inside? There was such a strong padlock on the doors outside. Who are you?' he was asked.

He was staggering even while sitting. When he wished to say something, he started stammering. His tongue was getting dry. His throat was getting dry. He hadn't drunk water in months. He had just kept on digging the tunnel. The water he had brought with him from home in a thermos had finished a long time ago. His tongue and lips were chapped completely. The tongue felt like it had twisted and his mouth felt as if it was made of resin. Still, he tried to speak. He told them that he had reached here after digging a long tunnel. He also told them that the Bazaar was following him, evading whom he had come all the way here.

The priests didn't understand the head or the tail of what he was saying.

What tunnel? Which tunnel was he talking about?

Even a tiny hole wasn't visible in the sanctum sanctorum.

And from which place was he talking about running away from?

How did he appear just like that in the sanctum sanctorum, which was sealed from all sides?

It didn't take long for the priests to understand the whole matter.

He surely was some miraculous, enlightened saint. And it was through sheer divine coincidence that he had appeared in their temple, just like that. He had emaciated his body in penance. Praise be!

He muttered 'tunnel, tunnel' again and again. This was the voice of an enlightened saint. He was giving, perhaps, some hidden signal to the world by saying 'tunnel'. The priests fell to his feet. His hand, too, automatically raised in the gesture of blessing. Fine particles started to flow from his dust-covered hands. The priests felt blessed. The ash of his penance was being showered on them as a blessing.

Tunnel Baba had appeared in their temple so miraculously—how pivotal this thing would prove to be in establishing the temple's brand value in the market of spirituality, who else knew this better than the priests?

And in this way, he was entrapped in another market after running away from one market. He wasn't able to, perhaps, grasp this thing right now. Or, perhaps, if one ran away from the Bazaar, they could fall into 'spirituality'—was this the bitter truth?

Who knew what the truth was? For now, he had become the Tunnel Baba.

Gradually, a crowd of devotees and disciples started gathering in the temple and around it. By noon, a queue of thousands had formed to the temple. A whole market of offerings had sprung up. There was a fair there. The news of this miracle had spread far away in the city that some magical Tunnel Baba had miraculously appeared in the temple; that he could grant every wish.

He had appeared in the bazaar of religion with the status of a new star on the horizon, and he was astonished himself.

Within the outside boundary wall of the temple's courtyard, there was a marble platform.

Right now, he was seated on that platform. All the priests were standing surrounding him. He had been bathed, dressed in new clothes and decorated, and had been seated on the platform. Long hair. Flowing beard. Huge forehead. Silk orange robe. He had turned out to be quite grand and stately for no reason whatsoever.

A stream of people was all around the temple; the noise of exultation, all around. Every devotee wanted to get some of the dust from Tunnel Baba's feet. Miraculous Tunnel Baba was gazing at the crowd with his eyes half-closed. The devotees were feeling blessed. And he? He looked as if, was lost somewhere. He was closely looking at his surroundings.

A narrow road had come all the way to the temple gate.

On either side of this road were huge shops of offerings, and other things required for worship. Nestled among them were restaurant-type narrow shops. And then the shops for clothes, soap, oil and cosmetics, etc.. A devotee too, eventually, is nothing but a customer. The street was filled with customers of spirituality. He was earnestly looking at this street.

This long street seemed like a narrow tunnel to him.

So, was he entrapped in a different type of tunnel after getting out of one type of tunnel? And if he was entrapped, then why was he getting so much joy in all of this? So, if one runs away from the Bazaar, is spirituality the only support left? Don't know.

For now, he was sitting, smiling amidst the loud chants of exultation…

Tunnel Baba!

He had closed his eyes. He had dug the tunnel for months. He hadn't slept for months. Right now, he was taking a nap, sitting.

This, too, might be Tunnel Baba's spiritual gesture—the devotees believed that. Perhaps, Baba is immersed deeply in meditation!

The chanting had grown louder.

## He Was Martyred And Nobody Came To Know

The dawn has just broken. But even in the wee hours of the morning, there was a lot of hustle-bustle in the street.

The residents of the street were out on the road. A police car was parked nearby too. Three policemen. Two folks were there from the local TV channel as well. And some more strange faces. There was quite a commotion in the street. There was an ambulance parked at the mouth of the street, next to which a hospital worker was standing and yawning.

His dead body was lying in the street.

In the morning, he, tearing the fogginess of the dawn, had come crashing down on the street from the roof of the third floor of his house. The street was completely empty at that time. A yawning dog of inquisitive nature and an old man standing idly next to the grill of a house—these two were the only entities in the street at that time. The dog was laying on the street and lazing when he came crashing down from the roof. In one corner of the street, right next to the gutter, a handcart had been parked. He had fallen straight onto that cart. He crashed on the cart with a loud thud, he bounced towards an iron grill fixed in the verandah of a house from there, and then after colliding with the grill, he had come crashing back into the street and fallen facedown on the ground. Receiving a push from the falling body, the handcart quickly rolled towards one side and, after dragging alongside the wall, eventually turned upside down. The handcart had almost climbed over the lazing dog. The dog ran after those dogs' whining who had already started running, startled by the loud bang and turning-over of the handcart.

His skull had cracked open as soon as he had hit the street. The blood oozing from the cracked skull had spread next to his head on the ground, and turned into a thick, dark brown puddle by now. While falling from the roof, his vest had turned upside down. The broken, weak cage of the ribs was exposed. A few hair. Bald head. One hand was stretched out in front, jutting into the gutter. The other was getting crushed under the dead body.

The police believed the case to be a suicide. This was of such great relief. All the people standing on the street were praising this truth-telling and honesty of the police because, let's be honest, what the heck could they—or anybody else—have done had the police believed this to be a murder? His son had shown the prescriptions for his treatment to the police though. The psychiatrist used to say that his father was in a deep depression; he was given medicines for the same. That means, that he was taking medicines for insanity? Why, sir? Yes, you can say that. The people from the street, too, had affirmed what the son had said: 'Babu ji, these days, did seem anxious quite a lot, day and night. He was frightened of everybody. He had started to remain silent and lost in his own thoughts for the past three years. For the last two years, nobody had ever seen him getting out of his house. He had stopped meeting people. He was always seen peeking out from his window but if somebody from the street even as much as said "Hello" to him, he would quickly and anxiously draw the curtain… He would be seen on the roof at odd hours of the day as well. He didn't even take his medicines and treatment regularly, sir. He used to say that the medicines made him sleepy. If he fell asleep, then who was going to keep a watch?'

'Watch?'

'Oh! Don't even ask, Inspector Sahab! He had started talking kooky. He used to say that somebody was going to come and capture his house. He always kept his house shut. If a door or a window was left open by mistake, he would make a spectacle. He would be on the rooftop all the time. He would say that he was guarding his house. He would say that if people came to capture the street, he would be able to see them first from his rooftop. Same, kooky talk. We had him treated a lot, sir. How expensive the treatment has become these days. But we didn't hold back. The problem was that Babu ji never took his medicines. And that's why the illness increased further and further. Last few days, he had been in a dire condition. He would be on the roof day and night. He would ask for his food to be sent there as well. He just wouldn't agree to climb down from the roof. He would take his plate and go back to the roof. He had spoiled everybody's sleep. He would do something or the other, and make noise the whole night. He would scan the surroundings from the rooftop. He would draw the curtains on the window and then sneak a peek outside. All day long, he would caution us to be alert, "the assault can happen anytime" he would say.

A constable had started laughing loudly hearing all of this, and said, 'Did the oldster lose it completely or what?'

The other policeman, too, had agreed. 'Who can say when such a crazy man would jump off the roof or hang himself with a noose around his neck? You can't catch a crazy man? Yes, sure, what can you do to a crazy man? See, he did jump after all, did he not?'

The police inspector finished his paperwork slowly and leisurely. Till then, his dead body lay on the street.

His son thanked the police inspector again and again. He was quite obliged that the police didn't entangle the matter, and that they didn't try to ensnare the family members in this incident. Suppose they had started saying that someone from the family had pushed him down from the roof? Then, what would anybody have done? He hadn't left any note either. As a rule, it is imperative for someone committing suicide to leave a note before dying. If seen from this angle, he had gotten almost everybody killed while dying. Thank God for the police who made things a lot easier by considering this to be a suicide.

But, was it really a suicide?

No, this wasn't a suicide.

And this, only he knew. But he was no more. Now, it was only the Bazaar who knew this, because he had been martyred while battling the Bazaar.

The truth of the matter was that he hadn't committed suicide. He wasn't a coward who would commit suicide.

Agreed that he remained frightened these days. But this fearfulness wasn't because of his cowardice. He was alert because he knew the enemy well, that was all. He had every moment's information about the enemy. It was this alertness of his that people understood to be, and called, his fear. The world slept and he stayed awake. 'If times are so bad, then somebody has to stay awake', he often said. He would stay awake. He would keep an eye on the enemy, day and night. And he was doing exactly that even last night, when that moment of the encounter with the enemy came in whose anticipation he had been living for a long time.

That was how it happened.

Last night, too, he was on the roof all night long—as was his habit. Nowadays, even the family members didn't say anything to him. They'd say to him, 'Well, if you want to spend the whole night on the roof, then please spend as many nights as you can. Be my guest! How much is one going to spoil their own sleep because of you? If we try to talk some sense into you, you say that you're keeping a watch. Who knows which enemy you keep talking about all the time! These days, you believe the mall at the mouth of the street is the enemy. Tell me! Isn't that craziness or what?'

Anyway, whether the family members understood or not, he understood his duty very well.

He was on the roof last night too. He kept an eye on the enemy all night long, without blinking even once. His son was an idiot; he was unable to see such a gargantuan enemy. And when told about the enemy, he said that it was just a building, just a mall. How many times had he tried to explain to him that a mall was just a mask for the enemy...that the Bazaar had come all the way to their street, wearing the mask of a mall. That it was standing right outside their house, on the lookout for just one chance. The enemy could enter the street anytime. This street and this house, all of it were going to come under the Bazaar's possession.

'If you won't remain alert, it will turn out to be very bad. The Bazaar would evict you from your own street. Everywhere, this is its trick. It comes to every place in such a way that people don't even realise. After getting you entangled in beautiful masks, it would evict you from your own life. It was doing just that in the whole world. People were becoming homeless within their own homes. It is about to enter our street,' he would say. But nobody listened to him.

His son had told him off, 'You've lost your mind, reading all these nonsensical books. It would be better if you watch movies of your era on TV and visit the temple on the street in the evening. Better yet, just don't read these useless books. That's what happens when someone reads too much!'

So, nobody was with him anymore.

He was on the frontline, *all alone*. But he knew that even if one man stood in attention facing the Bazaar, it wouldn't dare enter this street. Even one man who was awake could make the enemy bite dust. So, he was alert. He kept an eye on the enemy at the mouth of the street from his roof. Nothing had happened all night long.

The enemy remained at the mouth of the street. It was testing his patience, perhaps. Or, perhaps, it was looking for a perfect opportunity.

The dawn was near. That he fell asleep…

He must have fallen asleep for barely five minutes before he woke up again, startled. When he woke, he stood up in anxiety. He had fallen asleep leaning on the parapet wall. Now, he stood up holding on to the parapet. One such nap could also give an opportunity to the enemy. If the enemy sensed that he fell asleep, then? 'Hey, Ram! What have I done?' he exclaimed, stood up and looked toward the enemy. And when he looked, he was stunned. It was good that he was holding on to that parapet, otherwise what he saw was so terrifying that he felt darkness in front of his eyes and he almost fell.

He saw that the enemy had disappeared from the mouth of the street.

And right at that moment, the lights of the whole city went off. Only ghosts of light were standing, here and there. Around the dazzling mall and its nearby areas, all that was seen were a mixed haziness of the darkness of the night, the hazy illusory light of the dawn, and some weak lights. More than whatever was visible, there was the scattered magical enchantment of seen and unseen. And the enemy wasn't visible anywhere in all of this.

Where did the enemy go? He took a look all around in panic.

There was darkness on the street. The weak lights of the invertors of some of the houses were trying to take a peek into the street from the verandah. Look, he had shut-eye for a teeny bit and the enemy shut off the city's lights and stealthily entered into his street.

After all, he was the one who was awake. The enemy waited for him to blink his eyes. His eyes blinked and the enemy came into the street. He took a peek into the street. He tried looking into the darkness. And he was able to see the enemy as well. The enemy, taking long strides, was spreading in the street. This street of his, too, was going to be under the Bazaar's possession.

He screamed in a loud voice from his roof itself. He warned the enemy in a raised voice.

'If you don't quickly leave the street, then…' he shouted.

'What's coming after then?' the enemy mocked him.

What should he say? He couldn't figure anything out. Here, on the other side, the enemy, completely ignoring his warnings, kept on marching into the street. He tried to wake up the neighbourhood and his family members by screaming more loudly.

He even started beating the drum kept on the roof loudly. But nobody in the street listened to him. Arre, what's the point of sleeping like that when one doesn't even know about the incoming threat to one's life, he thought. He ran helter-skelter on the roof in frustration. There were some bricks on the roof. And some junk too. Useless items of a household. He started throwing bricks down from his roof. And then a broken frame of a bicycle. Then some broken statutes. Old broken plastic buckets… The whole junk ended up on the street. There was lots of noise in the street.

But not a single citizen of the street woke up. The enemy, too, wasn't scared. He kept on marching. The bricks scattered in the street collided with the enemy's body. The other junk, too, rolled off here and there in the street after colliding with the enemy's body. The enemy didn't even get a scratch. It kept marching on as before.

Now? Now what? What to do now?

The enemy wasn't stopping even for a moment. Rather, it even raised its head and looked at him. The enemy even smiled after looking at him.

He ran towards the stairs now. Should he go downstairs and wake his son up? But he gets angry instantly these days. If one tries to talk anything sensible, he says, 'Babu ji, it's fine that you have lost your mind, just…please don't come down to make us lose ours too. You should just stay on the roof.' He stopped midway while climbing down the stairs. No…there was no point going downstairs now. He came back the stairs and ran to the parapet. And, in trying to look into the street, ended up half-hanging on the parapet. And while taking a peek, he warned the enemy again, screaming. It didn't have any effect on the enemy.

He will have to do something. The enemy has to be stopped somehow. If he has to carry out this task alone, then he alone will have to make an effort. When life itself is in danger, then this very life has to be put in danger. The enemy is marching in the street unconcerned. If nothing is done now, then the street was going to be in the Bazaar's possession soon. All these thoughts were racing through his mind.

He became very restless. What should I do now? Oh, God! What should I do now, he was getting restless thinking this, like the hero of a tragedy—running from here to there on the stage. If he delayed even for a moment, it would be too late. But what could he do, after all? He was alone. He was weak in his old age. And the enemy was so gargantuan. Hundreds of thousands of times larger than this street. Quite big. Wearing a shoe that would cross this whole street in one stride.

So?

He would have to work with a cool head. He was not going to get anything now by getting excited unnecessarily and screaming. He gradually started getting calmer. He stood on the parapet, looking at the street below.

He had made a decision. There was no doubt in his mind anymore. He wasn't restless. He wasn't pacing on the roof either. It was as if he'd taken stock of the enemy one last time by peeping into the street down below. Then, he put his other foot on the upper hole as well by putting it in a slot in the parapet. He leaned on the parapet on his hands, with his feet sticking in the ornamental holes in it. Had somebody seen him from afar, he surely would have chided him, warning him that he could fall. But who would have been able to see him in this hazy hour of dawn? He balanced himself on the parapet and started peeking down below, and took direct aim at the enemy. And then, he bounced off his lower foot after pressing it down like a spring. He added more strength to his leap from his other foot on the parapet, and he leapt into the air.

He leapt onto the chest of the enemy who was entering the street.

He leapt from his roof and died.

His neck broke. His skull fractured. It didn't take even a moment. He fell straight into the street and died. He martyred for the world, and the world didn't receive the news of this sacrifice of his. In the daily register of the world, this incident was registered in the account of his insanity. Suicide.

And in the history of the world?

The world's history, these days, was being penned by the Bazaar. When this incident was presented in front of the Bazaar to be registered in the world's history, it just scratched that place on its back slightly, the place from which he had leapt that morning from his roof. The Bazaar doesn't register such idiocy in its history, you know.

He had died. Just like that. A somewhat nameless death.

## Dementia

He didn't remember anything now.

His memory was completely gone. He remembered only that somebody had stolen his memories. It didn't serve him at all, but he hadn't forgotten the thief's name. He still knew it very well. The name of the one who had stolen his memories was still on the tip of his tongue. He even told that to everybody, here and there. But nobody listened to him anymore these days. Nobody listened to him. He would keep on talking about something or the other all day long. Who knew what he mumbled? He couldn't tell anything properly anymore. These days, he couldn't even construct a sentence properly. He couldn't use language properly…it was as if it had been forgotten. His family was used to his mumbling now. These days, they didn't pay any attention to what he said. Children laughed at him. Outsiders took pity on him, or just walked away with a polite smile. They talked amongst themselves about what the condition of such a learned man had become…that he was such a big economist in this city, going around giving speeches. And then who knows what happened, as if he slowly started getting crazier and crazier.

And now this condition… Everybody had forgotten him. He, too, had forgotten everybody. These days, he couldn't even recognise the children in his house. If a relative touched his feet and introduced themselves, he would either look far in the distance or just sit there smiling. His face had slowly turned into a desolate place where no expression had its residency left anymore. Even the doctors had given up. They would just say, 'Take care of him. He has dementia. You know Alzheimer's, that's what it is. There is no cure for this anywhere.'

He had been abandoned like a bleak, dreary ruin in the busy, blooming world. Memories didn't live here anymore. The mind was completely empty. Only one thought kept hounding him still, and he'd silently say to himself, 'The thief is still roaming scot-free. My memories are gone and everybody else's memories are also in so much danger… The whole world is in danger. Suppose it steals everybody's memories, then?' He got restless, just imagining a world where every citizen had reached his condition—memoryless, wandering, and completely dependent on everybody else. Wouldn't everybody be dependent on that one thief then? The whole world. Whatever the thief would say, everybody would agree to that because then it would be the thief who would have a memory. Then, the one with memory in the world would be only the thief. The thief with infinite memories. The master of everybody's memories. Then, the memories would be in possession of the Bazaar.

Everybody's memories. There wouldn't be any opposition, anywhere. Everybody would walk holding the Bazaar's hand, wherever it may take them. Everywhere, it would be the Bazaar, and only the Bazaar. Everywhere. In every street. In every home. And amidst this, memoryless people would wander like crazy. Completely dependent on the Bazaar, desiring the Bazaar, even to take a shit and take a piss!

He, too, had become dependent to take a shit or take a piss. He had forgotten where the bathroom was. He didn't recall what he wanted to do upon reaching the bathroom, and stood there thinking what to do. He couldn't open the drawstrings of his pajama. If he ended up opening it, he couldn't figure out what to do with it. Even tiny things had become a puzzle for him. He reeked all day long. How many times could the family members change his clothes, after all? These days, he was left with a diaper. Someone came periodically to check the diaper, and that was all. He, too, understood the exasperation of his family. This much he understood, even now. But what could he do? He was helpless. He couldn't remember anything. He was quite troubled. Not for himself. Whatever deterioration could happen to him, was already happening. But this thought haunted him, time and again, that one day this whole world could languish like him. If the world didn't recognise this thief with time in hand, then what would happen to this world? If this thief wasn't stopped, then one day everybody would become like him. Then, will everybody walk around like this, wearing a diaper? Would the whole world reek the way he reeked? Would stench become a man's identity?

He would get intensely anxious thinking about all of this. Anytime. Suddenly. And then stayed anxious all day long. Sometimes his heart got so agitated by this anxiety that he started slamming his hands and feet. And then he wouldn't calm down, despite consolations from anybody. The Bazaar, the diaper, the stench—who knows what else he keeps on mumbling… He started screaming against the thief. He wanted to warn everybody by screaming at the top of his lungs. But he found that his screaming didn't have much of an effect on anybody. The people around him seemed unaware, and were busy having fun. Nobody understood him; his speech had transformed into an undecipherable muttering. Getting irritated, he would mumble more and more. And then he would start crying. And then somebody would come and give him a pill. And then, he would finally fall, asleep, sobbing. The doctor had prescribed a few pills for his agitation. If he was agitated, he could be given one. If he fell asleep, then he was alright—and they will be 'free' from worry!

His memory was completely gone. He only remembered that once, he remembered everything. Now, he doesn't remember anything. He took his meal and just a while after having it, he'd start screaming, Will I be given food when I am already dead, he'd ask himself. It was just yesterday that he had opened the door, gone out, and stood stark naked on the road. The children of the neighbourhood gathered all around him and started laughing. His family members had to face quite a disgrace. His son chided him. He said that he wasn't naked at all! He said that he had been wearing the supreme loincloth all the time! That this was a fault in people's vision. He had forgotten how to tie the drawstrings of his pajamas though. What to do with the drawstrings, he just couldn't figure out. If somebody tied it for him, he would play with it and pull on it. Now, his family members had removed the drawstrings and put an elastic band in his pajamas instead.

He remained lost in his own thoughts. Yawning. Woke up in the night and started screaming. He had forgotten the difference between day and night. He didn't recognise anybody. He even saw things that weren't there. He heard voices and sounds that weren't anywhere at all. He even replied to these voices and sounds. He would say that he had employed a whole team to nab the thief, who spoke their findings in his ears. Sometimes he heard the footfalls of the thief and hid, and quickly got into the position of a soldier on the frontline. 'Let the enemy come! If he barged in here, we will attack!' was his mantra. Once, he had attacked his son. The doctor had said then, that if he had started attacking people like this after getting violent, he might need to be hospitalised.

A thief entered his house every night and stole some more memories from his bundle. There were hardly any memories left, but the theft was still ongoing. The thief was quite miraculous; he was making him a pauper every day. He was quite angry about that. If he got to lay his hands on the thief, he will tie its arms around his back, though he had long forgotten how to tie anything; and now, he couldn't even identify his arms. When the car was passing through the market while he was being taken to the clinic, he suddenly became excited and opened the door of the running car, and was about to leap out of it. The scooter passing next to the car almost collided with it. 'Have you gone crazy?!' the man on the scooter had yelled, dodging the opened door. The son leaped and pulled the car door shut, and chided him, almost cursing him, and saying that if they had collided with the scooter, they all would have been in some real deep shit! His son had taken the car to a side and parked.

'If you do anything like that then we will have to admit you there, Papa. They keep people's arms tied in the madhouse. In a straight jacket...' his son almost threatened him. He was silently looking out of the window. He was trying to look for that thief, looking out of the window, looking for the one he had just seen in the market, and who had disappeared in the market after emerging from it.

It was to catch that thief that he had opened the car door, and was ready to leap.

# The Death Of A Wealthy Man

An insanely wealthy man belonging to the city had been found dead in his own home.

The people in the city didn't know about this incident, of course, but you've been following this incident since the beginning. You are well aware that this is that same wealthy man who was digging a tunnel to safely stash all of his wealth. Well, he wasn't just digging; he had, in fact, almost completed it.

That same wealthy man was found dead under his bed in his bedroom this morning. And the cause of death had turned out to be so strange that the police and the doctor who performed the post-mortem were uncertain as to what to make of this. Murder, suicide, or something else? At the site of the crime the police had found that the clothes of the dead were covered in dust and dirt. How did such a wealthy man, in his luxurious bedroom where the entry of even a speck of dust was prohibited, get covered in dust and dirt from top to bottom? Which place would he have gone to, right before his death, that he ended up being covered in so much dirt? And his dead body had been found under the bed that way. What would he be doing under the bed? How did he end up under his bed at the time of death? The police were surprised. They had some hope from the post-mortem report. Perhaps, the report could clarify the cause of his death. But the doctors were puzzled even more. The windpipe of the deceased was found to be full of dirt. He had choked on this dirt. If everything was put together and seen, it seemed as if he had died crushed under dirt in some mine.

But why would a wealthy man die crushed in a mine? Actually, it was getting difficult to ascertain that after all... How did this wealthy man die?

His son had presented all the papers of his father's treatment to the police. 'He had a mental illness, sir. He was getting regular treatment as well. A case of suicide can be made on this basis, right?' he said. The police, perhaps, might even make it so. It was the matter of a wealthy man, after all. The approach to higher-ups had its own pressures. The money, too, wields its own pressure.

Still another incident had reached the police, percolating. The reporters had narrated a somewhat bizarre story in this incident.

The servants of the house were whispering about an incident that had occurred right before his death in the evening.

Father and son had had a sharp argument in the evening in raised voices for a long time. Perhaps, they had a brawl as well, a peon was revealing something like that. A tunnel was mentioned again and again. Nobody had been able to listen to the whole thing properly but some tunnel was being argued about, that was for sure. Whatever voices seeped out from the closed door, they face got so distorted that it became difficult to properly identify what actually was being argued about in the room. Yes, it was certain that the argument was quite hot. Raised voices. They must have been raised, that's why a few words were heard outside…otherwise the doors and walls of the wealthy are usually mute.

The police had asked a few questions to his son regarding the matter of this tunnel.

'What is this tunnel we are hearing about?' the police wanted to know from his son.

His son hesitated somewhat for a minute, but soon stabilised.

'Sir, there is nothing to it. Just…it was some mental disorder of his. He had completely lost his mind. He was even under treatment for it since last year under a psychiatrist. Here, please have a look. So many prescriptions from the doctor, and receipts of medicines. He would mumble all the time. He would keep on thinking something. It didn't feel good to yell at him and shut him up. It was a matter of my father, after all. But once in a while, I would have to yell at him. Just last evening I had yelled at him. What can one do, sir? How difficult it is to live with an insane man twenty-four-seven, nobody else can even begin to understand…' his son explained and while finishing what he was saying, he held his head in his hands and sat down.

From what the son told the police, about that tunnel and an argument between him and his father—these two things were getting abundantly clear from it. And then the papers of his treatment were also there.

But, what in reality had occurred that evening, nothing about that was told to the police by his son. Had he told anything to the police, they would have nabbed him, right then and there. Had he told the whole incident correctly to anybody, nobody would have believed him even a bit. Yesterday evening's incident was so unbelievable that his son hadn't been able to believe it himself, that something like that had occurred right in front of his eyes.

What really happened yesterday evening went something like this:

The son had returned home from the factory in the evening, just like every day. Two factories had been started by his father. With God's blessings and his son's hard work, both the factories were running great. When he returned from work, he had a lot of cash in his briefcase. When he was taking this money out and keeping it in the locker in the house, he found out that the bundles of cash worth fifty lakhs left there previously weren't to be found anywhere in the locker.

He was shocked and stunned!

After all, where did so much cash go from the locker? Who had taken all that money from his locked safe? Only him, or his father, had the means to open that safe.

So, was it his daddy who took it? Surely, he must be the one who must have done something. He cursed himself. How long had he been thinking of changing the code number of the locker! He was seeing very well that his father had been going crazy. He knew that well. Still! All he did was just think! He should have gradually freed his daddy from the ownership and liability rights of every property long ago. People do that to their fathers who are in good health. His daddy, in fact, was losing it. Still…to hell with it!

He ran towards his father's room, leaving the safe in his room as it was, open. His daddy was sitting, squatting on his bed, writing something in his diary.

'Did you open the locker yesterday or the day before yesterday?' he asked.

His father slowly raised his head from his diary. He looked at his son's bewildered face. Seeing his ashen face, a mysterious smile started playing on his lips. He smiled and nodded his head in affirmation.

'What did you do with so much cash?' he asked him, almost standing on his father's head.

He started laughing like a maniac.

He said, 'Okay, you tell me, what would I have done with it?' And uttering this, he started looking towards his son with so much playfulness, as if he had asked some tricky question from his son's school textbook, and his son seemed unable to answer it.

His son came closer to him. So close that if his son lost it, he wouldn't have to cover any extra distance to slap his father's face.

'Daddy, what did you do with that money, tell me that!' he barked, getting restless.

Seeing his son's restlessness, he deemed it appropriate to tell him the whole thing. Poor thing! He was fretting for no reason! So he told him everything as if he was disclosing a secret.

His son was speechless!

'What are you talking about?'

'I am telling you the truth,' he said, surprised at his son's reaction. He had, perhaps, anticipated a reaction from his son wherein the son would praise his prudence and foresight a lot. But hearing him talk, it was as if the blood had drained from his son's face. His countenance was totally pale! For a moment, darkness came over the son's eyes.

'You took the whole money!'

'Don't you worry son! Our whole money is safe there,' he became worried seeing his son's face.

'You've gone and left all that money in who knows which tunnel, and you're telling me that I shouldn't worry!' his son asked him, shaking him by his shoulders.

'I've even left two kilograms of my gold there. My tunnel is completely safe, son. Totally safe. Even safer than your locker. We'll gradually take everything there and hide it. Then, it wouldn't 't matter if they raid our house to their heart's content; they could do whatever they wanted—they wouldn't be able to find anything. I've dug that tunnel at such a place that no matter how hard anyone tries, they wouldn't be able to find it.'

He was so mesmerised by his own cleverness that after saying what he had to say, he started clapping and laughing uncontrollably, and just kept on laughing.

His son was left gawking at his father's face in anger and bewilderment.

Yaar, this father of mine has completely gone nuts! Perhaps, I was the one who was a fool who didn't realise such a simple thing in time. This bloody doctor didn't warn me in time either. What the…!? Papa always used to talk about digging a tunnel, being raided, hiding money, and other such kooky tales all the time, but that it would come to this extent, I hadn't the slightest inkling ever, the son thought to himself.

He had even seen his father jotting down something in his diary. The psychiatrist had consoled him saying that these were just the preliminary symptoms of schizophrenia. That his father was having hallucinations and becoming delusional. 'Your father will come to believe something anytime, and he will believe it to be totally true. Without there being a tunnel in reality, he will see one in person. Nobody would say anything and he would hear voices. But I am prescribing some medicines, and when you give them to him, he will get well soon. Surely,' the doctor had said.

To hell with surely. Now, see! See for yourself how big of a racket he has caused. Who knows where he has gone and buried so much money and so much gold, and see how he is sitting and smiling now! And he is looking at me as if he has reached the moon and is now expecting on receiving a pat on the back from me.

Fifty lakh rupees! And now he is telling me about two kilograms of gold too! These thoughts were racing through his mind.

His son's heart was filled with disgust.

He asked his father while grabbing him by his shoulders and shaking him, 'Have you gone totally nuts, you codger?'

He was astounded hearing what his son had just said. He had gone so crazy as to not realise that his son was chiding him.

'But at least listen to me…' he tried to explain to this son.

His son was still leaning on him. He was standing right in front of him, still tightly grabbing his shoulders. Staring at him with burning eyes.

'Don't you worry so much, son. Don't you worry at all! My tunnel is a lot stronger and safer than any bank locker.'

How much longer could his son tolerate?

When the son delivered a strong slap across his cheek, he fell from the bed. He was lying sprawled on the fabulous carpet laid below. He was so stunned that it was difficult for him to even think or understand anything. He stayed on the carpet, laying flat. His son didn't let him remain there either. He son bent down and grabbed his hand, and tried to make him stand almost by dragging him.

'Where is that bloody tunnel of yours? Take me there right away!'

He had stiffened like wood. It was difficult to make him stand up.

His son, raging with anger and pulling his hand, said in a menacing tone, 'Take me there right now! Right this very moment. I have to give cash to a business party *tomorrow*!'

He was laying flat on the floor. His son grabbed his hand and started pulling him upward. And because of this, one of his shoulders and his chest on that side rose from the carpet. His face became horrifying. He turned his neck and looked at his son with a lot of trouble, and said, 'I will go and bring all the cash tomorrow morning, son. For sure...'

'And if somebody moved it from there at night, then?' his son hadn't stopped pulling his father's hand yet. He was still pulling him.

The father's body had further stiffened now.

'It's difficult to reach there at night, son. In the morning...' he could barely eke out a few words at a time.

'What is so difficult?' his son asked sarcastically.

'The tunnel is deep. There is no light there either. The path is all zigzag. I have dug this tunnel in such a way that even the people raiding it won't be able to reach there. One can't reach there at night...'

He was slowly trying to stand up on his own; his son hadn't let go of his hand yet though.

'Have you gone completely bonkers or what?' his son said.

'No, I am not insane, son. Don't ever fall for what that doctor is saying. It's his business to declare people insane. That's his bread and butter. I am perfectly alright,' he said, standing properly now.

'Really?' his son came and faced him squarely. poor old man was getting scared to see him like this. He was standing next to the bed. Abutting it. The bed was right behind him.

'I am telling you the truth...'

'Okay, then just tell me where that tunnel of yours is? I'll go there myself and bring all the money back.'

'You won't be able to go there...'

'And you?' it seemed like the son was getting fed up.

'Even I in the night...nobody... I'll bring it first thing in the morning...'

His son shoved him in anger. He fell on the bed.

His son kept his one foot on the bed, and while leaning on him, said, 'You will get out of here right now and you will only come back after getting the money. Do you understand?'

He just looked at him in disbelief. He was unable to recognise this person. Who was this unfamiliar person? He sure looked like his son, but he wasn't. How could his son, who always addressed him as 'Daddy ji', change so much? So if the matter of money comes in between, does the face of every son in the world change just like this? Thinking all this, he started sobbing. Then, he slowly sat upright on the bed, and with his head in his arms, he kept sobbing for a long time.

'Don't show me your crying like this, codger!' there was so much cruelty in his son's voice that he was shaken to the core.

'Get out! Right now! Get out of this house. That tunnel, wherever you've dug it, go there. And get all the money, right now! And once you have it with you, come back home only then. Do you hear me?'

His son's face had turned menacing. Quite menacing. A blackish face. Burning eyes. Crooked nose. He had seen pictures of demons in the storybooks in his childhood. All those pages were fluttering in his mind right now. Was it the noise of all those pages fluttering in his mind or was it his heart that was pounding loudly?

He slowly got up from the bed and started walking towards the door.

'Return only if you have the money with you, otherwise don't even bother coming back...'

Only he knew how dangerous a job it was to go in the tunnel at night. Almost fatal. But his son wasn't willing to listen to him. If he stayed here, he will beat him to death. He will have to get into the tunnel. He will have to get into the tunnel, taking all the risks at night itself.

He opened the bedroom door and stood there. He stood there for a few moments thinking about something.

His son came from behind and pushed him, and threw him outside. He was thrown into the verandah, staggering, and the door slowly closed behind him. 'Go... Go on now!'

He could hear just this much when the door shut completely. It was quite possible that his son might have cursed him...but before he could hear that, the door shut completely.

The son had now reached his bedroom. His wife asked, 'What were you arguing about with Daddy ji in such a raised voice? Why do you argue with him? Don't you already know? His mind is not in its right place!'

He stared at his wife the same way, the way that his father had received a warning that he could start beating him any moment.

'Even my mind isn't in its right place! You better talk to me later…' saying this, he quickly took two shots of whiskey and lay down on the bed.

His wife remained silent. She, too, recognised this look of his.

And then, at night, without talking to anybody and without telling anybody, the son took sleeping pills and fell asleep.

And then it was morning again.

And his father was found dead in the morning.

His son woke up at the break of dawn. How could he have remained asleep like a log despite his worry for the money? He was surprised at himself.

When he woke up, he scrambled and reached his father's room almost running.

The old man was lying dead on the floor, next to his bed.

His clothes were covered in dust, his body was covered in dirt. His palms were muddy. His hair had mud in it too. And the mud was all over his head and hair. As if he had crawled somewhere to enter a tunnel.

So, had he come back after really going into a tunnel?

Right next to him, fifty lakh rupees and the gold was lying on the bed.

He was stunned and speechless to see the whole thing.

And then a sequence was initiated. First the doctor, then the police, and then the inquiry.

And today, the police informed him that it was found in the postmortem that he had died because his windpipe was filled with mud, and that he had choked to death. The matter had entangled, and had become quite complex. Though he was found dead in his house, the way dust and dirt had been found in his body seemed as if he died getting crushed under in some mine. That's why the police had talked to him about the tunnel too. He said only this that his father had gone insane, that he would say whatever came to his mind. 'How can we tell you which tunnel he was talking about? Yes, he was found dead in the bedroom and there is no tunnel in the bedroom, is there? the son said, feigning confidence.

The son, after all, couldn't truthfully tell the whole thing to the police anyway. Yes, he knew this thing quite well that there was some tunnel, somewhere... He surely would have taken the risk and entered the tunnel that night, that's why he brought the money which was kept there back with him. So, did the tunnel collapse on him? Did his father die, crushed under the rubble? Dirt being found in his windpipe surely pointed towards that.

So, how did he come back home at night? How did he enter the bedroom? How was he found here?

Or, was one end of the tunnel really in his bedroom, from where he crawled back with difficulty and died? But the bedroom was totally spick and span, and locked from everywhere. Where was a possibility of a tunnel here?

Then?

Don't know.

Yes, this much is true that daddy ji had turned out to be a fine father. And certainly, he wasn't insane. Some tunnel was there somewhere. Certainly. Daddy ji was digging it. He was definitely identifying some danger that we weren't able to possibly see, perhaps.

What could have been that danger?

He had always considered whatever his father said to be insanity. Had he been alive, I would have properly asked him about this danger, certainly. I would have tried to understand the whole thing. All I remember now are some fleeting things that seemed nonsensical, he thought to himself.

Whatever it was that daddy ji used to scribble in his diary, could some signs be found in there?

He had already hidden that diary from the police. He would certainly read that whole diary, from cover to cover, when he would be alone and free. Perhaps, he might get to know something from it.

## So What If He Can't See?

Although his eyes were said to be alright, he couldn't see anything.

These days, he was found wandering the streets of the city with a white cane in his hand and black sunglasses on his eyes—like a blind man.

His family took him to many famous eye specialists. After conducting hundreds of expensive tests, their opinion, in unison, was that his eyes were perfectly alright; that he couldn't see anything because, perhaps, he just didn't want to see anything. But was it possible that if somebody didn't want to see at all, he would stop seeing anything altogether? He couldn't see anything. He had even fallen into ditches here and there, colliding with things in his path. How was that possible?

The only thing which the ophthalmologist said in answer to these questions was that for this, they should get the opinion of a good neurologist. That, perhaps, he might be able to tell them something. Why a neurologist? When asked this, the ophthalmologist explained the whole system of sight to him, saying that even if the eyes in the body are alright, if that portion of the brain where vision is formed and where a picture of things seen is formed and sensed develops some dysfunction, a person is unable to see. His family even took him to a neurologist. The neurologist performed some more expensive—in fact, more expensive than expensive tests—and eventually concluded that he was alright even neurologically.

'Then? Then how is he blind? Why does he run into things while walking? Why can't he see a thing which is right in front of him?' they asked.

'You should take him to a good mental illness specialist. A good psychiatrist,' he said.

'That, we have been doing for the last five years. He used to complain in the beginning that somebody had stolen his dreams. That's what he used to shed his tears about. He would wake up in the middle of the night at odd hours and sit upright. The treatment went on for a long time. It didn't benefit him even a penny. And then, we simply stopped the treatment in despair. Now, this new problem! No, this isn't a new problem either. His old mental illness has increased further it seems.'

'You should take him to a psychiatrist once again. The answer to his illness can only be found with a psychiatrist. This is a type of mental disturbance. And there is no other physiological dysfunction. His eyes are perfectly alright.

His brain, too, is neurologically perfectly alright,' the neurobiologist said.

Then? Then what?

They went back to the same psychiatrist. Once again. What did the psychiatrist say? He had three-four long sittings with him and then concluded that he had drifted away from seeing anything. 'He has had enough of seeing and doesn't want to see anything anymore. And if somebody decides to not see anything anymore, then eventually their eyes stop seeing anything altogether as well. After all, everything is under the control of the heart and mind, the psychiatrist explained.

'So why doesn't anybody talk some sense to him? Why has he become blind like this despite having a good pair of eyes? Why don't you try to talk some sense to him? We've tried! We've tried to talk some sense to him. Everybody has tried. Everybody has been defeated. Friends, family members, doctors. Everybody. If somebody tries to talk some sense to him, he needlessly starts arguing with them. He starts giving illogical arguments. He says "I am better blind. Arre, what's there in the world which is worth seeing? Why should I see anything? What's left there to see in the world which has prohibited seeing dreams? The world is blind without dreams anyway".

'So, are you going to spend his whole life just like a blind man?'

'No,' he was quite optimistic. He said that one day he will start to see everything once again. That one day, all of his dreams will come back to him once again. The murderers had killed his dreams as per their understanding, this was true. But this was their illusion. The bigger truth is that dreams never die. They don't die despite their death. This is the miracle of dreams. They revive again and again. His dreams, too, will certainly come back one day. They will come. And from that day onwards, he will be able to dream from his eyes once again.

'Really?'

'Yes. Hundred per cent certain.'

'And till then?'

'Till then, I have all of this, no?' he pointed at the white cane and black glasses, and started smiling.

'Isn't this the mien decided for the blinds by the society? So, let this be. I am surprised by this…that if this is the uniform decided by the society for the blinds, then why doesn't the whole world walk with a white cane in its hand and a pair of black glasses covering their eyes?' he continued to laugh while saying this so that whatever he said should be considered to be said in jest. He didn't want the world to take offense for being called blind.

Anyhow, an amazing incident had occurred yesterday from which it became clear that he could see. A huge car had come speeding towards him. He was walking on the footpath with his son. And at the last moment, he jumped and moved away to one side from where he was walking. He saved his son, too, by shoving him to one side at the last moment. His son hadn't been able to see the oncoming car. *He* had seen it. Otherwise, that car would have run over them. The front wheels of the car had come onto the footpath already. The speeding car, moving zigzag, somehow regained control and went ahead. His son couldn't say a word for quite some time due to anxiety.

And then he said, 'Papa, you had seen the oncoming car, hadn't you?'

'Yes…' he replied.

'That means that you can see fine! Right?'

'I can see the assassins of my dreams clearly even with my blindness on.'

His son couldn't understand what he said. Anyway, why would somebody spend one's time and brains trying to understand what a crazy man was saying?

## The Rebellion Was Flourishing

These days, people avoided going through that road late at night.

They were afraid of running into him on the road.

He didn't do any harm to anybody though. Late at night, he would climb out of the manhole. Sometimes, people had seen him coming out. They had also told me that if he saw anyone by chance, he didn't say anything to them. He would just go back into the manhole after seeing them. Some crazies had surely tried to follow him though. But when he turned around and looked at them once, they got the chills and were stopped in their tracks. His eyes were shining, as if a hearth was burning under them. He didn't have normal eyes, Bhaisahab. His eyes were like that of a snake. They show it in the movies. You've seen them, haven't you? Just like those... So, could it be that some snake living in the manhole takes the form of a man and comes out? When the media doesn't get any other scintillating incident, they recirculate this incident again and again as a new one. Yes, many people dismiss this whole incident as just rubbish. Most of the rest of the residents of the city have accepted him to be somewhat of an invisible denizen of this city.

But who is it that keeps wandering through the city at night, scanning it?

After all, who is this that lives underneath a manhole?

Is he alone, or has a settlement come up there?

Who is it that keeps an eye on the activities of this city?

The word on the street was hot that could it be that rebels had started living underneath the manhole. A rebellion could flourish anywhere, after all. If the suffocation goes beyond the limit anywhere, a rebellion starts to bubble up. There was so much suffocation underneath the manhole too. The rising and popping of the bubbles in muddy waters was also there. It was quite possible that a rebellion was flourishing there too. There wasn't any less suffocation outside either though. So, were the rebels living underground waiting for the suffocation to rise above as well, so that they could come out then? Could it be that one of the rebels was coming out, again and again out of the manhole, to take stock of the suffocation above?

Who knows. But this was certain that somebody surely lived underneath the manhole and wandered around the whole city late at night, taking stock of it.

## It Was Noted In The Crazy's Diary That The Crazies Were On The Rise

His son had completely forgotten about his father's diary. After the mysterious death, it had taken quite a lot of time—and a lot of running around—in getting everything settled anyway. His father's real death by getting crushed in an imaginary tunnel had proved to be quite expensive. The police had charged double the rates. The haggling went on for a long time. The only heir to such large wealth would have come under suspicion anyway. Anyhow. In the end, everything had wrapped up pretty nicely.

It was after months that he was sitting and chilling.

He was sitting in the living room, with his feet spread wide and a large drink in his hand, when suddenly he remembered about the diary. He had left that diary in a drawer in his bedroom, but he remembered it suddenly, right now...don't know how. He placed the drink on the side table, got up, went to his bedroom and brought that diary with him. He had started turning the pages of that diary while slowly sipping his drink.

That diary was written in a somewhat strange and bizarre way.

For many pages, it was just calculations about the tunnel and record-keeping of the digging done. When, on which date, how much was dug, and in which direction. Plan. The tunnel's design. Description of the tools and such.

Some pages had descriptions of lending and borrowings.

Jotted down on some pages was the description, in a cryptic language, of the valuables which were going to be kept safe in the tunnel.

And then in many pages, there were many names which had their phone numbers (perhaps?) written in front of them. These names didn't match with any names in the family, or the circle of friends and acquaintances. The son knew the names of all the important friends of his father. There wasn't a single name jotted in the list which he was familiar with. He had a list of completely unknown names in front of him. Who were these people? What association did they have with his father? If he had written their names down, then this surely meant something.

He stopped at this page of list with the names.

The diary's pages were fluttering lightly in the soft breeze from the air conditioner. He sat there pondering something, gazing at the fluttering pages with empty eyes.

He made another drink, and kept on slowly sipping it. Pondering.

He had made a small bar for himself in one corner of the living room. This corner had a system of soft lighting. It was in this soft light that he was sprawled, half-reclined on a reclining chair. The diary was in his lap; the glass, in his hand.

He sat there with the open diary in his lap contemplating for a long time. And then it was as if he had had a flash of insight. He picked the first name from the names written on the open pages of the diary. And he dialed the number written in front of that name on his cell phone.

'This number does not exist', a recorded voice was heard from the other side. He tried again. But that voice continuously repeated 'this number does not exist'.

And then he started picking the names from that list, one by one. He tried the phone numbers of the next three names on the list. The first number was found switched off. The second was continuously found to be out of reach. The third one didn't exist either.

He was annoyed. He kept the glass in his hand on the small side table next to him. He then picked up the diary in his hands. Yaar, how could this be possible that every number I find is not working, he thought to himself.

He was too insistent now. He tried the fifth number. This was a landline number. A girl picked up on the other side.

'Could I please speak to Panna Lal ji?' he said, after carefully reading the name written in the diary one more time, and picked up the glass from the side table. There was silence on the other side. The girl didn't say a single word in response. Nor was there any answer for some time. Just deadening silence.

'Hello?' he repeated, thinking that perhaps the line had got disconnected.

'Yes…' the girl blurted a short 'yes' and went silent again.

'Yes, I wanted to talk to Panna Lal ji…' he repeated what he had said before.

There was a long silence once again on the other side.

'You are speaking from Panna Lal ji's home, correct?'

'Yes, but may I know who this is?' finally, the girl spoke a few words.

'I am the son of one of his friends. I wanted to talk to him for a moment…please.'

'If you are his friend, then you would already know, wont you?'

'What would I know?' he eagerly asked. The glass almost came to his lips and stopped.

'…that Panna Lal ji is in a mental asylum for the last six months…' the girl said.

'Sorry, I hardly knew. who am I speaking to?'

'I am his daughter-in-law.'

'Oh! What had happened to him that he had to be admitted to a madhouse?' he asked.

'I don't know. It was as if he was possessed by a desire. He talked about digging a tunnel, day and night. He used to say that he was digging such a tunnel that would take everybody to a new world. That's what he would tell everybody who would listen to him. Everybody laughed at him. The neighbours, the kids; and the kids in the neighbourhood would laugh at him and ask, "Uncle, will you take us too to the new world?" He used to say that once the tunnel is dug then he would take the whole world to that new world...' the girl started venting all of her anger on the phone.

He, too, got excited hearing the tunnel being mentioned by the girl. How can this be possible? Is this just a coincidence or is it something quite complex?

'And then?' he asked in an astonished tone.

'And then, he started digging the floor of the house one day. When all of us tried to stop him, he ran after us with the pickaxe to hit us. He had brought a pickaxe home from who knows where. He said that his tunnel was completely ready now. That all he had to do now was just dig a path from the tunnel to the house.'

'Arre!'

'Yes! When people tried to talk sense to him, he got further agitated. He almost hit my husband with the pickaxe. If he hadn't quickly jumped to the side at the last moment, his skull would have cracked open. He had gotten so out of control. That's why we decided to have him admitted…'

'Oh! How is he doing now? Can I meet him sometime?'

'He is in bad shape right now. Even in the hospital, he has to be tied to the bed many times. The doctor is surprised as to what type of madness this is, and no medicine is having any effect on him. Sorry, you won't be able to see him right now. And there is no point in meeting him right now anyway. The doctor let's even us see him from afar. May I know why you want to meet him though?'

'If he ever gets well, then please do let him know that Garg Sahab is no more…'

'Garg Sahab?'

'Yes, Garg Sahab. My father…'

'Oh! I am sorry to hear that. How? What happened?'

'He, too, used to talk about digging some tunnel. But he used to talk about hiding money in a tunnel. He never talked about going to some new world through a tunnel. We, too, had him treated for insanity…'

'And then?' the girl asked somewhat surprised.

'And then one day, he died. Crushed under that same tunnel he used to talk about.'

'Arre, had you seen that tunnel?' there was excitement in the girl's voice.

'No. How could I? When Daddy ji was alive, we always

thought of his mentioning of the tunnel to be his craziness… and when he passed away, we couldn't figure out where the tunnel was. Who knows where he used to go and dig it? But if this was just his madness, if the tunnel was somewhere just in his heart and mind, then how could he have died getting crushed under it? So, that tunnel has to be somewhere. For sure. Perhaps, your father-in-law might be aware of it. That's what I wanted to ask him. He, too, was digging a tunnel, wasn't he? You were telling me just now that he was digging a tunnel...'

'Very surprising!'

'Yes, if he gets well even slightly, then I would like to meet him. Please take my number,' he started dictating his cell phone number.

'Okay…' the girl didn't seem to have gotten over the shock of this surprising revelation. She took his number down, softly said okay and disconnected the phone.

The son kept the cell phone next to his side, and picked up the glass to finish his leftover drink. He slowly sipped his drink now.

The diary was still lying in his lap, open. The rest of the names were peeking out from the pages—as if the insane were peeking from behind the bars of a mental asylum.

He decided he will try every number, turn by turn. He had taken a peek at the diary, and he was now dialing the next number.

## Glad That The Number Of Crazies Was Increasing

That same psychiatrist. That same clinic of his. A similar crowd of insane. That same waiting room. That their turn comes first, that same restlessness.

Morning time. The doctor had just reached. He had just sat down on his soft, cushioned chair. He would start seeing the patients in a short while. For a while, he just sat there with his legs spread. And then he pulled open a drawer and took out a diary.

This was his private diary. You could call it a secret diary. You could even call it an unaccounted diary. Whatever name you want to give it, but it was in this diary that he noted down his real income, and his lendings and borrowings.

Every day, he cast a cursory glance at this diary before beginning his mornings. The accounting of figures of his income and the number of patients filled him with a new excitement to work. He got immense happiness seeing that the number of insane in the city was increasing. If the number of insane increased, his income will increase too. But these days, he was surprised by one thing. He was seeing that patients of a certain pattern were increasing more and more. Insane of a similar type. Similar story. Similar insanity. It seemed as if the same patients were being brought to him again and again in a different mien.

Just look at yesterday's cases, now.

Two of them were convinced that they were digging a tunnel. Three people were anxious and restless because of the stealing of their dreams. Five of them felt so insecure that they kept themselves locked under seven locks, and then there were some who couldn't fall asleep because of this fear that the government was going to seize everything they had and hand it over to the Bazaar—it was a crowd of such patients these days. Every day. New patients. They all shared one thing among them. All of them, who knows why, took the Bazaar's name in some context or the other. He was unable to understand this pattern. If the market was strong and Sensex was going so high, then in what context did they talk about the Bazaar—he couldn't figure that out. They were insane, perhaps, that's why.

The doctor wasn't able to understand their real disease.

It was becoming impossible for the doctor, who was enjoying the heights of the market, to understand what was bubbling up through the sediments.

## The Worry Was That The Number Of Crazies Was Increasing

The Bazaar's grand office.

Countless printouts were spread in front of the Bazaar, all over a huge table.

Standing near it was that same minion who had spread these printouts in front of the Bazaar.

The minion was the Bazaar's wave expert.

He ran the supercomputer which caught the mental waves floating in the society. The Bazaar already had plenty of information about every citizen whom it called its customer from a plethora of sources though. It had already been sketching a portrait of a customer's psyche through his cell phone, e-mail, topics of Google searches, comments on social media, etc. And on the basis of these, the Bazaar had been formulating its strategies. But now, a new weapon had been added to its arsenal in deciding strategies. The fine changes which occur in the magnetic field of the environment by a citizen's thinking—the supercomputer caught these changes and transformed them into waves.

Using these waves, one could probe deep into a man's psyche and reach there, where the person himself couldn't reach. This supercomputer captured the complex waves of the subconscious mind and analyzed them. And just like the fingerprints of any human being, the wave patterns of any person could be captured and analyzed too. The analysis of every wave was added to the already existing analysis of the old patterns of the customer, and analyzed again in its entirety. And then on the basis of this analysis, the wave expert presented his advice and comments to the Bazaar.

The Bazaar was the one who took the final decision. The Bazaar, through this analysis, decided the strategies to control the subconscious of its customers and gave directions to its minions thereafter.

The supercomputer expert minion had presented his latest analysis in front of the Bazaar right then. This analysis was perturbing for the Bazaar. It was worried after reading the comments of his expert on the printouts. The minion was standing respectfully in front of the Bazaar after making his comments.

'What's all this?' the Bazaar pointed at the printouts and questioned its minion quite sternly.

The minion was standing in that posture, the posture in which minions generally stand. It was evident from his posture that this man would rarely disagree on any topic with its master.

'Yes, sir. It is like that...' the minion replied in an apologising tone.

'But how could it be?'

'Sir?'

'I was just looking over your comments. Here, take a look...here, you have commented that many customers are going insane, and that this insanity of theirs is on the rise. I have read your warning as well, that this is not good for the Bazaar. Correct? But how could that be?'

'Yes. We found the analysis of waves to be surprising too, sir.'

'But hasn't this been our understanding to date that the more insane the customer is, the more beneficial it is for the Bazaar? Then why are you giving a cautionary comment on this observation of yours?'

'Because, sir, this seems like a totally different type of craziness.'

'What do you mean?'

'Sir, we are finding it difficult to fully comprehend the meaning of these complex waves as well. Even the supercomputer isn't able to process anything properly. The computer is giving out contradictory analysis on this topic.'

'So... What do you actually mean?'

'It seems that nowadays, a different type of thinking is being bred in society, sir. Currently, this different type of thinking is just in its subconscious. But the fear of it rising is real—at least that is what it seems,' the minion said somewhat afraid. The minions were quite afraid of telling the bitter truth to the Bazaar.

'And why does it seem like that to you?'

'That's what waves are telling us.'

'What's the matter with these waves? Tell me more, and tell me freely.'

'We are finding strange waves, sir. They are indicating people's hatred, and they are pointing at their rebellion too.'

'Rebellion from whom?'

'Sorry sir, but the truth of the matter is that something is developing against the Bazaar in their subconscious. It is this concern which I have noted in my comment.'

'But how can this be possible?'

'Sir, that's what the waves are telling us.'

'Arre, are these bastards getting insane or what? Arre, how can anyone even think against the Bazaar?'

'But the good thing is that even society thinks of these rebels as crazies. Though…'

'Though?'

'The speed with which the number of these crazies is increasing, it is feared that the mental waves of the whole society end up like that eventually.'

'Is that even possible?'

'Sir, at least the composite analysis of all these waves is pointing in that direction. I have completely noted this fear in my comment...'

'Would you just keep on noting this or do something about it?'

The minion went silent. He stood there with his head bowed.

The Bazaar, too, went silent. It is quite worried hearing all this. Its eyes were fixed on the papers presented by the minion. The Bazaar is thinking. It kept on thinking for a long time. And kept on looking at the papers, unblinking. And then, suddenly, it spoke:

'This computer of yours is working alright, no?'

'Yes?'

'I am asking if the computer has any virus or anything like that...'

'No, sir. This supercomputer of ours is perfectly fine.'

'Could it be that it is catching some wrong waves or anything?'

'No, sir. That is not possible.'

'Why isn't that possible? Arre, suppose your computer is catching the waves of cats and dogs as well, then? Don't the psyche of dogs and cats also emit some waves too?'

'Yes, they emit some waves too.'

'So? Suppose our computer is catching those waves in between, then? You know, like, interference...'

'Sir, the computer completely filters out the waves of animals because they can't directly become our customers right now. They aren't directly of any use to us right now. The computer ignores these waves. It only catches human waves.'

'So, can't we somehow control these waves rising in people's psyche at this stage itself?' the Bazaar as if asked itself.

'Sir, so far such computers haven't been invented which would control a human brain completely,' the minion said apologetically.

'I know,' the Bazaar said.

The minion stood there with his head bowed. The Bazaar, too, had sat down with its head hanging. Both of them were sitting with their heads down but their reasons were different. One head was down out of habit. The other was sitting with its head down in worry.

# Satisfied That The Number Of Crazies Was Increasing

The temple of the Tunnel Baba.

Quite the recognition this temple had in the city, and the surrounding areas too. The Tunnel Baba was quite miraculous. If he blessed someone, his blessings came to fruition in a great way. If he touched an ill man, even the dying man would stand upright on his two feet. A missing person would be found in which direction, at what distance, he could tell right away. He didn't speak. You just had to understand his signs. He, too, was now completely engrossed in playing the role of this Tunnel Baba character. He had started against the Bazaar; he had come to take refuge in spirituality. So many people bowed to him that he was under the illusion of being miraculous himself now. Tens of hundreds of people came to his refuge throughout the day. Yes, the morning was spent in the solitude of samadhi. And then after having breakfast, he saw his devotees for merely three hours. He gave solutions. He placed his hand on his devotees' heads. Handed them holy ash. Handed them sweets. And to some, he handed a flower. And on some, he just sprinkled some water. He looked at some and just smiled. Fifty types of gestures and spells. Devotees returned filled with gratitude. People of every type. Troubled. Defeated. Victorious. Poor. Rich. Distraught. Happy. Hungry. Satiated. Unsuccessful. Quite unsuccessful. Student. Mother. Father. Old. Young. Everybody sought blessings from the Tunnel Baba.

And it reached the highest extent one day when his own children, too, came to seek his blessings. Because of the crowd, because of not being able to see properly, because of shoving and pushing, or because of his long dreadlocks and his mien of a sadhu, the children couldn't recognise their own father. They started telling him that their father had gone missing a long time ago, asking for his help and wondering if he could tell them where to find him.

He stayed silent; only smiled a bit. And then raised his hand in assurance. That was all. Later, he kept on thinking about it the whole day. Suppose, if he had said to his children, right then and there, that he was their father? What would have happened then? And then he thought that it was alright that he didn't tell them. And then he thought that… And then he had been thinking about that every day. Home. Bazaar. That rebellion of his against the Bazaar. That restlessness of his to find a way to settle a new world beyond the Bazaar.

The tunnel. But look, all of his rebellion eventually vanished into spirituality.

Meanwhile, one of his worries had increased further.

One or two crazies were brought to his durbar almost every day. The troubled family members sought Tunnel Baba's blessings for these crazies. The doctor's treatment was ongoing but the crazies weren't getting well. If Baba placed his hand on their head, perhaps they might end up receiving God's grace. And all of them were crazy in various ways. Some were digging a tunnel and weren't ready to come even in Tunnel Baba's durbar without their pickaxe. A couple of them walked with a torch in their hand. An extinguished torch. They said that one day when they will light it, there will be light everywhere, and the trash from the Bazaar would be incinerated with it. They kept lighting up and extinguishing that torch all day long. They had even burnt their hands one or two times but they wouldn't listen. Some who were brought in were those who wandered in the market all day long and shouted slogans against the Bazaar. Their voices became hoarse but they didn't shut up. They barely slept a wink—they shouted slogans even in their sleep. They all had one thing common, and that was that the Bazaar had a huge role in their craziness... And it was this thing which was making him restless these days.

The Tunnel Baba continuously remembered those days when he, too, was digging a tunnel against the Bazaar. Seeing these crazies, he was remembering all of that; then leaving behind all that, he had come into the refuge of this temple. Was this spirituality of his a facade of a defeated man? Had he escaped making this tunnel, his way of escape while digging it against the Bazaar? So, does this mean that those stronger than him, more committed than him, and more combative than him were these people who were still fighting, without caring if society thought of them as crazies? Yes, perhaps. Perhaps, this was the truth.

Tunnel Baba hadn't met anybody today. It was said that he wasn't feeling well.

He was engrossed in his worship since morning. He had neither eaten nor drank anything. He was sitting in front of God with his eyes closed. Even the priests of the temple didn't know what type of worship was going on today. Tunnel Baba was actually thanking God that the number of such crazies was increasing.

So what if he lost? Other people hadn't lost yet.

Thank God that the number of crazies is increasing everywhere.

There were at least some who were continuing their fight further.

# The Time of Rebellion

The Clocktower area of the city.

Quite a famous area of the city this was.

An important vestige of the evidence of the old city's grand historical tradition. Talk about its heritage value travelled far and wide. Countless tourists from the country and abroad come to see this clocktower. The city was quite proud of this minaret.

The dense market surrounding Clocktower Square was the city's most prosperous market; it was called the Clocktower Market. This market, too, had quite a name around town. The city was proud of this market as well.

The clock was atop a four-story minaret, and it was two hundred years old. But it told time so precisely that the city was proud of this fact too—that the clock told precise time. This thing was told with pride to every tourist who visited the city.

This minaret was called the Clocktower.

The market surrounding the Clocktower, too, had been developed in the form of a heritage market. The Bazaar knew that heritage can be sold at a hefty price. The tourists saw the minaret, and then wandered around the streets of the market stretching far and wide around the Clocktower.

The Bazaar, too, was proud of the Clocktower.

The clock chimed every hour. On a small platform built right under the clock was a puppet; it would start dancing by going round and round, as soon as the bell of the clock tolled. It would go around once when the clock chimed one o'clock, and it then went round and round four times when the clock chimed four. The puppet was adorned with beautiful clothes. Its clothes were changed every day. Wearing the clothes of folklife of different regions of the country, this was how the puppet danced. The heritage value of the whole play was enhanced with the traditional attire of the folklife, that's what the city believed. The city was proud of this puppet too.

The Clocktower chimed every hour.

Once at one o'clock, four times at four o'clock. Ten times at ten o'clock. The puppet went round and round on its axis, with quite a style, those many times too. With every chime of the Clocktower. The tourists, too, stood in a crowd next to the minaret waiting for that moment. When the bell tolled, the puppet danced with it. People who were waiting in a circle around the Clocktower started clapping.

Hearing the bell toll, the Bazaar started smiling. It found this sound to be like a sweet symphony. The music of the sound of the bell tolling created a dream of a crowd of customers in the Bazaar's eyes.

And today was Sunday.

There was such a fearsome crowd here on Sundays, as if the whole world and their dogs had turned out. The market, too, was in full bloom on this day.

Even today, many tourists were roaming around. Many customers.

It was close to seven in the evening.

In the roundabout around the minaret, so many people had gathered that they were pushing and shoving each other for space.

And just then, the clock struck seven.

The bell of the Clocktower started tolling.

The puppet, too, started dancing along with it.

The whole crowd started looking at this scene, forgetting the shoving and pushing.

One. Two. Three… Six. Seven.

The clock was striking.

The puppet, too, was dancing round and round.

People were clapping and breaking into laughter.

But when the clock should have stopped after striking seven, it didn't.

The bell of the clock kept on tolling. And gradually, it started striking louder and louder. Now it was striking so loudly that all around, all one could hear was just the sound of the bell tolling. It was as if the whole universe was now filled with the sound of the bell tolling. Its sound had become so loud that it became difficult for people to hear each other talk.

The puppet, too, was going round and round along with it. As the sound of the bell tolling became louder and louder, the puppet started dancing faster and faster.

Hearing the loud striking of the bell, more and more spectators started gathering there. The crowd was gotten uncontrollable now.

It was swelling.

The police of the city came running. The management of the market, too, reached there. The maintenance staff came running to the scene as well. The workers of the Clocktower ran up the stairs. The mechanic tried to open the clock. He pressed a few switches here and there but the striking didn't stop. Then the mechanic grabbed the bell and tried to stop it, but it still didn't stop. He held on to the pendulum but it slipped from his hands. And while swinging back, the pendulum hit on the mechanic's head so hard that he almost tumbled down the stairs of the minaret!

The tolling of the bell had now turned into such a loud noise that the city's sky was filled with it. The gang of workers was still on the Clocktower and was trying to stop the pendulum's giant swings. But nobody was able to stop it. The bell was tolling, and the puppet was going round and round—faster and faster.

Down below, the crowd had swelled quite a bit by now.

And a lot of police, too, had arrived at the site of the incident.

The Bazaar had become very nervous about this spectacle. The crowd was becoming uncontrollable with every passing moment.

And just then, sparks started flying from some bearing of the moving puppet. The kilt of the puppet caught fire.

Now, the puppet was dancing with a burning kilt. A ball of fire was dancing on the minaret. A frightening scene it was. The workers on the minaret ran toward the ground in pandemonium. A worker fell from the roof in the ensuing chaos. He cracked his skull.

There was pandemonium in the square down below as well.

The crowd ran and went into the streets of the market.

It went into the shops.

Looting started.

The shutters of the shops started coming down quickly.

The market shut down within minutes. People were running breathlessly in the streets with shuttered shops.

People were trying to break the shutters by kicking, punching and hitting them with rods. Behind closed shutters, the Bazaar was sitting, cowering in fear.

The bell was tolling so loud now that it could be heard loudly even behind the closed shutters.

There, on the other side of the market, the burning puppet was still going round and round on the minaret.

The Bazaar, hidden within a closed shop, had sent its minions, and called for higher officials, police, and a maintenance mechanic.

Right now, all of them were standing behind the closed shutters as well.

Outside, the street was filled with the sounds of running footsteps and the bell striking. The noise was increasing further and further. The atmosphere was that of riots.

Although shades of fear and apprehension were wafting over the Bazaar's face, this belief was also there that it will be able to bring the situation under control.

'What's all of this happening, sir?' the Bazaar asked the higher official in a complaining tone.

The official looked at the mechanic.

'What's going on, Mister? Who maintains this clock of yours?' the official asked.

'Sir, I am the one who maintains it…'

'Then, what the heck is going on?' the constable said.

'What can I do in this situation, sir?' the mechanic asked.

'Arre, what do you have to do? Just stop this gong! You are the one who is going to stop it, who else will do it?' the official said in anger.

'Please stop this bell right away, Brother! Whatever the cost be, take it from us…' the Bazaar coaxed him.

'It is not possible to stop it, sir! I did everything I could. It's impossible to stop its wheel now…' the mechanic gave up.

'Something could surely be done? After all, its a bloody machine! If nothing else, just hit the bloody thing with a hammer!' a constable said.

'Sir, I told you, didn't I? Nothing can be done now. The clock is out of our hands.'

'Arre, how can you say that? If I cancelled your contractor's contract of maintenance tomorrow itself, you will be out on the streets,' the officer's authority woke up.

'Yaar, please do something! Understand the market's sentiments. If we lose control of the clock, the market would be looted,' the Bazaar pleaded.

'Sir, nothing can be done in this matter anymore…' the mechanic informed them again.

'Why can't anything more be done?' the constable asked.

'Sir, didn't I tell you that Time is out of hand now,' he said.

'How come?' the officer asked.

'Sir, at least try to understand. Actually, Time has revolted…'

'Who? Who has done what?' the Bazaar started asking.

'Sir, Time has revolted,' he said again.

'Time has revolted?' the Bazaar asked, astonished.

'My Lord, if Time has decided to revolt, then nobody can do anything...' the mechanic had ended up saying quite a philosophical thing while talking.

The official and the constable's attentions were towards the banging of the shutter. It seemed that the mob was about to break the shutter and barge into the shop.

The Bazaar was shellshocked.

Even Time could rebel against it—it had never thought of that even in its dreams. It hadn't made any arrangements in its scheme for this. The Bazaar had always thought of itself as beyond Time. It was finding out now just how wrong it was.

Time had revolted.

This was the time of revolt.

The Bazaar, perhaps, still wasn't able to understand this right now.

But one day, this was bound to happen.

My heartfelt gratitude goes to Mr Nirmal Kanti Bhattacharjee and Mrs Tultul Niyogi for being extremely patient and caring with this project—and with me as well, for I often became incommunicado for long periods as I was dealing with my father's demise during and after the pandemic.

Lastly, this acknowledgment would be severely found lacking if I didn't profusely thank my editor Vibha Chakravarty Kumar. Her work ethic, attention to detail in editing, and love for the language and literature were, definitely, an asset. But most importantly, the warm, free-flowing discussions with her regarding the novel and its language, and her zeal to bring the out best in expression were a true blessing.

## Acknowledgements

'Each age, it is found, must write its books; or rather, each generation for the next succeeding. The books of the older period will not fit this.' Though Ralph Waldo Emerson wrote these words in *The American Scholar* many decades ago, when I read *Pagalkhana* these words resonated so strongly that they became the impetus for its translation.

My sincere gratitude goes to Dr Gyan Chaturvedi—the author of the novel. The gratitude is not only for agreeing to let me translate this novel but also for the conversations that helped me understand his thought process while writing it.

I must thank my father, Mr Prabhu Joshi — a Hindi short story writer and a painter — for it was he who had quoted Emerson's words; and suggested that *Pagalkhana* should be translated into English for it so beautifully captures the zeitgeist of our consumerist society and deserves a wider readership.